TWELVE
TENDER
TEARJERKERS

TWELVE
TENDER
TEARJERKERS

From the Editors
Of *True Story* And
True Confessions

Published by True Renditions, LLC

True Renditions, LLC
105 E. 34th Street, Suite 141
New York, NY 10016

ISBN: 978-1-938877-64-3

Visit us on the web at www.truerenditionsllc.com.

Contents

UNFAITHFUL
HUSBAND

Everyone thought we were the perfect family. There was my husband, John, my son, Alex, my daughter, Devan, and me—along with assorted dogs and cats, two horses, and several hives of honeybees. We lived on a small farm near a town where we were active in the local government, church affairs, and social life. My husband was able to commute every day to his job in the city, and I took care of our honeybees and vegetable garden.

Our nearest neighbors were a widow, Mrs. Leland, and her son, Ed, who had returned to her home after the death of his wife. He was quiet and moody, mourning his loss for what seemed like a long time, and not mingling much in the community. His mother, on the other hand, was a social butterfly, apparently making up in her golden years for the fun she'd missed when she'd raised her five children. They were good neighbors, and Ed sometimes helped us out when the crops were ripe or the hives needed attention.

It was Christmas the year our world turned around, although we didn't know it at the time. I was at home with the kids, baking cookies and preparing for the holidays, when my husband called and said he wouldn't be home that evening. He had gone out with someone from the plant, to talk about a problem, and the two of them had ended up in a bar and had too much to drink. Now he would spend the night on a couch in his office rather than risk driving in his condition.

Although I was disappointed, I thought he was doing the right thing. He was not a heavy drinker and if he thought he shouldn't drive, he was probably right. I made excuses to the children, and we went out to a Christmas party at the church.

When John came home the next night, he was apologetic, but a bit moody. Perhaps that was to be expected, and I thought nothing of it when he went to bed early and fell immediately to sleep. He seemed a little preoccupied over the holidays, and frequently worked late.

In the middle of January, we all went to a scouting event for Alex's troop and watched with pride as he received some special awards. The scoutmaster praised our son highly, and said that he was a credit to our good and loving home. "A loving family is the greatest start in life a young man can have," he said.

I was very proud, and we all stopped at the neighborhood restaurant to celebrate on the way home. Suddenly, a change came over John. A tall woman came by our booth and stopped. He introduced her as Heidi Ford, and said she was someone he knew at work.

1

There seemed to be nothing unusual about that, but John was very quiet for the rest of the evening. Only weeks later would I know the reason. He told me one day that he had a special project and would need some time away from home. He came home late many evenings, and sometimes stayed away for a week at a time.

When Devan played in the school band concert, John failed to come at all. We made excuses to the other parents who exclaimed, "It seems so strange not to see John here with you."

Finally, the riddle was solved. John told me that he had found another woman. He wished it hadn't happened—but it had. She worked with him, and was brilliant in her field. The woman was Heidi Ford, the woman we had met at the restaurant.

Now it was clear to me. All the weeks that John had acted so strangely and said he was working late, he had been with his new ladylove. It was an old, old story, but I had not been smart enough to see it happening. I thought how ironic it was that while we were being praised and admired for being a perfect family, John was having an affair on the side!

He told me he wanted to move out, and that he would be taking an apartment across town. My heart was broken and I was humiliated. We had a big fight in which I called him all kinds of names, but in spite of it all, I was sorry when he packed his things and left. Even though he had betrayed me, I still loved him.

He asked me for a divorce, but I refused, telling him that I needed some time to get adjusted to the idea and to think. Before long, I learned that Heidi had moved into his apartment. It was hard telling the children. Alex was just old enough to know that men and women sometimes lived together when they weren't married, but it was unbelievable to him that his own father would do it, when he was still married to me!

Devan was horrified. At first, she got mad and said she would never speak to her father again, but late at night, I heard her crying in her room, and I knew that she still loved him, too.

We tried to imagine it had not happened, that some evening he would come home just as he always had. But after awhile, everyone in town knew he was gone, and they were shocked. He left some of his things at our house, explaining that he could always get them later, because I had plenty of room and he didn't in his new apartment.

When our neighbor, Mrs. Leland, found out, she came over to console me. She was very angry and told me that men never seemed to know when they had a good thing.

"The fool!" she said. "He thinks he can stay young forever. Have you noticed that his new woman looks a lot like you?"

The thought horrified me at first, but when I thought it over, I realized she did have much the same coloring, and perhaps people would think

2

she looked like me. I thought about this a lot, and convinced myself that he was just going through a phase, trying to hold onto his youth. Perhaps he wasn't really rejecting me, but simply rebelling against the responsibility of taking care of me and our two kids.

After much agonizing, I decided that the best thing for me to do was to stay on the farm, continue the gardening, and go on with the honey business. I refused to agree to the divorce, and told John that he should pay me a nominal sum each week to support the children. He agreed to this, and we worked out all the arrangements without going to a lawyer.

During the next few months, John came by to see us rather often. He went with Alex to a father-son banquet, and when winter was over, he dropped off some sports equipment he said he had no place for.

Devan got pneumonia late that spring and I had to take her to the hospital. I called John and he came and sat with me until the crisis broke. It was good to have him around, and after that, he came to the house a couple of times each week. He arranged for the gardens to be plowed and helped with the planting.

But he always went home—home to his apartment and the woman he lived with, even though he was still married to me.

Mrs. Leland came by one day and told me that everyone was talking about me. She said they all felt it was foolish of me to allow my husband to come to our home at his own convenience, to use it to store his stuff, and to take advantage of our kids and me. She said he was using me, and that I should kick him out for good and hold him up for all I could get out of him.

I listened to what she had to say, but after thinking it over, I had to tell her that no matter what happened, I was still John's wife. I didn't believe in divorce, and no matter what he did, I still loved him and thought he would be back someday.

"He never had much fun as a kid; his folks were poor, and he went to work early. He just has to get this out of his system," I told her. "But he can't turn his back on our life together and his family. Sooner or later, he'll get tired of Heidi and come back to where he belongs."

I could tell she thought I was wasting my time—and humiliating myself in the bargain—but I thought my husband was worth waiting for.

As for John, he found that the world went on as usual even if he had adopted a different lifestyle. No one seemed much interested in what he did, and so he continued doing it. He resumed his bowling league, and although he took Heidi to their year-end banquet instead of me, no one had much to say about it. He worked as usual, and even went to church once in awhile. At first, he sat alone. Then one day, when I sang in the choir, he sat with the children. He never did sit with me, but he might have had he attended more often.

3

So life went on. The children and I continued much as we always had, and their father became almost like an uncle who dropped in from time to time to help when things went wrong. When Christmas came again, John brought presents for all of us, although he didn't come on Christmas Eve or for Christmas dinner.

We had our usual guests, however, and Mrs. Leland and Ed came early and helped with the preparations. Ed carved the turkey and sat at the head of the table. None of the guests mentioned John, but Mrs. Leland scolded me in the kitchen, and Ed said he couldn't understand it. When everyone had left, Ed stayed behind and we had a glass of wine together. He told me that he would always be around if I needed him and that he cared about the children and me very much.

I told him I was grateful for all he'd done for me. He took me in his arms, but I didn't feel at home there. I told him I loved him like a big brother, but I still had a husband, and thought I would one day have him back. Ed said he wouldn't push me, but I should remember he was close enough for me to yell for help if I needed him.

From time to time, I did. When the washing machine overflowed, when the car wouldn't start, when we all had to go in different directions and needed extra wheels, he was there when John wasn't, but John continued to come around, too. All in all, it was as if the children had two doting uncles, so they fared pretty well.

As for me, I felt I could never get romantically interested in Ed. He was like a faithful dog—always around to greet us. But John was still the man I loved. I made him a pie once in awhile, and mended a jacket for him because he and Heidi didn't have a sewing machine. Our relationship was cordial, but he always went back to Heidi—and no one could understand why I continued to wait.

I was the only one who had any sympathy for him. He had worked since he was a kid. We'd married very young, and he'd probably only had a few girlfriends before he met me. I felt he had just become infatuated with Heidi. She was always well dressed, while I sometimes wore grubby jeans and no makeup. He probably wanted romance again. She was attractive, she made no demands on him, he could come and go as he pleased, he still had a family which loved him, and he encountered only a little criticism in the community. He had the best of both worlds.

But I felt he would one day tire of her and want to come back to the home and family we had built together.

Whenever I talked to Mrs. Leland about this, she told me I was a fool. "Have you no self-respect? Kick him out for good! Make him pay for his fooling around."

But I wouldn't listen. I still felt like a married woman and avoided the company of other men—except for Ed Leland, who was like one of the family. Although he had made it clear that he would be ready

4

whenever I was, I couldn't take him seriously. In my heart, I was still married to John.

The turning point came when my husband's mistress, Heidi, become seriously ill. John stopped by one day and explained that he had been up all night and had taken Heidi to the hospital. She was suffering from cancer, he said.

We didn't see much of him after that. Apparently, he spent all his free time at the hospital. After a number of weeks, she died. I felt it was only right to attend the funeral, but I made it a point not to get too close to John.

When spring came again, I called Ed to help me. We spent a long day opening and cleaning the hives and setting them in their spring locations. I realized what a good and faithful friend he was, and told him that he would always be dear to me. He kissed me good night, and there seemed to be a jaunty bounce in his step as he walked away.

The next day, I had a telephone call from John. He said the silence in his apartment was unbearable. He wanted to move some of his things back to the house, and until he decided what he should do, he would sleep in his office.

Within a week, he came to see me. He was thin and looked drained. He said he wanted to talk and literally fell on his knees in front of me. He begged my forgiveness and said he had made a serious mistake. He said he had realized for some time that he really didn't want to spend the rest of his life with Heidi, but, when she got sick, he felt he had to stick by her. She was suffering enough, he said, without being left alone as well.

He wept and asked me to forgive him and take him back. Or at least, to let him come back in the house and try to earn his way back as a husband.

So it had happened. Just as I always believed it would. My husband had come back to me, because this was where he really belonged!

Somehow, I knew what he would say even before he said it. The words sounded old to me, as if I had heard them all before. Moreover, they didn't make me feel as happy as I had thought they would, and I found myself not listening, but thinking instead about the hives Ed and I had opened that week.

John appeared to be in agony, but I told him that I needed time to think. He agreed to leave and wait until the next evening for a decision from me. He said he knew he had treated me badly and didn't deserve to be forgiven. But he declared that he would make it all up to me because he now knew I was the only one for him.

Early the next morning, Ed banged on the door. He had seen John's car and suspected why he had come. He told me not to listen to John, that he might leave me again if the mood struck him, and that he couldn't stand by and see me hurt again. He told me he loved me and had only waited until I could see it for myself. Now, he begged me to

5

marry him, and said that we could move away for a fresh beginning, away from old memories that had grown hollow.

So I had a choice. I could take back my erring husband, who now said he had never really stopped loving me, or I could marry my faithful neighbor, who had always been there when I needed him. I shut myself in my bedroom and thought about it all day.

I couldn't decide. After all these years, I couldn't imagine myself as anyone but John's wife. And Ed, always faithful, always there, but I still couldn't think of him romantically. I was torn and scared.

Suddenly, the telephone rang. As I picked it up, I still didn't know what I should do. Then I heard John's familiar voice, and all at once my future was clear.

"I love you," he said. "I've always loved you."

These were the words I had waited so long to hear, the same words that had started my home and family years ago. I took a deep breath.

They could start my life all over again, set my days back on track, and give my children their father once more. My mind was made up.

"It's no use, John," I told him. "It's too late."

I told him I was now ready to give him the divorce he had asked for earlier. I had considered what he said, but finally realized I had been holding onto a dream—there was nothing left for us.

He was devastated and begged me to reconsider. He babbled on about how I was his "whole life," and it became repulsive to me. I hung up the phone.

Immediately, I called Ed. He was ecstatic to hear my voice.

"I knew you'd call," he said. "I'll be right over!"

But I stopped him. I told him I appreciated the fact that he had always been there to lean on, and that I had come to realize that I loved him dearly, as a brother, and that no matter how hard I tried I couldn't make myself want to marry him. I must say he took my rejection much more easily than John had.

I hung up the phone again and walked into the living room. I poured myself a glass of wine and looked at myself in the mirror.

"Here's to you, you hussy! You may look like the mother of two children, a keeper of bees, a tiller of the soil, but you are really a heartbreaker! Tonight you have smashed the dreams of two men!"

I laughed out loud, and felt as if I had dropped a heavy burden. I didn't love the John that was, only the John who used to be. I had been clinging to my dreams and my first love. If he had never left me, things would have been different, but I finally realized the hurt and humiliation I had suffered when he had lived openly with another woman could never be erased.

And I could never love Ed. He would always be part of my old life. He apparently thought he would become a hero by righting a wrong done by another man.

It was time for me to set some goals for myself and think about how I would reach them.

That night I slept a long, deep sleep. When I woke up, I felt ready to take on the world. I dressed myself carefully and applied my makeup as best I knew how. Then I set out to look for a job, a new life, new friends—and who knows what else.

I have found a job, and I'm taking classes in the evening to prepare myself for a better one. I have had a few casual dates, and have met a man who seems genuinely interested in me. I don't plan to encourage him to move too quickly, but I do think I shall listen to what he has in mind. But now, at last, I can hold my head up high as a real person . . . and do what's right for me.

THE END

STILL IN LOVE
WITH MY EX

I suppose I always knew I would run into Lyle again. I didn't dwell on it and I didn't dream about it, because when I'd divorced him, I'd made up my mind not to look back. But I knew that someday we'd see each other again and maybe deep down, I also knew that, somehow, I wanted that. I didn't want to begin again with him and I certainly didn't want to be married to him again, but I wanted to see him just one more time. Maybe I was hoping that he'd changed in the five years since we'd been divorced, that his ideas about how life should be and what was really important would be different. After all, we were nearly nine years older now than when we'd first met. I knew I hadn't changed much, at least not in my fierce determination to live my own life in the way I thought best for me, but I thought maybe Lyle might have changed his outlook. Maybe he'd finally come to know that money wasn't all that important. That there were better things to do in life than worry all the time about making lots of it.

When he did come back into my life, it was as sudden and unexpected as the first time we'd met. The first time, I'd been an art student and Lyle had come to the art school with a wild scheme to get a bunch of students to go to Paris for a month, with him as their guide. It didn't work—the director at the school thought he was a little crazy, but I fell in love with him the very first moment he smiled at me.

One thing led to another, until I was divorced and at home, in my little house in Mapleleaf. I'd just gotten off from my job as a waitress at the Silver Lining Café. It was November, damp and chilly, the time of year when a wet wind would come in from the sea and out across the mountains like a knife. I had a fire going and the big portion of stew the cook had given me was bubbling away on my ancient stove. I had my dog Otis's big plastic dish out, nearly filled with dog food. My plan was to give him some of the stew, have my own dinner, and then get to work on my latest project. From the kitchen, I could see it there in the tiny spare bedroom, a huge, as yet unformed piece of beautiful buried redwood, waiting for me to give it form and life. If all went well—and I knew it would—I would not only be paid well for it by the lady who'd commissioned me to do the work, but the statue would stand on a grassy hill just beyond the road that led to the lighthouse. It would be my first real success here.

I heard the sound of an approaching car and realized that was why Otis had been barking his head off. Usually, he barked at nothing, as if he was pretending some danger lurked outside and he wanted to

8

impress me. But this time, it was a visitor. I stood at the front window and rubbed a little spot clear so I could see through the mist and oncoming darkness. It wasn't a car but a pickup truck. Since most of my neighbors drove pickups, I mentally made a quick count of my supplies—plenty of coffee, enough of the stew for two people, and some bread I'd made. Plus a bottle of wine, unopened and leftover from a still life I'd done the winter before. I'd sold that watercolor for fifty dollars, which was exactly my bill at the local grocery at the time.

Otis was still barking wildly, showing off. I rubbed a bigger place on the steamy window and pressed my face against it. The truck had parked; someone was getting out. In the gloom and drizzle, I saw a man get out of the truck and walk around it. He stood for a moment, looking at my little house.

"Otis," I said automatically, "will you please keep quiet?" I narrowed my eyes, trying to see. The man stood there in the rainy night, legs apart, hands jammed into his jacket pockets, wide shoulders somewhat hunched against the wind. He was looking intently at the lighted window where I stood staring back.

I let my breath out slowly. I stepped away from the window then and looked quickly around my tiny house, almost as if to hold it close to me, hold close the life I'd made for myself here. I had a job and friends and good neighbors and privacy to do my sculpting. In that other little room stood my beautiful piece of redwood, waiting for me to finally produce something that was beautiful and important. . . .

Maybe, I told myself, *I'm mistaken.* After all, it was nearly dark outside and it was raining and it had been five years since I'd seen him. It was probably my mind playing tricks on me. I turned back to my clear spot on the steamy window and watched as the man headed for my front porch. He seemed somewhat uncertain, as if he wasn't sure he had the right house.

It was, I realized, Lyle. No doubt about it. I knew well enough how that body moved, the set of the shoulders, the impatient stride. He was on the porch now, knocking, and my dog had retreated under the table, snarling softly.

"Anybody home in there?" Lyle called.

Go away, I thought wildly. *Go away and leave me alone! How dare you find me—how dare you knock at my door?*

"Hello," Lyle said, and I could see he was trying to peer in through the glass window at the top of my front door. "Does Brittany Johnston live here?"

I opened the door. I looked up at him, into his clear eyes, and I saw him smile slowly, with great charm, exactly the way he'd smiled nine years earlier, the first time we met. There was rain on his eyelashes and rainwater had soaked his hair. His face needed a shave. He looked wonderful, and for a heartbeat, I couldn't answer him.

9

"Yes," I said, trying to smile and be casual, "I live here. But my name is Brittany Romaine now. I use my maiden name, remember? Come on in, Lyle."

I knew that his presence, his masculine, electrifying presence would change things and it did, almost immediately. Otis stopped snarling and came out from under the table, his tail wagging, and his big eyes adoring. As if by magic, the newscast went off the radio and music came on—soft, because my radio was so old it couldn't project anything very loudly.

"It took me all day to find you," Lyle told me. "I forgot about the name change."

He was still looking at me. He seemed a little shy and uneasy, and I found myself remembering that quality about him, that dear, little-boy quality I'd nearly forgotten.

"Well," I said, tugging at Otis's collar, "sit down, Lyle. You can sit over there in the rocker if you like—the other chair is sort of horrible. Otis chewed most of the stuffing out of it so now it's his bed."

Lyle took off his jacket, and handed it to me as if he' d just come back home from some long trip. He was still watching me, a smile on his face. "You haven't changed," he told me as I hung his jacket up on one of the pegs I'd carved for the hallway. "Turn around, Brittany, and let me have another look."

I felt my face go hot. I had on one of my smocks—not a very nice one—and my hair probably looked crazy from the dampness. I'd worn it up to work that day, because my boss didn't like long hair around the kitchen, but I'd unpinned it when I got home. Without turning around, I took both hands and smoothed at my hair, hoping to tame it. *Stop,* I thought then. *What are you doing, anyhow? What difference does it make how you look to him?*

"I'll fix some coffee," I told him, not standing there for him to look at me the way he'd wanted to. "I brought some food home from work. Have you had your dinner?"

"Not yet. I was going to ask you out to dinner."

I was in the kitchen, trying not to let my feelings show. I was excited and giddy and angry, all at the same time. My life had been going along just fine and I had a dead-certain feeling that Lyle could change all that if he wanted to. I began to wonder why he'd shown up on my doorstep; I knew he wanted something from me.

"There isn't anyplace to go except the Silver Lining Café," I said from my kitchen. "And I spent most of the day there, working." I got out two plates and two bread-and-butter dishes and started to set the little round table in the kitchen. *Like old times,* I thought, and I glanced into the next room at Lyle. He had settled himself into that old rosewood rocker, stretching out his long legs toward the fire. My dog was happy to see Lyle again, and had settled himself at Lyle's feet.

10

Like old times, I thought again. *Me in the kitchen, trying to please, Lyle waiting to be waited on, everything cozy and warm.*

I'd been clearing the dead flowers from the bouquet on the table. I took a deep breath to steady myself. Then, still carrying the plates, I stood in the doorway.

"Would you mind telling me why you're here?" I asked him quietly.

He turned his head to look at me. His hair was drying from the fire; he needed a haircut. His eyes didn't reveal a thing.

"I came to see you, of course. And it's about time." He grinned. "I got to thinking, Brittany, that you and I should get together once in awhile. Maybe every year. Maybe more often than that." His grin widened. "Like old friends. We'll have a reunion; we'll talk things over. We can let each other know how we're doing."

It seemed I had begun to come back to my senses. "I asked you a question, Lyle. After all this time—you never tried to get in touch with me before. Not even a postcard or a phone call. Nothing. Why now?

He looked at me for a brief second. "Okay," he said finally. "Aside from the fact that I thought we should get together and renew . . ."

"What's the real reason?" I was beginning to feel better. I was beginning to feel more like my old self, or rather my new self, the self I'd discovered after divorcing Lyle. To look at him out there in the rain, big and male and gorgeous as ever, to let all those feelings of excitement take over the way they'd done, that had been a mistake. To rush out to the kitchen almost immediately and start fixing a meal for him, just as if he'd only been gone a few hours—that was very likely a mistake, too.

"I'm beginning to get the feeling," he said, "that you're mad at me for something."

Mad at you? Mad at you? I thought to myself. He had taken six years of my life away, that was all. Six years. I'd gone out with him for two, been married to him for two, and it had taken two more years for me to find myself after all the heartbreak. He had charmed me, made me promises, caused me to love him with such a wild, abiding passion that I thought I surely must be insane, and just when I was ready to do anything, anything at all to save our marriage, he cheated on me. Why on earth should I be mad at him?

"You know what?" I asked softly. "I think maybe it might be a good idea for us to go out to eat after all, Lyle. We can drive into Rosewood if you like. I'll get dressed. I won't be more than a minute, okay?"

He looked puzzled. He couldn't understand how I really felt. This place that was my sanctuary—I'd come here to be healed. I didn't want anyone, not even Lyle, to spoil it all for me.

I deliberately didn't take much time to get dressed up. I took a quick shower, brushed my hair, put on a skirt and sweater and somewhat scruffy shoes, and I was ready to go.

11

I'd never known Lyle to drive a truck before, usually his car was a fast, expensive sports car with huge payments to be made that he couldn't afford. Not only did it seem strange to be riding in a truck with him, but there was something very heavy banging around in the truck bed in back.

"What's that?" I asked as we headed down the highway toward Rosewood.

"Probably my dredge. I guess I didn't fasten it down real tight." He glanced at me. "Would you believe me if I told you I've thought about us a lot, Brittany? Even though I didn't get in touch, I thought about us. I couldn't figure out where we went wrong."

I stared out the front window into the dark rain. "Maybe," I said quietly, "it was that girl you slept with. The one I found you in bed with."

"That wasn't it," he said. "I mean, I don't think that was the real reason."

"That reason," I said coolly, "was about as real as it gets. I divorced you right afterward, remember?"

"But she—whatever her stupid name was—she wasn't the real reason, honey. The real reason was something else. And I still haven't been able to figure that out."

Neither had I, but I'd given up on it long ago, when I decided to put my life back together again. It didn't seem to matter too much to me, anyhow. What mattered was that our whole thing, our whole love affair and marriage had been like some bright, shining promise that was like gossamer, like stardust. What should have been lasting and solid just melted away. I was too much in love to understand all that at first.

"Let's not talk about the past," I said. "Lyle, I'd still like to know why you came here looking for me after all this time."

"You're suspicious," he said almost under his breath. "You always were like that. You never really trusted me."

"Are you going to tell me or not? I'm not stupid anymore, you know."

"You never were," he said quietly. "You always were too smart for me, Brittany. I mean, you were in art school when I met you, and I was more or less trying to scratch out a living. You had—class." He glanced at me again and his eyes were warm and admiring. "Real class. I liked that. You've still got that."

"I work as a waitress," I reminded him. "I live in a one-bedroom house that's about one step up from a shack. I live from paycheck to paycheck."

"That doesn't matter. You've still got it," he told me. He slid one arm around the back of the seat, letting his warm, strong hand rest lightly on my shoulder. "I think about us," he said quietly. "Believe it or not, I do. Anyway, I'm glad I came down here. I'm glad we're

12

together right now, even if you are still mad at me."

So, he wasn't going to tell me the real reason he'd shown up. Not just yet, anyway. I sighed softly and let myself enjoy the moment—the dark, steady rain all around us, the warm, cozy truck interior, Lyle there beside me, beautiful and strong, and as thrilling as ever.

I could love you again, I thought clearly. *I could love you as I did before, only more so. I could love you as a woman now, not as a moonstruck young girl.*

Maybe Lyle sensed my thoughts—he'd always been able to do that. He'd slowed the truck down and then he'd pulled off the highway, and down a country road. Then he stopped the truck.

"Lyle, what are you doing?" I asked.

"I just wanted to kiss you," he said softly. His hand touched my face, smoothing back my hair. "I just wanted to hold you for a minute, and kiss you. Okay?"

Sure, it was okay. I knew it really wasn't okay, but now, at that moment, in this place, safe from the rain and darkness, just for now, it was okay.

"Only one kiss," he murmured. "Promise."

I didn't say anything. I closed my eyes as if to gain some sort of strength, as if to fight off some powerful spell, some sweet and tender trap. .

But it didn't matter. He was kissing me and it didn't matter about any of those worrisome things that had plagued me since he'd come back into my life.

"Wow," Lyle said under his breath. "You haven't changed, Brittany. I used to think I only imagined what you could do to me when I kiss you, but after all this time, it's still the same."

"Lyle, we'd better not continue with this." I struggled to sit up all the way. My heart was beating harder than usual and I was so full of sudden, sweeping pleasure that it frightened me. "We're not kids anymore. We shouldn't be pulling off the road, parking like—"

"Like we used to do," he said, finishing my thought.

"Lyle, I mean it. You promised to take me to dinner."

I had to give him credit for having charming manners, in the best old tradition. He started the truck at once, and within seconds, we were back on the highway. Not only that, he didn't behave as if he were in the least bit annoyed with me.

I found myself watching him as we drove through the darkness toward the village of Rosewood, sneaking looks at his nice profile. If anything, he was more handsome than he'd been before, when I'd been married to him.

That handsome face and body are what gets Lyle through life, I thought. *That and his great charm, and that sweet, unexpected little-boy quality about him that he doesn't even know he has.*

13

I suggested the restaurant, first of all, because it wasn't the dark, quiet sort of place I felt sure Lyle expected me to pick.

"This isn't exactly what I had in mind," he told me as we settled ourselves across from each other. "I can afford to take you any place you want to go." He kept looking around. "I didn't expect a glorified diner on our first night back together."

I leaned toward him and kept my voice low. "Lyle, we are not back together again! You—you showed up on my doorstep, asked me out to dinner, and now—"

"Going out was your idea," he said dryly, looking hard at the menu. "You want a hot dog or a tuna-fish sandwich?"

But he made me laugh, even giggle, as we sat there at that old, nearly worn-out table with the wildflowers stuck in a jar between us, and once again, I felt myself giving in to joy. Not the crazy kind, where you jump up and down and scream, but some quiet, sweet, and reflective kind that I hadn't experienced since—since the last time we were together.

We tried, more or less, to get sort of caught up with each other. As if we had to do that, as if we owed it to one another to talk a little about where we'd been and what we'd been doing since we'd split up. Everything was funny, at least everything Lyle told me about his various get-rich-quick schemes. They were all wild and if they hadn't been Lyle's ideas, maybe a little weird.

"And now?" I asked finally, secretly relieved to know he hadn't remarried in all that time, or at least he hadn't mentioned that. "What're you doing now, Lyle?"

He seemed uneasy, all of a sudden. "Well," he said carefully, "remember the idea I had to do private advertising on the side for up-and-coming business guys just starting out?"

"That must have been after I left—after the divorce," I said. There had been so many ideas, schemes, all of them charming and crazy, but surprisingly, most of them brought him money. Not enough, though— never enough to let him get whatever it was he wanted out of life. I'd never been able to figure out what that was, all I knew was it had something to do with being rich, although he never told me that.

I was watching him carefully. I had the clear feeling that he was working up to telling me something, something he knew I wouldn't like hearing. I waited for the hammer to fall. Whatever he was working up to tell me—well, I wondered where I'd fit in his newest plans.

"I decided to try being a guide again. Not to try," he said. "To do it. As a sideline. Apart from my other work."

"Other work?" I leaned closer to him. "Lyle, what are you getting at?" I might as well have said: What the heck are you up to?

He was looking at me, into my eyes. This was a sure sign that whatever it was, he wouldn't turn back. Not until he'd tried as hard as he could to make whatever it was work.

14

I'd often thought it was a shame he didn't feel that dedicated to our marriage.

"Brittany," he said, his voice low, "I don't know why I didn't think of this before! It's so easy—it's there, waiting for somebody to find it—waiting to be taken in and weighed, honey. It's still there, lots of it. Don't let anybody tell you it's all played out because they don't know what I know."

I let my breath out. Gold. That had to be it. *Of course,* I thought, *this is the big venture he's been looking for all along. The real thing— gold. Knowing Lyle, if there really was some around, he could find it.*

"You mean you're going to—"

He nodded. "I've got just about everything I'll need," he said eagerly. "I met this guy in a bar and we started talking and he told me he has all this equipment—everything to look for gold. He even had a nice big tent and cook stove and the whole works. Plus the heavy stuff."

"You're talking about the dredge, right? In the back of your truck."

"No" he said, looking worried again. "I'm talking about heavy machinery, like the backhoe and the bulldozer. But, Brittany, you'll get used to the noise. I mean the sounds. And I promise to finish up by evening." He smiled. "In time to take you to dinner someplace fancy. Okay?"

"Outside my house!" I cried. "Are you saying that all this—this craziness is going to be happening right outside my door?" When he didn't answer, the panic grew in me. "A backhoe and a bulldozer right outside my door, Lyle? Is that what you're saying?"

He looked around uncomfortably. "Brittany, it seems to me if you didn't want to be bothered when somebody decided to mine the creek again, you'd—"

"Lyle, nobody has mined that creek since the Gold Rush when they gave up on it after years of breaking their backs."

His eyes were smiling. "All those years and nobody's been back to try. Like I said, it's all there, just waiting to be picked up and weighed."

"Then why didn't whoever it was you met in the bar claim it? He had all the equipment, didn't he?"

"He's too old. And he kept falling off the mountain."

"What?" *Of course,* I thought. *It has to be dangerous. The only time he'd done something that wasn't, was the time he wanted to take my class to Paris and that was probably the only time he ever completely failed in one of his wild schemes.*

"Yes, he fell off the mountain a few times. Anyway, he's the one who told me about the creek, and how he always wanted to try there. I'm sorry it happens to be next to your place, Brittany. But that's just the way it worked out." He smiled. "Looks real neat to me—I'll be close to you while I'm getting richer and richer. I figure I can give you

15

a daily—or nightly—report on how well I'm doing. Okay?"

"No," I said through clenched lips, "it's not okay, Lyle. Look, I have a life, too, you know. I realize it may be very hard for you to believe that I'm not still moping around over you, but—"

"So you did that? How long did you do that, Brittany?"

He was teasing me now, pleased that he'd all but won. "I'll make it all up to you," he told me. Then, his hands covered mine across the table and his beautiful eyes were suddenly serious. "I mean it, Brittany. I want to make it all up to you. All my failures. I knew you were living in Mapleleaf, but I didn't know you'd be this close to my camp."

"You're going to have a camp there, too?" I asked.

"The tourists won't bother you, honey. I'll take them further up the creek, where I won't be working. Did I tell you I'm going to be a guide on weekends for people from the city who want to come down here to pan for gold?"

Of course, it wasn't very likely there'd be any gold where he'd be taking them, not if I knew Lyle. But it would be a big party, and everybody would have a great time and some of the women would come on to him or even think they were in love with him. That's the way it usually went. Lyle had a pattern. He'd only cheated on me once, though, in spite of his many chances. Just once, when things between us were so rocky, when we were both in agony because we couldn't stop the end from coming.

"Is that why you took me on that country road and kissed me, Lyle? To get me to see things your way? To come around and not file any complaints about the noise and the wanton spoiling of this beautiful land?"

"I've got legal papers," he said flatly. "So you can forget all that, Brittany. The main thing now is for us to be able to get along. Because if you start giving me big problems in the legal area, then I'll complain that you're cutting up too many trees to do your sculpture."

"You know I mostly have my wood shipped in. The only local wood I use is from fallen trees. You know perfectly well I wouldn't—"

"Sure," he said gently, "I know. You've still got a tender heart, Brittany. You still want to take care of everything within your reach—stray dogs, flowers, even the mountains. I was married to you once, remember. How could I forget that about you?"

So I agreed to his plans, more or less. I gave in—he wouldn't be on my little piece of property anyway, and he'd obviously done it all quite legally. There was really nothing I could do about it. I had wanted Lyle to come back into my life one last, final time. I had wanted to see him, hear his voice, and see him smile. Instead, he hadn't only fixed things so that he'd be practically sleeping in my flower garden, but he had somehow managed to make me fall in love with him all over again. Or maybe I'd just never stopped loving him. Maybe that was it.

16

Yet, I was genuinely angry, and with good reason it seemed to me. We finished our food in silence, and when we were outside and Lyle asked me if I wanted to walk to the beach, I declined the offer.

But on the drive back to Mapleleaf, it was the same thing—the cozy truck, romantic music from the radio, Lyle close to me, wanting to make love to me. I knew he did. I knew that as well as I knew I was in love with him. After all, I'd been married to him once, as he'd said—and I couldn't forget a thing like that. I couldn't forget the look in his eyes when he wanted to take me in his arms.

"I'll wait until tomorrow to fix up my camp," he told me at my front door. "Tonight, I'll just sleep in my sleeping bag in the truck." He looked down at me in the dim amber glow from the porch light. "Unless . . ."

"Good night, Lyle," I said fiercely. "Maybe we can talk tomorrow. . . ."

"What about tonight?"

"I'm too tired to talk about it," I told him. "The fact remains, I have been commissioned to do a statue, a very important piece depicting all the pioneer women who came to Mapleleaf and survived. You've no idea how hard it must have been for most of them. I've been researching, and—"

"Look, Brittany," he said. "I'm not going to stop you from doing your thing."

I hated it when he put it that way. Lyle had always put down my work, as if it were somehow silly. Like the watercolors I'd done when we were first married and living in a tiny apartment. Lyle had behaved as if that was just a woman's pastime, until she got pregnant and her real work began. Now, he seemed to be doing the very same thing.

"If it's too noisy," I told him coolly, "I'll sue you. Good night, Lyle."

I closed the door softly, but firmly, behind me. Lyle hesitated—I felt sure he was going to knock and ask if he could come in but he didn't. He turned and went quickly down the porch steps, got into his truck, and took off. I listened, there in my tiny kitchen where the only other sound was Otis, wanting to bark, but knowing he'd get scolded if he did, so he just whined.

The truck could be heard on the narrow road outside, all the way down toward the creek, and then it stopped. *He's close,* I thought, a quick surge of pleasure going through me.

If one of us wanted to, we could call out a name in the night and the other would surely hear.

When I found I couldn't sleep, I finally got up and crept to the kitchen to get a glass of water. I wasn't the least bit thirsty and I woke up Otis, and he immediately thought it was morning and whined to be let out. As I opened the door for him, I could see Lyle's campfire, burning low, just an orange glow in the darkness. My dog headed that

17

way. I smiled a little at the thought of Lyle in his sleeping bag, with Otis pouncing on him.

I had to work at the Silver Lining Café the next day. I was waiting on tourists mostly. I didn't have time to think much about my situation. I knew there was really nothing I could do about getting Lyle to move somewhere else to look for gold. But I really didn't want him that close to me. I knew I'd just have to put up with the problem of the noise and the tourists—and Lyle. There would be some extra dust around, plus the garbage, but that didn't bother me, at least not a whole lot.

What bothered me was Lyle. Having him so near, watching his charm get to me once again. Those first few days, we didn't do much more than wave at each other. I'd thought he'd appear on my doorstep at least once a day, but I was wrong. In the morning, as I got into my ancient car, I'd see him down the ridge, cooking his breakfast. He'd hear the sound of my car and he'd stand up and wave. More than likely, Otis would be there, too, right by Lyle's side. Otis had reverted back to puppyhood, with Lyle as his daddy.

I began to worry about Lyle and hating myself for doing that. He was out there, all alone, except for Otis, working his heart out on that backhoe. He had his tent set up and every morning and evening I could smell food cooking. Actually, Lyle knew how to look after himself very well. So I didn't bother him—not at first. I was busy working at the Silver Lining Café until after two, when we'd finished with the lunch customers, and when I got home I immediately began working on my statue. I had a nice piece of pitch burl from a redwood tree, a dead one I'd come across while walking in the nearby woods, and I wanted to cut it to use it later on for the pedestal. The immediate noise from my saw drowned out the sound of Lyle outside on his tractor, so I had no idea he'd been knocking at my door until Otis dashed around to the back of the house where I was working and began barking.

I ignored him at first. It wasn't dinnertime, and he'd had plenty of fresh, cool water in his dish. Besides, I thought it a bit disloyal for him to be gone all night at Lyle's camp, the way he'd done the night before.

When Lyle gently touched my shoulder, I think I jumped a mile. I turned and looked up into his smiling face. His hair was wet—he and Otis had probably just come from a swim in the creek. "I didn't mean to scare you," he said, when I'd shut off the saw. "I just came over to invite you to a party."

"I don't go to parties," I told him, taking off my big denim work apron. "I'm too busy for that."

"But I've been working out the details for two days. I've got beer and food all iced down—maybe you noticed the tarp over the bed of my truck. Will you come, please?"

I hadn't noticed. I'd made a promise to myself not to snoop, not to creep around peeking out of windows at his camp, and not to try to

18

watch for him. "I may not have time," I told him, remembering how it had been when we were still married and we'd go to parties. Women were always after Lyle. Although he might look at me from across a crowded room and wink, as if to say it was all in fun and he only loved me, and me alone—still, I used to feel hurt and jealous. I'd always been shy and a bit reclusive. Maybe that's why I'd felt so at home in Mapleleaf where neighbors were polite but tended to live far apart and minded their own business.

"Take the time," Lyle told me. "It won't be a party without you, Brittany. I washed my shirt in the river, just so I'd look nice for you."

You big liar, I thought. *The day you do your laundry in the river is the day hell freezes over. He more than likely had zipped into Rosewood and had his clothes hand washed and ironed while he shopped for his favorite beer, imported and expensive.*

Still, I could tell he really wanted me to come. I ended up not only promising to come to the party the next evening, but I found myself lending him a cooler and some glasses. When he left, he gave me one of his brief looks, a kind of message that somehow told me we shared some lovely secret. That had been the message I'd silently gotten from him the first time we met, there at the art school. The look held some kind of promise, as if sometime, maybe not now or tomorrow even, but sometime soon, he was going to make love to me. And I would love it—and I would be hooked.

The next morning as I showered to get ready to go to work, the delicious aroma of cooking barbecue sauce floated in through the open windows of my house.

As I drove off to work, I raised my hand in greeting and there on the ridge, Lyle did the same thing, with what looked like a big, wooden spoon in his hand. I could see my dog sitting there, totally happy, by Lyle's tent.

What would it be like to wake up in his arms again? I thought to myself.

That was the sort of thinking I had all that day, while I waited on tables, while I sat in a back booth with the other waitresses, getting our free late lunch, and while I fixed a cold sandwich for myself much later that evening. I knew I was in trouble as far as that kind of thinking went. I knew what it all meant. It simply meant that I was very likely going to make love with him again. It was only a question of time. Not of place—we only had two choices, my bed or his sleeping bag. The question was: How long could I hold out?

All the next day, I could see Lyle on the ridge, doing things, getting ready for the party. The smells were glorious, floating down on the autumn air—the sauce, whatever meat was on the spits he'd rigged up, spices, and a heady, musky smell. I felt myself getting more and more excited. I waved my usual greeting that morning and my dog showed he still thought of me now and again by chasing my car until I'd nearly reached the Silver Lining Café. Then he turned tail and headed back to Lyle's camp.

"What's happened to you, Brittany?" one of the waitresses asked me as we sat in the kitchen taking a coffee break. "Did you finish whittling that statue they're going to pay you for doing? It must be a lot of money you're making by the way you look. You look—kind of wildly happy."

I'm losing it, I thought. *Lyle is definitely making me crazy again. I hadn't really spent a full evening working on the sculpture since he'd come back.*

Instead of going right home the way I usually did, I drove into Rosewood to a shopping center and bought myself a dress. I hadn't meant to do anything quite that foolish; what I'd planned on buying was a new shirt to wear with my usual jeans. But I saw a dress I liked in a window, so I tried it on and bought it.

It was soft and filmy, not overly long, but long enough to give it a kind of back-in-time look. It had lace on the front and on the full, soft skirt, and it was too pretty to pass up. Back home, when I was dressing for Lyle's party, I took a look at myself in the full mirror with the crack at the top. The dress was beautiful—I looked very much the way I'd looked nine years before at school, flushed and happy and excited and full of longing for Lyle.

I had bought some bright paper napkins to take to him because that was the sort of thing he'd probably forgotten when he'd done his shopping. From my front porch I could gaze at the ridge and see some sort of colorful little flags waving in the evening breeze. And balloons, strung up from tree to tree. And all those heavenly smells wafting around, scenting the whole countryside. I packed up the napkins, smoothed my hair down one more time, and walked up the ridge to Lyle's camp.

Otis greeted me with yelps and his tail wagging as I walked over the ridge. Lyle was stirring a big black pot of barbecue sauce and he smiled admiringly as I walked toward him. I could tell he liked the dress.

"I was getting a little worried," he told me. "You're late, kind of."

"I went into town," I told him. "Am I the first one here?"

"Yeah," he said, and at once, he changed the subject. He wanted me to stir the sauce while he fixed the salad. He gave me a barbecue apron to wear. I felt so pretty and happy and protected—all the things I'd learned to tell myself not to wish for, all the elusive, passing things I'd learned not to expect from life, because after Lyle and I split up I felt I could never have them again.

The very person I'd expected to protect me from life's hurts had himself hurt me so badly that I'd thought I might never recover, might

20

never find myself again, might never rise and stand and be sane and creative—after all that heartbreak. And now, there I was, quite ready to let it happen all over again.

"Lyle?" I put down the long spoon and headed for his big tent. He was just outside the door, breaking off pieces of fresh herbs, dropping them into a salad bowl. "Everybody's late?" I questioned, a feeling of worry beginning in me. Something was wrong, but I didn't know what. "And that one chicken on the spit won't feed very many," I told him. "Even if it is a nice fat one." I managed a smile at him. "Would you mind telling me what's going on here?"

"A party," he said, not looking at me. "A celebration, that's what! I've got a nice little deal going here and every day, Brittany—every single day I get closer to being rich—I mean really rich—so that, my Brittany, calls for a celebration. Look—I've even got champagne! Hold your glass, Brittany. I hope you're hungry."

"They aren't coming, are they? The party—it's just for the two of us."

"Well," he said, his face beginning to redden, "I guess I made a little mistake."

"What's that supposed to mean?"

"Well, I invited all these people, I really did, honey, but you see, I invited them for tomorrow. And I invited you for tonight. But never mind, you can come to the party tomorrow, too."

"You tricked me," I said. "You lied to me and then you tricked me."

"No! I didn't lie. I said there's going to be a big party and there is! And I didn't trick you, Brittany." He paused.

"Well," he said softly, beginning to smile, "maybe I did, just a little. I just wanted to spend some time with you, that's all. Just to have you near me by the fire. I thought we could talk. Like old times."

"You could have asked me," I said, my throat getting full, as if I had tears somewhere deep inside me, unshed and bitter. "Lyle, why do you always do this?"

A shadow crossed his face. His voice was oddly cold. "Do what?"

"Play games," I said. "It was always this way—you never knew how to be completely open and honest with me. Everything was always some kind of con, some trick, some scheme to get me to see things your way. Never," I said, my voice shaking. "We were never able to sit down and talk things over, decide what was best for both of us. It always had to be your way."

"You want to know something, Brittany?" His eyes were icy. "You sound just the way you used to. You sound just the way you did when we were living in that dump and I was busting my neck trying to get us out of there, trying to figure out how I could get a nice place for us. You always manage to twist things around so that I came out a bad guy."

21

"It wasn't a dump," I said faintly. "I loved that little place. If you hadn't been so—so greedy, thinking about getting bigger place, a better address—"

"You should have married a slob," he said, his face quite red with anger. "You should have married one of those friends of yours from that fancy art school! You had no place being with a guy who has ambitions, who wants to have the best out of life—" He stopped short. There was a terrible, frozen silence between us.

Very carefully, I put my glass of champagne down on the crate Lyle had set up by his tent as a table.

"I'd better be going," I said quietly. "I'm sorry, Lyle."

I felt blinded with sorrow as I walked toward the path that led to my house. It was nearly dark, the big swinging beam from the lighthouse had just been turned on, lighting up the dark sea beyond. I could smell the musk of the woods and the mingled scent of the flowers that grew on the mountain. About halfway down the path I stopped, hearing a sound behind me. I turned around, ready to tell him I was sorry. Then I saw that it was Otis, padding along behind me, switching his allegiance for the moment. I stumbled on and by the time I reached my crooked little front porch, I had begun to cry.

I wanted to scream, to sob, to just let all those unshed tears, all the pain and bewilderment and anguish he'd brought up to me pour out of my soul, and then—then maybe it would be over. The past could be left behind, forgotten forever, and I would emerge clean and whole and refreshed. What Lyle did or didn't do wouldn't bother me. Because we were separate now, two different people. We weren't married any longer.

But I couldn't. Maybe I should have done that right after the divorce, instead of holding everything inside me, counting on my work—my sculpture and my painting—to see me through.

I made myself a cup of instant coffee and walked into the room where the big piece of wood stood, covered with a sheet. I took the sheet down and stood back and narrowed my eyes. I thought I would begin working as soon as possible. The sculpture would be a woman. She would be slender, even fragile, and her strength would come from within. She'd have the pioneer spirit.

I took off my new dress and left it on the floor. I took off my new shoes and they landed somewhere near the back door. Otis was delighted—he thought I'd given them to him to chew on. I didn't care. I put on my jeans and my hideous old shirt and tied my hair back in a scarf. Barefoot, I climbed the ladder to rub oil on the block of sanded wood. In my mind's eye, I could see her, small and defiant and determined. Like all of the pioneers, all the women who'd been living here, living and dying here, making jam and having babies and keeping on even when their men had either left them or died. Strong women. I got to work and I kept on sculpting.

22

I worked far into the night. Sometime between night and morning, I went back out to my kitchen and made myself another cup of instant coffee. I sliced two pieces of brown bread that Juana Vila, my neighbor, had given me earlier that week, when I drove her into town to see the doctor. I spread jam on it that another lady had sent over when I'd been sick with the flu.

I felt good. I felt strong. Even though I looked out the window on my way back to my workroom, even though I stood for a moment looking at Lyle's campsite, I knew I was going to be okay. There was no fire tonight—no amber, warm glow, no fragrant smoke. It was dark over there, and lonely.

I don't need you anymore, I thought. *I'm strong now, not like I used to be when we were married. Maybe I still love you, but I don't need you. I'm free.*

My boss at the Silver Lining Café wanted me to work a double shift the next day, and because I could use the good tips the dinner shift brought, I agreed. I was dead on my feet, when I finally pulled up in front of my house, around eight that night. I'd hardly slept the night before and I knew I wouldn't get to work on the statue at all that night. I could barely manage to take my shower, but I fed Otis, wherever he was, and crawled into bed.

I woke up to the steady sound of a hard rain. I thought I heard Otis barking to be let in, but I couldn't be sure, because of the thunder. I thought he'd probably been at Lyle's camp all night. I pushed my hair back. I hadn't heard the usual party sounds, probably because I'd been so tired.

I put my feet down on the cold wood floor and padded to the front door. It was just like that dog of mine to decide to come home in the middle of a thunderstorm and get me out of bed.

I flung open the door and looked up into Lyle's wet face.

He wore a heavy jacket and he still looked soaked. Water dripped down his face into his clothing. Otis dashed in beside him.

"Hi," he said, leaning against the door. "Look, I know it's late, but could I come in, Brittany?"

"I don't mean to be inhospitable," I told him, "but this is pretty crazy, Lyle. I mean, I have to work tomorrow and—"

"I've got kind of a problem," he said, looking down at me. "Have you got a first-aid kit anywhere?"

"What?" I asked.

"A first-aid kit." And he withdrew his hand from the jacket. I stared at it in disbelief and horror. He had it wrapped in a bloody towel.

"Come with me." I pushed him down the hall. Then I rushed to the bathroom, where I kept bandages and tape and bottles of stuff that I never used. "Sit down," I said in a voice not my own. "Just sit down a minute—and let me look at it. Then I'll drive you to the hospital."

23

He sat and I knelt in front of him, gently taking the towel from his poor hand. I let my breath out in a sigh of relief. "It's a cut," I told him.

"Well," he said, "I knew that. I knew it was a cut."

I nearly giggled. I was beginning to feel somewhat lightheaded, maybe from overwork, maybe from the wild sound of the rain and thunder.

"I mean," I told him, "it isn't a puncture wound. That way, you might have lost the use of some of your fingers."

"Couldn't play my old guitar anymore," he said, beginning to smile at me.

"I'll get some warm water and soap," I told him, my heart beginning to beat faster. "You just stay put."

It didn't really look bad, in spite of the blood. We bent our heads over his hand and after a brief argument about whether or not it needed stitches, Lyle won. No hospital for him.

I got the fire going in the fireplace and once I'd cleaned and bandaged his hand, we sat close to it, me in the old rocker and Lyle on the floor, his long legs stretched out in front of him. I didn't dare look down at him—all sorts of feelings were beginning to filter into me.

"How was your party tonight?" I asked.

"What?"

"Your party. For the weekenders who've signed up to look for gold with you as their guide. How was it?"

"It was okay. About ten, twelve, showed up. Most of them got drunk. I hope they don't do that next weekend; somebody could fall in the deep part of the creek."

"I didn't hear a thing," I told him. "I came home from work and I was so tired that—" I'd looked down at him and he looked at me with those clear eyes, sending me some silent message of need. I heard my voice trail off.

"Come down here with me," he said gently. "Just for a minute, Brittany, let me hold you in my arms—please."

I didn't want to. I didn't want to give in that way. I didn't want to lose all those brave, beautiful feelings I'd had before, the ones about being free to be my own self and to live my life without him.

"It's not forever," he told me softly. "It's just for now, Brittany. Just for a little while. Please . . ."

And I slid off the chair and went down there, into his waiting arms.

"Be careful," I said. "Your poor hand is hurting enough."

"It's okay," he said, and he touched my face. "Thanks for taking care of me, Brittany."

His mouth was very close to mine. I shut my eyes briefly and then I felt the kiss begin. Again, all the years, the bad times, washed away, and they didn't matter at all. It was Lyle and me together—safe, safe from the storm outside. I could hear sounds at first, the mantle clock ticking busily, Otis snoring softly in his old chair in the corner, the heavy rain, and the maple tree outside creaking in the wind.

But very soon, I heard nothing but Lyle's heart thundering, next to, mine. I felt nothing but the closeness of us being together.

And I wanted nothing but this—to be with him.

The next morning I was in the kitchen when I heard Lyle's voice from my living room.

"Hey, Brittany, where are you?"

"Fixing coffee. You can get your own breakfast. I have to go to work." I put my coffeepot filled with water on the stove. I wasn't really sure how I felt. I knew if I allowed myself to, I'd feel wonderful, but I wasn't sure that would be good for me. So I just felt sleepy instead. Last night Lyle and I had made love again and again, almost as if to make up for lost time. It had been wonderful, but now I was feeling afraid. Maybe I shouldn't have tried to get close to him again. . . .

Lyle was up and in the kitchen then, looking unshaven and gorgeous. I looked at him and quickly got out two coffee mugs. "Last night," he began. "Brittany, about last night—"

"I've had my shower," I told him. "You can take one if you want to." I put out the pitcher of cream on the table. "I expect you'll get tired of bathing in the creek, except for all that gold floating around in it."

"You're upset," he said quietly, from behind me. "What is it, Brittany?"

"It isn't anything," I told him. "I just have to get ready to go to work, that's all. And when I get home, I want to spend at least six or seven hours on my sculpture. When it's finished, if the people who commissioned me like it, I'll have enough money to expand a little bit here. I might be able to quit my job as a waitress. Good-bye, Silver Lining Café." I turned around and looked squarely at him. "So I'm going to be very busy, Lyle. I can't—I mean, I don't want to—"

"You're too busy to work me into your schedule," he said. "Is that what you mean?"

"I didn't say that. But if you want to put it that way, I suppose that's true." I took a small breath. Behind me the coffee had started perking, warming the small room, scenting the whole house with its fragrance.

"Things ought to be really great this morning," Lyle said quietly. "After last night, I thought maybe we could talk about—about starting over. But I can see I was wrong. All you wanted was what I gave you last night."

His words were like a slap in my face. "Think whatever you want," I told him. "It really doesn't matter. What matters to me is not letting myself become the way I was before, when we were married. I'm my own person now, and I have faith in myself. I'm not going to let you or anybody else take that away from me!" Then I left.

But at work, I felt miserable. All day long I told myself I'd feel better when I got home, but I didn't—not very much, any how. For some crazy reason, I thought Lyle might still be around my place, maybe waiting for me, but, of course, I was wrong. He would never do that—hang around and wait to talk things over after an argument. He'd never done it before, when we were together, so he wouldn't do it now. I realized my attitude that morning had very likely ended things between us, maybe forever.

I threw myself into my work. Whenever I could find time, I was working on the statue. I felt almost at peace—chipping, carving, and cutting away at that beautiful piece of wood. Bits and pieces of my work were all over. I had sold many tiny, carved animals I'd made when I first left Lyle. I hadn't made a whole lot, but it had helped to make my initial payment on the house. During the divorce, Lyle had offered to send me money every month for as long as I wanted it, but I had refused. I'd wanted to stand on my own two feet—nobody had helped me very much in my entire life and I wasn't about to start taking money from the man who had hurt me so much, after turning my life around completely.

Anyway, my work was important to me, even though I'd never made a good living doing it. I guess I thought the man I loved and married ought to understand my work, but Lyle never did. It was like he was obsessed with making money. He wanted me to be his partner—to fall in with all his plans, no matter how wacky they seemed to be. My work really didn't interest him at all. He didn't like or understand my friends from art school. He thought they were all crazy. His friends were mostly in business, different ventures that were going to make them rich. I didn't understand them and I didn't feel at ease with their wives and girlfriends. Once, coming out of the bathroom at somebody's swank apartment where Lyle and I had gone to a party, I overheard one girl refer to me as Raggedy Ann. I went to a store the next morning and bought some new dresses and shoes, but the truth was, it wasn't my style. Afterward, I hated myself for giving in, for trying to be someone I wasn't, for trying to look like all those other women.

During the next few days, I could hear Lyle on the ridge, working hard. That next weekend, I tried hard not to peek out my window, when all the people showed up at Lyle's campsite, tramping around, having what looked to me like a real fun time. They came mostly by way of Lyle's truck, some crammed in the front with him, and the rest sitting in the truck bed. They seemed to drink a lot of beer, and the good-time sounds lasted far into the night. When I came back from work I'd see them knee-deep in the creek, panning for gold, or pretending to. The girls had on skimpy bathing suits and one of them didn't even try pretending to be panning for gold—she was stretched out on a big flat rock, taking in the sun.

Well, it was none of my business what went on there. I had my own

26

thing to do and Lyle would never change. He probably was having the time of his life, getting paid very well for having a party all weekend.

It was very busy up on the ridge. I'd glance as I went to work in the mornings and again as I drove home; the scene on Friday, Saturday, and Sunday evenings remained the same—loud voices, laughter, giggles, and splashing in the creek.

When I'd finished working on my sculpture, maybe after seven, or sometimes eight straight hours, I'd take a hot shower to ease my muscles. Then I'd look out my window, into the darkness, over to where the campfire burned low and the loud voices had ceased.

I wondered if anybody was with Lyle, there in his tent. Maybe that girl who'd been on the rock.

The following Friday, I ran into Lyle in Rosewood. I'd gone in to pick up a few supplies at the big supermarket at the mouth of the valley and there was his truck, parked in the lot. To my surprise, Otis was sitting calmly in the truck, looking important, obviously waiting for Lyle to come out of the store.

I felt unreasonable anger go through me. I went over to the truck and tapped on the window and Otis began to bark with great joy. He put his big paw on the window and slobbered, but when I opened the unlocked door, he made absolutely no effort to jump down.

"You're terrible," I told him. "You're a terrible dog! I'm supposed to be the one you love, do you hear that? I'm the one who raised you from the time when you were a little puppy, and you don't show one bit of gratitude—"

"Hi," Lyle said from behind me. "Sounds like you're mad at Otis."

"I'm not at all mad at him," I said coolly, trying to control my sudden outburst. "It's only that I don't understand why he hangs around your place all the time. He's my dog."

"Well, maybe he prefers being with me."

I took a deep breath. "Look, Lyle—Otis is my dog and I don't have to explain anything to you. I want him back."

Lyle was looking at me in the same way he had when I'd insisted on inviting all my friends from the school over to our house, before we split up. I knew he thought I was being stubborn and vengeful.

"Sure," he said quietly, "he's your dog. But I don't think he'll stay. Not unless you tie him up and we both know he'd hate that."

"I don't have to tie him up," I said coldly. "He'll stay."

Lyle opened the door to the truck, and I tugged at Otis's collar. Finally, he sort of tumbled out and began whining.

"It isn't me, exactly," Lyle told me. "Brittany, there's another dog, a female—one of the girls brought her last weekend and I think Otis fell in love. The dog's a poodle."

I was trying to get Otis into my tiny car. "Well, if the poodle was there last weekend, Otis shouldn't still be acting this way. I think it's—I

27

think it's whatever you feed him. Too much meat. He'll get fat."

"No," Lyle said firmly. "It's the poodle, all right."

"But the dog has been gone almost a week!"

"Well," Lyle said, beginning to look a little uneasy. "Not exactly."

"The lady left her dog?" I felt my breath catch. "Oh," I heard myself saying.

The lady didn't leave—she's been there all week! I thought to myself.

"No," Lyle said quietly. "You don't know. It isn't what you think. And the only reason I'm talking about it at all is because—because I figure you'll drive by and see this woman around my place and you'll get the wrong idea."

"You mean I might think you're sleeping with her? I'll see you around, Lyle."

I started my car but Lyle had remained where he was, his face dark with anger. Finally, he tapped on the glass. "I don't care what you think," he said. "But for your information, it isn't what you think."

"I don't care," I said. "Get out of my way, please. I don't want to run over your foot." I took off. Fortunately, I didn't run over Lyle's foot.

Saturday was my first full day off in a long time, so I slept in until seven-thirty. When I got up and put the coffee on, I heard Otis whining to be let in.

"Well," I told him, holding open the screen door, "what an honor. Come to think of it, you've been around since yesterday. Did the poodle leave or—" I stopped talking. If the poodle was gone, so was the woman. Of course, Otis had hung around the camp before, when there wasn't another dog there, so it was hard to tell why he'd come back really.

All the same, around noon, when I went outside to bring in the piece of lace burl from the downed redwood tree I'd been weathering, I paused for a moment to look over at the ridge. All was quiet. Then, I saw Lyle out there, by himself. He seemed to be measuring, stretching something—some kind of rope, maybe, across the ridge, up through the rocks and then down and across the creek. I watched, fascinated. I felt certain the woman was gone. I nearly smiled. Maybe Lyle had told her to pack up and leave. Maybe Lyle knew I was jealous!

At any rate, I felt a lot better when I went inside to begin my work. The statue had begun to take on definite form. I had been working away at the neck for well over a week, and that morning, I decided to have her wearing some sort of hat, the kind I'd seen the older women in Mapleleaf wear as they worked in their gardens or chopped wood. At noon, I got down from the ladder and surveyed my work. I had to think about her face. I went out to the kitchen and began to slice bread to make a sandwich, and then the idea came to me that maybe I wouldn't

28

give her a face. Maybe she'd be better off if she didn't look like any woman in particular, but more like all the women pioneers who'd lived there, ever since the first women came there.

It was such an intriguing idea that I wished I could talk to somebody about it. That's when I noticed Lyle climbing up out of the creek, carrying what looked like a fishing line. Usually at noontime I'd see smoke from his campfire, which meant he was fixing a meal, but not today. Very quickly, I grabbed a big bottle of orange soda, some apples and peaches from my neighbor's tiny orchard, and spread peanut butter and jam on some of my bread. I also grabbed some carrots, and put everything into one of the baskets I kept hanging from the ceiling in the kitchen. Then I started out for the ridge, with Otis loping along beside me.

"Hello," I called, a bit out of breath. Lyle appeared from the far side of his tent. He looked totally surprised.

"Hey," he said. "It's nice to see you. Are you still mad at me?"

"I brought you some lunch," I said, ignoring the loaded question. But I looked around very quickly. The woman was gone. Not a trace of her—or her dog. I sat down on the soft grass, opening the basket. "I thought you might like to picnic," I said. "If you aren't too busy."

"I'm busy," he said, folding up the threadlike line he'd been measuring with. "But I can get back to it." He knelt close to me, peering into the basket.

"We could go the lighthouse if you want," I told him, flustered. "Unless you want to stay here, that is."

"I'd love a picnic at the lighthouse," he said, picking up the basket. "I can do more measuring when we get back. I'm making a lot of progress."

He seemed quite proud of himself. I didn't ask him what had happened to the usual weekend gold hunters, because I felt sure none of them had showed up that weekend. But that didn't seem to bother Lyle, at least not very much. He talked enthusiastically about the gold he felt certain he'd find.

It was a wonderful afternoon. We didn't argue, not even for a minute, and deep down I knew Lyle had told me the truth about the woman who'd been staying there. I knew he hadn't been sleeping with her, because I was so close by and he still cared about me. I knew he cared, and for that day, at least, he even seemed interested in my work.

"How's the sculpture coming, Brittany?" His eyes were teasing me.

Usually, that would have annoyed me, but not then. Nothing could have spoiled that perfect day for us.

"Moving along just fine," I said, stretching back on the soft grass. "Just fine," I repeated, turning my head to look at him. His eyes were very bright, as if he felt the wonder of this moment. "Would you care to come over and have a look?"

29

"You mean that? I thought you'd kicked me out of your house for good."

I couldn't help but smile. "I didn't ask you to move in with me, Lyle. I just invited you to come over and have a look at my work."

"You're very lovely, Brittany. More so than when—"

I sat up quickly. That was what that look meant, of course.

He wanted to make love to me—outside, by the lighthouse. "We'd better be going," I said, changing the subject

"Okay," he said cheerfully. "I'll carry the picnic basket. Where's Otis?"

But he knew something had changed between us. The feeling of anger between us, of misunderstanding, seemed to be gone. For a short time, at least.

We'd spent hours there by the lighthouse and it was nearly dark when we got back to my house. I went around turning on lights, chattering about how great it was to be able to heat the place by way of the fireplace and only having to pay a small heating bill.

"Well," he said finally, "when do I get to see it?"

"You mean the statue?"

"Yeah. Of course, I mean the statue."

"Well—now, I guess." We headed for the small bedroom feeling a little hesitant, and I reached up and yanked off the old sheet.

There was a small silence.

"Where's the face?" Lyle asked matter-of-factly.

"The face? Well—I may not do a face. I mean, I may just leave that a blank. I don't mean a blank, but kind of empty."

"Oh." He seemed uncomfortable. Either he didn't understand or else he thought it was stupid. Stupid and awful. I felt my heart sink—all my happy, cheerful feelings seemed to vanish. Lyle simply didn't understand me. He probably never would.

But I hid my disappointment, much the way I'd done when we were married. While he watched television, I hurried around in my kitchen, fixing a meal. I knew well enough the things that were Lyle's favorites, and I was glad I had some of them on hand. He loved bread and butter, and fried eggs with potatoes and mushrooms. I also had a lovely strawberry pie I'd baked and put in my freezer for a rainy day, only I had thought it would be when I was alone and maybe feeling kind of blue. But this was the perfect time—I popped it in the oven, and in no time my little house was filled with the heavenly fragrance of strawberries.

We ate our meal in front of the fireplace, where the fire crackled and logs gently broke open to reveal glowing embers. My old radio softly played music from the nearest station, which was the only one I could get. Outside, it had begun to drizzle.

"My tent has a leak," Lyle told me. He didn't look at me so I couldn't

30

tell whether or not he was lying. Lyle was a poor liar—those clear eyes always gave him away. "It'll be cold in there tonight," he said.

"Lyle," I said carefully, hoping against hope that I wasn't already persuaded, that I wasn't already charmed beyond reason, "it didn't work before when we were together—and I have no reason to believe this time would be any different."

"I didn't ask you to marry me just now," he said, finally looking at me. "I was only asking if maybe I could stay here to keep from getting wet. In fact, I really didn't ask that. I just said my tent leaks."

I let my breath out. "Lyle, what's going on with us?"

"I don't know exactly," he said softly. "I thought it was all over. I thought it was all a big mistake and we were finished. Now, I'm not so sure."

I wanted to cry.

"Please," I heard myself saying. "Please stay tonight. We don't have to think about anything beyond that. Just for tonight." I smiled at him. "I wouldn't want you to catch cold out there in your tent."

And so the magic words had been said and we suddenly became like happy children. We did the dishes together, and then, while Otis watched us with sleepy interest, we danced to the music on the radio, with my head resting lightly on his shoulder.

"You haven't changed," Lyle whispered to me. And I was captivated by his charming spell.

I wanted to reserve a little piece of myself, some tiny corner of my mind and heart, keeping it separate, so that I wouldn't be totally lost in love with Lyle, and so that afterward, I could find myself once again, be myself once again—independent, cool, lost in my work, and needing nobody.

But that didn't happen. I was a woman in love.

He was still asleep when I left early the next morning to go to work. I fixed coffee and turned off the stove, and I put a plate and cup out for him. I worried all the way to work about whether or not he'd be able to find the blackberry jam I meant for him to have with his toast and eggs.

It wasn't until my coffee break that it dawned on me that I had gone right back to behaving and thinking the way I used to. Lyle had been my entire life when we were married—I had put all my own ambitions aside. When I'd been with Lyle somehow I'd felt I had to totally concentrate on pleasing him. It was his quest for money, big money, that ruined us. His frantic drive to make more always got in the way, somehow. It had been awful for me.

And now, it was as if none of that bad stuff had ever happened. Just being with him, making love with him, had wiped away all the past.

I got off work at the usual time, and stopped by the big kitchen to pick up my usual take-home foods like all the waitresses did. But

31

instead of going right home, I drove into Rosewood and picked up a few art supplies. What I was really doing, I guess, was trying to get things sorted out.

I still loved him. And making love with him was a delight that brought such joy to me that it would be very hard to say no the next time he asked. But I'd already begun to regress into my old pattern; I became a kind of mindless being who couldn't think or create or do much of anything except worship Lyle.

Surprisingly, I felt relieved to find that he wasn't there at my house, waiting for me to show up and fix a meal for him, before rushing back to bed with him. But he hadn't even fixed himself breakfast—the cup and plate were still where I'd left them.

I skipped supper, fed Otis, and went to work on the statue. I'd have to try to get more work done on it before the week was out. Two members of the Mapleleaf Society were due to come see what I'd been doing with the grant they'd paid me.

At first, I was glad that Lyle wasn't around. I managed to get a surprisingly full day in, working at the Silver Lining Café, and then working far into the night on the sculpture. It finally began to take on a definite shape and form and the head looked quite good, with the hat and the strong, but slender, throat. I hadn't even let myself take as much as one peek out the window, over to the ridge and Lyle's camp. Even Otis was staying at home with me instead of going over there, probably because my house was warm and cozy and Lyle had no heat in his tent.

But after a few more days, I found that it had become hard for me to get to sleep at night, even though I was exhausted from a long day of waiting tables and then standing on the ladder for hours, chipping away at the sculpture. I would close my eyes and think of Lyle, of being close to him.

The next morning, as I drove to work, I could see him out there on his backhoe, working in the rain. His camp looked dreary, cold, and waterlogged. There hadn't been any campfire smoke for days, although sometimes I'd hear his truck roaring up the crooked road, heading for town. At first, I thought he was just going in to eat but one night, I heard him coming back very late, past midnight. *He's been drinking,* I told myself, *lying there in bed.* And Lyle only drinks when something is really wrong in his life. . . .

Me. Maybe it was me. Or to be more specific—maybe he regretted having made love to me. He'd never told me he still loved me. He'd told me I was pretty, sweet, desirable, and that I hadn't changed—but he hadn't said he loved me, not once, not even when he was making love to me.

No wonder I hadn't seen anything of him lately. He was probably scared to death I'd march up there to his campsite and invite him to move in with me.

The people from the Mapleleaf Society that had given me the grant to work on the statue came to visit me the next Sunday. Two elderly women puttered up the road in a shiny antique car. Their names were Cordelia and Lucia Fiske. They both wore white gloves, which they took off only when I served a nervous tea on my best tray. Then they began chatting about the statue.

"It's very big," the one named Lucia said. "Don't you think it's rather too big, Cordelia?"

"I have to agree with that," Cordelia said, nibbling on a piece of cake I'd made for the occasion. "We thought it would be smaller," she said logically.

"It's for outdoors," I told them nervously. "It's to go on—on a hilltop, or at least a rise. It needs to be big enough to be seen."

"Lovely cake, dear," Lucia said. She seemed to be constantly sniffing, and it occurred to me that maybe Otis had left a dog smell in the house. "I noticed—if you'll forgive me—that there isn't any face."

"Lucia," Cordelia said, "that's because it isn't nearly finished. It has taken rather a long time to get this far though, hasn't it?"

"There isn't going to be any face," I told them, beginning to feel desperate. Nothing was going right, nothing. Come to think of it, nothing in my life was going right. "It's symbolic that there isn't any face, I mean."

The women looked at each other behind their glasses. They both put down their cups of tea, almost in unison.

"Well," Lucia said. "I think there ought to be a face!"

"Maybe faces are the hardest part to do," Cordelia said.

"Look," I said in desperation, "it isn't that I can't—that I don't know how to carve the face! It's that I wanted it to represent all pioneer women who came here with a dream and stuck it out—stayed through the worst of it—"

They stared at me blankly. *There goes my grant,* I thought clearly. The second half of the money was due in a week. I knew I'd never get it. They didn't understand the statue and they didn't like me very much, and they definitely didn't like Otis. He showed up just as they were leaving and jumped up on one of them—I'm not sure which one—with filthy, muddy paws. Still, I was determined to finish the sculpture. I felt I had to. I felt that unless I could do that, I wouldn't be a person at all. Like my statue in there, I'd be incomplete.

Twice, I saw Lyle that following week as I was driving to work. He waved at me and then continued whatever he was doing. He was trying to get the tractor started Wednesday evening, when I saw him up there on the ridge as I was driving home from the post office. There had been a letter for me from the board of the Mapleleaf Society. They wanted me to appear before their committee in the city to explain my work. I knew what that meant. They would tell me they'd decided not to renew the grant. It didn't really matter at that point. What mattered to me was getting the piece done.

But somewhere deep inside me there was a terrible longing, a feeling of pain. It had to do with Lyle, I knew. It definitely had to do with Lyle, some kind of aching disappointment because he didn't he love me again. I knew he liked me; he thought I was funny and strange and a good lover—but he didn't love me.

All the same, the day before I had to go up to the city about the grant, I came home from work and instead of rushing in to work on the sculpture, I fixed coffee and a few sandwiches. I put them in a little pail with a lid and headed for the ridge. It was misty, cold, and dark. Even Otis had elected to stay home by the fire.

I was a bit out of breath when I'd reached the top of the hill. There was no sign of life anywhere around Lyle's camp, just a soaked pile of ashes where the campfire had been and some long underwear and some socks hanging wet and forlorn-looking on a clothesline he'd put up. I walked over to the tent. There wasn't anything to knock on but I didn't want to open the flap, either.

"Hey," I said, "anybody home in there?" I heard a sound, kind of a sudden movement. But then the tent flap opened and there was Lyle, wearing jeans and a sweatshirt.

"Hey," he said. "I didn't expect to see you around here, Brittany. Something wrong?"

"No, I—I just thought—I brought you some supper," I said. He didn't seem glad to see me.

"Thanks. I was going to go into town."

"Oh. Well—"

"No, no, save me a trip. Come on in," he said, standing back. I went inside the tent. It leaked, just like he'd said that night, and it was cold.

"I haven't seen you for a while," I told him, sitting gingerly on one of the crates. "I was wondering about you."

"About me?" he asked. "I'm fine. I'm just great. I probably will be moving on tomorrow or the day after." He opened the pail and began eating a sandwich. "Good," he said. "You make this?"

"Moving on? You mean you're through here? But—"

"Well, sometimes a guy makes a mistake. I made one here, that's all. To tell you the truth, Brittany, there isn't any gold here. At least I didn't find any. I dug holes and panned and dug more holes but I didn't find even a little nugget. Nothing. And you have to have a little something to convince people before they'll come around. Unless it's just strictly a party, but I suppose they can do that anywhere without paying me to do it. So you might say my idea was a gigantic bust."

"Oh," I said somewhat feebly. Well, maybe it was for the best. Without Lyle, maybe I'd start to feel better. Knowing he was close on the ridge—that had bothered me.

34

"So you're leaving right away then?" I asked in a quiet voice. "Did you say tomorrow?"

"Maybe. Or the next day. As soon as I can get somebody to come and haul the backhoe and the tractor back to the guy who told me there was gold to be had up here. I bet he'll even think I'm a failure."

"I'm sorry it didn't work out," I told him. "I mean—I don't mean about us—I mean I'm sorry you didn't get rich."

"Yeah." He looked at me, his eyes guarded. "About us, I hope you don't think . . . I hope you don't think I did a number on you, Brittany. I didn't plan to come down there to your place and spend the night a couple of times and then . . ."

"Oh," I said in a strange, cheerful voice, "I don't think anything like that, Lyle. Things are different now. We're different people now. I don't expect the same things of you that I did before," I lied to him.

"Good. I was afraid maybe you'd think I ran out on you or something." He smiled, as if it couldn't be so. "Took advantage of you. I wouldn't want you to think that. I wouldn't want it to end like that for us, Brittany."

"No." I had to get out of there, get away, before he saw what was happening to me. I was starting to fall apart and any second, it would have showed. "Well," I said, "enjoy the supper."

"Hey—don't go so soon! I mean," he said, "aren't you going to stay while I eat?"

"No," I said. "I have lots of work to do."

He was looking at me, his eyes direct. "Okay, then."

"Well," I said. "Good-bye, Lyle."

"Take care of yourself, Brittany."

"Yes." The tears stung my eyes. "You, too."

The next day, I drove to the city to meet with the Mapleleaf Society elders. It was a disaster. I didn't get the second half of my grant. Not only that, but Cordelia and Lucia had nothing nice to say about me. Those people didn't understand my work—and they didn't understand me. In fact, nobody did—not even Lyle. And he was the only one who mattered.

I was in a dismal mood that evening as I steered my little car toward home. I just wanted to curl up by the fireplace—in that place that was all my own—where I'd be secure and comfortable. I wanted to forget Cordelia and Lucia and the entire Mapleleaf Society. I turned on the radio to cheer me up. That's when I heard the news—there was a big fire in Mapleleaf—maybe threatening all I had in the world. I kept thinking of Otis, trapped in that fire, too scared to find a way out.

My little car seemed to take on wings. I drove faster than I ever had in my entire life, and when I got to Mapleleaf, I could see the reflection of the flames in the night sky. I hadn't thought it would be so bad. When I saw all the fire trucks and all the people and activity, I suddenly thought of Lyle. Where was Lyle?

Just for a flash of a second, just for a heartbeat, I saw life as it would be for me if something happened to him. Not being married to him, or even seeing him ever again, would be bearable. I could take that, live my life and get by okay. But if he were dead, I knew I couldn't. I loved him!

Then I saw his truck. He must have driven it out. It sat parked, along with a lot of other pickups belonging to my neighbors. I parked my little car, got out, and headed for Lyle's truck.

Otis sat inside, staring out the front windshield like he owned it. His tail wagged when he saw me, but he made no move to get out. He was waiting for Lyle.

And so was I.

Sometime around midnight, my neighbors set up a coffee, sandwich, and donut table for the volunteer firefighters. Every once in awhile, a group of exhausted men would come out of the woods and eat and drink coffee and go back in. But not Lyle. I began to pray for him. I didn't ask that he'd love me again, just that he'd be alive.

By dawn, the fire was contained. Volunteer firefighters were straggling in from all directions. One of them was Lyle, who came on the back of a fire truck with a lot of other volunteers. He climbed down, shook hands with everybody and headed for the coffee table, where I stood, silently thanking God. I had begun to wish that I had prayed that Lyle not only be alive, but that by some miracle he'd love me.

"Hey," he said when he saw me, "how'd you get here?" His eyes looked tired.

"Drove. Thanks for saving my dog."

"You're welcome. I had to carry him out. He's a coward when it comes to anything more serious than a cat near the woodpile."

"I know. Lyle, is my house gone?"

He looked at me then. "I'll drive you there. I'm not sure what happened over that way."

I didn't want to, but I began to cry silently as we drove along. My neighbor to the east had lost her house. I knew that little house had been there for over a hundred years, and now it was gone. There were big trees down everywhere and when the wind shifted, there was still smoke. We drove on.

"Well," Lyle said finally. "It's gone." We stood looking at the burned beams; all the windows had shattered. And, my sculpture was gone. It had burned along with the rest of the house.

"I'm sorry about the statue, honey," Lyle said gently from somewhere behind me. "I know it was important to you."

"Let's walk out back," I told him. "Let's take a little walk out back."

He held my hand and we walked along in silence. The woods hadn't

36

burned; it was fresh and green and as sweet smelling as ever in there.

It didn't really matter about the sculpture. I didn't really care about it—not anymore. All I cared about was Lyle.

"Are you okay, Brittany?"

"Yes." I turned to him. "I'm fine."

"I guess you ought to know that the reason I didn't come around after—after we—was, well, because I knew my big idea was a flop and I guess I was ashamed." He looked at me with tired eyes. "I always wanted to make it big, Brittany. I always wanted to impress you, to give you the best. And I never could."

Well, he didn't have to say anything more. I knew that my unsaid prayer had been answered. Lyle did love me. He'd probably never stopped.

I leaned against him. He smelled of soot and smoke and sweat. I felt his arms go around me and it was as if my poor, frightened, tired spirit just let go and stopped fretting. So we didn't have any money right now. And my house and sculpture were ashes. We still had each other, and Lyle understood me. What he'd said about my sculpture was proof.

"Well, my tent is still okay. Tonight we can sleep there," Lyle said.

"Okay, and tomorrow I'll figure out what to do about the house," I said.

"Then let's go to sleep and tomorrow, we'll get married," Lyle said matter-of-factly.

"It takes longer than that, I think."

"Well," he said, "whatever. In the meantime, we can build a fire and talk it over." Otis came running over to us then. It was like old times. And Lyle wanted to marry me again!

We climbed wearily up the ridge, to the tent, which became our home for the next few weeks. And after spending that time together I knew we would make it. We'd both been through worse. This time, things will be different. They say love is better the second time around. And you know what? I think they're right.

THE END

A LOVER'S
MEMORY

It all started on the last day of my sophomore year of high school. Mike Powell had called to cancel our date for the end-of-the-year party on Saturday night.

"My grandfather's had a stroke and we don't know if he's going to make it. I have to leave for Montana tomorrow morning with my parents. Megan, I'm really sorry."

Mike knew as well as I did that everybody was already paired off for the dance. He must have dreaded making that phone call.

"It's okay, Mike. Of course, you have to go," I told him.

"My grandmother's going to need help with the farm. But, Megan, this is some time to just walk out on you for Saturday night."

"Don't worry about it." I tried to sound casual, as though I didn't care at all. "There'll be other dances. I'm sorry about your grandfather."

"Tell you what. If you're still speaking to me, we'll have a special date when I get home," Mike suggested.

"How long will you be gone?"

"I don't know. Dad will have to get back to his job in a couple of weeks but—" There was a slight pause. "My mom thinks she and I may have to stay awhile."

"I'll miss you. Do you know much about farming?" I asked.

"I may have to learn in a hurry." He chuckled. "Can you see me milking a cow? I'll probably squirt myself in the face the first few times." His voice got serious. "Thanks for understanding, Megan. I'm really sorry."

It wasn't that Mike was the love of my life, but I knew I'd miss him. We'd known each other since fourth grade, when his family moved into the green-and-white house on the corner of our block. We'd built snowmen in each other's backyards and climbed the big apple tree outside my house. Without him, I'd have probably flunked eighth-grade math. I was just used to him, and I knew it would seem funny, not having him around that summer.

I was still sitting at the table after Mike's call when the phone rang again.

"Have you decided what to wear?" It was Christy Pollan, my best friend. Christy thought clothes were the most important things in life, after boys. Every day that week, she had decided on a different outfit for Saturday night.

"Christy, I'm not going," I told her.

"What are you talking about? Look, Megan, you can't back out now.

Where do you think Mike's going to find another girl at this late date?"

"I'm not backing out. Mike's grandfather had a stroke."

"So? That's too bad, but he wasn't planning on taking his grandfather, was he?"

"He has to go to Montana with his family. They're leaving in the morning," I explained.

"Oh, no!" Christy moaned. "And he was supposed to drive!" she added in her end-of-the-world voice.

"He couldn't help it, Christy, and I think it's nice his family cares enough to make the trip," I said.

"I guess you're right," she conceded. "But it leaves us with a problem."

"You and Jeff can find somebody else to drive with."

"I didn't mean that. I'm talking about you. We have to find you another date."

I'd much rather have just quietly missed the party than have my best friend advertising all over school to find me a date.

"Christy, please, I'll just sit this one out. There will be plenty of other parties," I said.

"I'll work on it," she insisted.

"That's what I was afraid of."

"In the meantime, don't forget we're going to the movies tomorrow night. We can walk up to the theater and Dad said he'd bring us home. See you tomorrow," she said.

That's the way it was with Christy. She liked to call the shots and, unless I strongly disagreed, it was easier to just go along with her. Christy belonged to the drama club and the school choir and was always telling me I had to get out more if I wanted to have any fun. "You never know where Prince Charming will be hiding out," she'd say with a toss of her hair. "You have a great personality, Megan. You just have to let people get to know you."

I knew she was trying to tell me I couldn't get by on my looks. My eyes were a little too small and my nose wasn't the greatest. My hair was unexciting, too.

"Okay," I said. "I'll come over about seven."

I knew I certainly wouldn't be doing much socializing that weekend—a movie with Christy on Friday night and a cozy evening at home alone on Saturday.

Our small town didn't have much variety in entertainment. Most of the kids hung out at the movies or the bowling alley. It seemed funny not to see Mike milling around with the crowd. *Maybe he won't have to be gone all summer,* I thought hopefully.

After the show, we were watching for Christy's dad's car when she cried, "There's Dan!" She waved as a little car pulled up to the curb beside us.

39

"Hi, squirt," the driver said. "Dad told me where to find you."

"Hi, jerk!" Christy answered happily. "Are you home for the whole weekend?"

My friend had mentioned a twenty-two-year-old brother, who had his own truck rig and was on the road a lot, but I'd never met him.

"Your timing's perfect. We need an extra man for tomorrow night," Christy said.

I wanted to crawl under the car. What a way to meet a gorgeous guy like Dan! I'd seen his pictures around their house and knew he was really good looking, but I still wasn't prepared for the real thing.

"No comment until I've heard all the details," he answered.

He smelled slightly of after-shave and, as I sat beside him, I felt a tinge of excitement. He made the high school guys look like first graders.

"Who's the pretty creature sitting on my right, and I don't mean my ugly sister," Dan teased.

"That's right, you two have never met. Dan, this is Megan Parker. Megan, this is my black-sheep brother, Dan. Where shall we give him the privilege of taking us?"

"How about popcorn and hot chocolate at my house?" I suggested. Maybe I could put my best foot forward and convince Dan that he wouldn't be getting stuck with a wallflower. That is, if he wasn't already working on an excuse to get out of going to the party.

I measured corn and put it into the popper while Christy melted butter in the microwave. Dan put the teakettle on the stove and spooned cocoa into three cups. We'd talked about Dan's last trip on the way from the movie, so he still didn't know I was the one in need of a date. I felt dowdy in my old jeans, bulky sweater, and sneakers. I usually dressed with a little more care to take in a Friday-night movie, but with Mike out of town . . .

"Hi, kids." Mom came out to the kitchen long enough to meet Dan and chat for a few minutes, then went off to bed. Dad wasn't around, which wasn't unusual. He seemed to be spending less and less time at home lately.

The three of us sat around the kitchen table and Dan told us funny stories about his road trips. I was having such a good time I forgot all about the party until Dan said, "By the way, little sister, what's the trap you're setting me up for tomorrow night?"

Christy just smiled smugly and looked at me. I felt my cheeks burning in embarrassment.

"Christy, I already told you—" I began.

"Oh, I think I just put my big foot in my mouth," Dan interrupted. "What's the story?"

Christy explained about Mike. "It's not fair for Megan to have to sit home tomorrow night just because somebody's grandfather got sick, right?"

"Right." Dan looked at me and my heart began to race. It was all so embarrassing! With Christy backing her brother into a corner, he could hardly do anything but take me to the party without sounding rude.

"Look, it's really not necessary. I'm sure there are plenty of girls you'd rather—"

"Dozens," Dan teased, "but they're used to waiting in line. Let's just call it a thank-you for tonight. I've had a really good time, and you make a great batch of popcorn. If you wouldn't mind being seen with an old man like me, I'll do my best to give Mike a run for his money."

He sounded so sincere my embarrassment faded. "I'd love to go with you, Dan, if you're sure."

"Consider it settled." He turned to Christy. "Come on, squirt. We'd better let Megan get her beauty sleep. You can fill me in on the details on the way home."

The clock on the living room table chimed midnight as I closed the door behind them and leaned against it. Dan couldn't possibly see me as anything but a tag-along friend of Christy's. But I could hardly wait until the next night. I was already sure I was falling in love.

I spent most of Saturday deciding what to wear and then changing my mind. *I'm as bad as Christy,* I told myself. Things had certainly turned around in the past two days.

The car carrying Dan, Christy, and Jeff pulled up in front of my house about eight-thirty. Cinderella's chariot couldn't have excited me more. Even Mom's remarks that afternoon hadn't put a damper on my spirits.

"Well, it's nice of him to fill in while Mike's out of town," she'd said. "But don't let him turn your head. He's much too old and experienced for you." I didn't know those words would come back to haunt me.

The garden setting from the Thursday-night prom the seniors had held took care of most of the decorations. The juniors added some balloons, streamers, and posters. Traditionally, the sophomore class came back on Sunday for the cleanup. I wondered if Christy would talk Dan into that, too.

CDs blared through the loudspeaker and the soda machines gobbled coins all evening.

"Where'd you learn to dance like that at your tender age?" Dan asked as he handed me a diet soda.

"Maybe our generation is more liberated than yours." The teasing banter came more easily to me then. I wasn't about to admit that most of my limited experience had taken place in front of my bedroom mirror.

About halfway through the evening, I thought of Mike and felt a pang of guilt because I was having so much fun. At midnight, one of the chaperones announced the last dance, traditionally the school

41

song. Dan held me close as we swayed together, falling under the spell of the slower music. School songs aren't noted for their romance, but as the lights dimmed and Dan put his arms around me, pressing his cheek against mine, I could have danced with no music at all. Magic turned back to reality as the last strains faded and about two hundred kids pushed their way toward the exits.

The four of us piled into the car. "Shall we have a bite to eat?" Dan asked.

We divided a pepperoni pizza, the only one that got a unanimous vote. Christy explained the sophomore cleanup tradition to her brother. "You've been to the dance, brother dear, so it's only fair that you share in the cleanup."

"My diploma's five years old. I don't think they'll let me in in broad daylight," he teased.

"You did all right tonight," I assured him. "For an extra pair of hands, we'll overlook your not having a student identification card."

"Well, if it isn't Dan!" A voluptuous female descended on us from nowhere. She stood behind Dan, covering his eyes with long fingernails. When he reached up to pull her hands away, she grabbed his wrists, and her flirtatious laugh made our table the center of attention. "Where've you been, honey?" Her swaying body told us she'd had one too many beers. "Aren't you sort of robbing the cradle?" she drawled.

Dan stood up, mumbled introductions, and led her back to her noisy crowd across the room.

We finished our pizza and drinks, but that girl, Patty, had put a damper on our festive spirits. Her condescending laughter seemed to stay with us, a fifth and unwelcome member of the group.

When Dan walked to the door with me, I wondered if I'd ever see him again. "Thanks, Dan, it was fun." I felt his hand under my chin, tilting my head up as he bent toward me. His lips moved toward mine and I wanted to bottle that moment and make it last forever.

"I'll call you tomorrow," he whispered.

I closed the door softly behind me and heard the car pull out of the driveway.

"Megan? Is that you?" Mom called from the top of the stairs.

Who else? I thought. "You didn't have to wait up, Mom," I said aloud.

"I worry when you're out." She'd never expressed worry when I was with Mike.

"We went to the dance, Mom, and then to have pizza. There was nothing to worry about."

"Kids aren't safe in church these days," she said.

I tried to smile. "You don't need to worry about me, Mom." I kissed her cheek. "See you in the morning."

I got ready for bed and climbed between the sheets. The memory

42

of Dan's gentle touch started butterfly wings quivering inside me. His kiss still felt warm on my lips as I fell asleep and began to dream.

When the phone rang at noon the next day, I crossed my fingers and raced to answer it. My heart skipped a beat when I heard Dan's voice.

"Last night was great. I don't remember my high school dances being that much fun. Must have been the company," he murmured.

I found it hard to believe that the attentions of a guy already established in the business world were turned in my direction.

"Ready to clean up the gym? We'll pick you up in a couple of hours," he reminded me.

But when Christy and Jeff turned in our walk that afternoon, my new self-confidence took a nosedive.

"Where's Dan?" I tried to sound as if it didn't matter.

"Somebody came down with flu and he had to make an unexpected run to Boston. He said to tell you he'll call you soon."

Is he really on the way to Boston? I wondered. And I couldn't help thinking about Patty.

The sophomores turned out in full force to clean the gym. I went through all the motions, pulling down streamers, posters, and paper flowers—but the fun wasn't there. I managed to work alone most of the time, to avoid the banter and gossip about the night before. By four-thirty, the gym looked as though the party had never taken place.

"How about a hamburger?" Jeff suggested.

"Great idea," Christy said. "Come with us, Megan."

"Thanks, but I think I'll just go home."

"Jeff, make her come with us," my friend persisted. "She needs cheering up, after Mike taking off and Dan canceling today."

Christy's tactless words not only mirrored my mood, but they made it worse. I wished they wouldn't talk about me as if I weren't there. I felt like a hospital patient with two nurses discussing what to do with me next.

"I'm fine, just not hungry. See you later," I said quickly. I could feel their eyes on my back as I hurried through the crowd of kids. I just wanted to get out the door and be alone.

The month of June was filled with restless nights and empty days. For a week after the dance, I kept vigil by the phone. During the second week, I made hourly checks on the mailbox, but the results were no better. *What do you expect, you little jerk?* I asked myself. *A big brother helped his little sister's friend—that's all there was to it.* Once or twice, I found myself getting mad at Mike for beginning the whole thing by canceling our date, but then I'd see the ridiculous unfairness of that. By the third week, my hopes were fading fast. Christy and I avoided the subject. Whether it was as deliberate on her part as it was on mine, I had no idea, but I think she realized her big brother had made quite an impression.

43

On the Fourth of July, Mom told me that Christy was on the phone. No matter how often we saw each other, we still talked on the phone at least once a day. But when I answered, it wasn't Christy after all.

"I'll pick you up at eight, and we'll go over to Central City for the fireworks."

Dan! All my attempts to settle back into a dull routine flew out the window. The thrill of hearing his voice had me reeling with excitement. As the afternoon dragged by, I felt a little annoyed that he'd assumed I'd be available and willing to go. But he was so right!

I had to talk fast to get Mom's permission.

"Don't make a habit of this, Megan. You should be dating boys your own age," she insisted.

"We'll be with Christy and Jeff, and they're my age," I assured her. But when Dan came alone, I called a quick good night to Mom and hurried out of the house.

"Wasn't Christy ready?" I asked.

"Would you mind if it's just the two of us?"

I could hardly believe what I was hearing. A whole evening alone with Dan! He reached for my hand and the butterflies were back in business.

The drive passed quickly. Central City was much larger than my town, and the annual fireworks display there drew an audience from all the surrounding areas. Dan pulled a plaid blanket from a picnic basket and spread it on a patch of grass. The hill where we were sitting was packed with people.

"Coffee?" Dan poured some from a thermos he'd brought.

"You've thought of everything." I took the cup and held it between my knees as I opened a box of cookies.

The fireworks were just one lovely burst of color after another. Rockets hissed straight up and then exploded in tiny red, blue, and green stars, and the finale stirred the admiring crowd to cheers.

We made our way to the car and started home. After about a mile, Dan pointed toward a truck stop beside the highway. "There's my rig." He pulled up in front of it. "Come on, I'll show you."

Twelve or fifteen trucks were lined up in the parking areas around the restaurant. I followed Dan to a red-and-white cab with POLLAN TRANSPORT written in big letters on the door.

"Where's the trailer?" I asked.

"I delivered it this afternoon. What you see is mine, free and clear. I pull trailers that belong to other people wherever they want to go."

The way he stroked the shiny surface, I could tell he was proud of it. "Climb in. I'll show you," he offered.

"Don't you mind being on the road so much?" I asked.

"I love it. Except for a destination deadline I'm my own boss. This is a sleeper cab. When I'm tired I just pull in to a truck stop and catch some shut-eye. I don't think I'd like driving all night by myself."

He reached across the seat and pulled me toward him. "Well, I agree a voice on the CB is no substitute for the real thing." Dan's kiss was long and lingering. "Especially when she's female." He held me closer and kissed me again. I wondered if any female would do, but then I pushed the thought aside. Tonight, he was with me, and that was all that mattered.

"I'd better get home, Dan." I moved reluctantly away from him, hoping he wouldn't let me go. But he only smiled, offering no resistance. The doubts swept over me again as we walked back to the car without a word. Was he mentally comparing me with Patty? Did he have another girlfriend?

Had I acted too childish? I knew there were plenty of girls who could handle a love scene without turning into a prude. I knew my inexperience was showing. When Dan had graduated from high school, I was still playing with dolls! I felt torn in two directions, part of me wanting to stay in his arms, and another part of me afraid of getting into a situation I couldn't handle.

Dan didn't kiss me when we got back to the house. He only smiled the same way he had before. "I won't rush you, honey." He brushed my cheek with his hand and was gone.

I wasn't sure exactly what he meant but it sounded hopeful, and I knew I'd be available whenever he called. *Oh, please, Dan, please call!* I thought.

Christy told me he left the next day. "He never phones when he's on the road," she warned, "and he's never sure exactly how long he'll be gone."

But he could have called to say good-bye, I told myself.

That time, he was back in six days, and the four of us went bowling on Saturday night. "Dan really likes you," Christy confided to me in the ladies' room.

I put on fresh lip gloss. "What did he say?"

"Nothing, but I can tell. He's taken you out three times in a row. He usually plays the field."

"Is Patty one of the players?" As much as I hated to, I had to ask.

"She was for a while, but just for kicks. He'd never get serious about somebody like Patty."

Christy must have been right. For the rest of the summer, Dan and I saw each other usually every week or ten days. Sometimes we'd double with Christy and Jeff. We picnicked at the park and swam in the lake at the edge of town. Once, the four of us drove to Central City for a rock concert. I really had to do some fast-talking to get permission for that one. Christy told Mom that Dan had gotten the tickets for her birthday, and, of course, she wanted me, her very best friend, to go with them. She didn't leave Mom much choice. If she said no, Mom would be the bad guy.

As Mom realized my involvement with Dan was becoming more

45

than a passing fancy, she never missed an opportunity to remind me of what a nice boy Mike was, and to ask me if it would be nice when he came home again. She became more and more vocal about her disapproval of Dan, making vague references to dangers I was supposedly too young to understand. The more she protested, the more defensive I became. I was sure I was not only old enough to choose my own friends, but smart enough to choose them wisely.

Dan's parents weren't too happy about us, either, but Christy became a staunch ally. It wasn't long before we were planning devious ways for Dan and me to meet without our families knowing about it.

When Mike came home at the end of August, Mom was delighted. "I hope this will put an end to this summer's nonsense," she commented.

I didn't argue, but I was determined to keep on seeing Dan. I began telling Mom that Christy and I were going to a movie, or double-dating with Jeff and Mike, or watching television at Jeff's house—any story that she'd accept, so she wouldn't know I was really with Dan. Secrecy made our meetings all the more enticing, and being with him became a challenge worth any deceit. But we kept our feelings under control, and I couldn't understand what all Mom's fussing was about.

It was around this time that Mom and I talked about teenage pregnancy. Kim James, one of the seniors, was expecting a baby in the spring.

"Kim says they're getting married at Thanksgiving," I told her.

"You kids think you have all the answers. It's not easy when the marriage certificate, the birth announcement, and the high school diploma all come in the same year."

"What if it were me?" I asked her.

"Heaven forbid!" she said, giving me a suspicious glance. "Would you want me to get married?" I persisted. "Well, I suppose so, if it came to that and if you really loved the baby's father. Just behave yourself and we won't have to face that decision."

I repeated the conversation to Dan at the library, one of our many meeting places.

"Well, if we keep on getting all of this static we just might have to hold your mother to that." He winked and kissed my cheek.

"Behave," I teased, "or we'll get thrown out of here." One Saturday night in the fall, Christy and I were invited to a slumber party, which had Mom's approval. About four o'clock, Christy called. "Guess who just drove in?"

"Oh, no!" I whispered. "What about the party?"

"Bag the party. I'll say you got sick," she suggested.

"Christy, you're a doll!"

"Come for dinner," she said. "No, you'd better not. The way you two look at each other you'd just make things worse. Come over about seven. Dan and I will work something out."

I rolled a change of clothes into my sleeping bag and threw a

46

toothbrush in my purse. "I'm going to walk over to Christy's," I told Mom later. "Christy's dad will take us to the party. See you tomorrow."

I hadn't seen Dan for two weeks and my heart was pounding with excitement. Christy met me at the door and hurried me to her bedroom, where we huddled like two conspirators planning a bank robbery.

"It's all settled," Christy whispered. "Dad will drop us off, but we won't go in right away. Dan will leave a few minutes later and pick you up on the corner."

"What'll I do with my sleeping bag?" I asked.

"Just throw it in Dan's car."

Fortunately, none of the other girls were arriving when we pulled up in front of our friend Sue's house. We started slowly toward the door while Mr. Pollan turned the car around and headed back home.

Suddenly, I thought of one important detail we'd both overlooked. "Christy, where am I supposed to sleep tonight? Mom will think I'm here. Sue will think I'm home sick. And I can't go to your house without you."

"Oh, boy," Christy moaned.

"Well, I'll just have to go to my house. I'll tell Mom I didn't feel well and Sue's mother drove me home."

Dan's car pulled up at the corner. I raced toward it and two seconds later, I was in his arms.

"I've missed you, baby." Dan pressed me against him and kissed me passionately.

"I've missed you, too. It seems like two months instead of two weeks."

He kissed me again and again. I could feel my reserve slipping. "What would you like to do?" I asked, pulling away.

"Just what we're doing, but I guess that's not a very good idea." He let me go and I moved over toward the passenger door.

"There's a new place about halfway to Central City. They have a band on weekends. Feel like dancing?" he asked.

"Let's go," I said.

Dan started the car and pulled away from the curb. "No, that won't work."

"What won't work?"

"Your tender age, my sweet. They won't let you in."

"Oh, no!" I said in disgust. "How can you put up with such a baby?"

He laughed. "It's part of your charm. You're sweet and natural. It's a nice change from girls who wear too much makeup and know all the answers."

Patty's image flashed across my mind, with her wild hair and long fingernails. How many other girls was I a "nice change" from? *Stop it, Megan. He could have called one of those others if he'd wanted to, but he didn't. He called you,* I told myself.

47

"Maybe we could find a nice children's movie somewhere—" I suggested. "That shouldn't get anybody into trouble."

We both started laughing and I forgot about Patty. We drove to Central City and went to the movies. Later, we stopped for hamburgers and coffee.

"Are you going to stay at Sue's tonight?" Dan asked.

"I can't. Christy told her I got sick. I'll have to go home and hope Mom stays asleep. I'll think of something to tell her in the morning."

"At least she isn't sitting up worrying about the terrible trucker who's leading her little girl astray."

He put his arm around my waist as we left the coffee shop and crossed the parking lot. We got in the car and he turned on the radio to a romantic station.

"Now there's just you and me," he said softly.

I slid across the seat and melted in his arms. Our kisses became more passionate and I could feel my resistance weakening.

"Dan," I whispered.

"Hush, honey. Nobody's waiting for you. We have plenty of time."

"I'd better go home, Dan." I started to pull away, but he held me closer and we kissed again. A few minutes later, I'd passed the point of no return. Any will to resist melted like snow in the tropics. I belonged totally to Dan.

I woke up as daylight began to filter into the cab. Dan stirred beside me, and I remembered what had happened the past night. I sat quietly and tried to figure out what to do.

Why didn't I use my head and make Dan take me home after the hamburgers and coffee? What a jerk! I thought. I'd been so sure I could handle any situation. What if someone I knew saw me climbing out of Dan's cab in time for breakfast? I felt trapped and scared. How could it have felt so right to be there just a few hours ago and then so wrong?

I shook Dan awake. "Please take me home," I whispered.

He sat up, rubbing his eyes, and glanced at his watch. "It won't look too good if your mom sees you walking in at dawn."

"She'll be asleep. Please, Dan!"

"Okay, honey. I'm sorry, I guess things got a little out of hand."

"It wasn't all your fault. I knew what I was doing. Now I just want to go home."

When we reached the house, Dan got my sleeping bag out of the back.

"Don't come to the door," I told him.

He kissed my cheek. "I'll call you later," he assured me.

I wanted to jump back in the car and shout, "Take me away! I just want to be with you." I was tired of hiding my feelings and telling lies.

Mom wasn't asleep. As I started down the walk the front door flew open. Mom's face was a mixture of anxiety and anger. Dad stood

48

behind her, staring at Dan's disappearing car.

"Well, it's about time!" Mom yelled. Her anger was winning out over the worry. "We've been frantic! Where on earth have you been?"

"It's obvious," Dad said. "That was Dan's car."

"Dad, it was my fault. I can explain!"

"There's no explanation for walking in at dawn from a slumber party you've never been to. Looks like you've been doing more slumming than slumbering," he snapped.

Mom gave him a withering glance, which surprised me, since she felt so strongly about Dan. "Go to bed, Megan," she said coldly. "We'll talk later."

I hurried up the stairs, welcoming the escape, but dreading the confrontation I knew I'd have to face later. How did they know I wasn't at Sue's? My room was a welcome haven, but sleep wouldn't come as my mind played a rerun of the last few hours. In my excitement to see Dan again, I'd certainly let things get out of hand. When and how I'd get home had seemed trivial compared to being in his arms again. *Well, it wasn't all our fault,* I thought. If our parents hadn't tried so hard to keep us apart, we wouldn't have had to lie. In the comfort and security of my own room, the emotions of last night came flooding back. I knew it would be harder than ever to be away from Dan, and tougher than ever to find ways to see him.

I stayed in my room Sunday morning for as long as I could, but by noon, I decided I might as well face the music. Instead of yelling and demanding an explanation, Mom and Dad gave me the silent treatment. Apparently, they thought everything had been said, and the time had come for action.

For the next few weeks, the house became my prison, except for school hours. Even my phone calls were monitored, and Christy's became particularly suspect. But I was so out of circulation hardly anybody called anyway.

By Thanksgiving, life had begun to return to normal, at least on the surface. I was allowed to date Mike, and to attend gatherings of my friends who were on the "approved list." But by that time, I was pretty sure I was pregnant. I didn't know who to talk to or where to turn for help.

During Christmas vacation, I finally confided in Christy. "Well, they'll have to let you see Dan now," she said. She promised to keep it a secret until Dan came home again and she had a chance to talk to him. I felt scared, trapped, and very much alone.

"Maybe I should talk to Mrs. Carlson."

"That's a good idea," Christy agreed.

Mrs. Carlson was my counselor and I was hoping she would break the news to my parents. The first day after Christmas vacation, I went to her office. I'd rehearsed what I would say, but when I finally sat

49

in the chair beside her desk, the words stuck in my throat. Unable to meet her eyes, I stared at my hands and burst into tears. She let me cry for a minute. When I calmed down, she asked, "What's the problem, Megan?"

I still couldn't find any words. It was almost as if talking about it would make the whole terrible nightmare true, and silence would make it go away.

Surely that wasn't the first time around for Mrs. Carlson. I wondered how many other scared, embarrassed girls had come to her, forced to blurt out their version of the same sad story.

"Mrs. Carlson, I'm—I'm pregnant."

The inevitable set of questions followed. "Have you told your parents?"

"I was hoping you would," I admitted.

"Do you know who the father is?"

Was it possible to get pregnant and not know who the father was? "Of course," I answered.

"Some girls don't, Megan. And some won't tell. Does he know?" she asked.

"It's Christy's brother. She's going to tell him."

"Megan, you're the one who's pregnant. You're going to have to take the responsibility."

I knew I was sounding like a real jerk. I'd been foolish enough to get pregnant and then I was expecting Mrs. Carlson to break the news to my parents, and Christy to tell Dan. I forced myself to look at her and spilled out the whole story—how we'd started dating just so I'd be able to go to the dance, how our parents disapproved right from the beginning, but how we fell in love and continued to meet secretly.

The counselor listened quietly, then called Mom and made an appointment. "Your mother will be here at two o'clock, Megan. Come back then and we'll get started on some plans."

I met Christy in the cafeteria, but I couldn't eat. A thousand questions raced through my head: *What if they throw me out of the house? Will Dan want to marry me? What if he doesn't? What will it be like when I begin to show?*

Facing Mom and having to tell her that I was carrying Dan's baby was the most agonizing experience of my life. I expected her to rant and rave, or at least cry. Instead, she sat in shocked silence, looking bewildered. Finally, she turned to me and said in an icy voice, "How could you?"

All my pent-up resentment and frustration burst out. "It's your fault!" I yelled. "You treated me like a little kid. You knew I loved Dan, but you didn't care. You were worrying so much about my being 'nice' you wouldn't even let us see each other!"

Mrs. Carlson cut into my tirade. "Recriminations won't help now,

Megan. Important decisions have to be made and we'd better get on with it."

Mrs. Carlson was obviously the only one thinking clearly. She outlined our options. "You'll have to choose soon between abortion or full-term delivery."

Mom spoke in a monotone. "Abortion is out of the question."

"In that case, you can take your time with other decisions. Megan, come in tomorrow after lunch and we'll talk again."

I didn't know what I'd have done without Mrs. Carlson.

Mom treated me like a delinquent, which made it impossible to confide in her. She and Dad weren't getting along and I assumed I was the cause. One night, their voices were louder than ever and I could hear fragments of the conversation, even through the closed bedroom doors—something about tramps, and setting a bad example, and being forced into marriage. Dad packed a bag that night and left the house.

Two weeks later, Dan came home and Christy broke the news. Dan called me, but Mom policed the phone. Then, he came over and Mom refused to let him in. Mrs. Carlson finally convinced her that no matter how my family felt about Dan, he was not only entitled, but obligated to be involved in the decisions. Mom agreed that we could meet in Mrs. Carlson's office.

"That's the best I can do, Megan. Do you have any idea why your mother is so adamant?"

"My dad walked out and she blames me. He thinks I'm a tramp."

"Did he tell you that?"

"No, but they had a big argument right after they found out about the baby. Dad packed up and left."

Mrs. Carlson looked thoughtful. "Don't blame yourself for everything, Megan. Your own problems are enough right now."

Dan came to school and we talked with Mrs. Carlson. She explained all the alternatives, but Dan told her he wanted to marry me and we wanted to keep the baby. The stumbling block, Mrs. Carlson explained, was my being a minor, which meant I could neither marry nor keep the baby unless my parents agreed. With Dad out of the picture, this meant convincing Mom, but, in her present frame of mind, it was a hopeless task to get her to budge an inch. She ranted about how I'd ruined my life before I'd even had a chance to grow up, and how hard it would be to find "a good husband" willing to accept someone else's child.

"Mom, I've already found a good husband and we want to keep our baby. You've said you thought kids should get married if the girl gets pregnant, and I believed you."

"Megan, are you telling me you planned this baby?"

"Yes!" I'd come too far to back out now. One more lie at this point couldn't make the situation any worse. "You wouldn't let us see each other. You didn't even try to get to know Dan. You just assumed that

51

older meant not good for me. It's my life, Mother. This is my baby and Dan is my choice for a husband. And I'm not a tramp—no matter what Dad thinks. At least Dan and I are willing to face our responsibilities, which is more than I can say for Dad."

I expected Mom to yell back, but she only sat quietly for a minute, then got up and left the room. I found myself feeling strangely sorry for her. Wrapped up in my own problems, I'd never stopped to realize what all this turmoil must be doing to her.

It helped to get rid of all the pent-up frustration, but the only thing that changed was my waistline. By the time I finished feeling sick every morning, my clothes were too tight. It didn't take long for the news to spread all over school that I was carrying Dan's baby. I resented the casual attitude of the girls who made no secret of their experiences with boys, but thought "getting caught" was stupid. They made sex seem cheap and sordid and bragged about their formulas for being "safe."

Winter faded into spring. When I asked about Dad, Mom snapped, "He won't be coming back." Her tone of voice shattered any hope of making him an ally and deepened my sense of guilt for having driven him away.

One rainy Saturday afternoon in May, I slouched at the kitchen table across from Mom and reviewed my dilemma. Being sixteen, unmarried, and seven months pregnant didn't paint a rosy picture. But it didn't have to be nearly as grim as Mom was making it. Dan had called to say he was coming over to try to break the stalemate. Mom had stood firm in her decision against the marriage and kept telling me that adoption was the best thing for the baby and the only way I could "get on with my life."

"Pregnancy, Megan, is not a sufficient reason to marry."

"But don't you remember what you said when Kim James got pregnant? I asked you how you'd feel if it were me and you said you'd probably want me to get married."

"That was a different situation entirely. Kim was a senior and the family liked the boy. Dan is so much older. He's gone most of the time and probably has a girl at every truck stop. You're using this baby— you call it a love child—to force me into letting you make a foolish mistake. Just because he's Christy's brother. . ."

We seemed to be arguing in circles. "This is a love child, Mother," I hissed at her as I got up to leave the room. "And we're going to keep it no matter how much you threaten us."

The jangle of the phone cut off my sentence and I picked it up.

"Megan? The highway patrol just called." I recognized Dan's mother's voice and she sounded terribly upset. "There's been a bad accident. Very bad. It's Dan. I hope you're satisfied."

In stunned silence, I dropped the phone back into its cradle and fainted.

The next few days swung back and forth between dream and nightmare. A drunk driver had run a red light and hit Dan's car broadside. The drunk driver walked away with a few cuts and bruises, but Dan died on the way to the hospital.

At the funeral, his relatives glared at me as though I were responsible for his death. His mother couldn't forget that he was on his way to see me when he died.

I hibernated in my room, unwilling to see or talk to anyone. Mom brought me trays of food, which I left virtually untouched. Marrying my baby's father was now a dream beyond reach. All I could do was fight to keep my child—and I was determined to do that.

Mom's attitude softened after Dan's death. Maybe she realized it was a rough way to make her point. Two weeks after the funeral, she urged me to have lunch with her in the kitchen.

"Honey, we need to talk," she began as we sat at the table, but I interrupted her.

"I know how you feel," I told her, "and you know how I feel. What is there left to say?"

Mom looked at me with a gentleness I hadn't seen for months.

"I was carrying you before your father and I were married. We were both seniors in high school. Our parents thought we were seeing too much of each other, so we'd sneak out during the week and meet in the park."

Mom, always so prim and proper. I'd never pictured her as a young girl in love. And Dad, no longer caring enough to even stay with his family. Would Dan's and my love have turned sour, too?

"What if it hadn't been for me? Would you have married?" I asked her.

"I really don't know. We'd talked about marriage after he finished college. But with you on the way, we had a quiet wedding right after high school graduation. Your dad had to work and settle for a few night classes. He's been a good provider, but I think he always felt trapped. I guess I have, too, at times.

"Your dad's leaving had nothing to do with you and the baby, Megan. He'd been seeing another woman for quite some time. Your being pregnant just gave him a handy excuse to leave, but he'd have left anyway. It was unfair of me to let you think it was your fault."

I felt closer to Mom than I had in years. "I haven't been very honest, either, Mom. Dan and I didn't plan to have me get pregnant. It was the night of Sue's party, and it was the only time. How did you know I wasn't there?"

"She called to say she was sorry you were sick. Lies have a nasty way of tracking us down."

"I'm sorry about lying, but I did love him, Mom."

"Love isn't always enough, honey. And I didn't want you to end up like me."

"Mom, I want this baby."

Mom smiled. "So do I, Megan."

53

My daughter, Carole, was eleven months old when I graduated from high school. Mike took me to the senior dance and we talked about the last two years.

Another year has passed. Mike just completed his first year at the university. We celebrated Carole's second birthday yesterday. While we watched her feeding the ducks in the little pond in the park, Mike reached for my hand. "I've always loved you, Megan. I want to marry you when I finish college, if you'll wait for me."

My love for Mike is different from what I felt for Dan, but I know it will last. He'll be that "good husband" Mom talked about, and he'll be a wonderful father to Carole.

Dan's parents have chosen not to accept her as their granddaughter, but Christy is a devoted aunt and has continued to be a good friend. Mom, of course, is a doting grandmother, and Mike assures me his parents already think of Carole as their granddaughter.

I've learned the hard way that we can't always have everything we want. Sometimes, there's a master plan that's better than ours. When Mike graduates in three years, we'll be married and we'll have the rest of our lives to live happily ever after. *THE END*

MY LOVER—
MY KILLER!

I was giving myself a last look in the mirror when my husband, Robbie, came up from behind and put his arms around me. "You look beautiful, Paula," he said softly, kissing my neck.

I turned in his arms and pushed a lock of silver-streaked hair off his forehead. "And so do you," I replied, smiling.

He kissed the tip of my nose and turned away. "I'd better get down and check the bar. Our guests should be arriving any minute."

I picked up a pair of earrings from the dresser. "Tell Kay I'll be down in a minute to help her."

"Listen here," Robbie protested, turning back. "I don't want you overdoing tonight, you hear? That's what we've got Kay for."

"Oh, Robbie." I felt that familiar drag on my emotions. "Stop treating me like a child."

His half-smile was bittersweet. "You could be my child, you know. If I'd married at nineteen and had a child at twenty, she'd be just your age."

"Darling, don't," I said.

It wasn't often that Robbie brought up the twenty years difference in our ages, just often enough to make me aware that it bothered him even after five years of marriage. I was twenty-five when we married, Robbie forty-five. And though our marriage hadn't been wildly exciting, it had been happy. Robbie was a sweet, considerate man, and although I often felt he was more like a father than a husband, our marriage was good. Sometimes I wondered what it had been like for him with his first wife, who'd died several years before we married.

Robbie wagged a finger in my face. "I repeat—take it easy tonight. We still haven't had the results of your last visit to the doctor."

He walked out, and I dropped on the edge of the bed for a moment, succumbing to the weariness I hadn't dared show when Robbie was around. I was tired. But Kay couldn't be expected to do everything for the annual party Robbie gave for his employees, and I'd helped more that day than I'd admitted to Robbie. Besides, what was the use of waiting for the results from the doctor. They never changed. They'd show what they'd shown for so many years, since I was a child. I had a bad heart, and although I was under the constant care of a doctor, there was no foretelling how many years of life remained for me. My mother had died of a similar ailment when I was a child.

I rose, took a deep breath, and pasted a smile on my face as I heard the first faint tinkling of our doorbell. Soon I was caught up in the flow of arriving guests, all of whom worked for Robbie in his small, but flourishing, plastics business which he'd started on a shoestring.

Most of the guests had arrived and I was circulating among them when Robbie came up to me with a man about my age in tow. "Paula, this is Ken Tyler, my new sales manager."

I was startled by his handsomeness—he was tall and romantic looking. My ever-erratic heartbeat doubled for a moment. I held out a hand. "Hello. I'm happy to meet you. Robbie has talked about you often."

"And I'm happy to meet you. He's talked about you often, too."

"Ken's done a bang-up job since Dan's retirement," Robbie said with a pat on his back. "But then, I'm not surprised. He was a crackerjack salesman before."

I glanced around. "Where's your wife, Mr. Tyler? I'd like to meet her."

His complexion turned ruddier. "I'm sorry. At the last minute she wasn't feeling well. It was too late to call. I hope her absence won't upset your plans."

"Of course not. We're having a buffet. One more or less won't make a bit of difference. I hope it's nothing serious?"

"No, not really."

"Well, it was nice meeting you. I'll see you again before the evening's over. Do have fun," I said, moving away.

Somehow I felt his intense eyes boring into my back. I searched my memory for tidbits of information I remembered about him, little items Robbie usually revealed about his employees. Yes, of course, Ken Tyler was the one who'd lost a young son in an automobile accident about a year ago, I remembered. The child had been in the backseat and was thrown from the car. His wife had been badly hurt in the accident, while Ken had suffered only a few bruises. Robbie said Ken had been badly shaken by the affair, and had thrown himself into his work ever since.

I was extremely conscious of Ken Tyler that evening. Whenever I looked up I found his eyes on me, thoughtful, studying. Although I knew it was ridiculous, I felt a magnetic pull between us and felt crazy inside every time our eyes met. My experience with romance was limited. I'd been ill and was restricted most of my life. But even so, no one had ever aroused the feeling in me that Ken did on our first meeting.

My romance with Robbie had been a strange one. My father had worked for him, and when I was twenty-three and unable to work because of my illness, Dad had been killed in a freak accident at the plant.

Robbie knew all his employees personally, as well as their families, and had been deeply grieved by Dad's death. He was a fortress to me in my sadness, visiting me daily after the accident. He fell in love with me, and I came to admire and respect and love him. Although my love wasn't as deep as Robbie's, it was enough, I thought, when he asked me to marry him. And it had been enough until the night I met Ken.

It was quite late when, weary, I sneaked away from the party for a few moments to a small den, wanting only rest for a while before resuming my duties as hostess. I was surprised to find Ken Tyler standing at a window staring out into the black night. , I didn't know anyone was here," I said. Then I said, "I hope you're not finding the party dull."

He smiled. "It's a great party, not dull at all. It's just that tonight is a night for couples, not one for singles."

"I'm sorry. I guess everybody else is in couples. How unfortunate your wife couldn't make it."

He hunched his shoulders, and for a moment his face twisted with an emotion I couldn't read. "Debbie doesn't socialize much these days. Robbie probably told you about our son's death. Although it's been over a year, she can't seem to pull herself out of her depression."

"Maybe you should push her to go out more. It would occupy her mind, get her thinking about something else."

"Yeah, I guess I should. But Debbie's face was somewhat scarred from the accident. Not badly," he said hastily, "but she imagines it's much worse than it is. That gives her a good excuse for refusing most invitations." I didn't imagine the undercurrent of bitterness as he said the last words.

He gave an apologetic laugh. "I'm sorry. I don't usually talk about this to people I've just met. But somehow you're very easy to talk to. I feel as if I've known you for a long time."

"Sometimes we need people to talk to about things that are upsetting," I said. "Please don't feel badly about having done it."

I had dropped into a chair as we talked, and now I rose. "I should be getting back. Robbie will wonder what happened to me."

"I hope you and Robbie won't mind if I leave. It's been a very nice party. I hope I'll get to see you again sometime."

"I'm sure you will," I said, holding out my hand.

His hand was warm and firm, and our eyes met and locked for an overly long moment. I felt a strange stirring within me and quickly pulled my hand from his. With a quick, "Good night," I hurried from the room.

For the remainder of the evening I couldn't get Ken out of my mind. There was something sad and haunting about him, which somehow matched the feeling that was so often in me.

At last the guests were gone and I allowed myself to submit to my weariness. Robbie put an arm around my waist and led me to the bedroom, saying, "Get to bed. You look tired. I'm sorry, darling, that I have to put you through this."

57

"Don't be silly," I replied. "You have obligations. And I will not live as an invalid." The last words were said with rebellion.

"Okay. But get to bed."

By the time Robbie checked the lights and doors, I was already in bed. "It was a good party, don't you think?" he asked as he undressed.

"Yes. I think everyone enjoyed themselves."

He talked about some of his employees, and in a few minutes crawled into bed beside me. I was tired, but there was a feverish feeling inside me. I needed Robbie that night. Heart problem or not, my physical needs were as strong as anyone's. But Robbie simply leaned over and kissed me, saying, "Sleep well—and late. I don't want you exhausted for days because of tonight."

Make love to me, Robbie, I wanted to shout. *My heart may be weak, but my needs are strong. Stop treating me like a child and treat me like a woman.* But Robbie didn't sense my need. For a moment I felt a spurt of anger, but it quickly ebbed. I couldn't blame Robbie when I knew it was his love and concern for me that kept him from making love to me more often.

It did take a couple of days before I felt rested again. A week passed, then two. I kept thinking of Ken Tyler, wondering why I did, and cursing myself because I did.

Then Robbie came home one night and asked, "Are you up to a dinner party at a restaurant next Saturday? The packaging show is in town, and we'll have a couple of important customers and their wives in for it. I'd like to take them out to dinner."

"Of course. I feel fine."

"Good," Robbie said. "I talked to Ken about it today. He'll make the arrangements."

A trembling began in the pit of my stomach. "Oh? Will he be there?"

"Yeah, since he's our sales manager." He shook his head. "I don't know about his wife."

"What's she like? Have you ever met her?" I asked.

"Once. Before Ken became sales manager and before they lost their boy." He frowned. "She's not the type I'd have expected Ken to marry. Pretty, but in sort of a flamboyant way. And kind of loud, not the quiet type I'd have expected Ken to go for."

I picked up a magazine from the table, not wanting Robbie to see the look on my face. *The quiet type! That's the type I am,* I thought.

I looked forward to the dinner both with dread and anticipation. The thought of seeing Ken again aroused an excitement that baffled me. It was so incomprehensible. I'd only met him once, yet the thought of him could set my heart racing.

I dressed with special care the night of the dinner, in a simple green dress that complimented my hair and skin. We were the first to arrive, then Ken and his wife. I looked closely at her. She had hair in an elaborate hairdo with curls wisping around her face. I saw the faintest line of a scar peeking through one of the curls. Ken introduced us. "Mrs. Murray—my wife, Debbie."

Her face was serious-looking, but she smiled a pasted-on type of smile as she said, "How do you do, Mrs. Murray."

"Please call me Paula," I offered with a smile. "Mrs. is so formal."

Our other guests arrived a short while later, and when Robbie asked what everyone was drinking, Debbie said, "I'll have a martini."

I saw a frown flash across Ken's face, but it was quickly gone, replaced by a forced, teasing grin. "Hey, that's pretty strong stuff. Wouldn't you rather have—"

"I'll have a martini," she interrupted, her chin jutting out stubbornly.

Two martinis later, Debbie was talking too much and too loudly, her throaty laughter rising above the voices. *Poor thing,* I thought. *She probably had the martinis because she needed courage to face the evening.* If as Ken said, she rarely went out since her son's death, it probably took a lot of courage to spend an evening with a group of strangers.

After dinner, a small band played for dancing. Robbie held out a hand to Debbie. "I haven't had the pleasure of dancing with Ken's wife."

Debbie rose, smiling coquettishly. "I love to dance. But Ken has two left feet," she said with a tinkly laugh.

The other couples rose, and Ken turned to me. "Would you care to dance with a guy who has two left feet?" There was a trace of anger in his voice.

"Since I also have two left feet, I don't think we'd do very well. Besides, I shouldn't dance. We can just talk if you don't mind."

"I don't mind at all. But why shouldn't you dance?"

"I'm afraid I have a rather tricky heart. The doctor doesn't advise it."

A look of concern twisted his face. "I—I'm sorry, I remember now. Robbie did mention it once."

I put a hand on his arm. "Please. Don't look so worried. I've lived with it for thirty years. I'll probably live with it for another thirty." I said it lightly, but felt a pull of depression. Thirty more years were more than I expected.

Tactfully, Ken started talking about other things, and I was strangely pleased we had so much to talk about, and that it came so easily and comfortably. Once Debbie and Robbie danced by, and Debbie was doing more talking than dancing.

"I'm afraid Debbie can't handle martinis too well. But, then, she hasn't been doing much drinking of any kind for a long while. I really had to do a lot of convincing to get her out tonight," Bill said.

"Please don't worry about it. Let her be herself. Maybe it will do her good."

He sighed. "I'm really worried about her. She's either very low or very high. But she won't see a doctor. Sometimes I—" He stopped, running a hand through his hair. "There I go again—telling you things I shouldn't. I guess it's like I said the night of your party. You're a person someone can talk to." His voice was wistful, with a strange little-boy sound to it, as if there were no one else he could talk to.

Robbie and Debbie returned to the table. The band was playing a rock tune, and Robbie dropped into his chair with a laugh. "I'm afraid I'm too old for this kind of music." He turned to Ken. "Your wife's quite a dancer."

"He wouldn't know," Debbie said with a pout.

Ken's face reddened, and I thought angrily: *Why does she do this to him? And why does Ken take it?* He seemed to be a strong man in all respects except when it came to his wife. Then suddenly it seemed clear. Obviously, Debbie blamed Ken for the death of their son, and Ken, obviously, felt guilty about it himself. The currents of unhappiness between them were clearly evident.

Robbie's voice interrupted my thoughts. "I invited Debbie to our cottage some weekend. I told her she could even bring her husband." He laughed, poking Ken in the shoulder.

Ken had recovered his poise. "That sounds great," he said. He glanced at Debbie, looking for a word of confirmation from her, but the serious look had come over her face again.

Later, driving home, I said to Robbie, "Do you think it was wise inviting Ken and Debbie out to the cottage? I have a feeling those two aren't getting along very well."

Robbie frowned, shaking his head. "I think you're right. The drinks loosened Debbie's tongue and she made a couple of cracks about Ken, talked a little about the accident. I could sense resentment—that Ken came out of it with barely a scratch while her son died and she'd been scarred. She's very self-conscious about the scars, although you can barely see them."

"Then why did you invite them? It doesn't sound as if it'll be a comfortable weekend."

"I don't know, except I like Ken. He's a good man. Maybe it'll help them if they get out more."

That night Robbie did turn to me in bed, pulling me close. "Are you too tired, darling?" he asked softly.

I was tired, but Robbie asked so little of me I couldn't turn him away. Besides, my body always needed Robbie more than he needed me.

But our lovemaking left me unsatisfied. Robbie always treated me too gently, as if I were a piece of bone china. And I wanted to be loved

60

passionately, roughly, wildly. Perhaps it was because I had been treated too gently all my life.

When it was over, I lay awake for a long time thinking how it would be if Ken made love to me. I hated myself for my thoughts. I thought about his marriage and couldn't suppress my resentment toward Debbie for the way she treated him. I'd never known a deep love for a man before. My feeling for Robbie was so different—a love born of respect and affection and gratefulness. I'd always known it wasn't the deep, passionate love a woman yearns for. And Robbie knew when I married him that that's the way it was. Maybe he represented the father I'd adored, and I the child he never had.

A week after our dinner, Robbie told me he'd invited Ken and Debbie to the cottage the following weekend. My heart began to pound. "Did they accept?"

"Ken said they'd love to come."

"What about Debbie?"

Robbie shrugged. "If he said yes I'm assuming she'll agree, too. After all, she's got to realize that Ken's moved up in the company and, as his wife, she's required to do her part."

Another couple, friends of ours, Barbara and Myles Lynch, were also invited. Myles and Robbie took the day off and the four of us drove up Friday morning. Ken and Debbie weren't due until that evening. I loved our small cottage, situated in an isolated spot surrounded by lovely big trees and half a mile from the lake. It was simple and unpretentious and peaceful.

We were sitting on our small screened patio having a drink before dinner when Ken drove up. I was surprised, and pleased, when I saw him climb out alone.

"Hello," Robbie called. "You're just in time for a drink."

"I could use one," Ken answered. But although he was smiling, he looked tired and drawn.

I introduced him to our friends and as Robbie handed Ken his drink he asked, "No Debbie?"

"No Debbie," Ken answered. The words were short and clipped. "She wasn't up to it."

"That's too bad. I'm sorry," I said, even though I felt a joyous lilt that she wouldn't be around to spoil our lovely weekend.

Kay, who'd been with Robbie and taken care of him since his wife's death, served dinner a short while later.

After dinner we played cards, but it was still well before midnight when Robbie said, "We retire early out here, Ken. Myles, Barbara, and I have an early reservation for a game of golf. Care to join us?"

Ken made a face. "Sorry. I'm afraid I don't play. It used to be because I couldn't afford it. Now that I can, I can't find time."

"Well, everyone does what they want around here," Barbara said

61

with a laugh. "You look as if you could use a nice, restful day, Ken. You can spend it sunning on the beach with Paula. That's her thing." A slight shiver went through me at the thought of spending hours alone with Ken.

It was close to nine before I woke up the next morning. Robbie and the Lynches were already gone, so I dawdled at my shower and getting dressed, a little frightened at the thought of being with Ken. When I finally went downstairs, dressed for the beach, he was sitting on the patio in swim trunks, sipping a cup of coffee.

"Good morning," I said.

"Good morning." His smile was soft—sweet. "You're a sleepyhead."

"I'm afraid I am. I don't always sleep well. But when I'm here, in this wonderfully fresh air, I sleep like a baby."

Kay stuck her head in the door. "Breakfast, Paula?" Kay was like one of the family, and called us by our first names.

"I'll get it, Kay. You've enough to do. I just want coffee and juice anyway."

"You sit still," she ordered. "Getting you juice and coffee isn't going to wear me out! Of course that's not what I call a breakfast," she said as she disappeared.

I sighed. "Not only does Robbie treat me like a child, but Kay does, too."

"I'm sure it's because they love you and worry about you," he said. Then, softly, "And I'm sure you're very easy to love."

A hot flush flooded my body at his words, and the look in his eyes. I stammered, not knowing what to say. "Thank you. That's a very nice compliment. I don't know that I deserve it, though."

Then Kay came out with my juice and a fresh pot of coffee and spared me further comment. We talked then, of inconsequential things, with cozy silences in between as we relished the loveliness of the day. Finally I said, "I'm off for the beach. Are you joining me?"

"As you can see from my swimming trunks, I've already anticipated an invitation," he answered with a grin.

We walked slowly down a narrow dirt road to the secluded beach, mounded with sand and brush. Huge, frothy waves broke on the shore, and the wind was quite strong, so we spread a blanket between two high mounds of sand to shield us.

"Ready to go in?" Ken asked.

I looked at the waves. "I don't know. I'm more of a wader than a swimmer."

He held out a hand. "Come on. I'll hang on to you. We'll stand in the shallow water and let the waves do the work."

I took his hand, and felt excited. Shyly, quietly, we walked to the sea. I felt like a young girl on her first date. When the first wave hit us, bubbling around our waists, we squealed at the cold shock. Then, clinging tightly to each other's hands we stood, letting the water beat against us.

Suddenly a large wave crashed against us, toppling us over. Ken's arms reached for me, trying to lift me to my feet, but we stumbled and fell again as another wave hit us. Gasping and laughing, we crawled to the water's edge, arms entwined. Then the laughter died on our lips, and in a brief intense moment our eyes locked. Slowly we moved toward one another and our lips met, our pulsating bodies pressed tightly together on the wet sand, the breaking waves foaming around us.

We clung to each other until finally, struggling for control, I pushed against his chest and clambered to my feet. I ran to the blanket spread on the sand and threw myself on it as the blood raced through my veins.

Ken ran after me and threw himself beside me. "Paula! My God, I'm sorry."

I picked up a towel and buried my face in it. "Heaven help me, but I'm not," I said, my voice muffled.

"Paula," Ken breathed against my cheek as he pulled the towel from my face and enfolded me in his arms. "If you only knew how badly I've wanted to hold you and kiss you from the first moment I met you."

"Ken—this is so wrong."

His lips moved softly against my throat. "Lord, don't you think I know it? What could be worse than a married man in love with a married woman—a woman who's the wife of his boss at that."

I took his face between my hands, wanting to drink in every curve and hollow. Then I kissed his warm, soft lips, and we fell back on the blanket, and all the words we said were as nothing. We forgot everything in the tornado of love and need sweeping over us—and we were powerless to resist it. How beautiful Ken's lovemaking was— how different from Robbie's. It was so deep, so intense, that my mind went blank in ecstasy.

When it was over, and the world came crashing down on us again, I grabbed for my bathing suit, deeply ashamed of what we'd done.

"Paula, I love you so much," Ken said softly.

"We barely know each other," I answered, knowing even as I said the words that our love needed no knowing.

"It was there the instant we met," he said. "You felt it as I did—I could see it in your face."

"It doesn't make sense," I protested.

"A lot of things don't," he said softly.

His arms reached for me again, and I rested against his broad shoulder, knowing a fulfillment I'd never known. "What do we do?" I asked.

"I don't know," he said sadly. "But let's not think about it now. Let's just enjoy whatever brief time we have."

"We have to think about it," I insisted.

"Not now. Please—not now," he said softly as he kissed me again.

After awhile we talked. Ken told me how bad things were between him and Debbie. "I knew we were different when we married. But I fell in love with her because she was like a child—vivacious and full of life. And it was a good marriage until Sean's death. But since then she's a different person. I didn't expect that it would affect her so harshly. My God, when you lose a child—when you feel you may have been responsible for it . . ." His face twisted in agony, and his voice was low as he continued, "I needed her more than she needed me. But she wasn't there. It's been over a year and she's become bitter and hateful. She barely lets me touch her—only in anger sometimes—and it's a violent thing."

"Maybe that's why you think you love me," I said, my voice small.

"No—no," he protested. "I'd have fallen in love with you no matter what. You're the kind of person I should have fallen in love with."

"But there's Robbie, too," I said. "I can't hurt him. He's been too good to me."

"Don't you think I know that? He's been good to me, too."

"Oh, Ken," I cried, "what can we do?"

"Darling, I don't know."

Eventually we knew that talk solved nothing. We went back to the cottage where Kay was preparing lunch. A short while later Robbie and our friends drove up from their game of golf. I could barely look at Robbie, I was so full of guilt. But he was enthused about his game, and the three of them regaled us with a blow-by-blow account. The talk flowed around Ken and me, and I felt as if I were a million miles removed from them.

I don't know how I got through the remainder of the weekend. Ken and I weren't alone again, but I was conscious every moment of his presence. Then Robbie and I and the Lynches drove home Sunday evening. After we dropped off Barbara and Myles, Robbie said to me, "Did you enjoy the weekend?"

"Of course. You know I love going to the cottage."

"I wondered. Don't you like Ken? You had so little to say to him."

"Why, yes. I—I like him very much. I didn't realize—"

He patted my knee. "Just wondering, honey." I spent a restless night, filled with guilt and with a love and yearning for Ken that was like an ache.

The next morning Ken called me. "I've got to see you," he said.

"It's so useless, Ken. So—"

"I've got to see you," he said again.

"I'm going out of my mind with wanting to see you."

"And I want to see you."

"I'm leaving for Elmdale in a few minutes. Meet me there right after lunch. It's only a half-hour drive. I'll have seen our customer by then and we can talk. There's a little restaurant on the outskirts. Please, Paula."

Weakness flooded through me, and I couldn't resist the pleading in his voice, and the yearning in me. "All right."

We set a time, he named the restaurant, and that was the beginning of a double life that made my life both a nightmare and a heaven.

Ken and I met whenever we could in little out-of-the-way places. It was rarely more than once a week, sometimes twice. We'd make sweet, frantic love, and try to cram days of loving and talking into a brief hour or two. The times we spent together were both ecstasy and agony. The joy of being together was overshadowed by our guilt, the shame of what we were doing to Robbie and Debbie.

We talked and talked about solutions, what we could do to be together. Sometimes Ken would cry, "Let's just go away together, darling. We'll forget everyone but ourselves." But we both knew that wasn't the solution, that we could never be happy living with the knowledge of what we'd done to Robbie, who'd been good to both of us, and to Debbie, who obviously wasn't well.

I don't know how long we would have gone on, stealing a few hours together, if it hadn't been for my regular checkup with the doctor. Although I wasn't feeling well, I attributed it to the terrible tension of the way I was living and the guilt that was corroding my insides. Still, I didn't attach any more importance to my visit than I did to previous visits. But a few days after my examination and the usual tests, Robbie came home early one afternoon. His face was drawn, his skin pale and papery-looking under his tan.

"Robbie," I exclaimed, "what are you doing home so early?"

Silently, numbly, he took me in his arms, then led me to the couch and pulled me down beside him. My heart began to pound frighteningly. "What is it, Robbie?" My voice sounded scratchy.

"God, Paula." His voice was filled with agony as he held me tightly. "I don't know how to tell you. But I have to, for your sake as well as mine. Dr. Maltin called me this morning. I went to see him. Dearest— your tests have shown increasing deterioration of the heart these last months. This last test—how can I tell you?"

I felt a coldness creep over my body, until I seemed to have turned into a block of ice. "How long have I got, Robbie?" My voice was flat. I felt numb.

His eyes were shiny with unshed tears. "He thinks about six months."

I'm going to die! The words resounded in my head, repeating themselves over and over. Strangely, I felt no fear. I was too frozen— dazed.

"Darling, if only it were me," Robbie cried.

"There's nothing that can be done?" I asked huskily.

65

"Nothing." He tipped my face to his. "I've been thinking and thinking ever since I left his office. I'm going to turn over the business to Ken to run. He knows the production end as well as the sales, and I can trust him. We'll go away somewhere together, where I can spend every moment with you. Where we can just be together to savor every second."

I leaned my cheek against his shoulder, my head whirling. I loved Robbie, but I loved Ken more. I didn't want to spend my last days and weeks with Robbie—I wanted to spend them with Ken. But how could I? How could I leave Robbie with a hurt so deep it would grind into him for the rest of his life? He thought I was good. How could I stain his image of me? Especially now.

"I—I've got to think, Robbie," I said finally. "I can't talk about it now. I just want to think."

"All right, darling. But, please, don't shut me out. I want to share your burden—to help you bear it."

I sat in the yard the remainder of the day, sometimes conscious of the loveliness of the day, the soft wind rustling through the trees, the sky a deep blue with fluffy white clouds scudding across. But sometimes I was only conscious of the fact that I had but a few months to live, and I had to make a choice as to how and with whom, I wanted to spend them.

I lay awake all that night, with Robbie's arms around me, knowing he was lying sleepless, too. I knew, because he loved me so much, that the agony was as great for him as it was for me, maybe more so. My death would bring me peace, freedom from hurt and worry and sorrow. But Robbie would have to live without me. As the first pale fingers of dawn thrust themselves into our room, I was still undecided.

In the morning, I insisted Robbie go to work. "Are you going to be all right?" he asked in concern.

"I'm going to be all right," I said.

That afternoon, Kay took the car to do some shopping, and I was sitting, staring into space, my thoughts going round and round, when the doorbell rang. I opened the door to find Debbie standing there. Her hair was lusterless and drab-looking, her eyes purple and shadowed. "Mrs. Murray—can I talk to you for a moment?"

I felt weakness flood over me, but said, "Of course. Come in."

I led her in, pointing to a chair. She dropped into it, clutching her purse tightly so her knuckles shone white. She didn't waste any time getting to the point.

"I—I know about you and Ken," she said simply. She held up a hand before I could speak. "I just want you to know that I don't blame you—or Ken. I've been a horrible wife since Sean's death. I kept blaming Ken for it even as I knew, deep down, he wasn't to blame."

She rose and started to pace. "But I couldn't seem to help myself

66

from being so mean. Sean and Ken were my whole life—and I'd never had much of a life before them. And suddenly, half my life was wiped out—dead. I guess I was so mad at someone or something that I had to place the blame somewhere. And—and so I blamed Ken."

"Debbie—

Her back was to me and she turned, her eyes pleading. "Please—let me say what I came to say." She swiped at tears with the back of her hand. "I—I know you're not a bad person. So I came to—to beg you to give Ken back to me. I'll be a good wife to him. I'll do everything in my power to make him happy again, the way we used to be."

My tears were flowing freely by this time. In a few short moments, Debbie had helped me make the decision that had been so hard for me. "Debbie, you can have Ken. He's yours," I said. "I—don't think he's ever really been mine."

She whirled on me, her eyes wide. "Do you mean it? Really? I know how much he must care for you. Ken isn't the kind to just—just have an affair. And, except for his guilt, he's been so happy these last weeks. I can always tell the day he's seen you. But how can you bear to give him up?"

And because I knew there'd always be the questions, and the fear in her, I said simply, "Debbie, I just learned yesterday that I don't have much longer to live."

Her mouth fell open and she dropped into a chair.

"I'm not telling you because I want sympathy," I continued hurriedly. "I'm telling you because I want you to believe me. I love Ken. I love him as I've loved no one else in my life. But I also love Robbie. And—and I can't hurt him, not in the short time I have left."

She put a hand to her lips. "I—I'm so sorry."

"Thank you." I rose. "And now, if you don't mind, I'd like to be alone." I knew in a few moments my composure, held so tightly in check, would crack. "Go home," I said wearily. "You have nothing to worry about."

When she was gone I ran to my room, and throwing myself on the bed, cried as I'd never cried before. That night when Robbie came home I told him I was ready to go away.

But I had to see Ken one last time. I called him and made arrangements to meet him at a secluded spot in the country. I told him everything—simply and unemotionally. Watching the horror contort his face at the news of my impending death, my heart ached for him. I listened to his impassioned plea that we go away together for whatever time I had left.

"Darling, I can't," I said as the pain, as real as an attack, twisted at my heart. "I have nothing more to bring you except hurt. And I'd be hurting not only you, but Robbie and Debbie. She's going to change, darling. I know she's going to. You'll be happy with her again. And you can have more children. Don't throw all that away for whatever fleeting happiness we may have."

We didn't make love our last time together. But, then, our love had been so much deeper than a purely physical relationship.

It's been two months since I last saw Ken. Robbie and I left a few days after and have been living in a rented home on an ocean shore. I think of Ken often, yearn for him. But my days with Robbie have been peaceful and happy. I've never regretted my decision. If I'd made any other choice, I wouldn't have been able to face myself.

THE END

FIRST AFFAIR

When you come from a town that has a whopping population of 344 at the best of times . . . and when you know, just know, that life has more in store for you than watching reruns on TV, or wearing clothes ordered from a catalog, why then, you're ripe for somebody like Kate Ellison.

Oddly enough I met Kate through Pete Stuckey, the boy from back home. Pete was tall and kind of skinny with hair so yellow and straight, Kate and I later giggled you couldn't tell the hay in his hair from the hair itself. Don't get me wrong. I liked Pete. I'd been happy to go to the school dances with him during high school, and I liked knowing he was there when I needed him.

But I wanted more out of life than anybody from Marrow Falls could ever offer, and that's why I worked during high school as a waitress at The Friendly Smiles Inn. I saved every penny I made, and all the extra money I could get from baby-sitting and housecleaning, for college.

Pete drove me to the city when it was time to start school. His lower jaw stuck out, and he kept saying, "I don't see why you want to go to college. Why don't you just work on your hope chest until I get through Recruit Training, and then maybe we can think about getting married?"

I drew a deep breath. "Pete, honey, I've told you. I don't want to think about getting married. To you or anyone else." That wasn't exactly the truth. If the right man came along. . . . But I couldn't tell Pete that.

I tried another plan. "Why are you joining the Navy now? There's no draft. You could stay home just as easy as I could. Your dad would be glad to have you help him on the farm."

Pete's ears turned red. "It's different for a man. I want to see what's going on out there in the world. But that doesn't mean I don't love you."

"Don't love me, Pete. Please. I've got itches you just can't satisfy," I whispered.

But I guess Pete didn't hear me. "I've got to go see my Aunt Katey while I'm in town. I promised my mother," he said. "Want to go with me?"

I certainly didn't want to tag along while Pete visited some tacky old middle-aged aunt, just to make his mother happy, but I changed my mind as soon as I saw Seton Hall, where I'd be living the next year, and the other students.

69

Pete didn't seem to realize how much like a couple of country hicks we looked as he carried my bags inside—but I sure did! The other girls' patched jeans and skinny, ribbed tops made my neat skirt and sweater look like a relic from an old Annette Funicello movie. As I stared at the sexy, long-haired boys wandering through, and the sophisticated with-it girls, I knew for a fact it was further than seven hundred miles from Marrow Falls, where Pete and I lived, to here. It was more like forty light years away, and that was a fact.

Pete swallowed hard as a girl, obviously not wearing a bra underneath her clinging knit top, bounced by. Another girl, her hair cut in the latest style I'd seen on TV, stared rudely at me. No wonder. I couldn't have looked more out of it if I'd worn a sunbonnet and trailed a cow behind me.

"Hey, Betty, can I borrow some birth control pills till I get to the doctor on Tuesday?" somebody hollered. My face turned a bright red, and I was glad Pete was still staring after the bouncy-breasted girl and didn't seem to hear.

"Let's, uh—leave my things and then we can go see your aunt," I murmured, suddenly reluctant to face whoever would be my roommate. Any one of these polished, poised girls was going to be horrified when they saw me.

If I thought, though, that Pete's Aunt Katey would be a familiar touch of back home, I was in for a big surprise.

The house Pete drove up to, after peering at a city road map and zigzagging up the nearest hill, was brand-new and beautiful. It looked like a picture in one of the home decorating magazines Mom was always pouring over—as if those magazines would have ideas on how to make a dumb old farmhouse that had worn linoleum and leaky faucets fancy.

The woman who came to the door, clad in a bright, flowing caftan, had shining reddish-brown hair cut in a short page boy. She was anything but typically middle-aged and tacky, but she was apparently Pete's Aunt Katey!

"Pete! Come in, come in," she cried in a low, husky voice.

Wide friendly eyes rested on me, and Pete introduced us. "Aunt Katey, this is Kim. My girl. She's starting at the university this fall, so I drove her up."

"Kate, please!" She groaned, winking at me. "Not Katey. Katey sounds like a little girl with braids and freckles on her nose. And, darlings, I'm not a little girl anymore, much as I wish I were. The freckles are gone, too, thanks to all the luscious makeup available today," she confided to me, linking an arm through mine.

"I . . . I'm so glad to meet you," I stammered. Oddly enough, though her sophistication and glamour made me feel ill at ease, there was something about Kate Ellison that I really liked. Maybe it was that she looked at me as though she really saw me. As though I mattered.

She served iced tea and wafer-thin cookies, chiding Pete all the while for not letting her know we were coming so she could have been prepared to entertain us. "I'd ask you children to stay for dinner, but George—"she turned to me and smiled charmingly—"he's my husband, dear. George's got a late business meeting and all I have in the house is a lone little lamb chop."

"I've got to start back anyway," Pete said. "Dad needs the truck back tomorrow afternoon. Mom said to tell you you're overdue for a visit."

Kate wrinkled her nose. "Dear, as much as I love my sister and her family, Marrow Falls is dull, dull, the dullest." She turned to me. "I'll bet you agree, Kim. You look like I felt twenty years ago when I left Marrow Falls. Scared to death of the big wide world, and yet determined to see more of it than wheat fields and rundown farms."

I had to laugh. "I'd never have dreamed you came from Marrow Falls," I said, thinking that the closest thing to Kate's silken caftan any woman in Marrow Falls wore was an old chenille bathrobe. And then I felt ashamed of myself for laughing, even to myself, at things like that. Mom had wrapped her faded, old chenille-robe around her many a night, to come into my room and soothe me if I was sick, or to brush away the scaries left by a nightmare.

Kate took my hand in her thin, manicured one when Pete and I left. "Come and see me anytime, Kim. What with George being so involved with his business, I'm really at loose ends now that I've got the house fixed up like I want it. I'd love to hear about college life. You're a lucky girl. Things at the 'U' are really swinging these days. It's a fun place to be."

Maybe it was, but for me, in the next few weeks, it definitely was not the fun place I'd vote for first. How in heaven's name, I fumed, could everybody there except me seem to know so unerringly how to act . . . dress . . . make friends. I didn't fit in at all, anywhere, and I was miserable.

It wasn't just that none of the kids in my classes spoke, or even seemed to see me. But I was miserable at Seton Hall, too. To begin with, it was a co-ed dorm, and I couldn't get used to the way the boys popped in and out of the girls' rooms, often without knocking.

Take my roommate's boyfriend, Kevin. He was tall and lanky, and very, very sexy. He and Caren were obviously "doing it" as we'd said back in high school, and sometimes, from the proprietary way he acted when he came into our room, I actually suspected they were doing it in the room I shared with Caren.

I tried not to be shocked. After all, this was after the Sexual Revolution. Maybe, someday, I'd stop hanging onto my own virginity, when the time was right for that sort of thing. But I was embarrassed.

71

And Caren's treating me like a half-wit who'd been forced on her by the dorm committee didn't help, either.

Neither did my growing suspicion that maybe I was a half-wit. The first five weeks of school I pulled D's on three major tests, C's on two reports, and an F for some lab work I did.

The day I got the F was the day I skipped my afternoon classes, went back to my room, and found a "Do Not Disturb" sign on the door. Puzzled, I inserted my key in the lock and turned the knob. Suddenly Kevin's loud voice blared out, "Get the hell outta here! Can't you read, you dumb klutz?"

Heat reddened my face as I realized what I'd walked in on. Hastily I slammed the door, but not before I heard Kevin groan to Caren, "How did you ever draw such a dud for a roommate?"

That was the last straw. Tears stung my eyes. My books weighed down my arms, and I quickly shoved them behind a couch in the TV lounge down the hall from our room. Then I stumbled down the emergency stairs and out of the building. I didn't know where I was going or what I was going to do, but I knew I had to get off campus. Fast.

Somehow I ended up downtown, wandering through Miller and Sons, the biggest, swankiest department store in the city. Not that I was in any mood to appreciate the beautiful clothes displayed on the counters and hangers. Blinded by unhappiness, I barely saw them.

I didn't see Kate Ellison, either, until I all but knocked her down. "Hey, watch where you're—Kim!" she exclaimed in that soft, husky voice.

Dressed in a pink crepe blouse and maroon velvet skirt and jacket, she looked even more terrific than when I'd met her before. I tried to smile, and she shook her head as she gave me a knowing look.

"Uh-oh, love," she said. "The lights have gone out of those eager, sweet little eyes and, if I'm not mistaken, I see tears in the offing."

My lips really did start to tremble then, and I had to blink fast. It had been so long since anyone had seemed to care about me or what I was feeling. Kate took my arm and said, "Come on, honey. Nothing's that bad. Have lunch with an old friend and tell me about it."

We weren't really old friends. I'd only met her once. But, over the delicious iced tea Kate insisted on ordering for me in the mezzanine lunchroom, I told her all about everything. "I just don't fit into the university world," I concluded.

Kate frowned. "Another roommate?" she suggested. "Or a single room?"

"I can barely afford the dorm now," I told her. "There are all sorts of extra charges that weren't mentioned in the college catalog. And the dorm officers keep coming around, collecting for this project and that one. My bank account's going to be as low as my grades if this keeps up."

Kate sipped her tea. Then, counting off on her fingers, she said, "Okay, your problems are, one, you don't fit in with the other kids. Two, you don't fit in with the dorm life. And, three, you aren't making it grade-wise." She brightened, and lifted an eyebrow. "Boyfriends? Or are you too loyal to my little nephew to want other men?"

"Oh, I want other men. Pete's nice, but—" I swallowed hastily, not wanting to say he was too much Marrow Falls for me to be serious about him. "The problem is the other men don't want me," I admitted.

Kate winked. "They will, darling. I promise." She took a sip of tea. "Look, you're not the first high school brain to run into trouble in college. College takes different study techniques, and once you learn them, you'll have no problems." Kate went on to say that she'd show me a few tips she'd learned when she was a coed. "As for the rest of it, you'll get with it fast. I'll help you there, too. Now, I've got a gem of an idea, so listen and then don't say no. Because this idea is too good to turn down."

Eyes sparkling, cheeks flushed with excitement, Kate came forth with her big idea. I was to move in with her. "We have an extra bedroom upstairs. You could help pay for your room and board by helping with the house on Saturdays. You'd have solitude to study, time to find yourself without a roommate sneering over your shoulder all the time, and we can work on your clothes and everything much easier if you're right there in the house with me."

"Oh, Kate, that's awfully good of you, but I couldn't—"

She lifted a hand. "Uh-unnnh. You're not allowed to say no, love. Remember I come from Marrow Falls myself. I know what you're going through. Now go home and pack. You're moving in with me."

I was so low that day I'd have gone off with the Wicked Witch of the West if she'd offered to help me as Kate had. As it was, I could hardly contain my excitement at the idea of moving in with Kate.

She assured me George wouldn't mind. "He doesn't care what I do, love," she said, looking almost sad for an instant. I guess she saw the quick look I gave her because she said, "We married too young, dear. In those days people actually thought marriage came before bed. Or they did if they were country kids like you and me." She laughed, then said, "Don't blush, honey. When the right man comes along, you'll know exactly what I mean."

The next few weeks I felt transported into a fairy tale, with Kate my fairy godmother. Luckily, we paid our dorm rent by the month, so I was able to move out of Seton Hall within a week without losing any money. And Kate took me in hand right away. "Don't be silly, Kim, this is fun for me," she said when I tried to tell her how grateful I was as she went over my wardrobe, putting this sweater aside, that pair of jeans in a pile.

Finally, she sat back. "You need a few new things to look with-it.

73

A couple of ribbed tops, and maybe one of those cute jackets that are all the rage now. The main thing, though, love, is the right bra. Those pointed cup things you've got don't go with today's look. Or"—she paused, looking at me—"better yet, don't wear any bra at all."

"Oh, I couldn't go braless!"

Kate laughed. "Okay, okay, don't look so scared. I'm not going to make you do anything you don't want to do, love. But let's get you one of the new 'nothing' bras. They give a natural look."

My clothes were just the beginning. Kate taught me how to use just the merest hint of makeup, so that it looked as if I was wearing none at all, and yet my face took on a new sexiness. She even took me to her hairdresser and had my hair cut.

And, sandwiched in between were pointers on how to take notes in class and underline my texts so the material I had to remember got stuck in my brain. She gently taught me about wines and how to order in nice restaurants. Things city girls learn naturally, I guess, but stuff you just don't pick up in a town of 344.

Thanks to Kate, I began to feel a self-confidence that I think helped more than the clothes and makeup. Though I don't think Jake Bell would have ambled over to me in the Student Union building a couple weeks later, if it hadn't been for the magic changes wrought by all three.

"Hey, aren't you in my Civics class?" he asked, leaning over the table so I got the full effect of the most divine blue eyes I'd ever seen. His shoulder muscles were so broad and strong looking, his knit shirt looked about to stretch apart at the seams. "I'm Jake Bell. Mind if I join you?"

"Why not?" I managed to say calmly, as though sensational guys like this one came up to me every day of the week. *What a fitting finale to Kate's Make-Over-Kim project,* I thought excitedly.

"I noticed you in class," he said. "You always look so serious when the prof's lecturing. As though you're eating up the whole lecture bit. It's kind of sweet."

I laughed. "Maybe it's because, where I come from, there wasn't anything like big group lectures. The biggest group I ever heard lectured to before was fifteen. My senior class in high school had fifteen kids in it."

Jake's mouth dropped open. "You're kidding!"

"No, I come from a little town that's so small we got our first paved sidewalk last year," I said, making a joke out of Marrow Falls, the way Kate had advised me, saying that as long as my unsophisticated background didn't bother me, it wouldn't bother others.

Jake seemed fascinated by everything I was saying. And by me! He said he was an "Army brat" and, though he'd lived all over the country, and in Europe he'd never lived in a small town. When we finished our coffee and I said I had to get to my next class, Jake stood up.

74

"I'd like to get to know you better," he said, looking down into my eyes with those divine blue eyes. "How about it, Country? Want to go out Friday night with this jaded old Army brat? We could have pizza and go to the Blue Owl for coffee afterward. They have this guitarist on Friday nights who's great."

"I'd love to," I exhaled, knowing my eyes were showing my excitement and somehow not caring a bit.

Kate was as excited as I when I got home and told her about Jake. "He sounds wonderful! Sort of like George was when I met him," she exclaimed, sparkling with happiness for me.

My eyes avoided hers. She'd told me often enough how hard she'd fallen for George when she met him, how special she'd thought he was. So special, in fact, she'd done everything she could to get him to marry her without delay, even though he'd wanted to wait until he was settled professionally. Now, though, I wondered how special she found him. George was so wrapped up in his business, he hardly knew he had a wife. His waist had spread and his hair was thinning.

Once Kate saw me staring at George as he left for work. He was always very polite to me, but I always had this crazy feeling he was never quite sure who this young stranger in his kitchen was. It was a vague, sort of detached way George had of meeting everything except business. Kate's eyes had met mine and she'd shrugged.

"When you get to be my age, love, you stick with what you've got, unless you're darn sure there's something better on the horizon."

I'd laughed, but I hadn't been altogether sure Kate had been joking. Now, when I told her about Jake, she said softly, as though she was remembering when she was my age, "He's going to be important in your life, Kim. I can tell."

"Well, let's wait and see," I said, hoping, but trying not to count on it too much.

Kate's eyebrows rose. She pointed to a pile of letters on the kitchen counter. They were mine, from Pete, who was now taking his Basic Training in San Jose. I hadn't answered the last two, or even opened the one that had come three days ago. "Your eyes never sparked like this for my dear nephew," Kate pointed out.

"Pete's nice, but Jake—" I didn't finish the thought, but I knew Kate knew exactly what I meant.

And, when Jake came by to pick me up Friday night, I could tell she sympathized with the way I felt about Jake totally and completely. Marrow Falls had never produced anything like him!

Jake was an architecture major and, as we dated more and more in the next few weeks, I began to daydream of having a lovely home like Kate's, of floating through it in a silken caftan, entertaining Jake's clients and business associates. It was a life like I'd never seen before and, one I had a feeling I wouldn't mind living.

Jake had dated another girl on campus before me, a girl who lived in Seton Hall, he said. When somebody pointed her out to me, I saw it was the girl who'd so fascinated Pete that first day with her bouncing braless breasts. I knew now that half the girls on campus didn't wear bras and, knowing Jake preferred girls with the natural look, I listened the next time Kate urged me to stop wearing mine, too.

"Get with it, Kim, get with it," she said. "Your generation has the world by its tail, what with the Pill and the lack of sexual hypocrisy in today's society! Don't be afraid to enjoy the goodies."

"It's more a case of other people enjoying the goodies," I said dryly, examining my braless form in the mirror. I wasn't exactly flat-chested.

"Well, when it's Jake enjoying the goodies, you don't mind, do you?" she asked, smiling widely.

I supposed I didn't. And, when Jake said, "Hey, ni-ice. I like the scenery," the first day I went out in a ribbed top without a bra, a warm feeling went through me. More than anything, I wanted to please Jake.

Toward that end, I pretended to like the art films he was crazy about and the monotonous, static guitar music he could listen to for hours on end. "You'll learn to like it, love," Kate insisted. "It's just a matter of getting used to something different."

All those first weeks of dating Jake, I didn't know what I'd have done without Kate to advise me and listen to my problems. I'd finally begun to make girlfriends on campus, but talking to them wasn't the same. With Kate, I could pour my heart out, knowing that because she came from the same sort of background, she'd understand.

Naturally, when Jake started complaining because I didn't "care" enough about him to cement our physical relationship in bed, I told Kate. "Jake says I'm a throwback to frigid, puritanical times. And that if our relationship is to mean anything, it has to be total," I quoted over a cup of midnight tea. George had gone to bed early and Kate had come down, restless, at midnight and found me still sitting over my books. I was doing more thinking about Jake than studying.

Measuring the tea, she turned to me and wrinkled her nose. "Well, don't you think he's right?" At the look on my face, she laughed. "Kim, Kim, this is the day of condoms and safe sex. If you love Jake, for heaven's sake, go to the doctor at the college and get on the Pill. If you don't, the inevitable will happen and Jake will get you pregnant some night when you're not prepared."

"But I've never gone all the way—"

"I know you haven't. But why miss out on a wonderful aspect of life with a terrific guy? Heavens, Kim, had things been different when I was your age, I'd have been in Jake's bed the first night he took me out!"

So would most of the other girls on campus, I knew. Sleeping with your guy was considered normal and natural. After all, hadn't the sexual revolution taken place?

Why, as Kate pointed out, shouldn't I as well as everybody else, enjoy the results of that revolution? The way Kate put it, it sounded downright unpatriotic not to be having sex if there was someone you cared about!

Besides, I had to admit, I wanted sex with Jake. I loved him so much I woke up every morning with his name on my lips. What was I holding out for? Jake couldn't marry me for two or three years, not until he was through college at least, I knew. And he certainly wasn't the type to put up with a celibate relationship with a woman for that long.

So, trying not to think about what my mother would say, and telling myself I didn't have to use them if I didn't want to, I went to the university's doctor and got the Pill and a package of condoms. And, of course, once I was on the Pill, it was easy to go ahead and say yes.

It happened one night a couple weeks later when Jake parked his car in front of the rooming house where he had a single room. He lived just a block from campus, in a place popular with the students.

"Country girl, I'm crazy about you," he whispered in my ear, his lips doing things to my pulse rate.

Jake's room was small, but there was, indeed, a homemade quilt on the bed. There was a desk and a chair in one corner, and a chest of drawers next to the bed. I saw all that, and yet I didn't, as Jake's tanned face filled my field of vision. His hands reached for me, and then all thought stopped as Jake and I became lovers.

The next couple of months were wonderful, and I couldn't have been happier. Kate was as thrilled as I by the way things had worked out with Jake, and she insisted I tell her all about our dates and everything we did.

Oh, not the details of our lovemaking, of course. But the other things . . . how Jake and I met for lunch every day in the Student Union at school . . . the way his voice always dropped when he called me "country girl," giving it more meaning than most men give the word "darling." How happy I was that I hadn't kept on holding back, like some movie virgin out of touch with real life.

I was too busy to write, too. Jake took up so much of my time, I hardly got enough studying done to pass my courses, and it seemed I was constantly forgetting an assignment or running late on something. But I didn't care, really. Graduating from college or learning a profession didn't seem nearly as important as it had when I left.

Then, so subtly I hardly noticed it at first, things began to change. For one thing, Jake stopped pressuring me to move out of Kate's and into a room with him. I thought at first that he'd just finally come around to understanding that I couldn't do that and take a chance on my folks surprising me sometime.

But the reason Jake stopped pressuring me had nothing to do with accepting or understanding my feelings. Just like his starting to be late for our dates, or even not showing up to meet me for lunch in the Student Union had nothing to do with being busy, like he said.

Then Jake stopped asking me out. That's when I found out he was interested in another coed, and considered everything "over" between us. "Come on, Kim, these things don't last forever," he said when I cornered him. "We had a good time and the vibes were great there for a while. But everything has to come to an end sometime, Country."

"I thought we'd get married someday," I protested.

Jake's eyes widened and he held a hand up in alarm. "Oh, now, wait! I never said one word about marriage, and you know it. I've got years and years to go before I'll be in a position to think about marriage."

Tears filled my eyes and I forced my chin up. "Army brat, you are being a brat," I said, trying to humor him into telling me that this was all some sort of joke. That he still loved me, and always would.

But Jake backed away like I was contagious. "That's the trouble with virgins," he growled. "You make it with them for a while and they think they've got you tied up forever. But not me, baby. I never promised you anything."

Pride froze my tears and gave me the strength to turn around and walk away from him, knowing that I was walking away from Jake for good. My heart felt shattered and I couldn't have told if the day was snowy or sunny as I walked up the hill to Kate's.

She was all sympathy, but, to my shock, not surprised. "You should have known it wouldn't last, honey. Jake's a man of the world. He's been everywhere, and done everything, thanks to his Army background. He wouldn't have stayed content with any one woman for long. But he was a wonderful experience for you. Look at it that way."

Through the tears streaking down my cheeks, I stared at her. "That's all you thought it would mean in the end? A 'wonderful experience' for me? If you didn't think it was going to be a permanent relationship, why didn't you tell me, Kate? Why did you let me stick my neck out and get hurt?"

"Who can ever tell a woman in love anything?" she scoffed, laughing lightly. "Besides, darling, in time you'll be glad you had this experience with Jake. Don't turn your back on anything you can get out of life, honey. In time you'll be glad you didn't. And sorry if you do. Oh, so sorry."

Right then I saw the truth about Kate's "friendship" for me. She'd missed out on what she thought of as a lot of fun. But people go to college to learn something. And I guess I couldn't hide from the truth forever. Finally, I had to face the fact that it had been my own decision in the end to sleep with Jake. After all, I hadn't been forced to follow Kate's advice, had I? My own common sense should have told me that

I didn't really know Jake and that he was really a very shallow person, not at all the kind of man who'd want anything lasting in a relationship.

It took me awhile longer to admit that I'd never really loved Jake. Oh, I'd been infatuated, and because he seemed like the "ideal man" I'd dreamed of meeting someday, while I was just a kid in Marrow Falls, I'd mistaken that infatuation for love. He hadn't had a trace of hay in his hair, and I guess that had done it for me.

Well, Pete Stuckey doesn't have hay in his hair now. I saw him the other day when he was headed for home on leave from the Navy. He grinned that big wide grin of his when I walked into the rooming house lounge.

"Hi. Think you could have lunch with a lonely sailor?" he asked. "I don't have a girl in this port." Then a questioning look came into his eyes. "Or do I, Kim?"

My heart did a funny little dance, and I suddenly realized how many good times Pete and I had shared. We'd gone together through most of high school, and a lot of good memories came to mind.

Pete wasn't just the boy I'd grown up with, though. I saw right away that the last few months had changed him as much as they had me. "You should see San Jose," he told me during lunch. "It's really a nice city. I'm thinking of maybe going back there after I'm out of the Navy, settling down, and maybe trying to get a small business going."

Pete and I are corresponding now, and I guess you could say he does have a girl in this port, after all. I won't say for sure we'll end up being serious, but I kind of think we will. I'm sorry now that there was a Jake in my life before I grew to appreciate Pete, but maybe I wouldn't feel the way I do about him now if it hadn't been for my experience with Jake.

Pete and I may end up lovers before we get married. A lot of people do these days. But I know one thing for sure; if we do, it'll be because it's what we want, and not because we're trying to live up to some phony image of "liberation." Real sexual freedom means deciding for yourself the sexual lifestyle that's right for you.

THE END

WHEN LOVE
IS A LIE

Our marketing department secretary, Carla Sue Tyson, winked at me as I ran around the end of the partition separating her office from mine. It was almost twenty minutes after nine, and I was nearly an hour late, which was sure to bring a lecture from our manager, Felix Sisk, on the "rights and responsibilities of professional employees."

Felix was a slightly overweight manager in his mid-fifties. And although he could be a sweet and funny guy—when you caught him on a good day—his "good" days were few and far between, and he was a hard, demanding boss the rest of the time. I tried not to let him get under my skin. I figured there was at least one like him in every company, and I tried to be as pleasant as I could be. His last "good" day had been on Christmas Eve, nearly seven months before.

Felix's office was on the far side of Carla Sue's, and I figured I'd probably be safe if I talked softly. "Carla Sue," I hissed. "Carla Sue, are you there?"

Carla Sue poked her head around the shoulder-high partition and grinned. I hated those partitions. They were just high enough to give people the illusion of privacy without really providing any. It drove me crazy to know that there were at least twenty people who could hear every word I said whenever I opened my mouth.

"Hot date last night?" Carla Sue joked.

I knew she was joking because she knew that I had sworn off men forever when my first marriage ended in a prolonged divorce and custody battle. I'm also very religious and my church doesn't sanction premarital sex, so Carla Sue knew, without even asking, that even if I had been out on a date, it would never have been a "hot" one!

She walked around my small file cabinet and sat on the edge of my desk, sliding my purse into the open file drawer to make room for herself.

"Come on, what gives?" she asked, leaning forward so I could hear her. "You're always the first person here in the morning. I've never seen you even five minutes late before."

"Shhh," I said, putting a finger to my lips and standing on tiptoe to look over the partition in the direction of Felix's office. "He'll hear you. Maybe if I get busy right away, he won't notice I was late."

Carla Sue laughed and patted me on the head as if I was a small child. "I hate to burst your bubble, kiddo, but he noticed you were late at eight-thirty. He was in and out of here like a cuckoo at midnight, complaining about unreliable women."

I reached under her into the file drawer and rummaged around blindly in my purse for the key to my desk. "Terrific!" I said, unlocking my desk with a savage twist of my key. "This is the first time I've been late in eighteen months, and suddenly I'm unreliable. He's late at least once a week!"

Carla Sue stood and smoothed her skirt. "I wouldn't worry about it if I were you. He's at his Friday morning meeting. By the time he comes out of that, he'll be so angry at somebody else, he'll have forgotten all about you." She glanced at the clock on the wall. "We have at least an hour before he comes back." She leaned down, and in a conspiratorial whisper she said, "So where were you, anyway?"

I stood on tiptoe again and looked out over the partition to see if any of the office nosies were listening. Carla Sue and I called them the "Three Spies." Sylvia and Jean were single, and Gail had been widowed. They were all in their early fifties and firmly convinced that everyone, except them, lived a wild, totally uninhibited life away from the office. They did more harm than good with their eavesdropping and gossiping and I wasn't about to let them hear my personal problems.

"I had a run-in with my ex-husband. He kept me on the phone until two o'clock this morning letting me know what an incompetent mother I am, threatening to have the kids removed if I didn't let him off the hook for child support."

Carla Sue wrinkled her nose and waved her hand in the air as if she was fanning away a bad smell. "He's history, Karen," she said with a sniff. "I wouldn't worry about him. Ignore him! There's nothing he can do to you. Hang up on him the next time he calls."

I smiled at her, grateful for her loyalty and support. "I can't hang up on him. It seems like such a rude thing to do."

"Oh, please!" she said, settling herself again on the corner of my desk. "God would never ask you to deal with a jerk like that for the rest of your life."

I leaned back in my chair and thought about that for a minute. The only reason that God would have sent me Larry would have been to give me my boys. The ten miserable years I had spent being married to Larry seemed like a more than fair price to pay for my two kids. I smiled as their sweet, mischievous faces popped into my mind.

Davey was eight, and a more loving and gentle child had never been born. He was always on my lap, snuggling and hugging me, and I looked forward every day to one of his special, welcome-home hugs. Matt was just eleven, and although he was hyperactive and a little difficult to deal with at times, he was honest, bright, friendly, and responsible, and I loved him with all my heart. Both boys were miniature replicas of their father in looks. Our divorce and the court fight had taken them through some rough times, and they were finally beginning to relax and act like normal boys again.

I was born and raised in Tennessee, and my father had started molesting me when I was eight years old. I kept quiet about it for three years, but when I realized that he had started in on my little sister, I blew the whistle on him. I found myself in a courtroom on my twelfth birthday, holding a doll and describing what he had done to me.

My mother divorced him, and we moved in with my grandma for a couple of years. Then Mama had remarried, and our new father was exactly the same kind of guy as my real father. He left us alone because I got him one night behind the tool shed, pointed a pitchfork at him, and told him he'd be singing soprano if he ever laid one finger on me or my sisters or Mama. He drifted away a week or so after that. Although my mother didn't know where he went, I think she had a pretty good idea why, even though she never said a word to me.

After that, there was a whole series of one-night stands for Mama. The men were creeps with slicked-back hair and candy in their pockets for us kids, who gave Mama a few dollars for a night and went away without looking back. Mama used to cry at night and pray to God for forgiveness, but I figured God would understand that she didn't have any other way to feed us. I knew what she was doing was wrong, but it also seemed pretty wrong for us kids to have to go hungry three nights a week. She was my mama, and I loved her, and that was all that mattered to me.

The day I turned eighteen, I hitched a ride to the Navy recruiter's office in town and joined. They promised to teach me a trade, and I figured I could send Mama enough money so she wouldn't have to share her bed with anybody ever again.

Uncle Sam sent me to boot camp in a town outside of Chicago, and when I graduated I went to a naval base outside of San Francisco. I met Larry. One night I was getting off watch and he was my replacement. This guy was a dream come true—tall, well built, and handsome—just like in the movies. His hair was clean and he smelled like after-shave, and I fell head over heels in about five minutes. I wasn't exactly sure what he saw in me, but I didn't wait around asking any questions. We were married six weeks later, and two weeks after that, Larry shipped out for an eight-month stint in Japan.

The two weeks we spent together taught me a lot. In fourteen days, I learned that my handsome dreamboat was really a selfish, lazy, lying rat with an eye for anything in spike heels. He also had an incurable yen for a poker game. The day he shipped out, I told him I planned to divorce him. He just laughed and said I'd have to hurry or he'd beat me to it. I marched straight to an attorney's office, filled out the paperwork, and arranged to have him served when he came into port. Exactly one month after that, I found out I was pregnant.

It wasn't easy being pregnant and alone. The Navy gave me an early discharge, and I ended up on public assistance. I started going to church to make friends and maybe find somebody who would give me a part-time job. The church filled a lot of emptiness in my life, and about a month before Larry was due home, I accepted Christ as my personal savior.

I decided to try and give our marriage another chance for the sake of the baby. Larry was thrilled to have a little boy, and started going to church with me. When Matt was three months old, Larry accepted Christ and joined the church. I felt that this was a sign from God that things would turn out all right.

God must have been trying to tell me something different, though. Larry was a poor father and a terrible husband, and when he shipped out again six months later, I was glad. This time he was gone for over two years and I got pregnant again the night he came home. I had to admit one thing—when we made love, it was good, and he took away all the bad feelings I'd been carrying around about my father and stepfather.

We moved around a lot until Larry was discharged from the Navy. I went back to school, got my associate degree, and found the perfect job with a small electronics company. That's where I met Carla Sue, and that's when Larry met Sherri. She was a horrible woman, and there was no doubt, right from the start, that she was after my husband. She started begging rides to church with us, and I used to pray for patience while she flirted with Larry during the service.

The day I came home from work two hours early and found them together in my bed was the last straw. I didn't make a scene. I just packed my clothes and the kids' things, while Larry hopped around on one foot trying to put his pants on. We moved in with Carla Sue for a couple of months until I could save up enough for a place of our own. It was tough, and we didn't always eat well, but we were making it okay.

It had been just over a year since we left Larry, and I had my boys and my church and my friend, Carla Sue. I thought we could go on like this for a long time. And I accepted it.

Carla Sue poked me in the shoulder. "Earth to Karen," she said. "Come in, Karen!" I jumped about a foot and grinned at her. She really was a lovely lady, and I secretly thought of her as my second mother.

"I'm sorry, Carla Sue," I said. "I really was far away, wasn't I?"

"Oh, well," she said, "I understand. You know," she said, casting me a sideways glance, "what you really need is a terrific guy. Have I ever told you about my son?"

I put out both hands to stop her off before she got started again. "Only about a million times! Billy is handsome! Billy has two degrees in psychology, is a Cub Scout leader, youth group leader, makes good money, and loves children and dogs. Oh, Billy also owns his own house, too." I swiveled my chair around to face her. "Did I leave anything out?"

Carla Sue looked hurt. "He's a great guy, Karen," she said in her you-hurt-my-feelings voice. "I wish you would at least call him. He's single, and he's just waiting for a girl like you."

I shook my head. "Single? I thought he was engaged."

Carla Sue twisted the ring on her left ring finger. "He was, but she took off a month ago with his car and his charge cards." She absent mindedly rubbed the back of her hand. "She was such a nice girl, too. I couldn't believe it when I heard what she did to him."

I patted her shoulder, a little awkwardly. Comforting Carla Sue was new for me. Usually, it was the other way around. "Carla Sue, you're such a good person." I handed her a tissue. "It always surprises you when people act badly. Besides," I added, "you can't possibly know the whole story. Maybe she had a reason."

Carla Sue blew into the tissue. "Now who's looking for good in everyone?"

I smiled sheepishly. "Okay, okay—I give up. He's a paragon of virtue and she's a rat. It wasn't your fault you couldn't see through her. Lots of people are amazingly good actors."

She looked mollified. "Can't I at least give him your phone number? He really needs someone to talk to right now, and you haven't had a date in over a year."

I reached into the drawer for some typewriter paper. "Okay, give him my phone number. But be sure to warn him that I have absolutely no intention of getting involved. I was married once, and that was plenty!" I typed the date in the upper right corner. "Besides, can you imagine trying to get involved with a guy who lives in Tacoma? I can't even afford bus fare some weeks. Telephone calls alone would break me!"

Carla Sue smiled and started to say something, but her words were interrupted by our boss, who came storming around the corner into my office.

"Karen," he said in his calm, you're-in-trouble-now voice, "would you step into my office for a moment, please?" He turned and disappeared.

I peeked into the mirror in my top drawer and patted my hair, hoping I didn't look as uneasy as I felt. I had to admit, he always made me nervous. It wasn't as if I were chronically late—I had a perfect excuse made up, but I hated being put on the defensive. And there was absolutely no way to win an argument with him. He was the boss, and as far as he was concerned, that made him automatically right. I always counted myself lucky when I didn't lose too badly or start to cry. Crying was always a disaster in Felix's view. Teary-eyed women made him nervous, and then he really got mean. Unfortunately, I cry a lot, but I smile a lot, too. All of my emotions are right on the surface.

Felix was seated behind his desk when I walked in, and he motioned

84

me to a chair directly under the fluorescent light. I hated that chair. He always sat me in it when he was about to read me the riot act. I decided to try and defuse the situation. "Felix, I'm sorry I was late this morning. I'm having some trouble with my car." God would forgive the lie, I hoped.

There was a long silence. I learned a long time ago that if I don't have anything to say, it's best to keep quiet, so I stared straight ahead and tried to stop my hands from shaking. Finally, Felix looked up at me. "Karen, we simply cannot tolerate tardiness. It sets a bad example. It's a sign of irresponsibility, and irresponsible employees cost the company time and money."

His attitude upset me, and I picked up one of his pencils and tapped it on my side of the desk. "Felix, I had car trouble. There was no way to call. I apologize." He didn't respond at all, and I added, "What should I have done that I didn't do?"

He leaned back in his chair. "I suppose, under the circumstances, that there was nothing further you could have done." He stood up. "However, I don't want it to happen again."

Then I stood up, grateful that he wasn't going to launch into a long list of my problems and failures as an employee. "Felix, I promise! I'll have the car serviced tomorrow, so this won't happen again."

He smiled and nodded. "That will be just fine. Go on back to work now."

I sighed mentally in relief and turned to walk out. As I passed through the doorway, he added, "Oh, Karen?"

With a real sigh this time, I turned around. "Yes, Felix?"

"Make up the hour before you leave this evening, won't you?" It wasn't a request.

I smiled. "Of course I will, Felix."

He nodded, sat down again, and started shuffling through piles of papers on his desk. He'd forgotten about me already.

As I walked by Carla Sue's office, she gave me the thumbs-up sign. I laughed as I picked up my phone to call Carlotta, my baby-sitter, to see if she could watch the kids an extra hour.

She agreed, but reminded me that I'd owe her an extra hour's pay.

After I hung up, I fretted over my lack of money. If Larry would pay child support when he was supposed to, money wouldn't be so tight. Every time I asked him for it, he threatened to take the kids away from me. Still, the money wasn't for me, but for the boys, and I figured they were entitled to it.

I dialed my attorney's office and left a message with his secretary. I couldn't afford him, either, but he was letting me pay him a little bit each month.

Everybody in the office closed up shop and went home at five, leaving me alone with my thoughts and my typewriter. I loved when the building was quiet and empty. At home the boys were always so active and I was usually so busy that I really enjoyed the chance to be alone for a while, so I didn't begrudge spending the extra hour in the office.

After working the extra hour, I picked up the boys from Carlotta's, paid her, and drove home slowly to conserve gas. My gas indicator was on empty, but I knew I had at least thirty miles worth of gas left in the tank, so I wasn't worried. At least, not much.

When we got home, I let Matt play outside because he was full of energy. In fact, he was slightly overactive and sometimes he drove me crazy, but tonight I felt calm and peaceful, and his noise didn't really bother me. Davey fell asleep while I was preparing dinner, so Matt and I ate alone and talked about the weekend. We decided to go to the beach after we finished our Saturday chores.

Once the boys were tucked into bed, I washed the dishes and settled down on the sofa with the library book I had started the night before. I had been reading for over an hour and was deeply into another world, where I was gorgeous and rich, when the telephone rang, startling me. I glanced at the clock, wondering what sort of an idiot would call so late, and I realized it was only nine.

I picked up the phone. "Hello."

"May I speak to Karen Woods, please?" The voice was male, very deep, very attractive, and very unfamiliar.

I was still a little annoyed at being interrupted, and I let my tone of voice show it. "This is she." And who the heck are you?

"Karen, this is Bill Tyson." There was a pause while I tried to remember who on earth Bill Tyson was. Was he a bill collector? "I'm Carla Sue's son." The voice was hesitant now, not nearly so confident.

Light dawned in my brain. "Of course," I said. I didn't want to hurt his feelings. "Carla Sue's son." There was another pause. What on earth should I say to this stranger? I forced some enthusiasm into my voice. "Well, what can I do for you?"

"Well, not a lot really." He sounded a little more secure. "Mom's told me a lot about you, and I promised I'd call, so I figured I'd better before she flies up here and breaks my arm!"

Oh, great! I thought. *He doesn't want to talk to me any more than I want to talk to him.* I laughed. "Yeah, I know the feeling. Carla Sue seems to think that you and I were made for each other, and we're just two stubborn people who refuse to cooperate."

"Mom does seem to like to play matchmaker." There was another pause. "She said you have two boys. I love kids. How old are they?"

There is nothing in the world that I love to talk about more than my kids, and, before I knew it, I had told him all about Matt's hyperactivity, my rotten boss, my disastrous marriage, my worries about always being broke, even my dream of one day being a writer. He'd told me about his job and his house and his dog and his old girlfriend. We discovered we liked the same old movies and music, laughed at the same jokes, had the same favorite foods and television shows, and we shared a dream of getting away from the city and living in a cabin in the mountains.

I was enchanted. The next time I looked at the clock, it was almost midnight, and we'd been talking for nearly three hours. Before Bill hung up, he promised to call again in a day or so. And he did. He called again the very next night, and the night after that, and every night for the next three weeks. We shared our secrets and our dreams, and we laughed and cried together. I floated through my days at work in a dreamy state of euphoria, and when I let Carla Sue in on why I was so happy, she was ecstatic!

"I knew it!" she shouted, slapping me on the back so hard I choked on my coffee.

"Shhh," I said, wiping coffee off of my typewriter keys with a paper towel. "Felix will hear you."

"Who cares?" She did a little pirouette in my office. "I knew you two were made for each other." She leaned over and looked me straight in the eyes. "So," she asked, "when's the wedding?"

I choked on my coffee again. She had put her finger on the very thing I'd been thinking about but hadn't dared say out loud. "Carla Sue, don't be silly. The man lives in Tacoma, for heaven's sake! I can't marry someone who lives in Tacoma."

"Of course you can!" She put her face close to mine. "You have a right to be happy. This is your chance. Take it! You don't have to be lonely all your life. Besides, those boys of yours need a real father." She looked at me. "I can vouch for him, you know." She gave me a big grin. "I've known him all his life!"

"Carla Sue, this is all happening too fast. I've only known the man for three weeks. In fact, I've never even met him."

She looked thoughtful. "You're right. I hadn't thought of that." Her face brightened. "I know. I'll call him and tell him to come down." She disappeared into her office.

I stood up too fast and knocked my cup over, spilling coffee in my lap. "Carla Sue—don't—wait . . ."

But at that point, Felix came racing into my office with a stack of papers, heavily marked in red ink. "Karen, these need rewriting. How fast can you do it?"

I leafed through the stack of pages. There were heavy corrections to make, but with the computer, I didn't think it would take too long. "An hour?" I said hopefully, afraid he would say he needed them in fifteen minutes.

Felix's face lit up. "Oh, Karen, you're a doll! Thanks!" He leaned close and gave me a swift peck on the cheek. Carla Sue looked over the wall at me, eyebrows lifted. "Better circle this day on your calendar!" She laughed.

That night, when the phone rang, I was expecting it and caught it on the first ring. "I'm flying in tomorrow," I heard the now-familiar voice say. "Can you meet me at the airport?"

"I'll be there," I promised, my heart starting to hammer at the thought. "Oh, wait. How will I recognize you?"

"I'll be wearing a football jersey and carrying a red rose." His voice was gently teasing now. "The flight gets in at three-thirty."

"I'm not sure I would recognize a football jersey," I said doubtfully. "But I know a rose when I see one."

He laughed, his voice full of delight. "Oh, Karen, I've been looking forward to this so much!"

"Me, too," I said. "Go get some sleep and I'll see you tomorrow."

"Okay, sweetheart. Sweet dreams."

"You, too." I was longing to say, "I love you," but I didn't dare unless he said it first.

"Oh, Karen?"

"Yes?"

"Don't bring your car, okay? We'll rent something cool when I get there."

I laughed. "Aye-aye, sir! Cool, it is!"

After I had replaced the receiver, I wandered around the house, locking doors and turning off lights. Before I crawled into bed, I made a list of all the things I wanted to get done before Bill arrived. The last thing I remembered before falling asleep was something Pastor Jones had said to me the previous Sunday.

We were standing on the front steps of the church, just looking around at all the bright dresses and the sunshine, and listening to the happy shouts of the children playing tag on the grass.

The pastor had turned to me and said, "Karen, you look as if you have a secret—as if sunshine has come to live in your heart." I had laughed and given him a quick hug.

"Pastor, I have sunshine in my soul!"

I smiled, remembering, and the next thing I knew, it was morning.

The boys had made themselves breakfast by the time I got out of the shower. I wrapped myself in my blue robe and, rubbing my hair dry with a towel, bent down to kiss them good morning.

"I'm going to need your help today, guys." They looked up at me, distracted momentarily from their cartoons. "Bill is coming today, and I want to have the whole house sparkling clean by the time he gets here."

Matt leaped up and shot into his room, returning with clothes for Davey and himself. The next thing I knew, he and Davey were completely dressed, their toys were put away, and there was a pile of dirty laundry overflowing the hamper by the washing machine. Between the three of us, we managed to finish in four hours what it usually took me all Saturday and Sunday to complete. I put on makeup and set my hair. Later, we walked the three blocks to the bus stop.

The bus was running late, as usual, and we got to the airport just as they were announcing the arrival of Bill's flight. There were butterflies dancing in my stomach as I waited by the gate, and Matt and Davey were excited.

When Bill came through the security gate, I knew him immediately, even without the red rose or the baseball jersey. I said a silent prayer as he came near, and the four of us stood looking at each other.

Davey broke the silence with typical childish innocence. He looked up at Bill and asked, "Are you Bill? Are you going to be my new daddy?" and he held out his arms to be picked up.

I heard Bill say, "I hope so, Davey," and the next thing I knew, the four of us were hugging and laughing together, and the surrounding people were beginning to point and whisper. As Bill kissed me on the cheek, I heard him whisper, "Thank you, God," and my heart overflowed with happiness and joy. I felt a peacefulness and a sense of "coming home" that I'd never experienced before.

Still carrying Davey, Bill took Matt by the hand and we walked towards the car rental desk. "What kind of car should we get?" Bill asked, looking at me. "Something big and fancy, or something racy?"

The boys jumped in before I could answer. "Something red and fast!" Matt said, dragging Bill to the window to look out at the sea of rental cars. I shrugged my shoulders.

Bill came close to me and whispered, "Looks like we're outvoted." He smiled down at me. "We'll save the fancy job for our honeymoon."

Suddenly, my knees felt like rubber. It was all coming true, everything I'd ever dreamed. I could barely stand. I sank into a chair as Bill filled out the paperwork and signed the charge slip. Holding the keys out to Matt, he put his arm around Davey and pointed to a red sports car out on the lot. "It's that one, Davey," he said. "Think you and Matt can put my suitcase in the trunk?"

Davey nodded solemnly, and he and Matt ran off through the parking lot, dragging Bill's suitcase through the gravel.

"Watch out for cars," I shouted, but they were already too far away to hear me.

Bill put his arm around me. "They'll be all right," he said, giving me a gentle squeeze. "When I was their age, I was dodging trains on the old railroad bridge near my house."

I shook my head. "They're growing up so fast."

Bill stopped and turned me around so I was facing him. "I've been wanting to do this for a long time," he murmured as he kissed me. I thought I saw stars. Stars and fireworks.

As we drove home, Bill kept glancing over at me and running his hand across my knee.

"Where are you staying?" I asked, assuming he was planning on staying with Carla Sue.

"Well," he said, giving me a sideways glance and a smile, "I was hoping to stay with you. I have to fly home tomorrow night, and I wanted to spend as much time with you and these two little monsters"—he reached back and ruffled Davey's hair—"as I possibly can." He looked at me questioningly. "Is that all right with you?"

Suddenly, I was glad I had changed the sheets on my bed this morning. Then, in a flash of embarrassment, I blushed. Then I felt the peace and happiness steal over me. I realized that God had given me this man, and I felt blessed. Still, I wasn't sure exactly what his intentions were. "I only have a double bed," I said, too shy to look directly at him. "Or you could sleep on the sofa."

He smiled again and caressed my cheek. "I want to sleep with you," he said, stopping at a light. He looked directly at me. "But I want our wedding night to be the first time for us. Tonight, though, I want to hold you in my arms and cuddle."

I rolled down my window and waved at a neighbor, proud to be seen with this incredible man. "I want that, too," I said. He pulled into my driveway and turned off the ignition.

I got out of the car and ran around it, pulling his door open and hugging him. Then I stopped, horrified.

He looked worried and held me by both shoulders. "What is it, Karen? What's wrong?"

"There's so much to do if we plan to be married so soon. I have to give notice at work, train a replacement, pack up our stuff, call my attorney, have a new visitation agreement written up, and . . ."

He put his finger gently across my lips. "Shhh," he said, "don't worry about it. I'll be here to help."

I leaned against him, safe and secure for the first time in my life. It was a great feeling.

The rest of the day we spent playing with the boys and making plans. We saw a movie, went to a fast-food restaurant for dinner, and walked barefoot in the sand, watching the sun set. And when we put the boys to bed that night, it was as if we'd been together all our lives. We undressed and got into bed, and I fell asleep with my head on his shoulder and his arms around me.

By the time Davey and Matt and I took him to the airport Sunday afternoon, our plans were set. We had gone to church together and caught Pastor Jones before the service. In our church, weddings are public events to which every member is invited. The thought of sharing my joy with all my friends made me happier than I had ever been, and when Pastor Jones announced our engagement and named a wedding

90

date only two weeks away, the entire congregation gasped and then stood up and applauded. As they clapped, there was a shriek of joy from somewhere in the back and Carla Sue came flying up the aisle and threw her arms around us.

"Oh, I knew it!" she said, wiping tears of joy from her eyes. "I just knew it! You two are so right for each other!" It was a triumphant day for her, and, as she beamed at us, I felt bathed in warmth and love. She hugged me tightly. "I always wanted a daughter," she said. "I'm so glad it's you." I handed her a tissue from my purse, and we left the church together, laughing and crying and clasping hands with our friends as we passed.

Somehow, I got through the next two weeks. There were so many little details to take care of, and so little time to do it. I had to give notice at work, and of course, the Three Spies spread the news far and wide. They were aghast that I would marry a man I had just met. Finally, I stopped even pretending to be polite and told them that when I wanted their opinions, I would ask. They went off like hens with their feathers ruffled, cackling and sputtering, while Carla Sue fell out of her chair laughing.

Bill returned the Saturday before the wedding, and together we held a moving sale. We sold all of my appliances, and my bedroom furniture and living room set to members of my church. We made arrangements for them to come and pick the things up the following Sunday, the day after the wedding.

Felix's reaction was the biggest surprise of all, though. On Thursday, two days before the wedding, he called me into his office and had me sit in the chair I had always hated. He sat down opposite me and leaned back, fiddling with his tie pin. Felix had never been a fidgety type, so I knew something was up, but I wasn't expecting his next words.

"Karen, I want you to know that I'm going to miss you." His words came out in a rush. "You're the best technical writer on the staff."

To my astonishment, I saw that his eyes were glistening with tears, and I reached out and slid the tissue box closer, so he could reach it. I sat awkwardly for a moment. This was so unexpected that I was flabbergasted, but I knew I had to say something.

To my surprise, I found my own eyes full of tears. I reached for a tissue. "Felix, you know I would never have been able to say this if I weren't leaving, because people might have thought I was . . . well, you know . . . trying to get special favors or something from you, but I think you're the best manager I've ever had." And it was true. He was fussy most of the time, but he knew how to motivate people and make them work hard, and he always did his best. I blew my nose. "I'm going to miss you, too."

He stood up and walked around the table, patting me awkwardly on the shoulder. "Karen, I also want you to know that if you ever need

91

a job, you can always come back here and work for me. And if I'm retired by then, you can be sure that my replacement will know about your abilities." I stood and gave him a big hug, which surprised him at first, but then he relaxed and hugged me back.

"I'm going to be looking for work in Tacoma," I said. "Can I have people call you?"

Felix smiled, a big, broad smile. "Of course. I'll give you the best recommendation they've ever heard."

I smiled back. "Thanks, Felix. Thanks for everything."

I left Felix's office and walked back to mine, wishing for the millionth time that I could marry Bill and still somehow stay close to the people who cared about me. Larry and I had moved around a lot, and I wasn't afraid of making new friends, but I knew that I would be lonely for a while until I found a job and we were all settled in. Still, I knew I loved Bill with all my heart, and I was willing to follow him as far as I had to if it meant real happiness for me and my boys at last.

The next forty-eight hours went by quickly, and before I knew it, I was standing in front of Pastor Jones, holding Bill's hand as tightly as I could and repeating the words that made me his wife. He had been pretty jumpy all week, and a little short-tempered with the boys that morning, but I knew he was terribly nervous, and I loved him all the more for being human.

Our reception was held in a hotel near the airport. To my amazement, the Three Spies had given us a night in the bridal suite as a wedding gift, and since Bill had to leave late Sunday morning to fly home, I wanted it to be a night we would never forget. Carla Sue had given me a beautiful satin negligee, and I could hardly wait to put it on. My plan was to drop Bill at the airport the following morning, go home, and supervise, while the guys from the church loaded the truck, and then leave for Tacoma that night.

During the reception, Bill was drinking glass after glass of champagne and apparently having the time of his life. I have to admit, I had more than I should have had as well, and, by the time we went upstairs to our room, I was slightly drunk and Bill was stumbling over rough spots in the carpeting. We got to our room, undressed, and fell into bed. In my new nightgown, I was feeling sensuous and sexy. This was the moment I'd been waiting for. I rubbed Bill's stomach, tangling my fingers in his hair and inhaling the sweet, masculine scent of his body.

He opened one eye. "What are you doing?"

I nuzzled his chest. "Mmmm," I said lazily, smiling at him, "loving you."

He groaned and pushed my hand away. "Oh, Karen, not now! Can't you see I'm too drunk to do anything?"

A rush of disappointment mingled with love swept over me. Poor baby. The past few days had been such a strain for him, and here I was deviling him to make love to me. I kissed his shoulder.

"I'm sorry, sweetheart. Go to sleep. Maybe a little later." As I fell asleep listening to his even breathing and feeling the weight of his body next to me in the big, round waterbed, I hugged myself. It was going to be such a good life together!

I woke with a start a few hours later. Bill was standing naked by the big plate-glass window, staring out over the sea of cars in the hotel parking lot.

I smoothed my hair and drew my nightgown up my thigh invitingly. I patted the bed beside me. "Come here," I said in my best come-hither voice.

He turned to look at me, his features indistinguishable because of the light shining behind him. "Go back to sleep, Karen. I need to think."

Suddenly, I felt alarmed. I got out of bed and went to stand beside him. "Bill, what is it? Have I done something to make you angry?"

He smiled and stroked my cheek. "No, babe—it's nothing you've done. Go back to sleep now."

Reassured, I pushed my luck a little. "Bill, this is our wedding night." I stroked his arm with a fingertip. "Come back to bed with me? Please?"

He turned and pushed my hand away. "No!" he shouted, oblivious to the fact that I had begun to cry. "I can't right now! I just can't!" His voice softened slightly. "Don't you understand? I can't right now."

He's as nervous as a virgin, I thought to myself as I went back to bed. And then it dawned on me with blinding clarity. Of course! He was a virgin! The poor guy was probably scared to death. I snuggled deep into the fluffy comforter. "I understand, Bill. I love you." There, I thought, he knows that I care about his feelings. Ours was going to be a marriage where we shared and shared alike, and if he felt nervous, I was going to be understanding and let him take his time.

The next morning when I woke up, Bill was gone. I looked at the clock. We were going to have to leave for the airport soon. I showered and dressed quickly, and rode the elevator down to the mezzanine level. I finally found him in the hotel's weight room, on a weight bench, panting and dripping with perspiration. I walked quietly up and kissed him.

"You scared me half to death! Don't ever do that again!" he exploded, leaping up and showering me with droplets of sweat. He grabbed a towel from the shelf nearby and rubbed his wet hair vigorously.

I stood quietly, watching him. If anything, he seemed jumpier than ever, loaded with nervous energy. In fact, it looked as if he was about to fly out of his skin. As I watched, he took a small prescription bottle full of little blue pills out of his pocket and swallowed three of them without water.

Instantly, I was concerned. "Bill, are you all right?" I pointed to the bottle. "What are those for?"

He hastily stuffed the bottle back in his pocket. "It's a muscle relaxant," he said curtly. "I take it for muscle spasms."

I knew about muscle relaxants. Some people took them to calm down nerves. My doctor had given me a prescription for them when things got really bad during my divorce, and I knew darn well that the blue ones were ten-milligram tablets. And Bill had just swallowed three of them! I was worried. "Bill, thirty milligrams is an awful lot. If your muscles are cramping that badly, maybe you're overdoing it. Maybe you should let your doctor know. Maybe there's a more serious problem."

"I'm okay," he said. "I'm just especially tense this morning. I'll be okay once we get home and get settled in."

I could relate to that. I was feeling pretty edgy myself. I gave him a quick kiss on the lips and said, "I guess I'll go upstairs and pack. You need to be at the airport in an hour, right?"

He looked at his watch and made a face. "Is it that late already? I've been working out longer than I thought."

I ventured a casual question. "What time did you start?"

His reply was brief. "Six-thirty."

I gasped. "Six-thirty? You've been down here for four hours? No wonder your muscles hurt!"

He snapped me with the towel. It was meant to be playful, but it stung. "I need a shower, babe. See you upstairs in fifteen minutes?"

I nodded. "Fifteen minutes. I'll pack your stuff for you."

He had already started walking toward the shower, and he whirled around and shouted at me, his voice angry, "No, don't! I'll pack my own stuff!"

I held up both hands in a take-it-easy gesture. "Okay, okay. I won't pack your stuff. I'm sorry." I was starting to feel irritated by his attitude, but I wasn't certain how much was genuine irritation, and how much was the hangover I was feeling, so I decided to let the matter drop. I took the elevator upstairs and packed, and, by the time he came in twenty minutes later, I was reading the paper at the table by the window. He came over and kissed the top of my head. "I'm sorry I blew up at you," he said in a soft voice. "All this wedding stuff has really given me the creeps. Once we get settled in, things will be okay."

I knew he was right, and I hugged him. "I know," I said. "I'm jumpy, too. But we'll be there on Friday, and then we can really work to make things all right."

I listened, but didn't watch while he packed, and, by the time he was finished, it was time to go. He came over and stood by me. "Are you ready?"

I folded my paper and stood up. "As ready as I'll ever be, I guess. I hate to see you go so soon."

Bill picked up his suitcase and walked to the door. "I know. Me, too. But we'll be together soon."

"That's for sure," I said, and threw him a smile.

I dropped him off at the airport and drove home, thinking to myself that it had been a strange couple of days. Carla Sue had spent the night with the boys, and they were just finishing lunch when I arrived.

"So, how was it?" she said, glancing at the boys to make certain they weren't listening. "Tell me all the romantic details."

To my surprise, I started to cry. "Oh, Carla Sue, it was awful!" I sobbed on her shoulder as we walked to the sofa and sat down. "He didn't even make love to me!"

The expression on her face changed from joy to concern in a split second. "You're kidding!" she said, but even she could tell it was no joke. "Tell me what happened."

She held my hand and I told her everything. As I spoke, she got angrier and angrier. Finally, she stood up and headed for the phone. "I'm just going to call that boy and give him a piece of my mind!"

I jumped up and ran to stand beside here. "Carla Sue, don't," I begged. "Don't you see? We have to work this out together, whatever the problems are."

She gave me along, thoughtful look. "You're right," she admitted. "Besides, his plane probably hasn't even landed yet. Okay, I'll stay out of it." She waggled her finger at me. "But you let me know if you need my help," she said, "okay?"

Gratefully, I hugged her. "Okay," I said. "It's a deal." She turned to finish the packing she'd been doing earlier.

"And, Carla Sue?"

She turned to look at me.

"Thanks," I told her.

She nodded, smiled, and gave me the high sign.

We finished the packing just as the guys from the church arrived with the rental truck, and they had it loaded in a little less than two hours. I checked my watch. I told the boys to run and jump in the truck, and I stayed behind for a moment to say good-bye to Carla Sue.

"Tell everybody thank you, okay?" I said as I hugged her. She patted my back.

"I will. And don't forget"—she pulled away to look me straight in the eye—"if you ever need me, just call."

"I will," I promised, and climbed into the truck. As we pulled out of the driveway, I waved a last good-bye. The boys were so busy pointing and talking that they didn't even notice that I cried for at least fifty miles.

We pulled into Tacoma five hours ahead of schedule, and I decided to go straight to Bill's house—our house—and surprise him when he got home from work. He'd already given me a key and directions, and I had no trouble at all finding it. There was a car in the driveway I didn't recognize, and I pulled in beside it. As I unlocked the front door, I turned to the boys and said, "Well, this is it! This is our new home! Are you excited?"

In response, they began shouting, "Open the door, Mommy! Open the door!"

As we went in, I caught my breath. It was lovely! I knew Bill did a number of things well, but I'd had no idea that his taste in furniture and colors was so exquisite. The house was exactly what I would have chosen if I'd been there, and now it was all mine to savor and enjoy.

Suddenly, I heard Davey shout from an open doorway, "Mommy, there's a dog in the backyard!"

I hurried in the direction of his voice and found myself in the kitchen. As I peeked over Davey's head through the back door, I saw an enormous black Doberman sleeping on the back porch. Hearing us, she leapt to her feet and began scratching and scrabbling at the base of the door, her little stump of a tail wagging like a metronome gone wild.

"Can we pet her, Mommy? Please?" Davey tugged at my sweater.

"I don't think so, sweetie. We don't know for sure that she's friendly. We'll wait for Bill to get home and introduce us."

As I watched the dog, a man I didn't know came around the comer of the porch and stopped, apparently as startled to see me as I was to see him. Suddenly, he smiled, and, holding the dog away with his foot, opened the door and came through. "You must be Karen, and I'll bet you're Davey, and you're Matt," he said to each of us in turn. He held out his right hand. "I'm Owen, Bill's roommate."

Bill's roommate? Bill hadn't said anything about a roommate. I shook hands automatically. "It's nice to meet you." My voice was doubtful. "I didn't know Bill had a roommate!"

Owen laughed and brushed the hair out of his eyes. "Shut up, Jackie!" he said to the dog, who had begun to whine and bark. "Only until I can find another place to live. You two got married on such short notice that I haven't been able to find a place I can afford yet."

There was relief in my voice as I said, "Oh, I'm so glad!" Then I blushed, aware that I was being very rude. "I don't mean I'm glad that you're leaving. I mean . . ." My voice trailed off and Owen laughed again and winked.

"I know what you mean. Newlyweds need to be alone, right? Don't worry about it." He tapped on the door with his fist. "Shut up, Jackie!"

"Mommy, can't we please let her in?" Davey was tugging at my sweater again, and, this time, Matt joined in. "Mama, please?"

I looked at Owen. "Will she bite?" I had heard some pretty awful things about Doberman pinschers.

Owen glanced down at the dog. "Jackie? She wouldn't hurt a flea!"

He opened the door, and the next thing I knew, seventy pounds of black fur had hurled itself like a cannonball through the door and knocked me down, licking my face and snuffling in my ear.

"Jackie, stop!" I shrieked. Owen and the boys started to giggle.

"Gosh, Mom, she sure is friendly! Can we play with her? Can we pet her?" Matt asked.

I was breathless from laughter. "Oh, do anything! Just get her off of me!"

The boys ran out into the backyard with her, and I could hear their laughter off in the distance as Owen and I talked. He had just finished saying how surprised they all had been to hear that Bill had gotten married, when Bill walked through the front door, looking grim. He barely gave me a glance as he stalked through the living room into the kitchen. I heard the rattle of a chain and the sound of the back door opening.

"Jackie!" he called. "Here, Jackie. Come on, girl!" A minute or so later, he stalked back through the living room and out again, slamming the front door behind him.

I looked questioningly at Owen. "Where are they going?"

Owen shrugged. "Probably out for a run."

I stood and looked out the big front window. I could see them about a block down the street. As I watched, they turned a corner and disappeared. "How far do they run?"

Owen was engrossed in a football game. "What? Oh, about five or six miles."

When Bill and Jackie returned, I was waiting on the front porch. I crossed my arms. "How dare you brush me off like that?" My voice was less than pleasant. "I just drove several hundred miles, and I think I deserve a 'hello' at the very least!"

Bill unhooked the leash from Jackie's collar and patted her. "Go on, girl! Scoot!" As she bounded joyously around the corner of the house and into the backyard, he took me in his arms and kissed me. "There, is that better?" He smiled down at me and my knees went rubbery.

"Much better," I murmured, nuzzling his throat. "Do you do that every day?"

He took my hand and led me into the house. "Every day. I'm always pretty uptight when I get home from work, and she needs a run. So we go together."

I felt a little better. With Owen's help, it didn't take long to unload the truck and get our things put away. The three of us talked until about ten, and then Owen excused himself. "Early day tomorrow," he said, yawning, and then walking upstairs. Bill and I were finally alone.

He got up and went into the kitchen. I heard the clink of ice cubes, and he returned, carrying a tall glass full of brown liquid.

"What are you drinking?" I asked, hoping it was iced tea, and he'd share it with me.

97

His reply was sharp, almost defensive. "Bourbon."

"Bourbon?" I was appalled. "That must be a ten-ounce glass."

He sipped the drink. "It helps me sleep."

"Helps you sleep?" My voice went shrill. "I'll bet it helps you sleep! I'm surprised it doesn't put you to sleep permanently!"

He waved a hand in my direction, as if to brush me off. "Nah. I drink this much every night. I get too wound up otherwise."

I twisted my wedding ring around my finger. "How long has this been going on?"

He took another gulp. "Oh, a few years. Ever since my father died."

Great. This was just great. First, he wouldn't make love to me, then he took three times as much medication as had been prescribed, and now he was drinking bourbon every night. What had I gotten myself into? I decided to jump in with both feet.

"Bill, is that why you wouldn't make love to me on our wedding night? Or is there another reason?"

He stared morosely at a brass lamp suspended from the ceiling above me. "I can't." His reply was quiet.

"What do you mean, you can't?" I asked, watching his face.

There was a twitch under his right eye. "Just what I said. I can't."

Either I was crazy or he wasn't speaking English. "Bill, I know you can."

He looked at me for the first time. "Oh, physically I'm capable enough. Emotionally, I can't. It disgusts me."

I was horrified. "It disgusts you?" I stood up, knocking a stack of magazines to the floor. "What do you mean, it disgusts you?"

His voice was low and very patient, as if he were talking to a small child. "Don't you hear well? It disgusts me. The thought of making love to any woman makes me sick to my stomach."

Suddenly, it seemed as if there was a freight train rushing through my head. His lips were moving, but all I could hear was a dull roar. *This is a bad dream,* I thought. *Yes, that's it. This is a bad dream, and when I wake up, I'm going to be home in my very own bed.* I sank back into the chair. "Bill, have you tried to get help?"

He snorted. "See a psychiatrist, you mean? Oh, sure. They say it's my mother's fault." He started a long, rambling description of his miserable childhood. I listened in horror to his story of beatings and neglect and abuse until I suddenly realized that his mother was Carla Sue—my Carla Sue—and I knew there was something very wrong. "Bill, do you take any other medication?"

He looked at me sharply. "Why do you ask?"

I thought fast. "Well, if you combine alcohol with certain types of drugs, it can cause some really nasty side effects."

He relaxed slightly. "Well, I do have a prescription for lithium. But I haven't been taking it lately."

My mind started to churn. Lithium? A friend of mine had been acting strangely, and was eventually diagnosed as a manic depressive. She had taken that drug also. Dear God, what had I gotten myself into? This man could be anything from a harmless neurotic to a violent killer. Why hadn't Carla Sue told me?

Bill's voice startled me out of my reverie. "Karen?" The smile on his face looked evil. *Stop it!* I told myself. *You're scaring yourself half to death.* I decided to go along with whatever he said, act sympathetic, and then talk to Owen about it in the morning. I shook my head to clear it.

"I'm sorry. I was miles away."

His voice was gentle, but my fear persisted. "What were you thinking about?"

I took a deep breath. *Stay calm,* I told myself. *Everything will be all right.* I thought of my little boys sleeping upstairs. They trusted me to keep them safe. "Oh, Bill, I love you so much. We can work this thing out together."

I was astonished when he started to cry. "Oh, Karen, I've wanted a family so badly. And I knew you never would have married me if I had told you the truth."

Well, he was right about that. I walked across the living room and stood by his chair. "You're wrong, Bill. I would have married you. We'll work it out. Everything will be all right."

He caught my hand. "Your hand is like ice. And you're shaking." He kissed my fingers. "I'm sorry. This must be a terrible shock to you."

No kidding, I thought. My head hurt as if an atomic bomb had exploded between my ears. "Bill, I'm awfully tired. Let's just go to bed, okay?"

He looked at me warily, and I hastily added, "Just to sleep. I just need to be held right now."

I was awake long after he had fallen asleep. I lay in our darkened bedroom, listening to his even breathing, and prayed to God for understanding and patience, and the strength to get through this. I prayed for Bill, too. There was no doubt in my mind that he was the victim of circumstances entirely beyond his control, and although I was angry at him for lying to me, I knew that he wasn't being deliberately malicious, but that he was sick and needed help. By the time the sky had started to lighten, I had decided on a plan of action. At dawn, I finally fell into a light, troubled sleep.

Bill and Owen were both putting in a lot of overtime, and they were gone most of Saturday and Sunday. I spent Saturday unpacking and exploring the neighborhood with the kids. Sunday, I typed up my resume and made copies of it, along with samples of my work, addressed envelopes to local companies, and mailed them at the corner. Saturday and Sunday night, I watched without comment as

Bill took more of his medication and then settled down in front of the television with his usual glassful of bourbon. I knew the combination could kill him, but I reasoned that if he had been doing it steadily for a while, he would probably be in no further danger as long as his usage didn't increase.

Monday morning, I walked the boys up to the nearest elementary school, registered them for classes, and went with them to their rooms to meet their teachers. I promised to be back when school let out at three-thirty, and went straight home and tried to call Carla Sue at work. Her phone rang and rang, and I could hear the clicking of the relays as it forwarded around the building.

Finally, Sylvia picked it up with an impatient, "This is Sylvia. Can I help you?"

I swallowed hard and tried to make my voice cheerful. "Sylvia, this is Karen. Is Carla Sue around?"

Sylvia actually sounded glad to hear from me. "Oh, Karen! Carla Sue won the church raffle and she's on her way to Hawaii for two weeks. She left this morning!" Her voice changed from excitement to concern. "Is everything okay?"

Sylvia was not on my list of people to confide in. "Oh, everything's fine! Two weeks, you say?"

Sylvia actually gushed. "Oh, yes! She was so happy, now that you and Bill are together. I knew she made plans to fly back through Tacoma. I think she wanted to surprise you!"

Trust you to spoil the surprise, I thought. "Well, thanks, Sylvia," I said quickly before she could ask any more questions. "I'll talk to you again sometime." I hung up before she could respond.

My heart sank. Two weeks! How on earth would I be able to manage Bill for two weeks without Carla Sue's advice and support? I said a quick prayer and ran down the hall to Bill's study. There were no doctors listed in his address file, so I rummaged through his filing cabinet looking for bills, receipts, insurance statements, or anything that could lead me to his doctor. Finally, I found it: an insurance statement that reported a payment to a Dr. Nallison for "psychotherapy services." I pulled the telephone book from the desk drawer and found his number.

I dialed quickly.

"Doctor's office," a receptionist answered, sounding tired and bored.

I spoke quickly. "Hello, my name is Karen Tyson. May I speak to Dr. Nallison, please?"

"He's with a patient right now. May I have him return your call?"

"Yes, please. My name is Karen Tyson." I spelled my name for her. "I need to speak to him about my husband, Bill Tyson. Can you tell him that it's urgent?"

She sounded more alert now. "I will give him the message. Can you give me your phone number, please?"

I gave her the number. I was starting to feel shaky again, but I tried to keep my voice calm. "When may I expect him to call?"

"He usually returns calls between patients. He'll be done with this session at noon."

I looked at my watch. It was eleven-forty. I had twenty minutes to wait. I thanked her and hung up, and wandered out to the kitchen to make myself some tea. I stared out the big front window while I waited for the water to boil, made the tea, and carried it to the table to drink it. I was sitting and staring out the window, watching Jackie chase squirrels, when the phone rang startling me so much I spilled the tea.

"Hello?" My voice was quavery.

"Mrs. Tyson? This is Dr. Nallison." His voice was low and mellow, exactly the kind of voice I would have expected a psychiatrist to have. "What can I do for you?"

I was so grateful to talk to someone who might be able to help that my words came out in a rush. "Dr. Nallison. I married Bill Tyson after knowing him for only five weeks, and I'm afraid I may have made a dreadful mistake. I have to talk to someone who understands what's going on and can help me decide what to do."

There was silence on the other end of the line. "Dr. Nallison?"

I heard the rustle of pages turning. "I'm sorry, Mrs. Tyson. I was just checking my calendar. I'm tied up all afternoon today, but if you can come right now, I'm free until one."

I knew his address from the phone book. His office was only about six blocks away. "I can be there in ten minutes. Are you still at 1397 Garland Boulevard?"

"Yes, I am. I'll see you shortly."

"Yes," I said gratefully. "In minutes."

I replaced the phone, mopped up the spilled tea, grabbed my purse and keys, and flew out the door. When I pulled into the parking lot, I slammed the car door and ran inside. Dr. Nallison's receptionist motioned me through a door. The doctor was seated behind a big oak desk, making notes in a patient's folder, when I arrived.

"Dr. Nallison?"

He looked up at me and smiled. "Mrs. Tyson, how nice to meet you." He held out his hand and I took it gratefully, sensing a lifeline in the strong, tanned fingers. He led the way to a sofa. "Won't you please have a seat?"

I plunged in. "Dr. Nallison, I'm terribly worried about Bill. He's drinking bourbon every night, taking huge quantities of muscle relaxants, and he's not taking his lithium, which I know has been prescribed." There was a thoughtful look on his face. "Can you tell me what's going on?"

101

He tipped back his chair and stared out the window for a moment. When he finally spoke, his voice was grave. "Mrs. Tyson, it is my policy not to discuss my patients with anyone without their express written permission." My heart sank. "In your case, however," he continued, "I will make an exception if you have some proof of your identity."

I fished around in my purse. "I haven't had my driver's license changed yet, but I have it and our marriage certificate. Will these do?" He held out his hand and I gave him the documents. He studied them quietly for a few moments and handed them back.

When he spoke, his voice was solemn. "Bill is a manic depressive."

I leaned forward. My guess had been right, after all.

"Manic depression is a disease that we really don't know enough about, and is characterized primarily by unacceptable social behavior. It's probably physical in origin, stemming from a chemical imbalance in the brain. In some depressives, we can treat it with drugs. A person with this disease may be a violent sociopathic killer, or he may simply be harmless." I smiled in spite of myself. My uncle used to talk to trees.

"In Bill's case," he continued, "the disease is characterized by extreme hyperactivity, insomnia, an extreme fear of dirt or germs, and the inability to function sexually as a normal adult male." I nodded my head. "To the best of my knowledge"—he flipped through a chart that must have been Bill's—"he is not violent, nor is he likely to become so, as long as he continues to take the medication that has been prescribed."

I held up my hand slightly to stop him. "Excuse me for interrupting, but he is not taking the proper medication, and he is drinking heavily. What effect could that have on his condition?"

Dr. Nallison laced his fingers together. "Well, it could kill him. His heart would stop and that would be it. Or he could continue to deteriorate—become suicidal, maybe even violent. It's hard to say."

I began to cry. He reached over and handed me a box of tissues. "What am I going to do?" I said more to myself than to him. "Oh, God, what am I going to do?"

He handed me the tissues and sat back in his chair again. "Mrs. Tyson, I can't tell you what to do. That's a decision only you can make."

I blew my nose and looked up at him. "Dr. Nallison, what are the chances that, if Bill is treated properly, he will be able to live a normal life?" I corrected myself. "That we can live a normal life?"

He thought for a moment before answering. "There isn't much of a chance."

I took a deep breath. That was it. It was over. I stood up and walked over to the window, watching the fall leaves swirl in the street below. "Dr. Nallison, tell me one more thing: in your opinion, are we in any danger?"

He thought for a moment. Then he looked up at me. "We? Who do you mean by 'we?'"

"My children and myself."

All the color drained from his face. "You have children?"

I was confused by his reaction. "Yes, two boys." He started writing rapidly in his notebook. "What is it?" I asked. "What's wrong?"

"Where are they now?" he asked, still writing.

"In school," I answered, sitting down again. "Why?"

"Bill Tyson has been arrested twice for sexual offenses against young boys." This time my face went white. "Bill was placed on probation because he agreed to undergo psychiatric treatment." I held onto the aim of the chair for support. "You've got to get them out of the house." He handed me a slip of paper. "They can spend the night at this address. It's an emergency-care home for children in trouble. Once they're safe, I would suggest that you pack up your belongings, go home, and file for divorce."

I stood up, although my knees were shaking so badly that I wasn't sure I could walk. I held out my hand and he took it. "Thank you, Dr. Nallison. I appreciate your time."

He smiled and squeezed my hand. "I'm truly sorry, Mrs. Tyson. I wish there was some way that you could have been spared all this."

I smiled at him through my tears. "Thank you for your concern, but I probably wouldn't have believed it even if someone had told me." I turned to leave, and then turned back. "Oh, Doctor Nallison?"

He took a half-step toward me. "Yes, Mrs. Tyson?"

"Is there a church nearby?"

He smiled. "Three blocks down on the right."

"Thank you. Oh, one more question. What do I owe you?"

He shook his head. "Nothing at all. There's no charge for this visit."

I went out to my car and drove slowly down the street, looking for the church. When I found it, I parked toward the rear. There was a group just finishing up, and, as I waited for the pastor, I kept wondering over and over again why Carla Sue hadn't told me about Bill. When the pastor had finished, he came toward me and introduced himself. As I explained the problem, he led me toward the rectory and had me sit in an easy chair. I waited while he arranged for several church members to meet me at Bill's house with a rental truck the following morning.

I called Felix and tried unsuccessfully not to cry while I briefly explained the situation and asked for my old job back. His voice was gentle as he told me my office was still waiting for me, at a slightly higher salary. Apparently, they hadn't been able to find anyone to take my place for the money I'd been making. After we hung up, I went into the church and prayed. The pastor called Pastor Jones in Sacramento, and Pastor Jones promised to arrange for an apartment, some furniture and appliances, and enough money to tide us over until my paychecks started again. When I finished my prayers, I called my attorney and asked him to start the divorce paperwork right away. When I left, the pastor hugged me and promised to look in on Bill.

I drove back to the school, picked up the boys, and took them straight over to the crisis center. Dr. Nallison had called ahead, so they were expecting us. Then I hurried home to fix dinner.

When Bill arrived home, I lied to him and told him that the boys were spending the night with some new friends they'd met at school.

That night, I held him close as he slept and kissed him good-bye. In spite of what I'd learned about him, I couldn't help but grieve for my hopes and dreams and plans that had been so cruelly shattered.

The following morning, as soon as Bill and Owen left for work, I called Pastor Jones and had him go ahead and send the men with the truck over. While they loaded the truck, I wrote a long letter to Bill, explaining why I had to leave, and wishing him well. When I went out into the yard to say good-bye to Jackie, she whined as if she knew I was going away forever. I ruffled her ears and considered for a moment taking her with me, but I knew she'd have no place to play back home.

The last thing I did before leaving was to gather up all the wedding gifts. They would have to be returned.

I locked the front door and slid the key into the mailbox. As I slid onto the truck's big bench seat and put it into gear, I waved good-bye to the house and to my dreams of a happy life with Bill. I drove slowly to the children's crisis center to pick up the boys.

As we drove out of town, Matt turned to me and said, "Mommy, don't we love Bill anymore?"

I put my arm around his shoulders and hugged him. "Oh, baby," I said, "of course we still love Bill."

Davey looked up from the coloring book he was leafing through. "Then why are we leaving?"

I took a deep breath. This was going to be very difficult to explain. "Well, guys," I said, moving into the right lane so I could slow down and talk to them, "God gave Bill some very hard problems to solve. And he just isn't ready for a family right now." *There, that wasn't too hard,* I thought.

Davey and Matt were silent for a few minutes, each as wrapped in his own pain as I was in mine. Then Matt looked up at me. "Mom, will he ever be ready for a family?"

I pulled over and stopped by the side of the road. "Davey, come here." I pulled him onto my lap. "You, too, Matt." I patted the seat next to me.

"You guys really wanted to have a daddy, didn't you?" They both nodded solemnly, and I saw tears running down Davey's cheeks. I started to cry, too. "Guys," I said, wiping my eyes, "Bill isn't going to be ready to be a daddy for a long, long time. You'll both probably be

104

grown men before that happens. But I promise you, somewhere out there there's a stray daddy that's just right for us. And we'll find him one day, I guarantee it."

I scooted Davey back onto the seat, and started up the truck. "Now, if we don't get going, we're going to get caught in the first snowfall and have to camp here for the winter." I shivered as if I were neck deep in a snowdrift. "And we'll have to eat tree bark for our supper because I don't have any food in this covered wagon!" Both boys started to giggle.

"Wagon, ho!" I shouted, cracking an imaginary whip. "Head 'em out! Let's roll!" Both the kids were rocking with hysterical laughter. "Fasten your seatbelts! We're going home!"

I've been back at work for three weeks now, and even though things have been a little crazy, it gets better every day. Pastor Jones managed to find me an apartment, and the people from the church who bought my furniture and appliances brought them back to me. I haven't been able to pay them back yet, but my attorney says I'll be able to recover my moving costs and lost wages from Bill, so I'll be able to pay them in a month or two.

Things are a little strained between Carla Sue and me, but it hasn't been easy for her to accept the truth about her son, and I can understand how she feels. She'd had absolutely no idea that he was as sick as he is, and it was a terrible shock for her to find out from me the day she got back from Hawaii. I think we'll be friends again before too long. I left her a little gift this morning and a note that said, "Thank you for being my friend" on her desk, and I heard her blowing her nose a little while after she came in. Whenever she's ready, I'll be waiting.

There was a lot of buzzing around the office when I returned, and the Three Spies were especially curious, but I put on my best tragic look and told them I just couldn't bear to talk about it. They fussed around me like ducks around bread crumbs and shooed all the curious busybodies out of my office, so I've made three new friends.

I had a long talk with Pastor Jones after I got settled in, and tried to resolve my questions about why God would lead me into such a disaster. Pastor Jones didn't really have any answers. I truly feel that God is paying me pretty close attention right now. I feel loved and cared for and surrounded by my friends. And I still don't have quite enough money, but somehow, it doesn't seem to matter anymore. I've even started to date a bit.

I know somewhere out there is a guy with my name written across his chest. I can feel it, and I know I'm going to find him soon.

THE END

"DON'T FALL IN LOVE WITH ME!"

"The woods are lovely, dark and deep," a voice said quietly at my side.

I had been standing, hypnotized, beside the swimming pool, my eyes on the still water. I didn't know who had come to stand beside me, but I resented his presence. I wanted to be alone with my misery.

"But I have promises to keep," the voice went on. "And miles to go before I sleep."

"Please . . ." I murmured.

"I know," he said. "You want to be left alone, Leah."

"How do you know my name?" I asked. I turned now, unwillingly, my eyes drawn away from that deep, inviting pool. A young man stood beside me. He was wearing a white T-shirt and blue jeans, and his eyes were a beautiful shade of blue.

"I asked the manager this morning," he said. "After I'd seen you at the pool every night for a week, late and alone."

"I've been trying to get up my nerve to go swimming," I said. "I don't swim very well."

"Uh-huh," he said. "That isn't the kind of fear I've seen in you. You're wondering if it would work. You're wondering if you've got the guts to drown yourself."

My God, who was this person? "You're wrong!" I gasped.

"Not wrong," he said softly. "I've been there myself."

"You're impertinent," I snapped. I turned, feeling the sudden fearful thumping of my heart because he had hit so near the truth. I had nothing to live for anymore.

When I started for my apartment, I felt a restraining hand on my arm. "Leah? Leah, let me help you," his voice pleaded.

I spun, afraid now, jerking myself away from his touch. "Look! I don't know who you are, but I want to be left alone. . . ." And then I saw his eyes. They were glistening with tears.

"Please let me, help you," he said. "Leah, I know. Whatever caused it, I know what you're feeling. Never turn away from another human being."

"Oh my God," I whispered. I didn't know where my tears came from. I didn't know I had any left. But something in me answered his, and I felt the great, terrible well I had thought dry bursting open inside me.

"Take my hand," he said.

I couldn't take his hand. I didn't know how to reach out to a

106

stranger. I wanted to scream at him again to go away, but already he was raising his own hands, and before I could back away, he took mine and gripped them firmly. Then my tears came.

"All right," he said gently. "Right on, Leah. Come on. Let me help you back to your place."

I was being led, my eyes blinded with tears. "I don't know you," I whispered.

"Sure you do," he murmured. "I'm a fellow hurtee. Did you think you had a monopoly on all the pain in the world? Come on, come on now."

I couldn't get ahold of my tears. The gentleness in his voice was cracking my heart. He led me toward my apartment, holding tightly to my hands. "Those are surface tears," he murmured. "You're not down to the real thing yet. Leah, let it all hang out. All of it."

My God, who was this man? What was happening to me? Through all my pain, since those first days when I had cried hysterically and begged Derrick not to leave me, I had held onto myself in front of people. The children, coming home for a brief time because their parents were in crisis, had never seen me cry because I was too proud to let them see the depths of my pain. And now, here was a perfect stranger holding my hands and ordering me to cry, and I was responding like a child.

My nose had begun to run, too, and, numbly, I reached into my pants pocket to pull out a tissue, but he stopped me. "Uh-uh," he said. "You can't get over it if you block off even a little bit, Leah. Let your pain flow freely, all of it."

Now I was being led through my apartment door, and the sobs were coming in hideous, tearing gasps. He was a total stranger, and yet he led me to the sofa and pulled me down next to him, still holding my hands. And I went on crying as I had never cried before, not even in the beginning.

"Say his name," the man commanded.

When I looked at him in horror, he said more sharply, "Say it, Leah. Who hurt you?"

I struggled to get control of myself. But no one had ever spoken to me with such command. "Share it!" he ordered. "Say his name."

"Derrick," I whispered.

"I can't hear you."

"Derrick!" I cried. "My husband—my—ex-husband Derrick!"

"Tell me how, Leah. No! Don't try to get at that tissue. Let it out. Share it with me."

"He left me." I sobbed. "For a woman—a girl. He wanted someone younger, someone fun who could—could. . . ."

"Be a playmate to him?"

"Who are you?" I gasped suddenly. "What are you doing to me?"

107

"I'm a child of the universe," he said. "Like you, Leah. I'm someone who knows what it is to suffer, and who cares because you're suffering, too. I've watched you every night from my apartment across the pool. I've seen your face. I knew what you thought you wanted, and tonight you looked as though you might try it."

"I don't want to live!" I sobbed. "I can't go on without him. I kept thinking he would get over it, that he'd come back to me, but the divorce was final last week, and he—he——" When I thought the tears were gone, I began to sob all the harder.

"He married her?"

"Oh, please," I moaned. "Please go away. Please leave me alone."

"I won't leave you alone," he said gently. "But I will let you blow your nose now, Leah." Through my flooding eyes I saw him smile faintly.

I wiped my eyes and my nose. "Do you feel better now?" he asked calmly. "In spite of yourself. It's that way when you share the root of your pain, Leah. The only way to ease suffering is to let it out, not bottle it. Anyone who contemplates suicide is wearing one helluva cork."

"Are you—are you a psychiatrist?" I murmured. The sobs had eased now. My eyes and face burned, but it was strange that I felt something like release for the first time since I'd heard the news that had seemed to shatter the last of the flimsy strings that held me together.

"I'm a Psych major at the state college," he said. "But I'm not practicing on you, Leah. I saw a need."

He let go of my hands, and I got shakily to my feet, feeling suddenly very foolish. "Don't be embarrassed," he said gently. "Sharing is life. Haven't you ever had anyone to unload on before?"

"Only Derrick," I whispered. "He was the one I took things to, and when he left me it was like I lost my rock."

"Hey," he said. "The only place to look for that old rock to lean on is inside yourself."

"Not for me." I moaned. "I don't have any strength of my own."

"Then use mine for a while," he said.

It was an insane conversation. This young man was a total stranger. "Please go now," I murmured. "I—I appreciate what you're trying to do, but no one can help me. No one can give Derrick back to me."

"When I'm through with you, you won't want him back."

I stared in shock. He was grinning suddenly. "What do you mean, when you're through with me?" I gasped.

"I mean I'm not going to let you bottle up again now that I've popped the cork. We're going to talk some more—you and me."

Anger was returning to me. "I don't need . . ."

"We all need," he said quietly. "Now where do you keep the coffee, Leah? I'm not much for talking without a little sustenance."

I stared in shocked numbness as he headed for my kitchenette and

108

came up with a jar of instant coffee. I ran after him, furious now. "Go away," I said. "It wasn't what you think tonight. I—I'd never do that. I have children."

"Good," he said. "But I'm not going, Leah. I'm going to be your friend whether you like it or not."

I couldn't believe this young man! While I stood there sputtering with indignation over my invaded privacy, he pulled a pan out from under the sink. "I'm Tag Henderson," he said. "Stupid name, isn't it? My mother named me Taggart after some distant branch of the family. Taggart Henderson, isn't that wild? But then, we can't always help what our parents do to us."

I was about to lash out at him again, and then I saw his eyes. For just a moment something haunted had passed through them, and it brought me up short. Whatever it was, it matched the way I felt inside.

"Tell me about Derrick now," he said gently. "I want to know why a man would leave a pretty woman who can't be all that old herself."

"I—I'm thirty-nine," I said. Old. My God, I was old. "She was twenty-five."

"And Derrick?"

"Forty," I mumbled.

"A bad year," Tag said. "It hits some men at fifty, others earlier."

"What are you talking about?" I said.

"Oh, whatever they call it. Male menopause. Whatever makes them go out looking to start life over. It hit my father, only my mother wasn't lucky enough to get rid of him. He stayed with her, and she let him humiliate her with one affair after another."

The water was boiling. "Sit," he said.

It was a strange experience—strange for me, who had been taught never to air my problems or let my emotions show. Something had happened when I saw that haunted look in Tag's eyes. Something in me had responded as though two lost souls had suddenly found each other.

I told him about the honor of those first days when my husband had told me he had met someone else. "We're stagnating," he said. "Our marriage is dead, Leah."

I cried again when I told Tag how the children had come home, my two married sons flying in from northern Texas, and my daughter, who was in the Navy in Norfolk. "They wanted to comfort me," I moaned. "But I couldn't turn to them. I couldn't let them see that their father had nearly killed me."

"Chalk one," Tag said.

"Chalk one?"

"Blessing," he said. "It's not as trite as it sounds to count our blessings, Leah. Three kids who love you enough to come home to

109

support you, that's a pretty heavy blessing. You should have let them comfort you. But that's okay. I'm here now."

It was two o'clock before he left. "That poem I quoted you tonight?" he said at the door. "It's from Robert Frost. Some people think it's about suicide, that the woods represent death, inviting death. But there are promises to keep in life."

"Promises?" I murmured.

"One big promise maybe," he said. "To survive. No matter what hits us. To accept pain, whatever happens. To be examples to others with pain, to reach out to them."

I didn't quite understand what he was talking about. But, strangely, for the first time in many months, I felt something that felt like hope inside me. He leaned over suddenly and kissed me on the nose.

"Sleep tight," he said gently.

I watched him skirt the pool and stood there a long time after the lights went out in his apartment. And then I went to bed, and for the first time in months, I fell into a deep sleep. It must have been because I had shared my grief.

But in the morning, waking to my lonely apartment, the apartment I had chosen in a strange city because I could no longer bear staying in the same town where my husband lived with her, my depression came back. What was I going to do with my day? Derrick was giving me enough money to get by on, and I hadn't yet found energy to get a job. I had nothing to do with the long hours except brood.

And then, before I was out of bed, someone banged on the door. "Hurry up," Tag yelled, "before I drop everything!"

I pulled on a robe and hurried toward the door. "Grab these rolls and get the oven going!" he exclaimed.

I took the rolls and stood back bewilderedly while he charged into my apartment carrying a tray. "Spanish omelettes," he announced. "And my pineapple surprise rolls, home cooked by me."

It was strange, but I felt my spirits lift. By day, I could see that he was maybe only an inch taller than I. He had long hair, which I hadn't even noticed the previous night, and his blue eyes were even more beautiful than I'd remembered. He looked a little like my oldest son, Scott, and, in fact, they must have been close to the same age.

Thinking of Scott made my spirits sag for a moment. He was twenty-three now—the child that had forced my marriage to Derrick when I was barely sixteen. Words came flying back at me, hurting words. "My God, Leah, let me go. We had to get married, and I've tried to hack it all these years, but I want real romance now."

"A ghost just crossed your grave," Tag said, plunking two plates on the table. "But I'll let her get by this time. Come on and eat, Leah, and don't tell me you haven't got an appetite. You've got to keep up your strength."

I would have sworn that I couldn't touch a bite, but when I tasted the omelets I began to eat as if I hadn't seen food in years. I had lost fourteen pounds when Derrick left, weight I couldn't afford to lose.

"Now the rolls," Tag said.

I bit into one. "I don't taste any pineapple," I said.

He threw back his head and laughed. "That's my surprise. There isn't any! Hey," he said suddenly, "is that a smile?" He got up and ran for the window and tore open the drapes. "Hey, Universe," he called, "she's smiling!"

I couldn't help myself. I actually laughed out loud. "Oh, Leah," he said gently. "That's good to hear. And it feels good, too, doesn't it? I remember the first time I smiled after I'd been through pain. I felt like a whole well of peace had opened up in me."

He came back and, still standing, bit into his roll. "Hurry up," he said. "Get dressed. It's going to be a great day. Smog's gone. Clouds are rolling, and we should be rolling, too."

"What are you talking about?" I cried.

"About Project Open Leah Up," he said softly. "I'm willing to bet you woke up feeling low today. You had your up side working last night, but the old down side can come on pretty heavy afterward. It's sort of like we have to suffer because we're scared to stay up for fear we'll get knocked down again."

"You're right," I said.

"I have a week on my hands until Sean gets back. Classes are out at State until the fall session, and I've got some free time, Leah. From what you told me last night, you were so busy all those years being a wife and mother, you didn't get much chance to find out who you were or what the rest of the world is all about.

"I want to show you some things. Sort of give you some things to hang onto when the going gets rough. If you'd had the kind of parents who could have built supports into you, I wouldn't have to train you. But train you I'm going to. You've got to get outside yourself and think of other people. It's the only cure. Now get into some pants. And bring a jacket and scarf."

I started to protest. For some reason I wanted to stay at home locked inside my misery. But his eyes were flashing eagerly, and I didn't seem to have any power against him. When I came out of the bedroom dressed, he had the dishes done up. "Follow me," he said mysteriously, "into the heart of the universe."

A few moments later, I was standing in a garage, absolutely stunned. "I'm not going to get on that!" I gasped. "I don't even know what it is."

"It's called a chopper," he said. "It belongs to Sean. You'd never know seeing him on it that he's a Psych Masters candidate at State. Hey, how do you like this outfit?"

111

He had been wearing a shirt and now he pulled it off to reveal a T-shirt and a blue jean jacket with the sleeves cut out of both.

"Oh, my," I murmured.

"Scared to be seen with me?" He grinned.

"Tag, I'm thirty-nine years old," I moaned. I stared in horror at the strange-looking machine.

"And I'm twenty-seven," he said. "If I'm not embarrassed, why should you be? Get on, Leah."

"I can't," I gasped.

"Sure you can," he chortled. And before I could stop him he had swept me into his arms and had plunked me down on its back. There was some kind of steel thing behind me. "You lean against it," he said. "And when that wind hits you, you'll know what heaven is."

"Tag, what in the world are we doing?" I cried.

"I told you. We're going to explore the universe, Leah, so that you understand you belong to it. You're going to learn to stop fighting what Derrick's done and accept it. That's where your trouble is, you know. You haven't accepted it. I think you're still waiting for some miracle to bring him back to you. But it's not going to work that way, baby, and your only alternative is to learn how to handle it. I'm going to teach you some perspective, so you'll have something to fall back on when the miseries hit."

I'd never known anybody who talked in such a complicated way. But before I could argue anymore, he was on the front of the machine, and, in a second, the thing cut loose with a huge roar that nearly made my heart stop. "Lean back and relax," he said.

Within minutes we were on a freeway, and I was hanging onto Tag's waist for dear life. "Not so fast!" I yelled.

"Hey, we're only crawling." He chuckled. "Leah, get your mind off the machine and you'll become a part of it. Look up!"

Timidly, I raised my eyes. The Texas sky was blue and filled with soft clouds. It was only moments before they had me hypnotized. "Lesson one," he called. "Look up when things get bad."

I began to get a heady feeling, now that my fear of the chopper was easing. I still felt silly. I knew that the cars passing us were taking note of our ages. But suddenly it didn't seem to matter. Nothing mattered except this glorious feeling of freedom.

"Where are we going?" I asked once.

"To people watch," he hollered above the wind.

For the next two hours I rode behind Tag, feeling a freedom I had never felt before. Towns slipped by us. The clouds turned a little dark, but the sky was still blue.

I was so hypnotized I was startled when we came to an abrupt halt. My eyes had been on the sky, and I hadn't even noticed the town we were driving through. But now, I looked ahead to see strange

112

brown hills rising. "Where are we?" I exclaimed.

"Mexico."

"Mexico!" I gasped.

"Come on," he said. "We're going to walk over."

When he pulled me off the chopper, I felt let down, as if I could have gone on forever riding that machine. "Why are we here?" I demanded.

"Have you ever been before?"

I shook my head. "Then I'm going to give you some more blessings to count," he said. "Hey, muchacho," he called.

"Oye."

A little boy came running over and Tag spoke rapidly in Spanish. The boy nodded eagerly. "Cuando volveremos," Tag said. Then he took my hand, and the boy climbed up on the seat. "He's going to watch the chopper," Tag said. "I think the only thing that would make Sean part ways with me is if something happened to his beloved bike."

We joined a group of people surging past a pair of guards.

"Where are you going?" a heavily accented man asked Tag.

"Just into Tijuana awhile."

Then we were in the most unbelievable string of traffic. "We're going up to the big street," Tag said. "La calle revolucion."

We walked until my legs began to ache. Now and then Tag would stop and say something in Spanish. "Keeping in practice," he said. "When I get my degrees I want to work with minority kids. I picked up the language in the service. Picked up a hole in my leg, too."

"You'd never know you had a hole in your leg," I panted.

"Say, listen," he said. "I can't slow down. I only have a week to get you trained. Come on, I want to show you something."

We'd been climbing a hill, and now we came to a halt in front of the strangest sight I'd ever seen. It was what looked to be miles of cardboard boxes, except that there were people moving in and out of the boxes. Here and there smoke rose. "What's that odd smell?" I murmured.

"Could be anything cooking," he said. "Beef if anybody had a windfall begging on the streets today. Cat. Dog."

"Oh, Tag!" I gasped, feeling my insides rise to my throat.

"Leah, look around you," he said. "This is poverty. The kind that doesn't have any welfare to lean on."

We had begun to walk through the things that I now saw with horror were cardboard shacks. Suddenly there was a loud shriek. I stopped, stunned at what looked to be a hundred children surging toward us.

"Hola, muchachos," Tag cried.

"Chicle!" a boy cried and thrust a tray of chewing gum up. "Por favor, senora."

I looked helplessly at Tag. "He wants you to buy some," Tag said. "A penny buys a bread roll down here."

I reached into my pocket and pulled out a dollar, and the crowd around us went wild. "Oh, Jesus," Tag moaned. "You show that kind of money and you'll start a riot. Here, put it back. Let me."

He reached into his pocket and pulled out a roll of pennies. "Ripped these off from Sean's poker supply," he said. He began to distribute the pennies, and the kids screamed and laughed and fought among themselves.

"Come on," Tag said. "I don't like doling out money like I was God almighty. I just wanted you to see how these people live. Take a good look, Leah. And then when you get home, think about whether you've ever had a hungry stomach, or how you'd feel if your kids ever had to grub like this."

He pointed suddenly. One of the boys who had made off with three pennies had run to an old woman. She stared down at the pennies he thrust into her hand and tears glistened in her eyes. "Wait a minute," Tag said. He hurried toward her, and I saw a dollar bill come out, and she grabbed his hand and kissed it. "Lo siento," I heard him say.

She looked at me and smiled a toothless smile and made the sign of the cross. "What did you say to her?" I whispered. Tears had hit my throat suddenly, and I could hardly speak.

"I said I'm sorry," he murmured huskily. "It was the only way I could express my shame for the way she has to live."

"Your shame?" I asked.

"Poverty is the shame of all of us, Leah," he said gently. "If we ran the world right, there wouldn't be any scenes like this. Blessing number two next to your kids," he said. "You are not poor."

On the main street, Tag bought me a taco and a sweet drink. A lot of the laughter had gone out of his eyes.

We had to walk past the shacks again on the way back to the border, and I knew that as long as I lived I would never forget them. It was as if something new had moved inside me today, the awareness of a kind of pain I had never comprehended.

The little boy was still sitting alertly on the motorcycle. Tag dug into his jacket pocket and came up with two dollars. The smile on that little boy's face lit the day that had suddenly begun to darken with possible storm clouds.

"Tag?" I said before I got onto the bike. "Thank you."

"It's only the beginning, Leah," he said gently. "You've seen a tiny piece of the universe you're related to. Tomorrow there'll be more."

Instead of the freeway, he chose to take a back road home. "This is Indian country," he said. "Sometime you'll want to read about our past, Leah. It gives you perspective on the present. People have suffered all kinds of pain from time immemorial, like the Indians who were run off their land. I want you to learn to reach out your hand to everyone you can, because it's the only way to find yourself."

"You almost sound like a preacher," I said softly.

"I only have one message," he said. "Love."

We were halfway home when the first drops of rain began to pelt down. "Oh, Jesus," Tag moaned. "All I need is to get one spot of rust on this baby of Sean's. Keep your eyes open for any kind of shelter."

"There!" I cried suddenly. The rain was coming harder when I spotted the little cement shed just off the road.

"It'll do!" Tag cried, and we went bumping into a dry field. A moment later we were off the chopper, and Tag had wheeled it into the musty shed. The sky burst open suddenly.

Tag sat down in the middle of the dirt floor, and I shivered. "Cold?" he asked. "Come on. Sit here with me, Leah. I'll keep you warm."

It felt strangely good to have his arms around me.

"Storms are beautiful," he said. "All nature is beautiful. People are beautiful. Even Derrick, Leah, who probably couldn't help what he did. It wasn't done against you. When you realize that, you'll be over a lot of the pain. It was something in him. His problem."

"But it hurt me," I said quietly.

"It can only hurt you as long as you let it," he said.

We were quiet then, and I snuggled against him. He was still a stranger to me, and, yet, in some ways I felt as if I had known him all my life. Only twenty-seven. Only four years older than my son. But he seemed older than time.

"Leah," he said gently after awhile. "This is going to be quite a week for you. But I want you to promise me one thing."

I looked into his eyes. "Don't fall in love with me," he said quietly.

"For goodness sake," I gasped. "I'm old enough to be your mother."

"This isn't anybody's mother I'm holding," he said softly. "You're a woman, warm and vibrant. Someday you're going to know love again, and it will be a strong, sure thing because of what you've been through. It isn't our ages that must hold us back, Leah, it's something I can't explain to you. Only don't even let yourself think about falling in love with me."

"You're being awfully presumptuous," I murmured.

He laughed suddenly. "Oh, it's just my awareness of how devastating I am," he said. "Make me the promise, Leah."

"Okay," I said wryly. "I won't fall in love with you." I didn't tell him that already, crazy though it was, I was feeling something for him that went beyond the strange friendship he offered.

Late in the night I lay awake. The rain had stopped, and I was remembering our night ride through the smell of damp fields. The air had seemed sweet and clinging, and I couldn't remember ever smelling anything so wonderful.

My depression was back. It always came during the night when I had no defense against it. I would picture terrible things, like Derrick

115

and his new wife, Valerie, lying in bed together. But tonight, in between the hurting things, I kept remembering the smell of that air. And once I thought of the poor people in Tijuana, and for the first time since all my sorrow had begun, there were tears on my cheeks for someone else.

"No pineapple surprise!" Tag exclaimed when I opened the door to him in the morning. "We'll get something to eat on the way."

"On the way where?"

"I don't know," he said. "What sign are you?"

"Sign?"

"Zodiac."

"I don't know," I murmured. "I was born on February twenty-third."

"Pisces," he exclaimed. "Couldn't be better. Pisces is the fish sign. That's it!"

He grabbed my hand and pulled me off to where the chopper waited, and, in a few moments, we were tearing along the road again. Before I knew it, we were sixty miles away, high on a road above the ocean. "There, Pisces," he cried. "You've come home to the Mother Sea. Isn't she something?"

All that morning we roamed the beach. Tag found tide pools and showed me tiny living creatures in beautiful colors that lived inside. We explored a cave and ate hot dogs for breakfast and another at lunch, and in the afternoon he rented a sailboat complete with a young couple to guide it. I had never been on a boat outside of the amusement parks where we used to take the children, and this was heaven, drifting along on the bright blue waves. I felt so free that once I stood up and stretched my arms wide.

"Blessing three," Tag said quietly, watching me. "You have eyes to see the sea with, you have ears to hear the whooshing of the wind, a nose to smell the salt, and skin to feel the cool spray."

"Blessing three," I whispered. Derrick and his new wife seemed a million miles away.

During the night memories of Derrick returned, of course. But now that I had other memories lined up with those of yesterday. I had a sense of God's beauty that years of doing housework and shopping and running kids to and fro had left me little time for.

"Thank you, Tag," I whispered into my dark bedroom. At least if the depression was still there, there were sometimes other thoughts now.

"I'll see you in the morning," he'd said. A soft glow touched inside me, and I fell asleep with the memory of his gentle eyes in my heart.

"Don't fall in love with me," he'd said. That was silly. Love took a long time to develop, and I could hardly fancy such a feeling for a boy nearly young enough to be my son. And yet the glow was there, and I was shocked in my sleep to dream that a young man with a face I could not see was kissing me.

116

"Cherry Omelets Surprise," Tag announced in the morning, shoving past me with his tray again.

"These eggs really have cherries in them," I cried when I bit into one.

"Sure," he said. "That's the surprise this time! Learn to enjoy the unexpected in life, Leah."

This time he led me to a small sports car. "No chopper today?" I said a little disappointedly. I had begun to enjoy riding that crazy machine.

"Nope. Today is serious business," he said.

I was startled a few moments later to find myself walking down the hallway of the county hospital and into the section called ONCOLOGY. "What are we doing?" I whispered.

"You'll see," he said.

For three hours we sat on a long bench while people came and went. There were four children, one so painfully thin I wanted to cry looking at him. There were old people and a woman near my age and a man near Tag's. All with cancer, I discovered. All taking radiation treatment. And all of them smiling and cheerful as if this were just a pleasant outing. Everyone was so kind and so friendly to everyone else. "You here for treatment?" the young man asked Tag.

Tag shook his head and quickly said, "We're waiting for someone."

The young man nodded. "It's tougher on the waiters," he said. "The families—they're the ones who have it hard. My wife cried a week when she found out."

"You have cancer," Tag said matter-of-factly.

"Two operations," the young man said. "But they didn't get it all. We're hoping for some luck with the chemotherapy."

"Oh, Tag!" I moaned when the young man was called into the treatment room. "Why did you bring me here?"

"Blessing four," he said quietly. "You have your health, Leah. And I wanted you to see how people with a different kind of agony handle themselves."

He was talking in a whisper. "A lot of these people are dying," he said gently. "And they know it. But they're fighting with all they've got for whatever time these technicians can give them here. You don't see any of them standing beside a pool or in a bathroom with a gun in their hands contemplating ending it all. They love life, and almost any one of them would trade places with your agony if you asked and they could."

It was a sobering experience. I watched the parents of the thin little boy laughing and joking with their child who was obviously very ill. And all of a sudden I couldn't stand it anymore. I flew to my feet and ran down the hall until he was outside. Tag was right behind me. He found me sobbing into my hands outside the Emergency entrance.

117

"Leah, baby," he said gently. "I'm sorry. But I told you before. People who get into the state I found you in that first night aren't used to looking out around them. They think they own a corner on pain. I know because I was like you. But pain, all kinds of pain, is part of life. Suffering makes us whole, Leah. It matures us, and it makes us one with all of suffering humanity."

He took my hands and gently pulled them away from my face. "Do you understand what I'm trying to tell you," he asked softly. "I'm trying to show you that you aren't alone." He pulled me close against his body, and I stood there trembling a long, long moment. "Now come back inside," he said finally. "And look at all that courage, and let some of it seep inside you."

We went back down the hallway and this time a young woman with a toddler in her arms was waiting. Her baby was fretting, and she seemed to be uncomfortable, shifting him from side to side. "Would you like me to hold him?" I asked.

She gave me a searching look. "It's all right," I said quietly. "I raised three children. I'll bet I can quiet him."

Her eyes filled with gratitude, and she handed over the little boy. I opened my purse and pulled out the jeweled wallet my daughter, Sally, had given me for Christmas. In a moment he was completely enchanted with the bright jewels.

"Are you here with someone?" I asked the young woman.

"No," she said. "I don't have anyone. And Lenny's baby-sitter copped out on me today. I have to have a talk with my doctors. I—I've had one breast removed and yesterday I found a tiny lump in the other." Her voice had wavered, but the words came out strong when she said, "It isn't anything, I know. It's probably just a cyst, and I wouldn't want to go through that operation for anything again." Then she looked at the little boy in my lap, her eyes glistening. "But for Lenny I would. I want to live to see him grow up."

"But you will!" I cried.

"Of course I will," she said. I looked at her with wonderment. She had such magnificent courage.

The doctors called her name, and she picked up her little boy, who for some reason chose to cling suddenly to my neck. I don't know what prompted me, but on impulse I exclaimed, "I'm Leah Woodard. I live at the Alamo Arms. If you run into trouble with your sitter again, will you call me?"

"You mean it?" she exclaimed.

"I mean it," I said.

"Thanks then," she said happily. "I will."

"Beautiful," Tag said when she disappeared through a door. "Absolutely beautiful, Leah. You reached out to someone else and offered a hand."

118

"Like you offered me that first night," I said softly.

"You're on your way," he said. "The first step to for getting our own misery is to help someone else."

"You're very wise," I said gently.

"I got that way the hard way," he said. And he leaned over and kissed me on my nose and took my hand and led me out of that place where the brave people fought for their lives.

"Tag," I said quietly in the car. "Tag, you told me I couldn't fall in love with you. And God knows I wouldn't let a silly thing like that happen. Not with the age difference between us. But don't kiss me any more, okay? Not even on my nose."

He grinned. "A deal," he said. "It wouldn't be love anyway, Leah. It would only be gratitude."

That's what I told myself in the night when I dreamed of him again, dreamed this time that we were more than kissing. I woke in the morning feeling embarrassed and uncomfortable, not even stopping to assess that for the first time in months I had not had even one dream of Derrick.

It was Wednesday, and Tag took me to the theatre to see an amateur group perform Shakespeare's The Tempest. They were surprisingly good. "Blessing four," he said. "Great arts to enjoy, to lift us out of ourselves." He didn't kiss me on the nose, but he held my hand through the last act, and I was painfully aware of his presence when he drove me home. On the way, he stopped and bought me a gigantic ice cream sundae. I had never tasted anything so remarkable in my life.

I didn't think of Derrick at all that night lying in bed. I was remembering scenes from the play and feeling that ice cream slipping down my throat. And my hand in Tag's.

In the morning I wrote to all my kids, the first cheerful letters I had written them in months. They had left in such a gloom, it would do them good to know that some of their mother's depression was disappearing.

I didn't see Tag all that day, and in the afternoon my depression came back. I couldn't help thinking about Derrick and all the ugly days of blackness when he had told me he was leaving, days of bewilderment when I whipped myself again and again, trying to figure out what I had done wrong.

When Tag arrived at seven, he found me downcast. "Uh-oh," he muttered. "Old Lady Blues crept in in my absence. Come on, we've got an hour before we leave. Spill it out."

I told him how Derrick had said I would always be part of him, but how he wanted someone new. "I didn't mean it to happen, Leah," he'd said raggedly. "But I just feel we're in a rut, that life is passing me by."

"For a long time I thought I would lose my mind," I told Tag with tears on my cheeks. "I knew we'd settled into a rut, but I didn't mind. I

119

always thought we had each other, and that was all that counted."

"And than he knocked that prop out from under you," Tag said gently. "You still love him, and it still hurts." I nodded numbly.

"Blessing five," he said. "Time. Time will ease the pain, especially when you finally stop feeling isolated and feel like a real child of the universe." He leaned over and kissed the tip of my nose and then muttered, "Oh boy, excuse me. I forgot."

I remembered his words all the way to the restaurant where he was taking me. I had felt isolated, cut off, alone. But I never felt that way when I was with him. Tag made me feel like a part of things.

The restaurant was Greek, and we ate stuffed grape leaves and bread filled with green onions and chunks of delicious lamb. We drank wine, and afterward people got up to dance. In only moments, Tag had me on my feet. We were lined up with the others, arms entwined, and I was bouncing awkwardly up and down. The music swelled, and the dance grew faster and faster, and suddenly, out of nowhere, I heard myself laughing delightedly. Tag threw me a pleased grin.

"What are you laughing at?" he shouted above the music.

"Me," I hollered back. "Because I don't know how to dance, and look at me!"

"I'm looking," he shouted. "And what I see is a woman who's going to burst forth into a great human being one of these days."

Suddenly, the line broke up, and the music grew wilder, and a fat, balding man grabbed me and began to twirl me around the floor until I felt like a whirling dervish. Round and round couples whirled. Tag was with some young girl, and I felt a moment's ridiculous jealousy. But then the music stopped abruptly and everybody simply fell down in the middle of the floor in a big pile on top of each other.

The balding man pulled me down, and then kissed me soundly on the lips. "You're a good dancer," he shouted above the laughter. "You come here often?"

"Never before," I said. "But I will again."

"I'll be watching for you," he said. And then Tag came and pulled me off the pile, and we had more wine, and I got just a little tipsy. I had never been tipsy before in my whole life, and it felt good.

"Blessing six," Tag said, grinning at me as we finally wound our way out of the restaurant. "Fun. You have a sense of fun, Leah, and without that, nobody can really be alive. Lord, if you could have seen your face when that guy kissed you!"

"You weren't doing so bad yourself," I flared suddenly. "That girl kissed the daylights out of you."

"Forget that, Leah," he said quietly. "It was nothing. Any more than it's affection for a new and budding friend when I kiss you."

I don't know what came over me. The wine maybe. But suddenly, I stumbled against him in the parking lot, and when his arms came around me to steady me, I reached up and pulled his lips down to mine. The kiss was sweet, but there was no fire.

"I'm sorry," I mumbled. I felt a moment's depression again. Not in all the months since Derrick left had I allowed myself to think of other men. It was only in my dreams that sex came knocking with its need. And this man was nearly half my age at that.

"Don't be sorry, Leah," he said gently. "It's just a natural reaction. You like me. I like you. But that's all it can ever be, honey. Two friends. Now where shall I take you tomorrow?"

The incident was forgotten. Except in my dreams where the kiss I had begun turned into something wild and uncontrollable, and I woke in the middle of the night panting and shocked at a passion I had never felt before, not even for Derrick. Sex had never been wild with Derrick, only good.

In the morning the phone woke me up. "Hi, Leah!" Tag exclaimed. "Listen, honey, I won't be able to see you until tonight. But I want you to dress up, okay? Wear a dress, will you? I've never seen you in one. And let your hair hang long and maybe stick a flower in it."

"Whatever for!" I exclaimed.

"I'm going to have a few people in for a little party," he said. "Don't eat. I'm going to make my Spaghetti Surprise."

"I hope it's got spaghetti in it," I said.

"That's the surprise," he said. "You're not knowing ahead of time."

At noon the phone rang again, and I ran for it eagerly, thinking it would be Tag. "Mrs. Woodard?" a voice asked timidly. "This is Kathy Hughes. We met at the hospital and you—you offered to watch Lenny for me. Well, I've had an emergency. My baby-sitter has four of her own, and two are down with bronchitis. I have to see my doctor again today."

"Do you want to bring him here or have me come there?" I asked swiftly.

"Could you come here?" she said. "That way he could take his nap."

In moments, I was on my way. How different I felt driving across the city from the first day when I arrived here, lost and bewildered, and so depressed I could hardly keep the car on an even keel. Today I felt strong—strong and pleased with myself because I was actually going out into the world to help someone. I pictured Tag's eyes when I told him tonight, pictured how they would glow with pleasure.

"You think entirely too much about that young man," I snapped at myself. But it didn't do any good to rant.

Kathy was dressed and ready to go when I reached the tiny apartment where she lived in a run-down housing project. Lenny recognized me and said, "Pretty, pretty," and I drew my wallet out of my purse and handed it to him.

121

"I don't know how to thank you," Kathy said. "I—well, I lost my nerve the other day and didn't say anything about the lump. But I can't mess around no matter what it means. I'm going back today and lay it on those doctors. If it's only a cyst, they can whomp it out in just one night's stay."

"I'm sure that's all it is," I said. "And Kathy, I'll be glad to watch Lenny when you go."

"You're great," she said.

Tears hit my throat as I watched her hurry down the walk to her battered old car. "God, let her be all right!" I whispered. "Let her see her little boy grow up."

"Cry?" Lenny said suddenly. Impulsively, I grabbed him up and hugged him.

"I'm not crying, darling," I said. But I was. I was remembering all my own babies, and I was thinking of a blessing Tag had not thought about. I had been allowed to live to see them grow up, to see that I had raised the kind of children who would come home to be near me when I was in need. I thought back on all the letters I had written yesterday. Had I said, "I love you" to each of them? I had.

Kathy was jubilant when she returned. "It's just a cyst," she said. "They're pretty sure by the shape. But I have to go in tomorrow, Mrs. Woodard."

"Leah," I said gently. "What time do you want me here?" And when she threw her arms around me and thanked me, I had to get out of there so she couldn't see my fresh tears. Two blocks up the street, I parked the car and sobbed and sobbed. But they werenbad tears. They were good tears because Kathy was going to be all right. Tears for someone else. For a brave young girl. And for me, too. It felt so unbelievably good to care about someone else again.

"Come at eight," Tag had said.

On impulse I stopped at a shopping center on the way home and bought a low-cut black dress. "Good Lord, Leah," I gasped, riding home, "why that kind of dress? You wouldn't think of trying to vamp Tag Henderson, would you?" I really had to think about it.

"Don't be silly," I hissed back at myself. But the thought had been planted in my mind, and it didn't do any good to argue with myself over age or over the fact that I'd been warned not to develop feelings for him. My heart seemed to have grown its own line of thinking, and I dressed more carefully than I had in years.

Standing in front of the full-length mirror on the bedroom door, I was surprised to see that I looked rather good. The weight loss hadn't hurt my figure at all. "You should have taken if off years ago," I mumbled. "And you should have bought a dress like this and stopped wearing frumpy old nightgowns and bought something sexy for Derrick to see you in." But it wasn't good going over all those things again. When he first left I had spent weeks tearing myself apart with the things I might have done to save my marriage.

"You have to accept," Tag had said to me in the beginning. He was right. Dear God, going over the might-have-beens only made my heart squeeze tighter inside me. And then I remembered what Tag had said about time, and I felt better. I went outside to steal a late-blooming rose from the manager's garden.

Tag was waiting for me alone when I skirted the pool and knocked on his door. He was wearing a sports jacket. "I've never seen you dressed up," I said. "You're downright beautiful, Mr. Henderson."

He grinned. "I am, aren't I? Come on in, Leah."

I had never seen his apartment. It was very modern, with brown and white sleek furniture and modern paintings on the walls. He was playing soft music, and he guided me toward a chair and pressed a glass of wine into my hands.

"Are we alone?" I was a little shocked to hear the coyness in my voice.

"For a little while," he said. "I want to talk to you, Leah. Before the others come. Sean is back, and he'll be coming in from the airport."

"You haven't mentioned my dress," I said softly. "And I'm wearing a flower like you suggested."

But he seemed distracted, and he paced the room, checking his watch from time to time. "Honey, you look lovely," he said. "But there's something I want to tell you, something I want to share. Will you listen?"

I dropped all the archness. He looked so terribly nervous. "What is it?" I said quietly.

He came and pulled up a brown stool and sat down in front of me. Carefully, he lifted my drink from my hand and set it on a table, and then he took both my hands in his.

"Leah, we're friends now. You're a beautiful person, and I love you. I'm going to tell you something I tell very few people. We've been seeing a lot of each other lately, right? But we won't be seeing each other much from now on. School will start soon, and I'll have my studies, and Sean is home."

"I don't understand," I murmured bewilderedly. I felt lost suddenly. "Tag, you've taught me so much. But there's a lot I haven't experienced yet."

"Things you'll find on your own now, honey," he said gently. "Leah, listen. There isn't much time. I want to tell you about the young man I was before, the one who came close to shooting his brains out one night over a pain he didn't think he could handle. He didn't really want to die—he just had a problem so big he thought it was the whole damn world. Lucky for him, he unconsciously proved he didn't want to die by leaving both his apartment door and his bathroom door open that night.

"It was late, but old Jeff, the building janitor, had come up to try

123

and spot a leak in a hall heater, and he saw that twenty-two-year-old kid with that gun in his hand, and he talked him out of dying. You know how? By shouting at him and swearing at him and asking him who the hell he thought he was to cop out on life when there was suffering a helluva lot worse than his in the world."

Tag gripped my fingers so hard they hurt. His eyes held mine.

"You know what that old man shouted at me?" he demanded. "He said that when one person fails at life, the whole human race fails, and I didn't have any right to do that to other people. And he did something like I've been doing for you. He dragged me down the steps and made me look up at the stars and smell the night air. Then he told me that his son had died in Afghanistan, and what right did I have to deliberately take the life God gave me when he had a son who wasn't coming home?"

Tears glistened suddenly in Tag's eyes. "Leah, that old man sat up with me all night. He asked me when was the last time I had held a kitten or seen a baby smile, and I said I couldn't remember, and he said, 'Tomorrow you go out and do those things, and then tomorrow night see if you can lift that gun again.'

"I wandered the streets all that next day, Leah, and I lived a lifetime in those hours, seeing things, smelling things, touching things that my situation hadn't let me experience since I'd discovered it in the service. And that night when old Jeff came to check on me I broke down and cried, and he held me like a baby, and when I told him who he was holding, do you know what he said? He said, 'These old arms ain't got themselves around nothin' but a hurt, scared kid.' I couldn't believe it, Leah. He accepted me, even though I knew he'd never met anybody like me before."

"I don't understand," I said quietly. "Tag, who are you?"

"I'm getting to that," he said gently. "I just wanted you to understand why I recognized your intent that first night. It was because I had been there, and because to let you do what you were thinking would have been letting a life fail that would diminish mine and everyone else's.

"Leah, there are all kinds of pain in the world. You've seen a little bit of that this week. You've learned to accept that other people have something to battle, too, and that they can do it courageously, the way you can.

"Let me tell you about another pain now, the pain of turning completely against a self that you could not accept because what you were seemed so hideous you didn't think you could live with it. Until Jeff.

"Leah, you're holding the hands of a homosexual."

I knew that my shock showed in my face. But I didn't draw my hands away. "Promise you won't fall in love with me," he'd said. Oh my God!

"Do I repulse you?" he asked suddenly, his eyes anxious. "Because I wouldn't have told you if I thought it would repel you. I just wanted to show you one more kind of suffering, Leah. And another kind of acceptance. It took me two more years to work out the way I felt about myself, years with a psychotherapist. He didn't turn me into a heterosexual. He taught me what pain I was causing myself over the guilt of being what I was. He taught me to accept myself. Can you accept me now? Can we still be friends?" "Friends?" I murmured. "Oh, no, Tag!"

I saw his face fall. His hands dropped away from mine. But I grabbed them up again. "Oh, please!" I cried. "You don't understand. I meant that we're more than friends, Tag. My God, you taught me to live again! I—I love you, Tag."

"And I love you," he said. "We've been through hell, Leah, each in our own way. But we've survived. It's a chain, don't you see? A human being who has known pain reaches out to another who knows pain, and on it goes, on and on through the whole world. We're all part of each other, Leah, every one of us."

He pulled me to my feet and his arms came around me, and it should have been strange now that I knew who he was, but it wasn't. It was beautiful. "I want to wrap the whole world in my arms," he whispered. He was crying, and I was crying, too.

"Well, well," a voice said from the doorway. "I must say this is a scene I didn't expect."

Tag turned quickly, and his face lit up. "Sean!" he exclaimed. The other young man was smiling, too. "Come and meet my friend Leah. I've missed you!"

They only shook hands warmly, but I saw the quick look that passed between them. And I didn't feel the least bit awkward standing there. I felt one with a part of the world I had never experienced before.

"This is my flower," Tag was saying to Sean. "She was a dying bud when I found her, but she's opening up now. Isn't she beautiful?"

Sean came forward and gripped my hand. "Welcome, Tag's friend," he said quietly. He looked at Tag. Tag smiled. "She knows," he said.

Someone knocked at the door. "That will be Harrison," Tag said. "Sean, check my spaghetti sauce, will you?"

He hurried for the door, and then he turned back a moment to me. "Harrison is straight," he said gently. "And he's a very fine guy who lost his wife two years ago to cancer. I used to go with them for her treatments sometimes. He's only just now coming out of the pain, Leah, and I think the two of you will hit it off."

Harrison Montgomery was a pleasant looking man of forty-five. He had a deep, resonant voice that still carried the remnants of the sorrow he had suffered. "Another blessing to count," Tag whispered in my ear after we had eaten his delicious spaghetti with raisins for the

125

surprise. "A chance in life to try again. Harrison likes you—I can tell."

It was midnight when Harrison walked me back to my apartment. He didn't try to kiss me, but he did make a date with me for Saturday night. "I want to know you better, Leah," he said softly. "A whole lot better." He patted me on my cheek, and for a long time after he left, I stood there in the chill night air feeling the spot on my face where his hand had touched.

There was still pain inside me. But tomorrow I was going to baby-sit for a sweet little boy, and Saturday night I had a date with a man with a gentle voice who knew what suffering was. And in time, I knew the pain would go away.

"We won't be seeing too much of each other from now on," Tag had said. But I had all the memories of the beauty he had taught me. I looked at the pool where I had stood so forlornly only a few nights ago, nearly ready to take a life that had suddenly become very, very precious to me. "If one fails, we all fail," Tag had said.

"I have promises to keep," I whispered to that pool. Then I looked up at the star-filled night sky, and a soft peace stole over me. "I'm a child of the universe," I whispered. "I belong here just like you, stars."

And then I grinned a little foolishly at myself because I was talking to the stars. I was crying when I went inside my apartment. Crying because a beautiful young man had taught me out of his own suffering to accept pain as a part of life. Out of pain came wholeness, I knew.

"Thank you, Tag," I whispered. "Thank you, my very beautiful young friend." And I took those stars to bed with me.

THE END

YESTERDAY'S
TEARS

I don't know if the numbness in my body was from the January cold, or from knowing that my husband Rick was never coming back. I could hear the muffled cries of his brother, but they were soon drowned out by the uncontrollable sobs of my son Miguel. Even though Miguel was only three years old, he'd had a very close relationship with his father. Rick had nicknamed him Mike. I watched our friends and neighbors filing past the steel-blue casket, dropping flowers on it. The services were over. I would have to go back to an empty house. Rick had been the backbone of our little family.

My son and I were the last to leave the cemetery. We watched the men lower the casket into the ground. All I could think of was that Rick was gone—and Mike and I were all alone.

When we got back to Rayville, we went to our house and the rest of the people went to Rick's brother's house for the wake. I didn't want to go because it would only lead to another argument with Frank, Rick's younger brother. He hadn't wanted me to take Mike to the funeral.

"He's too young to understand what's going on. He'll only be in the way," Frank had argued. But I couldn't go along with his way of thinking. I called my priest for advice, and Father John told me that Mike had every right to be there.

When Mike and I returned home, I tried to get him to eat something. He only stirred the food around on his plate. When I tried to get him to take a nap, he wouldn't lie down without my being in the room. I put Mike on my bed and pulled down the shade to darken the room. He stuck his thumb in his mouth and turned his face to the wall. He only did this when he was upset.

I sat across from my son in Rick's easy chair. I could still smell his after-shave. Looking at Mike, I thought to myself: *How are we going to survive without Rick?* Mike stirred on the bed, and I got up to peek over at him. He had tears in his eyelashes, but he was asleep.

I tiptoed out of the room, closed the door, and went downstairs to the kitchen to fix myself a cup of tea. As I sat with the tea in front of me, I looked around at my re-done kitchen and thought back to the time that Rick had decided to have our old louse redecorated, starting with the kitchen, just to please me. I could feel the stinging tears welling up in my eyes as I went deep into thought. . . .

I had been upstairs in our room getting dressed, when I heard my husband shouting about the stove. I smiled and patted my swelling stomach, then stepped into my old, comfortable shoes. I went downstairs to find Rick running cold water on his hand.

"What happened to you?" I asked.

He looked at me with a sheepish grin on his face. "I was going to surprise you with some toast and tea," he said, "when that old stove flared up and burned me when I turned it on. Terry, I can't stand this stove or this house anymore. Let's go see a realtor tomorrow and look for a house that's not falling apart!"

Rick was always on a "let's move" kick when things went wrong, even though he knew how much I loved this old house.

"Rick," I coaxed, "we can't go moving away whenever some minor thing goes wrong. I'll call a repairman to see to it."

"No!" Rick insisted. "I'll get you a new stove. One that doesn't have a mind of its own."

"I thought you wanted to move," I said, trying not to laugh at the way his mind changed in two minutes.

He had a self-conscious grin on his face as he walked over to me and took me in his arms. "Even though you're as round as a beach ball with our baby, I can still hold you in my arms," he said, kissing me tenderly.

Then he got serious. "Honey, I only want what's best for you—and our little champ," he added, patting my very large stomach. "I'll tell you what. This afternoon I'll call Paul Stevens, our new accountant, and ask if he can recommend someone who can remodel this kitchen. But now I have to get to work or we won't have any food to eat in our new kitchen!" he joked.

Rick gave me a quick kiss on the cheek and a pat on the bottom, and then out the door he went. For an older man, Rick could do things that my ex-husband, twenty years his junior, wouldn't even attempt. . . .

The telephone rang, jolting me out of my memories. It was my daughter Carla.

"Mom?" she asked. "Are you all right? I thought you might be alone, so I called to see if you wanted anything."

"No, thanks, honey," I said. "I'll be fine. I got Mike to go to sleep for a while and I'm sitting here with a cup of tea."

We talked for a few minutes. Carla told me she would come over the next day. She had something to tell me. Talking to my daughter eased the pain for a while.

My twins, Carla and Juan, lived with their father and his wife. Jim was my first husband, and we had gone through a bitter, messy divorce. He'd ended up marrying the woman he was running around with while we were still together. She was very wealthy, and Jim loved money more than anything but himself.

He'd left me after I had our second son. We'd found out that Jerry was severely retarded and Jim couldn't deal with anything that was

128

less than perfect. He started to work days and stay out nights with his friends, coming home only long after Jerry was in bed.

The pressure on me trying to raise three young children alone—one of them severely handicapped—was overwhelming and eventually, I had a nervous breakdown. I was in the hospital for two months. When I returned home, the strange phone calls started. Whoever it was would have nothing to say to me, hanging up whenever I answered. Jim never seemed to be the one who picked up these calls. When he answered, it was, "Sure, I can come to work right away." He "worked" overtime three or four days a week, but his paychecks never showed it.

This led to bitter quarrels, with Jim storming out of the house in a rage. When he returned home late into the evening, we would argue again and end up fighting. I hated to fight with Jim. He was a big man with a violent temper, and I always ended up black and blue.

He knew I had to take Jerry to his special school and the teachers would look at my bruises and speculate on what had happened to me. Sometimes, I think he did it just for that reason.

On the day we had our biggest and last fight, Jim said to me, "Terry, I'm leaving you and taking the twins with me. All you ever think about is Jerry. You neglect the rest of us and everything else, including your appearance. If you try to stop me from taking the twins, I'll have my lawyers prove that you're an unfit mother. All I have to do is tell the judge that you were in the loony bin for weeks, and you haven't got a prayer."

I was too scared to put up a fight. I watched him pack his things and the kids' clothes and walk out of my life. He didn't even look back at Jerry or me.

He never sent anything for Jerry's support, either. He knew Jerry was getting a small disability check, so he told me to live off that. I managed to make do with that for a while until the bills started rolling in on the first of the month—mortgage, utilities, water. I tried to get on welfare, but all the caseworker would tell me was that as long as my son was getting disability, I'd have to go to family court to get them to make Jim pay child support.

This took just about all the fight out of me. Going from one agency to another was becoming difficult because I had to take Jerry with me. The bigger he got, the harder it was for me to try to handle him alone. Things were really piling up on me.

The last straw came one afternoon when I brought Jerry home from school. He hated for me to feed him, but he made a terrible mess when he tried to feed himself. Jerry became so angry with my attempts that he knocked the bowl of soup off the table and threw his grape juice into the air, leaving purple stains on the ceiling and dripping down the wall.

I sat in the middle of the kitchen floor and cried. Jerry sat quietly,

129

staring at me. Finally, I got up and washed my face and cleaned the kitchen walls. I cleaned Jerry up, too, and then got him settled down for his nap. But when I went into the bathroom to clean up his clothes, I heard a piercing scream. I dropped the clothes and ran down the hall to his room. His window was wide open. He had fallen out of the window and into the backyard.

I ran down the stairs, taking two at a time, to the backyard. Jerry was lying on the steps, screaming at the top of his lungs. I picked him up in my arms, took him into the house, and called an ambulance.

Jerry and I were taken to Rayville Medical Center. He was X-rayed from the top of his head to the bottom of his feet. There was not one broken bone. He only had a slight bruise on his right leg.

I gave a sigh of relief and started crying. I knew when I took Jerry to school the next day, I'd have to explain to the director and social worker about the bandage on his leg.

Dr. Handle was very sympathetic. She gave me a prescription for Jerry and told me to keep him home for the next few days.

When I returned home, I gave Jerry his medicine so he could sleep through the night. He fell asleep right away, and as I stood over him, I said aloud, "Dear God in Heaven, please help me to take good care of my son."

The only reply I received was a roar of thunder in the distance and the pitter-patter of rain on the window. My sweet Jerry looked like an angel sleeping so peacefully. I made a pallet on the floor beside him and slept in his room that night.

I woke up the next morning in a fog. I looked at Jerry still sleeping quietly. I left the room and called his school to tell them that he wouldn't be in and why. The social worker, Mrs. Sims, was very upset and tried to make me feel as if I'd caused the accident through neglect. I ended up telling her exactly how I felt about what she thought and slammed the phone down. *What else can happen to me?* I thought.

I went about my normal routine for the rest of the day, only stopping long enough to feed Jerry and supervise his play. He loved aluminum foil. He would sit in his chair quietly for hours twisting it into odd shapes.

I was exhausted by the time I had to feed Jerry. After dinner, I put him to bed and went to my room to relax and watch television. One of my father's favorite movies was being shown, and I was going to call him and ask him to come over and watch it with me. I never got the chance.

The telephone rang. It was my sister Lenore and she was almost hysterical. She told me that Dad had been rushed to the hospital. It didn't look good. I called Mrs. Foster, a woman down the street who sometimes baby-sat for me, and asked her to come stay with Jerry. When she arrived, her daughter took me down to the hospital.

But when I got there, I knew from the look on my mother's face that I was too late. My beloved father was dead.

The next few days were a blur. The arrangements were made, the casket and flowers were ordered, and Dad was laid to rest. I was out of my mind with grief. After all our family and friends left for their homes, I broke down and cried. It felt good to let it all out.

I took Jerry back to school two days later. He'd already missed too many days, and I couldn't stay cooped up in the house anymore. When I got to the school, I found out what hell is without dying.

Jerry's social worker ushered me into her office after my son went to his classroom. It seems she had called the hospital to see if I had taken Jerry there after his fall. Someone at the hospital told her that there was no record of his being there. I stormed out of her office and into Jerry's class, and then demanded that Mrs. Sims take us to the hospital.

When we got there, I asked to see Dr. Handle. She met us in her office right away. When she walked in, she smiled and said, "Hello, Mrs. Carter. I hope there isn't something wrong with Jerry." I could see Mrs. Sims start to squirm, and when she tried to explain to Dr. Handle what had happened, Dr. Handle told her off very properly for doubting my word.

I took Jerry home with me and withdrew him from the school the same day. Then, I went to every agency dealing with retarded children until I found one that could recommend another school. They tested Jerry and classified him as profoundly retarded. I was told that he would be better off in an institution. If I didn't put him away, the doctor who'd treated me before felt he could get himself into serious accidents, and that I could have another nervous breakdown. Then I wouldn't ever be able to take care of him.

I finally agreed, and Jerry was sent to a special school sixty miles south of Rayville. Once Jerry was settled there, the only thing on my mind was getting a job and making life a little easier for myself.

Every day I would buy two daily papers and circle the jobs I felt qualified for. I didn't have very much money to spare, so I walked to most of the prospective jobs. By the time I got there, they were either taken or I didn't have enough experience. There were times when I wanted to give up completely. It seemed so useless, but I kept at it.

One Sunday morning, I went out to get the paper. While I was out, it started raining. There I was, without my umbrella. The man at the newspaper stand gave me one of his old papers to put over my head to shelter me from the rain. As I started back across the dirt road, a car came speeding by and splashed mud all over me, causing me to drop the Sunday paper in the mud.

I was drenched, my paper was ruined, and to top it all off, there was a man standing across the street roaring with laughter! I tried to ignore

131

him but he made me very angry. I looked at him with a scowl on my muddy face and said, "What's so funny?"

He apologized as he crossed the street, and offered me his umbrella. "No, thank you!" I told him, and I hurried across the road and into my house.

I was furious when I got inside. I pulled off my coat and wet clothes, took a shower, and put on a dry robe and slippers. Then I made myself a cup of tea. The chilly March wind had gotten to me, and I was still shivering from the cold. As I sipped my tea, I wondered what I was going to do about a paper. I only had enough money for bus fare to go job hunting. But I couldn't look for a job without a paper.

Deep in thought, I was brought back to reality by the ringing of the doorbell. *Who could that be?* I thought. I wasn't expecting anyone, and when I opened the door, there stood the man who had laughed at me. He was soaking wet, even though he had an umbrella. And he still had a silly grin on his handsome face.

"I'm sorry to bother you," he said, "but I don't know anyone on this side of town. The pay phone is out of order. My car won't start and I have to call the auto repair. May I use your phone?"

"I'm very sorry," I told him, "but I don't know you and—"

He cut me off. Holding out his hand, he introduced himself. "My name is Ricardo Miguel San Martino—Rick, to my friends," he said.

I was hesitant, but he looked nice enough. "Well, Rick," I said, "my name is Teresa Maria Carter. Terry, to my friends."

He shook my hand and asked, "Is it Miss or Mrs. Carter?"

"Mrs. Carter," I answered. His whole expression changed. But when I added "Not for too much longer," he smiled.

Rick made the phone call and was told it would be a while before they could come back to look at the car. He put his hand over the receiver and asked if he could give them my number. I nodded, so Rick gave the dispatcher my address and phone number.

I invited him to have a cup of tea with me since he had to wait. He accepted eagerly. He put his coat and paper on the washer in the utility room, and then sat at the table across from me.

I tried not to stare at him, but I was trying to figure out how old he was. He had a sophisticated air, yet there was a touch of the little boy about him. He was very handsome.

"So tell me, Terry," he said, "do you live in this house all alone?"

I told him yes, and then we talked about all sorts of things. I found out that we liked the same kind of music and movies. We also shared the same religion and birth sign. Before long, the doorbell rang, and Rick had to go with the auto repair driver to get his car started.

"I'm very glad to have met you, Teresa Maria Carter," he said with a warm smile. "I hope to see you again—soon."

"I'm glad I met you too, Rick," I said. After he left, I washed up the few dishes and thought to myself: *Here you are, Terry, alone again on a Sunday.*

Things went pretty well for me the following week. I got a part-time job in a camera shop, and, most importantly, got along well with my coworkers. They helped me out with every detail until I got the hang of things. I enjoyed my work very much.

Every night, as soon as I got home, I called Jerry. He would just say "Mama" and "bye-bye." That was the extent of his conversation. I talked to his doctor and was told that there was no change in his condition—that there probably never would be.

The next day, I had to work just half a day. After work, I went shopping. I couldn't face going home. I bought a new dress, shoes, and a purse. I had no real occasion to wear them, but it made me feel good to buy something for myself.

Shopping that afternoon, I was very surprised to see how much weight I'd lost. The dress I bought was a size ten. I'd been wearing a fourteen! After that, I went to the hairdresser and got a completely new hair cut. I felt good about myself for the first time in months.

When I got up the next morning, which was Sunday, I called Jerry. "Mama loves you, baby," I told him over the phone.

"Bye-bye, Mama," he responded. After hanging up, I rushed to the bathroom to get showered and dressed for mass. After mass, I put dinner into the oven, made a cup of tea, and settled down to read the paper. I had just pulled out the television section when someone knocked on the door.

When I opened it, there stood Carla and Juan. They were nicely dressed in new outfits. We hugged and kissed each other and cried tears of joy. I couldn't believe my eyes. They had grown so much in the few months that I hadn't seen them.

We all went into the kitchen, and I wanted to hear all about what they'd been doing. The first thing Carla said was, "We can't stay long. Daddy doesn't even know we're here. We told him we wanted to go to see Grandma Carter. We have to call him when we get there. Mama, we miss you so much."

"I know, kids. I miss you, too," I said sadly. "When Daddy gets over being angry with me, maybe he'll let you come to see me more often."

They just looked at each other as if they knew better.

Carla and Juan left after just a short time, and I finished preparing dinner. But I had no appetite, so I put it away. I went back to reading the paper, but I couldn't concentrate. Finally, I went upstairs and lay across the bed.

Before I knew it, I fell into a deep sleep and was only awakened by the ringing of the phone.

"Hello?" I mumbled into the receiver.

"Hello, is this Terry?" a vaguely familiar voice asked.

"Yes," I replied. "Who am I speaking to, please?"

"Terry, it's me, Rick. Rick San Martino."

Suddenly, my heart started pounding. "Hi, Rick. How's everything with you?" I asked, trying to sound casual.

"Fine, just fine," he said. "I just called to see if you were busy tonight. If not, would you have dinner and see a show with me? I know it's short notice, but staying in this house alone is driving me crazy, and I really would like to see you tonight,"he blurted out.

I laughed and asked, "How long did it take you to rehearse that little speech?"

He laughed, too. "Did it sound rehearsed?"

"No comment," I said, and then added that I'd really like to go out with him.

"I'm taking you to a great French restaurant," he told me. "I'll pick you up around seven."

I took a long hot shower, did my nails and hair, and then got dressed. When I looked into the full-length mirror in my room, I was completely satisfied with what I saw. I hoped Rick would feel the same way.

At ten to seven, Rick rang the bell. When I answered the door, he gave me a long appreciative look and said, "Terry, you look fantastic." I grabbed my jacket from the chair and off we went.

Rick and I had a delicious dinner, saw a wonderful movie, and stopped for drinks on the way home. But he only had a soda. He told me he hadn't had a drink in years. "I would find myself a different person whenever I drank. And not a very nice one," he admitted. "So now I just leave it alone."

Rick took me home around two in the morning. He kissed me lightly on the cheek and said good night. I went in to bed and slept like a baby.

After that first date, Rick and I were constant companions. He took me to see Jerry every Sunday. We went to flower shows, horse races, and amusement parks. We were like two kids enjoying each other's company. I learned more about him, too. He was really a solid citizen. He owned his own home and had recently started a new restaurant.

My bubble burst just when I was really starting to have a little confidence in myself. I came home from work, and just as I kicked off my shoes, the doorbell rang. When I answered, the man standing there asked, "Are you Mrs. Teresa Maria Cordoza Carter?"

My heart was pounding so hard I could hear it. I couldn't speak, so I just nodded.

"I have your divorce papers. I've been trying to deliver these to you for two days. Sign here," the man said.

I signed the slip, and he handed me the papers. Then he left.

I opened the papers and read them. I couldn't believe Jim could be so cruel. He had listed grounds for divorce from infidelity to mental cruelty. I flopped down on the chair at the dining-room table and let the tears come.

"Why, God?" I wailed out loud. "Why me? Jim left me and took my babies. You took my father. Jerry is in an institution. How much more can I take?"

I let out some of my pent-up anger by getting our family photo album and tearing up all of Jim's pictures. Then I grabbed my coat, slipped on my shoes, and ran out of the house, leaving the divorce papers on the living-room floor.

I must have walked for hours. By the time I got home, it had gotten dark and a light rain was falling. The phone was ringing when I let myself in, and by the time I reached it, it stopped. It was probably Rick. I was supposed to meet him for dinner. But I didn't want to talk to or see anyone. I just wanted the pain to stop. I sat in the chair by the window until the light of early morning crept in. I prayed I would be all right.

During the months before my divorce became final, Rick was working very hard in his new restaurant, and we would see each other whenever we could. In all the time we spent together, Rick was always a perfect gentleman. He never pressured me to sleep with him. He always told me how much he respected me. That made me love him all the more.

I didn't know how deeply I had fallen in love with him until he had to go to New York for a week on business. I missed him so much. He wanted me to go with him, but I couldn't take any time off from work without jeopardizing my job. Rick called every night before I went to sleep, just to tell me he loved me.

My divorce became final a few weeks before Christmas. I felt very low because the holidays were coming. I missed Carla and Juan, and especially Jerry and Dad.

I threw myself into my job. I worked overtime. I took anyone's place who couldn't come to work. Then I would go home and clean two rooms a night and hang decorations. I wanted everything to be nice for the holidays, just in case Jim might let the twins come for a visit. I knew I would have Jerry home. I was looking forward to his visit. By the time Christmas week rolled around, I had everything finished except the cooking.

On the day before Christmas Eve, Rick and I went into town to do some last-minute shopping. He told me he always waited until the last day before even thinking about shopping. We laughed and talked, held hands, and sneaked a passionate kiss in the department-store elevator when no one was looking.

Before long, it started getting dark. I had to remind Rick that it was getting late and we still had to go to pick up Jerry. Rick helped me into the car and put all the bags into the trunk. He was very quiet on the way back to Rayville. I couldn't understand why. We'd had such a nice time in town. I asked him if there was something wrong. He shook his head no.

When we stopped at a light, he looked straight ahead and said very seriously, "Terry, do you mind if we stop at my place before we go get Jerry? I have something I want to show you."

I said, "All right, Rick. I don't see any problem in that."

In all the time I had been going out with Rick, I had never been to his house. We pulled up in front of a large, white Victorian house, with a white fence around it and the initials "R. S." on the slightly rusting mailbox. Rick fumbled with his keys and finally got the front door open. He turned the light on in the living room and told me to hang up my coat while he got us something to drink.

Rick had a very cozy home for a bachelor. It did lack a woman's touch, but it was very clean. He called from the kitchen to tell me to turn on the radio or television, whichever suited me. I chose the radio. I put on a station that was playing soft music.

Just as the antique clock on the mantel struck six, Rick came back into the living room with a large glass of ginger ale for himself and a glass of white wine for me. Before he sat down, he took out a small gift-wrapped package from the drawer in the coffee table. He then came over to sit beside me on the sofa. After that, he said the sweetest words I'd ever heard.

"Terry," he said, "I can't wait until Christmas to give this to you. I want you to have it now. I know I'm quite a bit older than you, but you have become the most important person in my life. You are very mature. You've been hurt so much, yet you bounce right back. I just want to make you as happy as you have made me. I love you very much."

Rick opened the little box for me and showed me the most exquisite heart-shaped diamond ring that I had ever seen. He took the ring from the box and placed it on my finger.

"Well, Terry, will you marry me?" he asked.

With tears in my eyes, I replied, "Yes, Rick, I will. I'll be proud to marry you.'

He took me in his arms then and kissed me intensely. I returned his kiss. He picked me up and carried me to his bedroom. I gave myself to him completely. We made love all night. I had never known that lovemaking could be so beautiful.

The next morning, we had to rush to the institution to get Jerry, so the nurses could go home and start their holiday. All the way home, Jerry gurgled, cooed, and waved bye-bye. Rick dropped us at my house and gave me a kiss, promising to call later.

I got Jerry settled in the wheelchair that Rick had rented from a hospital-supply place. I had bought Jerry a big Christmas bib with Santa and his reindeer on it, and I put a red and green ribbon on the back of the chair to make it look festive. Even though Jerry didn't know about Christmas, he seemed to be enjoying himself, watching the lights twinkle on the tree.

When I started preparing our holiday dinner, I let Jerry watch me. I gave him some cookies and milk while I decorated the ham with pineapple slices and cloves. Jerry liked to be with me when I cooked. He knew he would get some of the food to sample. I was so glad I had him home with me. I really did miss him.

Just as I came downstairs after putting Jerry to bed for his nap, I heard a car door slam and a lot of giggling before the doorbell rang. I opened the door to see my Carla and Juan, with packages all wrapped up in brightly colored paper. Jim was sitting in the car with a scowl on his face.

The kids ran in and smothered me with kisses. "We came to spend Christmas with you, Mama. It just isn't Christmas without you," Juan said. Then, they ran back outside and Jim handed them their suitcases before he drove off. I guess he had a heart after all.

Once the twins were settled inside, they went into the kitchen and helped themselves to all the cookies their hands could hold. I was pouring milk into their glasses when Carla grabbed my hand, spilling the milk all over the table.

"Mama, where did you get that beautiful ring?" she gasped.

I told them about Rick and me. When I finished, they seemed a little put out, but they soon accepted it. They knew Jim and I would never get back together.

After we finished Christmas-dinner preparations, we popped popcorn. We all gave Jerry his bath. The twins were a big help. They put Jerry in his pajamas and stayed with him until he went to sleep. When that was all done, we sat on the floor in front of the fireplace and played Monopoly. I lost, of course. I never could get the hang of the game. The kids had such a good time watching me go bankrupt.

The twins wanted to open just one present each before bedtime. I told them to get into their pajamas first. They scrambled upstairs to get to their rooms to see who would get back downstairs first. They almost knocked each other down the stairs trying to be first, and I had to call it a tie. Carla was more than pleased with the CD player she received, and Juan was very happy with his television.

It was after eleven when they finally went to bed. I was exhausted. I wanted to hear from Rick before I went to sleep. *I love him so much,* I thought. *I hope he calls real soon.*

Rick called after he had closed the restaurant at two. "Baby, can I see you tonight?" he asked. "I won't stay long. I want to hold you in my arms for a while before I go home."

I wanted him to hold me, but I knew the kids were in the house. I didn't want them to see me sleeping with Rick until after we were married. I told him that Jim had brought the children over to spend the holiday with me.

He sounded disappointed when he said he understood. "I'll see you tomorrow," he added. "Now good night and Merry Christmas."

When he hung up, I had a scared feeling in the pit of my stomach. But I'd be foolish to doubt his capacity for understanding. He came over for breakfast, loaded with gifts for Jerry and me. He gave Carla and Juan each a card with fifty dollars in it. They were overjoyed. He played peek-a-boo with Jerry while washing the breakfast dishes. We even managed to sneak a long kiss while the kids were watching television. Finally, he had to leave to check on the restaurant, but he said he would definitely be back for dinner.

Christmas dinner was wonderful. Rick carved the ham. He made it a work of art. He sat beside Jerry and fed him for me. He was just great with kids.

After dinner, he lined us all up in the kitchen to show us how to do dishes—"San Martino style." He looked so funny with my apron on. He washed. I dried. Juan passed the dishes to Carla and she put them away. We sang holiday songs as the dishes went down the assembly line. Even Jerry seemed contented. He went right to sleep after his bath. I could hear the kids squealing with laughter as Rick told them about him and his younger brother Frankie and about Christmas in Texas.

It was eight-thirty when Jim blew the horn for the children. They got all their belongings and gifts and piled into the car. I felt sad to see them leave. I promised to meet them in town for lunch on Wednesday. We were going to have lunch at Rick's restaurant.

As soon as we were alone, Rick and I settled down on the sofa to discuss our wedding plans. He wanted to get married right away. I wanted a June wedding. We finally settled for March. Rick and I made passionate love before he left for home in the early morning.

On Tuesday afternoon, we drove Jim back to the hospital. I felt so sad when the nurse took him to his room. He looked so tiny in that hospital bed.

The next day, the twins called to say they couldn't come downtown to meet me. Jim had decided he was taking them out for the day. I was very disappointed, but I was getting used to Jim's using the children to hurt me. I called Rick to tell him I would be home for the rest of the day. He told me he would see me later on in the evening. "I love you," he added before hanging up.

Rick and I spent New Year's Eve at his house making love in front of the fireplace. We spent New Year's Day at the restaurant and had dinner before going back to his house for the rest of the evening. After the holidays, I went back to work and Rick went back to taking care of the restaurant full time. He said it had been neglected since the day before Christmas Eve.

During the month of February, we were quite busy down at the camera shop. I was taking inventory in the back when Jackie Miller, my coworker, came to tell me there was a phone call for me in the office.

"Is this Terry Carter?" a man's voice asked.

"Yes, it is," I said.

"Mrs. Carter, my name is Charlie—Charlie Foster," the man went on. "I work for Rick. I'm down here at Memorial Hospital. Rick had some sort of seizure while we were loading supplies into the van. He passed out right on the dock. I thought I had better get in touch with you."

I thanked Charlie for calling me and told him I would be right there. I hung up the phone and asked Mrs. Smith, my supervisor, if I could take off. She didn't like to give anyone time off, but after I explained to her what had happened, she told me to take as much time as I needed. I grabbed my coat and purse and hurried out. I took a cab, and was at Memorial in less than twenty minutes.

When I arrived, I went to the information desk. The secretary told me that Rick was still in emergency. Room seven. The receptionist gave me directions without even looking up. I hurried to the elevator and pushed the down button. When I got to the emergency floor, the doctor was just coming out of Rick's room.

I asked the doctor if Rick was all right and if I could see him. The doctor wanted to know if I was Rick's daughter. I said, "No, I'm his fiancée."

The doctor looked at me very strangely and said, "You may see him for a few minutes. He has suffered a heart attack. He needs to rest. I'm going to have him admitted to the hospital as soon as the rest of the tests are completed."

I was really worried. I'd known Rick was under a lot of pressure, but I hadn't anticipated he would have a heart attack.

I went into the room and looked at my darling Rick. He had tubes in his nose and mouth and an IV attached to his arm. He looked sort of a bluish-gray color. He opened his eyes slightly and gave me a weak smile.

"Hi, honey," he whispered.

I leaned over and kissed his cheek. "Rick," I said, "I want to stay with you, but the doctor says you need rest. I'll be outside in the hallway until they take you upstairs."

He just nodded. He was so weak. Half an hour later, they took hi·
up to his room. I called Charlie Foster to come to get me in Rick's
Then I drove him back to the restaurant so that we could close up

I went to see Rick every night after work. He was in the hos·
eighteen days. When he was discharged, he looked more like·

had grown to love. The doctor made him promise to take it easy. I told the doctor I would make sure he did. Rick smiled and gave the doctor a wink. He told me later that the doctor had teased him about having such a young woman. I found it insulting, but Rick liked having the doctor take notice.

Things went along pretty well after that. Rick got stronger and did everything he was supposed to do. Almost everything. The week before we were to be married, the doctor told Rick that he could return to work, but that he shouldn't put in the same number of hours he had before. There was to be no heavy lifting at all. He told him to hire someone younger to do those things.

On March twenty-eighth, Rick and I were married. We had a small reception at the restaurant, with just a few close friends and relatives invited. Frank, Rick's younger brother, called from Texas to give his blessing; he couldn't make the trip to the wedding. I'd invited Carla and Juan, but Jim wouldn't let them come.

After the reception, Rick and I left on our honeymoon. We went to Mexico and stayed at a lovely hotel on the beach. All too soon, it was time to come home. As soon as we got back and had settled down in Rick's house, I went to get Jerry. He stayed for a week and was good as gold. He liked being home.

Time passed quickly. Rick and I enjoyed being together. He took me shopping for all the things we needed for the house: plants, towels, sheets, curtains. He told me to do anything in the way of decorating that I wanted to do. He would always come home for lunch to find me putting in new shelf paper or hanging curtains. He knew how much I loved this big old house. On the Fourth of July, we decided to have a cookout for our family and friends. My mother and sister adored Rick, and they promised to be there. Frank was coming to live in Rayville. He had gotten a new job just a few miles outside of town. This was to be our first meeting, and I did want to make a good impression on my only brother-in-law. I had called Jim to see if he would let the twins come to the cookout. He refused and hung up on me.

Rick could see I was upset. He put his arms around me and kissed me. He didn't say a word. He didn't have to. Just having him close made me feel better.

Frank and Rosa arrived early in the afternoon. Rosa was a small, frail, plain-looking woman. She barely said an audible "hello." Frank was the opposite. Big, loud, and very handsome. He had been drinking when he arrived and felt no pain. He grabbed Rick and swung him into the air. Rick just laughed and hugged his brother, then brought him over to introduce us.

Frank gave me a leering look that made me feel uneasy. He shook my hand and kissed me on the cheek.

"Hello, sister-in-law," he said.

I nodded, and then hurried back into the kitchen to get away from him. But even in the other room, I could hear him say to Rick, "She's quite a looker, big brother—young, too. About the same age as Trudy."

Trudy was Rick's only child. He hadn't seen her since she was two. Her mother had taken her and left town while Rick was in the Service. He'd never talked about either one of them after he had told me about them for the first time.

"My wife's age doesn't concern anyone but me," I heard Rick say.

I could tell he was getting upset, so I took some drinks out to the patio. The conversation was dropped. I gave Rick his ginger ale, and he gave me a quick wink. I could feel Frank's eyes on me. He made me very uncomfortable.

Mom and Lenore, my sister, arrived just then. When they came out to the patio to say hello to everyone, Frank and Rosa were having a heated discussion about his drinking. When he saw Lenore, he immediately started flirting. But bless my big sister! She put him in his place very nicely.

The rest of the day went peacefully. Rosa sat by herself in a corner of the yard and Frank fell asleep under the tree by the garage. Everyone left by eleven. Rick drove Frank and Rosa back to their house because Frank was still drunk and Rosa couldn't drive the truck.

When Rick returned, he helped me finish cleaning up, and then we went to bed. He told me not to let what Frank said bother me. I assured him it didn't. Rick's lovemaking made me forget everything that had happened that day. We fell asleep in each otherarms.

The sharp jangle of the phone startled me awake. I looked over at the clock. It was four in the morning. The phone rang again.

"Hello?" I said sleepily.

"Teresa San Martino?" a harsh voice on the other end said.

"Yes, this is she," I answered.

"My name is Sergeant Bell. Do you have a son by the name of Juan Jose Carter?"

"Yes, I do," I replied. "Is there something wrong? Is he hurt?"

"No, he hasn't been hurt," the sergeant said. "He's been arrested."

My heart felt as if it would stop. "Arrested? Arrested for what?" I asked. By then, Rick was awake and sitting up.

"He and two other boys were caught breaking into a record store," the sergeant told me.

I couldn't believe Juan could do something like that. He always had everything he wanted. "Did you call his father?" I asked.

"Yes, we did," the sergeant replied. "He refused to come down. Your son asked us to call you. If you don't come down here to get him, he'll be sent to Juvenile Hall."

"I'll be right down," I said.

Rick was pulling his pants on when I hung up. "Rick," I said, "you don't have to go. I'll be all right." Rick ignored my protests and continued to get dressed. "Rick, please, I can handle this," I persisted. He gave me a cold stare and said, "Terry, you are my wife now. What concerns you, concerns me. Get dressed. I'll go get the car started."

Before I could say anything else, he was out of the room and down the steps.

When we got to the police station, Rick took charge. He got all the information and posted the bail. Juan was brought in from the cell area. When I saw my son and what he had turned into in just a few short months, the shock was too much. The floor came up to meet me.

I woke up in the captain's office. I heard someone say, "She's coming out of it." Rick was leaning over me looking as pale as a ghost.

"Honey, are you okay?" he asked.

I nodded. Then I broke into tears.

Juan had gotten himself into a real mess. On the way home, he tried to explain to me why he was arrested. I couldn't believe one word he was saying. There was no excuse for his behavior or appearance. He looked as if he had never had a haircut or a bath. His loose-fitting jeans and T-shirt were filthy. The bandana he wore around his long hair looked as if it was growing out of his forehead. I told him to save his story until we got home.

Rick went upstairs to shower and dress and get ready for work. I started fixing breakfast. My stomach was in knots. My entire breakfast ended up in the bathroom toilet.

I called Jim after Rick left for work. He told me he couldn't put up with Juan. According to Jim, Juan had cut school for weeks at a time. He was smoking pot. He had been picked up for curfew, and he was causing trouble between Jim and his wife. He hadn't been home for at least a week. Jim told me if I didn't keep Juan, he would have him put away.

"I can't let you do that, Jim," I gasped.

"Well, what would you suggest, Terry?" Jim snarled. "Let him run wild and end up like my brother, shot to death in some alley?"

This was the first time in years that Jim had spoken of his brother. He was always ashamed of him. That was why he'd changed his name from Catorio to Carter. And he'd always thought that Juan was just like him.

I told him I'd speak to Rick when he got home and see if he'd let Juan stay with us for a while. Then, after I hung up, I made Juan take a hot shower and put on one of Rick's robes. I washed his jeans and T-shirt, and then I went to the shopping center and bought him a few pairs of pants and some decent shirts and underwear.

When I got home, Rick was waiting for me on the patio. He frowned at me and said, "What are we going to do with Juan, Terry?"

I explained that I'd talked to Jim and what we had said to each other. I asked Rick if Juan could stay with us for a while.

He was reluctant, but he said it would be all right temporarily. He was emphatic about the rules of his house. He went into the kitchen where Juan was and sat down. Juan was nervous and scared.

Rick told him, "If you are going to be with us for any length of time, you are to do exactly what I say. You are going to work with me at the restaurant to pay back your bail money. Anything that your mother wants done around the house is to be done without any of your smart mouth. If you find you cannot abide by these few rules, you'll have to leave. Understand?"

Juan said sarcastically, "Yes, sir! I understand, sir."

Rick ignored the sarcasm. He reached into his pocket and handed Juan a ten-dollar bill and said, "Go get a haircut."

Juan opened his mouth to say something, but he thought better of it. He gave Rick an icy stare and then went down the road to the barber shop in the shopping center.

Every morning, Juan would be up and dressed and waiting for Rick to go to the restaurant. He enjoyed working. Rick had to admit that Juan was a hard worker. He got along with all the help, especially Jeannie, the hostess. He was such a clown that he kept everyone laughing at his antics. By the end of August, he'd paid back his bail money so Rick put him on salary to work after school. He was a different boy from the one who'd come to live with us a few weeks before. There was nothing Juan didn't try to do to please Rick and me.

Taking care of Juan and Rick and the house was taking its toll on me. I had stopped working at the camera shop and helped Rick out at the restaurant from time to time. But lately, I was so tired all the time. After doing breakfast dishes, I would go into the den, put my feet up, and have a second cup of coffee to relax. I would always go to sleep and wake up in the late afternoon. Then I would have to rush to get dinner done on time.

When Rick and I finished dinner, it would be early enough for him to watch his favorite programs. I would curl up beside him on the sofa. While Rick watched television, I would fall asleep. He would always have to wake me up to tell me it was time to go to bed. By the time Rick had turned out the lights, locked the house, and come to bed, I would be asleep.

Finally Rick suggested that I go to see Dr. Clark. "I've never seen anyone as tired and weak as you are all the time," he said.

I insisted that I was okay—that I just needed some vitamins, but Rick wouldn't let it go at that. He made me promise to get an appointment with Dr. Clark.

The first thing I told Dr. Clark when I went to see him was that I thought I might be starting early menopause. He said, "Let me take some tests first, then we'll know better if you're right."

Several days later, he called me in to discuss the tests.

"Mrs. San Martino, how old did you say you are?" he asked.

"I'm nearly thirty-six," I replied.

"How old is your husband?"

"He's fifty-three," I said. "What have our ages got to do with my feeling weak and tired all the time?"

Dr. Clark chuckled. "Because, my dear young lady, you are not going through early menopause. You are going to have a baby."

"A baby?" I couldn't believe what I was hearing. "After all these years? My youngest son is almost eight. My twins are fourteen. Are you sure, Dr. Clark?"

"I am quite sure," he said.

I drove home in a fog. I was so happy. Rick and I had talked about having children, but I sure didn't know it would be so soon. Then the burning question came up: how would Rick really feel? He was a lot older than the average man starting a family. Well, I would find out very soon!

I made a special dinner that night. Grilled steaks, salad, baked potatoes, and deep-dish blueberry pie. I called Juan at the restaurant and told him to see a movie after work.

He said, "I was going to call you to tell you I'm going to Jeannie's this evening for a party for her nephew. I'll be home a little late, if you don't mind."

I told him I didn't mind, but not to be too late.

I took a long bubble bath and put on a new dress. I set a beautiful table for two, with candles, a bowl of fresh flowers for the centerpiece, and a bottle of non-alcoholic champagne in a bucket of ice.

When Rick came in, he looked tired. He perked up when he saw how pretty the table looked.

"Oh, my gosh, Terry," he said, "did I forget your birthday?"

I laughed. "No, honey, you still have two weeks and a day."

"What's the occasion then?" he asked.

"You'll find out soon enough," I teased.

Rick ate heartily. After we finished, he leaned back in his chair. "Okay, lady, what's going on? Are you buttering me up for something? Well, it's yours, whatever it is."

"No, Rick," I said, "I don't want anything but your love."

"You have that—that goes without saying, honey," he told me. "Now tell me what this special occasion is."

"Rick, I went to see Dr. Clark this morning," I began.

He looked very concerned. "You're not really sick, are you?"

"No, I'm not sick," I assured him. I paused, took a deep breath, and said, "Rick, I'm going to have a baby."

He just stared at me. My stomach started churning, I was so scared. Then he let out a wild, triumphant howl and picked me up and swung me around. "Oh, Terry, baby, I'm so glad!" he cried. "Are you sure?"

I laughed and nodded. I had worried for no reason. Rick wanted a baby as much as I did.

Rick told Juan the next morning. Juan came into my room, a big smile on his face, and said, "Congratulations, Mom."

"Thank you, sir," I replied.

On Labor Day, Jim called to ask when Juan was coming back home. Jim and his wife had settled their differences and felt that they could handle Juan better now.

"I'll leave that up to him," I said. "He's working with Rick at the restaurant and doing well at school. He seems to like it here."

"He can still work weekends if he wants to, but he has to finish school," Jim said.

"I know that," I said. "But he could finish school here."

"No, he can't, Terry," Jim said. "We want him to come back home."

When Juan came in that night, we sat and talked. He said, "Mom, I have enjoyed my stay with you and Rick, but I miss Carla and Dad. If you don't mind, I would like to go home. I want to go to school with Carla and my friends."

I told him the decision was his to make. He kissed me and went to his room. Rick and I drove him home the next morning.

The months flew by. Thanksgiving came and went, and Christmas was upon us again. Jerry came home for the holidays. Rick hired a nurse's aide to help out since I was getting so big I couldn't handle Jerry by myself. We took him back to the hospital after New Year's Day. Carla and Juan called just about every day to see if I was okay. I assured them I was fine. They made sure Jim wasn't around when they used the phone to call me.

For Valentine Day, Rick gave me a portable television for the kitchen. "This is so you don't miss your soaps while you cook dinner," he said.

I smiled. I only watched one soap opera, but Rick teased me about it. He thought I took it too seriously.

I was getting bigger by the day. I told Rick I must be carrying an elephant. "Sure looks like it," he agreed, hugging me. This was the month that the stove decided to act up.

Rick got in touch with Paul Stevens, our accountant, and asked him to contact a reliable contractor for my kitchen. He wanted the work to start right away so that it would be finished by the time the baby arrived. During the last few weeks of my pregnancy, I stayed at the restaurant with Rick for most of the day. The contractors had the entire downstairs of our house in a state of disarray. We would have dinner at the restaurant and then come home. We had to step over all kinds of lumber and ladders to get upstairs to the bedroom. I told Rick I sure hoped all this mess would be worth it. He just laughed and said, "We will see."

On the twenty-seventh of March, the day before our anniversary, Rick took me to pick out something special as a gift. I wanted a new copper kettle for the kitchen.

"Terry," Rick protested, "I want you to have something pretty to wear."

I picked out a white lace bed jacket. It was so feminine and pretty, I fell in love with it. Then I bought Rick a leather recliner for his den. It was one he'd admired for quite some time but never got around to buying. They promised delivery by the end of the week. We went home and practically fell into bed, we were both so exhausted.

The next morning I overslept. Rick had gone and I was feeling weird. I had an appointment with Dr. Clark in the afternoon, so I took time to straighten up what I could. The contractors were just about finished. I had told Rick the night before I wouldnbe going with him to the restaurant that day. I wanted to call Jerry to tell him happy birthday before I got prepared for the doctor's appointment.

When I got dressed, I called Rick to come and get me. I didn't feel up to driving. He told me he was too busy, but he said he would send Charlie Foster to take me. Charlie arrived, and we got there right on time. Dr. Clark examined me and said, "It looks like you're going to have your baby today, Terry, or early tomorrow morning. You get dressed and I'll call the hospital. You're my last patient for the day, so I'll take you there myself."

We arrived at the hospital, and I was hooked up to a fetal monitor. The doctors had a consultation and decided to induce labor. Dr. Clark called Rick. He said he would be there as soon as possible.

My labor was long and hard. When it was time for the delivery, I opened my eyes to see my husband standing over me, dressed in a hospital gown and mask. He was going to watch the delivery. I couldn't protest. I hurt too badly for words.

"Just one more good hard push, Terry," Dr. Clark said. "Just one more."

I pushed with all my might. I was rewarded when I heard the beautiful sound of my baby crying. It was a healthy, six-pound baby boy.

Rick leaned over and kissed me tenderly. "What else could I possibly want for our anniversary?" he said.

"Now we have two birthday boys on our anniversary," I reminded him. "Today Jerry's birthday, too."

Rick smiled and said, "Well, I'll be darned! Three reasons to celebrate."

We named the baby Miguel Manuel San Martino.

During my stay in the hospital, I could not have been happier. I had a great roommate, Christine Edwards. She was a comic. She even made the stone-faced morning nurse smile. Chris had a deep dislike for her mother-in-law and talked about her constantly.

The day before I was to be discharged, Rick came to see me early in the afternoon. He looked extremely handsome in a new three-piece suit, and gave me a small rosebud in a crystal vase for my table. He couldn't wait to tell me my kitchen we completed.

During the time he was there, I never received so much attention from the nurse; I know they came to get a look at Rick. Just before he left, he talked to Chris and her husband, Tony. Then he kissed me good-bye and said, "I'll see you tomorrow, baby. Everything is ready for you and little Mike."

That evening during visiting hours, I was really not prepared for my first visitor. Carla came in wearing heavy eye makeup high-heeled boots, and a very low-cut blouse. Her jeans were so tight, she must have greased herself to get them on. She looked like a hooker.

"What's up, Mom?" she said. "How are you? Where is my new brother and when can I see him?"

I bit my tongue and said, "I'm fine, Carla." Then I walked down the hall with her to the nursery. All the nurses we passed were staring and whispering among themselves, and I was very angry at Carla for embarrassing me in that outfit.

When we got back to my room, I couldn't hold my annoyance in any longer. I asked her why she was wearing that ridiculous outfit.

She said, "Because Anna told me not to." Anna was her stepmother.

I said, "Carla, Anna was right." Juan and Frank came in together just then. Juan went to see the baby, and came back smiling. "He's really cute, Mom," he said. Frank stayed in the room talking to Carla and Chris, while I walked Juan to the elevator. He had to get back home to get dressed. He was going to a party.

Frank and Carla were in a deep conversation when I returned to my room. I was hoping she had sense enough to know that this man was bad news. She didn't. He ended up taking her home. I hoped she would be all right.

Rick came to get me after lunch on Sunday. He and Chris's husband, Tony, came at the same time. Chris and I hugged each other good-bye and promised to keep in touch.

When Rick and I walked in the door to our house, I wasn't prepared for the surprise. Decorations were everywhere. Balloons were hung from the living room through to the kitchen. There was food and punch and a giant cake with a baby doll dressed in blue on top. Everyone yelled, "Surprise!" The waitresses at the restaurant had talked Rick into letting them give me a baby shower. Chris and Tony had had to hurry to the house to get there before we did. My sister-in-law was even civil to me that day. I had a really great time, but I was glad when everyone left. I was so tired. I wanted to be alone with my husband and our son.

Mike was a very good baby. I had no trouble with him at all. Rick was so proud of him. He took us everywhere he went to show Mike off. We even took him to see Jerry. Jerry had been taught to say "baby."

When summer rolled around, Mike was just at the stage where he smiled at everything. Rick bought him a combination coach and stroller so we could go out in the afternoon sun.

Rick was putting in long hours at the restaurant. I was worried about him. He worked so hard to make the restaurant successful. I didn't want him to have another heart attack, so I begged him to slow down. He would come home very late at night and fall into bed exhausted. I had to make him promise me he would take it easy. He said as soon as he could get some reliable help, we would take a vacation together.

Early one Monday morning in July, Jim called to tell me that Juan was in trouble again.

"What did he do this time?" I asked.

Jim said he robbed a candy store and stabbed the proprietor. "You know he is going to jail this time, Terry," Jim told me. "He was already on probation for the record store incident. This charge is a lot more serious."

I felt sick. "What can I do, Jim?" I asked.

"You can go to court when the time comes," he said. "Anna, my wife, refuses to do anything for Juan or Carla because they refuse to listen to her or respect her wishes. She did give me the name of a good attorney, but she refuses to pay out any money. If I have to pay for the lawyer myself, I certainly can't afford to miss any time from work." He sounded desperate.

"I'll see what Rick has to say and get back to you, Jim," I said.

Rick gave me a flat no.

"What did Jim ever do for you except give you a rough time?" he demanded. "He refused to let you see or talk to your own children unless it was convenient for him. I know Juan is your child, Terry, but I'm going to have to put my foot down. Jim will use you to get what he wants, and then spit in your face. Let him go to court and face this mess alone."

I called Jim back after I'd fed and bathed Mike for the evening. Rick was in the living room, so I called Jim from the kitchen. I told him I couldn't go to court.

"Why not?" he yelled.

"I don't have to explain anything to you," I shot back.

He slammed the phone down without another word.

Somehow, Jim must have managed to hire one dynamite lawyer. Juan was put on probation. I didn't know why or how and didn't ask any questions. Carla called to tell me about it. She also told me Jim had made it clear that she and Juan were never to step foot in my house as long as they lived with him. He made her tell me this while he listened in on the extension line.

148

It hurt, but I said, "If that's what he wants, that's what he'll get."

When my birthday came around at the end of September, Rick and I took a two-week vacation to the Bahamas. Rick was under a great amount of pressure at the restaurant, and I didn't want him to get sick again. Mike stayed with my sister. She said we really deserved to get away.

I was so worried about Rick. He and I had not made love since the baby was born. I thought it was because he was working so hard. But he didn't attempt to make love to me during the whole vacation. We enjoyed ourselves, but both of us were glad to get back to Mike and home.

In October, Rick had a surprise birthday party given to him by his staff at the restaurant. He enjoyed it, but it was a little too much for him. He was home in bed for three days.

The next couple of months were relatively quiet. Rick's business was booming. We didn't have a lot of time to spend together. The Thanksgiving and Christmas holidays were celebrated quietly. Jerry and Mike were both growing like weeds. We had Jerry home a little longer this time.

For our anniversary, and Jerry's and Mike's birthdays, we took them, Mom, and Lenore out to one of the best seafood houses in town. Rick wheeled Jerry up to the table so that he could see the two birthday cakes. Jerry just gurgled and hollered "baby," but Mike stuck his whole hand into his cake. Rick snapped a picture just as he stuck his hand up to his mouth. He had cake everywhere!

After the party, we took Jerry back to the hospital and a very sleepy Mike back home to bed. Mom and Lenore drove back to town after cocktails at our house, and then Rick and I went to bed. He tried to make love to me, but nothing happened. I was very disappointed and so was he.

The weeks flew by fast. When summer came, I made an appointment with Dr. Clark, even though I knew it would make Rick mad. There was something wrong, and I had to find out just what it was. I told Dr. Clark all about it. Rick and I had had a beautiful sex life before the baby was born. Now there was nothing. I was becoming a frustrated housewife. I certainly did not want to lose my man.

Dr. Clark was very sympathetic. He said he would call Rick and give us an appointment in a few days.

Rick not only got mad, he was furious. He refused to keep the appointment. "What makes you think that I want a stranger prying into my personal life?" he yelled. "What we have, Terry, is very sacred to me. I thought it was to you, too."

He slammed out of the house, leaving me to cry alone in the night. He returned very late and slept in the den. I got up early, and put a pot of coffee on. I went to the den to find Rick going over some papers. I begged him to talk to me and let me explain just why I had to do what I did.

Rick sat down in his chair, and said acidly, "Okay, Terry, tell me why you aired our dirty linen in public."

"Rick," I said softly, "I apologize. I'm afraid of losing you. You're always away at the restaurant working while I'm always at home. I've seen some of the waitresses you've hired. I can't compete with them."

His expression softened. He took me in his arms and kissed me tenderly. "Baby," he whispered in my ear, "you don't have to compete with anyone or anything. You'll never lose me if I can help it."

Then he asked me to sit down, saying he had something on his mind that he wanted to discuss. I sat in his old chair and put my feet up beside me.

"I didn't ever want to tell you this, and I am being honest with you," he began. "I had no idea what you had to go through giving birth to a child. Laugh if you want to. I have never had an experience like that before in my life. I was so afraid for you. I thought you were going to die right there in front of my eyes.

"Since then, I've been scared to make love to you for fear you would get pregnant again. I couldn't see you go through that experience ever again. It will take time, Terry, but I promise you I'll get over this. It might be a while, but someday we will be just like we used to be."

I was touched by his confession. I explained to him that I would be taking precautions so that I wouldn't get pregnant again. He was satisfied.

It didn't happen overnight, but after Rick got over his bad experience, our love grew deeper. We had our share of ups and downs, but we always talked it out.

The January before we were to have celebrated our fifth anniversary, my darling Rick had a massive heart attack on his way home from work. The doctor told me he went quickly, but that didn't soften the blow. My Rick was dead, and now I was all alone.

The first night after the funeral was unbearable. I didn't sleep at all. Mike tossed, turned, and whimpered all night. I gave him a bath in the morning and fixed him some hot cereal for breakfast. He ate very little. When he went into the living room and turned on the television, he just stared at it. I felt so sorry for him. I knew he would adjust eventually. I had strong doubts about myself.

Carla came over to see Mike and me in the afternoon. I asked her if her father knew where she was. She said, "No, Mom, I told him I was going into town to get some new boots with the rest of my Christmas money."

I was sorry she had to lie. She would be seventeen years old in a few weeks. She should have been able to sit and talk to Jim about how she felt.

150

"I had to come, Mom," she told me. "I want to talk to you about something."

"Can't it wait, Carla?" I asked. "I'm in no mood for any more bad news."

"What makes you think it's bad news?" she said.

"Carla," I replied, "every time I have ever heard from you and Juan, it has been bad news."

She looked at me defiantly and said, "Well, I don't think of it as bad news. I'm pregnant."

Her words exploded in my ears. I looked at my daughter. She was a stranger to me now. She was not the sweet little girl I had known just a few short years ago. She was looking at me as if she was waiting for me to congratulate her.

"Carla, I don't want to talk about it," I said quietly. "I have had just about enough."

She gave me an icy stare, turned, and walked out the front door. I knew what she would face when her father found out about her condition, but I put her out of my mind. Mike was my main responsibility now.

I tried to coax him into eating something for lunch, but he refused. He just sat and stared at the television the rest of the afternoon. He did manage to eat a little soup for dinner, and so did I. It was the first thing I had eaten since Rick died.

Mike sat in the kitchen while I put the dishes into the dishwasher. He was very quiet, only talking when I said something to him. We watched television for a while and then went to bed. I fell into a deep sleep and dreamed that Rick was still with me. When I woke up, I was really hurt. I had come back to reality. .

I pulled on my robe and went downstairs to the den. Rick and I always kept our bar stocked with different kinds of liquors, even though he didn't drink. He knew I liked to have a cocktail once in a while. I poured a big glass of Scotch and drank it. It burned my throat and made me gag. I didn't care. All I wanted was to stop hurting.

I went back upstairs and sat in a chair by my bedroom window. The liquor took affect. I fell asleep for the rest of the night.

When I got up, the pain in my heart had eased, but my head felt like it was in a vice. I took another drink.

The weeks turned into months, and still I hurt terribly. I wondered if I would ever get over the loss of my husband.

One Saturday afternoon, I got Mike dressed and got into the car. I didn't know where I was going, but I was not going to stay in the house. I rolled the window down on my side of the car and let the cool air hit me. It felt good.

I ended up at the restaurant. Jeannie, the hostess, gave Mike and me a big hug when we came in. She ushered me to our favorite table and sat with us.

"Terry, if there is anything I can do for you," she said, "please don't hesitate to ask. All of us around here were crazy about Rick. He was a wonderful person. We really miss him."

I thanked her, and then asked if she'd watch Mike for a little while. I wanted to go to Rick's office and I wanted to be by myself.

His desk was a mess. That was the only way he could find anything, he always said. He had one corner of the desk that wasn't cluttered. He kept the pictures of Jerry, Mike, and me in that small space. Pencils, pens, books, and bills were everywhere else. I thought I had better leave it as it was. I would come back some other time to straighten it up.

I came out of the office just as Jeannie and Mike were bringing a large dish of ice cream to our table. Mike dug into the treat with gusto. I couldn't protest. At least he was eating something. We left right after Mike finished his last bit of ice cream. I promised Jeannie I would be back one day the following week to go over the receipts and pay the bills.

When we got home, Mike settled down in front of the television while I fixed dinner. Just as the two of us were ready to eat, the doorbell rang. It was Carla and Juan. My two teenage children looked like derelicts. I made them wash up while I fixed each of them a plate of food. They ate everything and asked for seconds. After they had eaten, I put the dishes in the dishwasher and cleaned the kitchen from top to bottom. The twins sat and watched me and said nothing. Mike had drifted off into the living room.

After I couldn't find anything else in the kitchen to clean, I sat down and looked at my children. "All right," I said, "what in the world is going on with you two? Carla, I want you to start. Tell me everything. Don't leave out a thing."

Carla started talking. She said, "I told Dad about the baby. He said, 'You either have an abortion, get married, or get out.' So I got out, Mom," Carla told me. "I don't believe in abortion, and I can't marry the father."

"So what are you going to do?" I asked.

"Mom, please let me stay here with you," Carla begged. "I'll help out as much as you want."

She was crying, and I felt like crying, too. I gave her some tissues to wipe her eyes. Then it was Juan's turn to talk.

Juan had been thrown out of his father's house because he refused to do what he was told—stay out of trouble. He was stealing from Anna's purse to buy marijuana. He was suspended from school indefinitely for smoking pot in the boys' room.

I found out that my twins had not been home in a week. They had stayed at a shelter for runaways. The director had called their father after the week was up, but he refused to let them come home. They were only allowed the one week there, so they came to me.

I was sick at the way the two of them looked. I couldn't turn them away. But there was an insistent voice in the back of my mind telling me to be careful. *Maybe I should call Jim,* I thought. No, I would wait. Maybe he would call me, but I had my doubts.

As the three of us sat at the table and talked, I found out that Carla was pregnant by a married man.

"How could you get involved with someone like that?" I asked.

She was still crying softly. "I fell in love with him when he came to do some work in the house," she said. "He paid attention to me when I needed someone to talk to. He said he was going to leave his wife and marry me."

"Carla," I said, "that is the oldest story in the book of lies by married men. They tell you that to get what they want. I don't understand why someone didn't explain this to you."

"Dad is too busy with all his women," she blurted out. "And Anna doesn't talk to me at all except to criticize me."

"I want to know the name of the man," I said. "He's not going to get away with this. You're a minor. I'll have him put in jail."

"Please, Mom," Carla cried. "Leave it alone. I'll take care of things."

"How are you going to take care of anything?" I asked. "You're not working, you have no income. I'm going to see my lawyer about this as soon as he comes back from vacation."

Juan sat quietly. He knew when I finished with Carla, he was next.

The clock on the mantel struck two. I didn't know it was so late. I told the kids to go to bed. I said we'd finish our talk after breakfast.

The next morning, I woke up to the smell of bacon frying. And I could hear Mike giggling downstairs. I went to the bathroom and put a cold cloth on my forehead. I wanted to crawl back into bed, but my stomach told me not to. It begged for food.

I put on my robe and slippers and went downstairs. Carla had fixed breakfast for all of us. Juan was running the vacuum cleaner in the dining room, and Mike was waiting patiently to be fed. Breakfast was great. I didn't know how long it had been since I had eaten a good meal.

After breakfast, I finished my talk with the twins. I told them they could stay, but only on my terms. Carla was to give me the name of the baby's father. If Juan ever stole anything from me, I would have him arrested. I knew I had to take care of Jerry and Mike, but these two were old enough to know right from wrong in the adult world. When I'd finished, I went back upstairs to shower and dress.

I decided to go to the restaurant. Putting off getting Rick's office cleaned up would only make things worse. I went downstairs to tell the kids I was leaving. They were all busy cleaning the downstairs. I told them to carry on. I would be back after lunch. When I went to the garage to get the car, I saw it had been washed. Juan must have gotten up very early to have done it so nicely.

I arrived at the restaurant about ten-thirty. Jeannie was there, giving the waitresses their pep talk about the luncheon crowd. She waved and told me to wait for just a minute. Finally she came over and kissed me on the cheek.

"How is everything going now, Terry?" she asked.

"Okay," I replied. "I came to clean out Rick's office and take a look at the books. I know I have neglected quite a few things in the last few months, so I'm here today to catch up."

Jeannie smiled and said, "Terry, everything is in tip-top shape. Ramon, the manager, is just like Rick when it comes to figures. He has kept everything the same way Rick did. Except for the desk. He did straighten that out."

I thanked her and went down the aisle to the office. Jeannie was right. The desk was immaculate. Everything was placed on the desk in order. Bills were marked paid and the receipts were placed in the ledger. All I would have to do was check the figures and record them in the book.

Ramon had cleared the desk off and put Rick's personal things in a box, underneath the desk. Rick's pictures, pens, pencils, and a set of keys were on the top of the filing cabinet. I picked up the box and put the items from the cabinet in it. Then, I sat down at the desk and started the bookkeeping. By the time I finished, it was almost dinnertime. I had worked all afternoon. I picked up the box and took it out to the car.

When I arrived home, Mike came running to me and jumped into my arms. I buried my face in his neck. He smelled so good. He had been bathed and powdered and smelled terrific. I carried him to the kitchen. Dinner was cooking—spaghetti and meatballs. Carla was making a tossed salad, and Juan was slicing the freshly baked bread. "Mommy's home! Mommy's home!" Mike yelled. Everybody gave me a kiss and a warm hello. Then, Carla served the food. She had become quite a good cook.

"Okay, Carla and Juan," I said. "There's no reason that you have to wait on me. I said you could stay."

They both gave a strained laugh. My own children were actually scared that they couldn't stay with me unless they waited on me hand and foot.

After dinner, I took the things from the restaurant out of the car and put them in the attic. I would go through them at another time. Carla came upstairs to tell me there was a phone call for me.

"This is the second time that he called today, Mom," she said. "It's Rick's brother Frank."

Of all the people in the world, I didn't want to talk to him, but what could I do?

154

"Is this Terry?" he said when I answered.

"Yes, Frank, it is. What can I do for you?" I asked.

"Well, Terry, I haven't heard from you in a few months. Are you okay?" he said. He had been drinking. His voice sounded thick.

"Yes, Frank, I'm fine," I answered. Then I repeated, "What can I do for you?"

"I thought I'd ask if Rick had any clothes I could wear," he said. "I'm out of work now, and I need some decent clothes to wear for interviews. All I have is mechanics uniforms. Could you help me out?"

I didn't like the idea, but I said, "I'll go through Rick's clothes and get back to you if I find anything." Then I hung up. Rick's closet was still as he'd left it. I had no intentions of giving Frank anything. I had no intentions of calling him back, either. I put him out of my mind and went to bed.

The telephone rang, waking me up. It was one-thirty in the morning. Jeannie was calling from the restaurant. "Terry, I am so sorry to call you this late," she said, "but we've been robbed! They got away with quite a large amount of money."

"I'll be right there!" I said.

I grabbed a sweater and pulled on a pair of jeans and my old shoes. I scribbled the kids a quick note and jumped into the car. I was at the restaurant in twenty minutes. Police and spectators were everywhere.

I pushed my way through the crowd and saw Jeannie. She was crying and waving her arms. When I got to her, she was hysterical.

"Oh, Terry, I'm so glad you're here!" she sobbed. "It was awful. Just awful." Several policemen and a detective came over to ask Jeannie some questions, and she rambled on almost incoherently to them and me.

"Ramon called me to take over this evening," she began.

"His wife was taken to the hospital. She's having her baby. When I got here, I went into the office to change into my uniform. The safe was wide open and two guys were stuffing money into a white bank bag. They stuck a gun in my face and told me to lie down. They said if I lifted my head, they'd blow it off. I was so scared. They went out the window."

"How could they get out the window?" I asked. There are bars on the windows, with padlocks.

"I don't know, Terry," Jeannie said. "I guess they came in the same way. They must have gotten the locks off somehow."

The detective told the policemen to check out the windows. The police came back with the locks in a plastic bag. They had been cut. They were going to check them for fingerprints.

After the police were finished with Jeannie, I sent her home. I told her I would call her tomorrow. I went back to my car to get the keys. In my haste, I had left them in the ignition. I got my keys and unlocked the doors to the back bar. Rick always kept extra locks and supplies in the old cabinet. I got out two locks to put on the windows. Before I was finished, Detective Warren came in to speak to me.

"Mrs. San Martino, I am going to leave two policemen here with you," he said. "They will make sure that everything is locked up before they escort you home."

I nodded and said, "Thank you very much. That will make me feel much safer." The last thing I did before I left was hang a sign on the front door: "Closed Until Further Notice."

When I got home, the sun was shining brightly. I was tired. I fixed myself a large mug of coffee and sipped it slowly. I could hear Carla being sick in the bathroom. I went upstairs and found her sitting on the floor, her head almost in the toilet. She was really miserable.

"Are you ready now to tell me the name of the father?" I asked.

"I can't, Mom. I just can't!" she wailed. I wet her washcloth with cold water and washed her tear-streaked face. She was still just a kid. I sat on the floor with her and rocked her in my arms.

Sometime after that, I took a shower and crawled into bed. I slept until four in the afternoon.

True to form, Carla was making dinner when I got downstairs. "Where are Juan and Mike?" I asked.

"In the garage," Carla answered. "I'll call them."

As we all ate dinner, Carla and Juan questioned me about the robbery, and I told them the few facts I knew. Then, just when we were finishing, the phone rang and I rushed to answer it. I thought maybe it was the police.

When I picked up the phone and said hello, a very familiar voice asked to speak to Juan. When I asked who was calling, she hung up.

"Juan, come here," I called. "That was for you. Please tell your friends that if they can't tell me who they are, I'd rather they didn't call here."

"Yes, Mom, I'll tell them," Juan said. Even as I went back to the dining room, that voice on the telephone was nagging at me. I knew it was someone who'd tried very hard to disguise her voice. Finally, I shrugged it off. I had too much to do to let it keep bothering me.

After dinner, I went into Mike's room to put away some of his toys and other stuff. When I opened up the top drawer of his dresser, I pulled out a bunch of coloring books lying on top of his socks. In between the books were two money bands. I thought Mike must have been playing in my old trunk in the closet. I kept all sorts of junk in there. Money bands, clips, old baby clothes, shoes, and rags for painting. When Mike followed me to his room to see what I was doing, I told him to stay out of the trunk until I decided to clean it out. He looked at me sort of bewildered, but said nothing.

I went to the restaurant on Friday to meet with Detective Warren.

He had some information for me on the robbery. He was waiting outside when I drove up.

"Mrs. San Martino, I have to be honest with you," he said. "I believe that whoever broke into your office had to know where everything was. Either he had to have had a powerful flashlight in order to see the small numbers on the safe, or he knew the combination. I'm going to question your help again. I believe it was an inside job."

I put some coffee on for the two of us and sat down. "What you're saying," I began tentatively, "is that you think it would have to be the manager or the hostess."

"I'm afraid so," he agreed.

"I cannot believe that Ramon or Jeannie had anything to do with the robbery," I protested. "But besides myself, they are the only two who know the combination to the safe."

"Are you sure, Mrs. San Martino?" Detective Warren asked. "I inspected the locks that were taken from the windows. Those locks were cut quite a while ago. They had already started to rust."

It was all too much for me to figure out, but I said, "If someone who works here is mixed up in this mess, he'll slip up eventually and I'll be around to catch him. And no matter who it is, I will bring charges against him."

Detective Warren sipped the rest of his coffee slowly. I was on my second cup when he said he was going back to headquarters. He gave me a warm handshake and left. I had to stay at the restaurant to wait for Paul, the accountant. He had the figures on how much money was taken.

Paul arrived around noon. He told me over ten thousand dollars had been stolen. I was really shaken. I couldn't afford to lose that kind of money, not with all my responsibilities. I thought about the loss all the way home.

I pulled the car into the driveway. I had to go back out to do some shopping, so I didn't bother to put it in the garage. Frank, my brother-in-law, was sitting at the kitchen table with Juan. Mike was sitting on his lap. I was furious. The kids were always told that they were never to let anyone in the house when I was not home.

"Hello, Terry." Frank gave me that leering look of his.

"What brings you here?" I asked him.

"Do I have to have a reason to come to see you and my nephew?" he asked.

"Yes, you do," I said flatly.

"Well, I just stopped by to tell you I won't need any of Rick's clothes after all. I got my old job back. I promised my boss no more drinking on the job."

I knew that wouldn't last long, but I said, "I'm very happy for you, Frank. Good luck."

I was relieved when, soon after that, he left. As soon as the door closed behind him, I jumped right in on Juan. I told him never to let Frank in again when I wasn't home. Juan just shrugged his shoulders and mumbled something I couldn't understand.

My plans for going shopping never materialized. I'd no more than finished with Juan when Carla came down the stairs, bent over and moaning. I knew right away what was happening, and I told Juan to take care of Mike while I drove Carla to the hospital.

She lost the baby, and maybe that was a blessing. When it was over, she was okay and she had to stay for a few days for observation.

When I returned home, Juan was waiting for me with some news from his father. He told me that Jim wanted to take him shopping for clothes before he and his wife went on vacation.

"What about Carla?" I asked. "She needs some new things, too."

Juan told me that his father said he would get her a few things when he came back.

"He said his funds are limited until he gets back from vacation," Juan explained. "I told him I'd be over. I'll be staying overnight at his place. I want to go to the airport with Dad and Anna to see them off. I'll be back tomorrow afternoon."

I nodded and he went on his way.

Mike and I ate a quick dinner. Soup and sandwiches. Afterward, he went to the living room to watch television. I told him I would be in the attic if he wanted me.

Once up there, I took the box from Rick's office from the old dresser where I had stored it. I went through the box and found our pictures that we had taken on our honeymoon. Rick looked so handsome in his tuxedo. I found the monogrammed gold pen that his mother had given him, and a small paperweight that had a broken snowman in it. There wasn't much in there that I had to dispose of, the other things were just small keepsakes.

Then I remembered. Where were the keys and the gun? I'd put them on the top of everything in the box. I went through the box again. I had to find those keys and, more importantly, that gun. I had changed all the locks at the restaurant so the keys were not really important. But what if Mike had found the gun and thought it was a toy? I knew it wasn't loaded, but I didn't want to take any chances.

I went to Mike's room. I took all the toys from the toy box and shelves. No gun. I looked under the mattress. No gun. It just wasn't anywhere.

I called Detective Warren and he came right over. When I finished telling him about it, he said, "Mrs. San Martino, I don't know what to tell you to do except to search the house again. Then if you don't find it, question the children about it. It didnmake wings and fly away. I'm sure it will turn up."

158

He must have seen how upset I was. He asked me if he could have a cup of coffee. I said, "Sure. Please forgive me for not offering you some." But I knew he just wanted to stay till I calmed down.

After he left, I gave Mike his bath and put him to bed. Then, I called Carla to see how she was doing. She assured me she was okay.

Juan got home late the next afternoon. He seemed quite happy. Jim certainly had been generous. Juan had quite a few nice things. Pants, shirts, shoes, underwear, socks, sneakers, and a watch. He said, "Dad and Anna left on their vacation this morning. They'll be gone for two weeks. He gave me fifty dollars to give to Carla." I told him about Carla losing the baby, and said he was very sorry to hear it and would call her when he gets back.

In the course of our conversation, I asked Juan if he'd been up in the attic lately. "No way, Mom," he said. "You know I don't like to go up there."

I let it go at that. And when Carla came home the next day, I asked her the same thing. She assured me she hadn't been in the attic. I knew Mike couldn't have been up there. He couldn't lift the trap door. I had to stop worrying. Maybe the gun would turn up eventually.

Sunday afternoon, I was alone at home, reading. I had given the kids some money to go to the carnival down at the shopping center. The telephone rang just as I was about to go downstairs to get something to eat. It was Jim. He had called to speak to the kids. I told him they were not at home at the moment, and I asked how his vacation was and why he was back so soon.

He was quiet for a moment, and then said, "What vacation?"

"Didn't you and Anna go on vacation to Washington?" I asked. "Juan said you would be gone for two weeks. He said that was why you bought him all those clothes—so you wouldn't have to spend any of your pay for school clothes in September."

"Terry, Juan lied to you," Jim said. "I haven't seen Juan since before he stayed at the shelter. I haven't seen Carla, either."

I felt sick. Things were beginning to add up. I told Jim about Carla, the robbery, the gun, and all the clothes that Juan had bought. Jim didn't say a word. He listened to the whole story without interrupting.

"Terry, I'm so sorry," he said when I finished. "If you don't mind, can I come over to your house? I want to be there when you confront Juan. I didn't know anything about this. I'll be over in less than an hour."

Jim arrived about forty-five minutes later. It had been quite some time since I had seen him. He looked a lot older than his years. He had gained some weight and was quite gray at the temples, but he was still good looking. He came in and looked around and complimented me on the house. The both of us were a little uneasy. I offered him a drink and he accepted.

Carla, Juan, and Mike came in about twenty minutes later. I could

159

tell by the look on Juan's face when he saw his father that he knew he was in deep trouble. There could be no more lies. He had to tell us the truth.

Juan admitted the whole thing. He had stolen the gun and the keys. The keys had a tag with the combination to the safe on them. I hadn't even noticed that it was gone. The gun's firing pin wasn't even in it.

Jim was so angry he hit Juan and knocked him out of his chair. I asked Juan who was in with him on the robbery. He said, "Nobody." I told him that Jeannie said there were two men who robbed the place. He looked scared. He finally broke down and said that Jeannie planned the whole thing. My heart was aching. I had trusted her and she did this to me.

There were tears in Jim's eyes when he asked me what I was going to do. I think he knew me well enough to answer that question himself. I could never trust Juan again. Jim and I took him down to the police station. Detective Warren was called to come in. He listened to Juan's story and a warrant was issued for Jeannie's arrest.

She was brought down to the station for questioning. She confessed to having masterminded the whole thing. She said she wanted to get back at me because of Rick.

"I loved him so much, but all he wanted was you," she said. "I was humiliated. I swore I would get back at you and I did. I used your son!"

The police took her away, screaming to the top of her lungs about how much she hated me. I felt as if I was going to die right there. Detective Warren asked me if I wanted to press charges against my son. It was one of the hardest things I had ever had to do, but I said "Yes." Jim backed my decision all the way.

When they took Juan away, Jim and I both cried for our son. But we knew if I let him off, he'd only get in worse trouble. Jim drove me home afterward. I had to tell Carla what had happened. She cried for two hours.

Later that evening, Jim called to see if I was all right. He talked very nicely to me. "I don't blame you for what you did, Terry," he said. "I hope you don't blame yourself. I think you did the right thing. I don't want Juan to end up like my brother. I'm sorry I gave him his name. One other thing, Terry: When it is time to go to court, I'll be there with you."

I thanked him and hung up.

I called all the employees the next morning for a meeting at the restaurant. Everyone showed up on time. They were all talking about Jeannie and Juan. I told them all that no way would I tolerate stealing. "I pay you all good wages," I said. "Anyone caught stealing will be prosecuted." Everyone agreed. Then I said, "Now, let's all get back to work so we can open up tomorrow."

In September, I had to get Carla transferred to East High. She would be closer to her district. I knew she didn't want to go back to her old school. All her friends knew about her brother. I got Mike enrolled in parochial school.

Carla, Mike, and I had dinner and talked about what going to a new school would be like. Mike was really excited about his first day of school the next day.

The telephone rang and Carla answered it. It was Juan's lawyer. He said Juan's trial was scheduled for Friday at ten. I assured him I would be there. I called Jim and he said he would meet me there.

The trial was over in less than an hour. Juan was sentenced to a juvenile home ninety miles away. He was to stay there until he was twenty-one. That meant he would be there for four years. I felt sorry for him and so did Jim. When they took him away, he looked at me with hate in his eyes. I knew he would never forgive me.

Jim and I walked out of the courtroom and said good-bye to each other. For the first time in years, Jim kissed me on the cheek. Then he walked away. His shoulders were slumped and he really looked old. I wanted to comfort him, but I knew he couldn't be comforted. I went home to wait for Carla and Mike to get home from school.

When Carla got out of school, she picked Mike up and they walked home together. I told her about the trial and she started crying. She wanted to know if she could visit Juan. I said I was quite sure she could, but I didn't know when. I told her I would find out for her and let her know.

Things were quiet for a while. The restaurant was coming along fine, and I didn't have any trouble with my employees. Carla and Mike enjoyed school and I was contented for the first time in ages.

Shortly after the Christmas holiday, I got a letter from Jeannie's brother telling me that she took her own life on Christmas Eve. He asked me not to blame myself because Jeannie was always bad news to anyone who came in contact with her. I really didnwant to know about it. I wanted to forget everything that had happened to me in the past year. It was a brand-new year and I was going to have a good one. What a laugh that was!

It had been a year since Rick died, and I missed him terribly. I put fresh flowers on his grave on the anniversary of his death. I came home and cried all night. I had to shake the loneliness, so I worked all day at the restaurant. I even helped the waitresses when it got too crowded. I felt like I was going to crack up, but I refused to let that happen.

One Tuesday evening, Detective Warren came in to have dinner at the restaurant. I came out of the office to say hello and chat with him for a few minutes. He invited me to sit with him, but I declined. I told him I had to finish my work and close the restaurant. It was Ramon's night off, and I wanted to close early. He said he understood.

I went back to the office to finish up the paperwork. Alice came to give me her total and said she was leaving. "Everybody else has gone, too," she said.

A few minutes later, I locked up the restaurant, grabbed my coat and purse, and started for my car.

The light in the parking lot had burned out and it was really dark. There was a lone truck parked on the lot by the fence. Its owner had left the hood up. I didn't see anyone by it, so I figured it belonged to someone who'd gone to get a mechanic.

Then it happened! As I opened the door to get into my car, I was grabbed from behind. I could feel the man's hot liquor breath in my face as he picked me up and tried to carry me toward the truck. I fought with all my strength to get away, but the man was very strong. He half dragged and half carried me across the parking lot.

I started screaming. The man eased his grip slightly and I took that opportunity to fight harder. I pulled away and tried to run. He grabbed me again and hit me in the face. I refused to black out. I pulled the ski mask off his face and got a real good look at him then. It was Frank!

That just fanned the flames of my rage. I fought like a madwoman, screaming and scratching and kicking. Frank was panting and laughing and talking about my "hot Spanish blood."

I fought as hard as I could. I knew I would die rather than let this animal rape me. But then suddenly Frank's grip eased and he fell to the ground. I was still screaming when Detective Warren took me into his arms. He put his coat around me to cover my torn clothes. He called a wagon for Frank and an ambulance for me. He rode with me to the hospital and waited for me while the doctor treated my bruises. Then, I had to go to the police station to sign a complaint. After I filed charges against Frank, the detective and a policeman escorted me home.

Carla was waiting up for me. She became as upset as I was when I told her what had happened. She made a promise that she would never give me any trouble for the rest of her life.

Frank San Martino was given a suspended sentence. I couldn't believe my ears. The judge said that Frank had never been in trouble before. Since this was his first offense and he was the sole support of his family, he would not have to serve time. I was devastated. When he left the courtroom, he gave me a sneaky grin. Oh, how I hated him! It was hard to believe that he was related to my Rick.

That was the last time I saw him. He took his family and went back to Laredo, Texas.

Several years have passed since then, and at last, I have a peaceful life. Carla kept her promise. She finished school, and now she is married to a fine young man. They have a beautiful son who was born on Rick's birthday. His name is Ricardo.

Jerry is still in the special hospital. He comes home quite often for long visits, but he is just the same. There will never be any change in his condition.

Mike is just Mike. He is doing well in school and is making me proud of him—as proud as his father would have been.

Over the years I have kept up my friendship with Detective David Warren. We enjoy each other's company. He knows that I still love my husband and am not interested in another romantic involvement. He respects my feelings. I like that very much.

As for Juan—I've heard from him just twice since he was sent away. In the first short note he wrote, he told me he would never forgive me for what I did to him. I was devastated, and there was no one I would talk to about my feelings—not Carla or Mike or Jim. It wouldn't have been fair to burden them.

But in the second note Juan wrote me, one I received just a few weeks ago, he hinted that he now understood that my decision had been his salvation. He apologized for all the heartache he had caused me, and he asked permission to come see me when he gets out.

I can't wait for that day to come! Being reconciled with my firstborn, my prodigal son, will truly make life worth living again for me.

THE END

DON'T TELL ME NOT
TO LOVE HIM

It was raining cats and dogs as I drove home from the mall. It was my grandmother's birthday, and I felt warm just thinking of our home and family and the birthday dinner my boyfriend, Tommy, would share with us.

An inner glow heated up within me at the thought of Tommy. He'd come such a long way since we'd met. I said a silent prayer that Mom's stubborn distrust of Tommy would soon fade. The prayer was cut short when I pulled in the driveway and saw Mom running toward the car, wearing a shirt and no shoes. I groaned. Grandma must have wandered off again. The car had only barely rolled to a stop when Mom pounded on the window.

"I'm so glad you're home," she cried as I rolled the window down. "Grandma's been missing for over an hour. With the storm getting worse, I'm frantic. Please ride through the neighborhood and see if you can find her."

"Grandma's not missing, Mom," I told her. "She's just out for one of her usual walks. You're getting worked up for nothing. She always comes back by herself, or is brought back by a neighbor."

"Worked up for nothing?" Mom gasped. "My mother's roaming around in a rainstorm and I'm worked up for nothing? She could fall and break a hip or she could walk in front of a car. . . ."

I saw that there was no way to reason with her. "It's just raining, Mom, it's not a hurricane. But I'll go as far as the park. She couldn't have gone beyond that," I assured her.

I drove up one block and down another. The wind whipped through the trees, and leaves flew through the air, heavy with the rain. I covered five blocks, but I didn't find my grandmother. Finally, I decided to head for home. I wasn't surprised to find Grandma and Mom with a neighbor, Mrs. Gooden, in the living room. Mom looked relieved.

"Mrs. Gooden found Grandma confused and standing in front of her house. She was good enough to bring her home. I guess you're right. I shouldn't worry so much," Mom told me.

Grandma was already climbing the stairs to her room, muttering under her breath, "Sorry to be so much trouble. The rain looked so pretty, and I just had to get out and feel it and then I didn't know where I was and . . ."

We heard her door close. It was always the same—first, the vanishing act—then, the safe return and the excuses. Mom should have been used to it by now.

I said hello to Mrs. Gooden and thanked her for bringing Grandma home, and left them alone to talk. I was looking forward to a warm bath and a nap before dinner, but first I had to hang up the new dress I'd bought.

The minute I'd seen it, I knew Tommy would love it. It was blue, his favorite color. While I soaked in hot water and bubbles, I closed my eyes and pictured tomorrow, Grandma's birthday. Tommy would be quiet and very careful of his table manners. There would be lots of gifts for Grandma and a lovely dinner, with a cake for dessert. With that festive scene printed in my mind, I rubbed my skin to a pink blush, and then fell asleep for a nap on my bed.

Later that evening, after the dinner dishes had been cleared away, with Grandma in bed for the night and Dad settled down with his newspaper, Mom and I found plenty to do in the kitchen. There was silver to polish, a tablecloth to iron, and the big turkey roasting pan to be rescued from the top shelf. Mom usually tackled kitchen chores with enthusiasm, going from one thing to another, but tonight, she was very preoccupied.

"Is something bothering you, Mom?" I asked.

The knife she was using on a summer squash slowed to a halt. She looked up vacantly, with a smudge of breadcrumbs on the end of her nose. "Did you say something?" she asked.

"I asked you what's wrong. You're a thousand miles away," I told her.

She sank into a chair, with dejection written all over her face. "It's Grandma. These jaunts of hers have been making me a nervous wreck, and she's so stubborn. She paid no attention when I told her how much it worried me. I'm at the end of my rope."

"You're overreacting," I said. "Grandma's only looking for a change of scenery. She likes to get out of the house. She has always come back, or a neighbor's brought her back. I wish you didn't worry so much."

"Well, why couldn't she at least tell me when she's going out? Then I'd know where she is," Mom replied.

"Grandma has lived many years, Mom. Maybe she doesn't think she has to answer to anyone for every move she makes," I said.

It was time to change the subject. Mom had a way of making a mountain out of a molehill. I planted a kiss on the top of her head. "We still have a few things to do in this kitchen before we call it a night. Remember, Tommy is coming tomorrow. I want him to see what expert cooks we are."

"Tommy!" The name fell off her tongue as if it had a bad taste. I finished screwing the lid back on the polish jar with a twist that turned my knuckles white, and then I set it down with a loud thud. *Keep cool,* I warned myself.

165

"Mom, why can't you learn to like Tommy? At least give him credit for the effort he's making to turn his life around. And you can't pick on his manners. He's always respectful to Dad and the perfect gentleman to you and Grandma."

"Manners don't change a jailbird into a decent citizen," she said gravely.

That horrible word gave me a jolt. "That's a terrible label to pin on anyone, much less Tommy. He's not a jailbird," I said patiently.

"He served time, didn't he?" she asked.

"He did three months in prison and just finished a year on probation. Mom, we've been through this before. You know what Tommy's life was like, and what he's doing to change it. Why can't you see the good in him?" I asked.

"What I see is a daughter who had every advantage—a loving home, the best education, a wonderful career—throwing it all away on an ex-convict. I see a girl letting a stupid infatuation lead her smack into trouble."

If anything could have blown my fuse it was Mom calling my feelings for Tommy an infatuation, but I checked myself.

Obviously, Mom's nerves were frayed, with Grandma's escapade coming in the middle of preparations for her big birthday dinner. I glanced around the kitchen. All that was left was to put the squash in the oven and clean up. I made myself smile, and wiped the breadcrumbs off Mom's nose.

"It's been a rough day, Mom. Go to bed. I'll finish up here," I told her.

She must have been exhausted, because she went off without a word. And while I finished up in the kitchen, I let my mind wander back through those early months when Tommy came into my life.

A lot of what Mom said had been true. No one in my high-school graduation class had more loving parents and a brighter future than I. Mom and Dad had high hopes for me and even though my decision to take up social work as a career didn't please them very much, they accepted it with good grace. They sent me to the best college they could afford and supported me while I earned my degree.

All my plans went along like a well-oiled clock. I breezed through college with high grades, and soon after graduation went to work for my city's Youth Services Bureau. That's where I had met Tommy. My heart went out to him from the first time I saw him across the office.

Backed into a corner of the room, he looked like a fish out of water. His eyes warily followed the secretaries and clerks passing back and forth, until he finally decided to go to the information desk. If ever a forlorn soul needed a friend, he did. And after all, that was what I was there for.

Tommy was in a residential program for first-time offenders who had proved trustworthy and showed the potential to become lawful citizens.

I introduced myself and offered my services. "Come on," I coaxed. "I told you my name. What's yours?"

After a few seconds of staring at me as if he couldn't believe I was talking to him, he blurted, "Tommy. Tommy Hillson."

"Okay, Tommy. Do you want to talk awhile? You can tell me anything—anything at all," I said. I indicated he could sit in the chair next to me.

It came slowly at first, and then, in a flood of words tumbling over each other, he told me about his mother, who died when he was so young he thought she'd deserted him, and a foster home that had made his life such a misery he dropped out of high school and ran away. Unskilled, and uneducated, he drifted from one menial job to another until he joined the Navy, where he routinely got into trouble.

When he finished his hitch, Tommy had left the Navy with no regrets and made his way back home, where he soon fell in with a gang. Day after day, he was drawn deeper into a network of crime. The end came when the gang was picked up for petty theft. Because no weapons were found on Tommy, the judge was inclined to leniency. His sentence was short, and it was all behind him now.

By the time he finished his story, Tommy wasn't as uptight as he had been when he'd come in. All he'd needed was a willing listener to help him relax, and I was glad it had been me. Then he asked me about my life, so I told him about my parents, and my grandma, and our home.

"That's it," I said. "Enough. I'm boring you to death."

"No way," he protested. "I was just trying to picture your family. They must be great. I never had a family like that."

No family life. I couldn't imagine life without my family. Suddenly, I heard myself asking, "Why don't you have dinner with us sometime? Mom and Dad like to fuss over company and Grandma would love it. She gets a big kick out of being around young people."

He hadn't exactly jumped at the invitation. I felt his reserve surfacing again, the distrust of one who's been knocked down by life so often there's nothing left to believe in, not even human kindness.

"I don't know," he stammered. "I wouldn't fit in. I don't know the right things to say. And besides, I don't even have a car."

"Stop with the excuses," I broke in. "Dad and Grandma will talk your ears off. All you have to do is nod once in awhile. I'll pick you up and bring you back home."

While I waited for Tommy to overcome his reluctance, another thought filtered through my mind. Was I doing this for Tommy or for me? When at last, still with doubt in his eyes, he said he'd come, I ignored the premonition that warned me Tommy might turn out to be

167

more than just a social work case to me.

That was months ago, and to my relief, that first visit went well and set a pattern for those that followed. Mom was quiet and aloof, but polite. Dad, on the other hand, was as friendly as he could be. He welcomed Tommy with a hearty handshake, and soon they were chatting away like old friends. In no time, Tommy was out of his shell, talking a blue streak. Grandma and Tommy took to each other right away.

I brought Tommy home often after that and the habit grew into a ritual. My mother didn't like him, but she put up with him, knowing I was helping him out. Tommy and I grew very close during this time. Although our backgrounds were so different, we had a lot in common. We both liked picnics, hiking, and going to the beach.

The picnics we shared were the best of all. We'd drive until we found a shady place, stretch out on a blanket, and then we'd raid the picnic basket.

I don't suppose I'm the only girl who heard her first true declaration of love to the accompaniment of a bird's song, while sunlight beamed through the branches of a maple tree. The magic chemistry called love had been drawing Tommy and me closer inch by inch. In the beginning, my head was flashing warning signals to my heart. Social workers are not supposed to fall in love with the people they're helping.

But when Tommy drew me close it was my heart, not my head, I was listening to. And it was my heart that answered his whisper, "Do you love me, Carrie?" with a fervent "Yes, Tommy, I do, and I always will."

And from that day on, we were lovers as well as friends.

Now the kitchen was finally cleared and I was ready to fall into bed. In fact, I suspected I'd fall asleep the second my head hit the pillow!

The next day was a mixed blessing of bad and good. Grandma had forgotten it was her birthday, but the dinner was nice, anyway. Between the chestnut-stuffed turkey course and the ice cream for dessert, Tommy announced he had a new job. He'd been taken on as a part-time bus driver starting tomorrow. His eyes sparkled with pride. Dad jumped up and pounded him on the back with noisy congratulations. Grandma hopped up and down in her chair, clapping her hands. Mom didn't say anything.

After dinner, Dad suggested a game of checkers. Tommy was too polite to refuse, but I sensed his restlessness. I said something about him needing to turn in early because he was starting a new job in the morning, and we left.

While we rode through the streets, Tommy kept up an endless string of chatter. He was full of plans that all revolved around us and his goal of independence. If he proved satisfactory to the bus company, he told me, they'd give him a full-time job.

"You know what that means, Carrie?" he asked me, not waiting for my reply. "It means I'll be able to rent an apartment, and I'll get my first crack at being in control of my own life." On and on he went, pouring out his hopes and ambitions until we pulled up in front of the halfway house. When I stopped the car, he crushed me in a bear hug.

"Can't you picture it, Carrie?" he asked. "You and I, married, living in a home of our own. I can't wait."

"We don't have to wait, Tommy," I said in a clumsy attempt to be helpful. "I make a decent enough salary for both of us."

"No way," Tommy said. "It's important for me to do this on my own. I've always been leaning on someone else. Now I have to prove to myself and to you that I can stand on my own two feet."

"It's okay, honey," I apologized. "We'll wait."

It was only a week later that my world came apart. Tommy had been working a double shift since he started, and the only time we had been together was for a quick lunch or coffee break. I'd hurried home that night, eager for a cool shower. As soon as I walked in the house, I smelled trouble. Instead of fussing with dinner in the kitchen, Mom was standing at the window with her arms crossed irritably; her eyes were cold.

"Well, your great experiment has finally backfired."

I waited for her explanation of this strange remark and when it didn't come I said, "I don't have the slightest idea what you're talking about."

"I don't suppose you do. Your precious Tommy isn't about to tell you he's taken up his life of crime again," she said.

"Mother," I snapped, "get to the point."

"The point is that my heirloom brooch is missing."

My knees went weak. The insinuation behind those words was too ugly to even think about.

"Let me get this straight. You're accusing Tommy of stealing a piece of jewelry you've misplaced?"

"I do not misplace things, and certainly not an heirloom," Mom declared. "The only time I wear it is to the country club summer dance, and it never leaves the box in my bureau from one year to the next. Well, young lady, the box is there, but the pin is gone."

"Mom, I can't believe I'm hearing this. Tommy isn't a thief. He hasn't even been in the house for days. When could he have taken your pin?" I asked.

"Anytime," she fired back. It was as if she'd been anticipating this question. "I told you I never even look at it all year. He could have taken it anytime."

The scenario was getting more improbable by the minute. A mental vision of Tommy sneaking upstairs, knowing exactly where to go to steal a brooch, and then rifling through a bureau drawer was so ludicrous it was funny. But Mom was not amused, and the wisest course was to humor her.

"Okay," I said, "just calm down. We'll search. The pin will turn up, I promise."

I spun around and left her standing at the window. At the top of the stairs I had to pass Grandma's room first. On an impulse, I went in and sat opposite to where she was rocking. I spoke gently.

"Grandma, did you know that Mom's upset?"

"I know she's storming around like a caged tiger. I didn't ask why. Your mother gets in these fits," she replied.

"Well, Grandma, the heirloom brooch you gave her is missing. She thinks it was stolen. Have you seen it?"

"Brooch?" she repeated vaguely. "Oh, that thing." Then she shot me a sharp glance. "Stolen? Where did she get that idea?"

I shrugged. "I think Mom's imagining things. She says Tommy took it."

"Tommy!" she shrieked. She threw her head back and laughed so hard I was afraid for her high blood pressure.

The noise brought Mom to the door. "What's the joke?" she asked us.

"You've finally flipped your lid. How can you say Tommy stole your silly pin, or stole anything, for that matter?" Grandma asked Mom.

"Because it's true. Now, Carrie, since you're determined to go through with this futile hunt, let's get it over with. I have dinner to cook." And having said that, Mom marched off.

We looked, both of us, though Mom just went through the motions, idly flipping pillows, opening and shutting drawers without touching the contents. I went at it with a vengeance. Tommy's reputation, and maybe his future, was at stake. But after more than an hour of digging and rummaging, I had to admit defeat. I'd combed the house from top to bottom, every room, every corner and closet, under rugs and furniture, but I came up empty-handed. The brooch wasn't anywhere, including in the basement or Grandma's room. I had to give up, but I wouldn't give in. Nothing would convince me Tommy was a thief.

After an unpleasant meal, Mom retreated to her kitchen. I carried a few plates in, but the kitchen, that evening, wasn't big enough to hold both of us.

I spent the rest of the evening talking to Grandma, since Tommy was working a late shift. I went to sleep early and Mom was still angry at me.

The next day, Mom was mad at me for bringing Tommy into our lives. Dad tried to console me, but all I wanted was my mother's trust.

My first idea was to try to reach Tommy at work, but I was told he'd be driving a full shift all day, and maybe some overtime. They were really beginning to give him more responsibility at the bus company. They, at least, seemed to trust him.

When I went downstairs, Dad was pacing, Mom was weeping, and Grandma was nowhere to be seen. I guessed the situation before anyone said a word. "Grandma's gone off again, right?"

Mom whirled on me. "You needn't be so flip. I'm frantic. Please, Carrie, go out and look for her. She wanders around so much and she doesn't even remember where she is."

"It's okay. I'll go out and find her. I'm sure I'll see her in the park or at a neighbor's house," I told her.

It never occurred to me that I wouldn't find Grandma casually strolling along. But I didn't find her, even though I kept at it until the morning turned into afternoon, and then into evening. When the streetlights came on and darkness stretched everywhere, I finally returned home, dreading to face Mom and Dad, but especially Mom.

I was relieved to find that Dad had persuaded Mom to take a couple of aspirins and lie down. He'd been so sure I'd bring Grandma home. His stricken look when I arrived without her was hard to take.

"This could be serious, Carrie. I've called all the neighbors. The only thing left is to call the police."

He was right, but I hesitated. It would be a bad experience for Grandma if the police spotted her and tried to get her into a squad car. No matter how gentle or kindly the officers were, she'd resist to her last breath. I prayed for time.

"Give it another hour, Dad," I said. "Let's have some coffee in the meantime. I'd love a cup."

We sat with our steaming mugs, lost in silence. Dad was in a state, his hands trembling so much that he spilled his coffee. Eventually he just gave up, put the cup down, and drifted into the living room. I refilled my cup and joined him.

Then the doorbell rang. My mouth gaped wide when I opened the door and saw Grandma standing there, hanging onto Tommy's arm as if she owned it. I stood rooted to the spot.

She brushed past me, dragging Tommy along. "Good grief," she grumbled. "How long did you plan to keep us on this doorstep?"

Heels clicked on the stairs behind me. Mom was clattering down, sputtering between breaths, "What is going on? I heard . . ." The words hung in midair as she took in this unlikely scene. Then she was hugging Grandma, crying and scolding at the same time.

"Just where have you been all this time?" she asked. "We've been worried sick."

"Stop babbling. Can't you see I'm all right? I've been shopping, that's all," Grandma said.

Dad and I stared at each other, and I wondered if I wore the same dumb expression on my face as he did. It was Mom who asked the sensible questions. "Shopping? How did you ever get all the way downtown by yourself? And if that's what you wanted to do, why

171

didn't you ask? One of us would have taken you," she scolded.

Grandma gave her the kind of look reserved for someone who had made a totally ridiculous remark.

Mom was not smiling. "You still haven't told us how you got to town. Besides, I don't see any packages."

Grandma gazed at Mom with patience. "Look, I'm worn out," she said. "We'll talk in the morning." Then she started to go to her room.

Mom's mouth opened with the start of another barrage of questions, but Tommy intervened. "Perhaps I can fill you in," he said.

Mom swung her eyes over to Tommy for the first time and finally said, "Thank you for bringing my mother home, but I don't understand how . . ."

"I brought her on my bus," Tommy said.

"You mean she's been riding around with you all day?"

"Yes. I knew how worried you'd be, but I couldn't leave the bus long enough to call. Besides, I had a feeling if I turned my back, she'd scoot off." He paused long enough to grin. "Actually, I think Grandma had a good time. We talked and joked and she did a lot of sightseeing. She hadn't seen some of the sections we went through in years." He twisted his driver's cap in his hands and turned sober again. "I'm really sorry I couldn't notify you. I hope you understand there was just nothing I could do."

Mom was having a struggle to find the right words. It was going to cost her a lot of pride to acknowledge the fact that someone she'd pegged as a jailbird had done her an enormous favor.

I broke the silence. "We do understand, Tommy, and we can't thank you enough for taking such good care of Grandma. She couldn't have been in better hands." It was a short speech, but it gave Mom a chance to gather her wits.

"Yes, indeed, Tommy," she chimed in. "We appreciate your kindness. It must have been a trying day for you. Could you use a cup of coffee?"

"I sure could," Tommy responded. "But, first, I have to give you this. Grandma gave it to me to pay her fare. I figured it was worth more than she realized, so I brought it back."

He reached into his pocket and took out Mom's brooch.

The color left her face so rapidly I was afraid she'd pass out. I helped her to a chair.

I quickly said, "Mom thought the pin was lost. We never expected to see it again. It's an heirloom." I dug my hand firmly around Mom's shoulder. When she reached up and covered my hand with hers I knew she got the message.

"Yes, Tommy," she said meekly. "It seems we're in your debt for quite a lot today. It's true we'd given up the pin for lost. You can't know what it means to me to have it back."

She fell silent, looking fondly at the pin, smoothing the stone between her fingers. Then her shoulders began to shake, but instead of the tears we all braced ourselves for, she raised a face wreathed in smiles. Then came laughter. All I could think was that she was hysterical.

"Oh, I'm fine," she gasped, scarcely able to talk for laughing. "I was just thinking how funny it was that Grandma tried to pay her bus fare with an heirloom brooch. We're certainly lucky Tommy was there."

At that, we all collapsed in laughter. Tommy and I will announce our engagement soon. We have plans to be married at Christmas. I don't suppose it will be the most thrilling Christmas present Mom ever got—she's still a little cold with Tommy—but most of her antagonism is fading. Someday she'll love Tommy as much as I do.

In the meantime, we've all begun to keep a closer eye on Grandma. We took her to the doctor's for more extensive testing, and her failed memory is the beginning of Alzheimer's disease. All of us are very worried, but, for now, Grandma's going to stay with us and we're all doing our best to watch her carefully.

THE END

THE WAY HE
REMEMBERED ME

I was supposed to meet Maria at twelve for lunch. I left home
a little early so I'd have time to stop at the library. Lately, I'd been
reading until my eyes got so tired I was ready to fall asleep. I'd finished
my last library book the day before.

In the library, I quickly selected three books: one on applying for
a job, one on budgeting, and one on how to sell a house for the most
possible money. Those were the practical books I needed.

I saved the ones for fun—my "dessert ones," as I called them—for
last. I found an interesting-looking romantic novel and then I went
to my favorite section of the library, the travel section. I hesitated
between a book on Maine and one on New Zealand. Maine might be
possible someday if I scrimped and saved, so I pulled that book out of
its place and put it in the plastic bag I carried to help me manage my
increasing number of books. I started to walk away; then I went back,
put the book about Maine on the shelf, and pulled out the book on
New Zealand. After all, if I was going to dream, I might as well do it
in a big way!

"That was a hard decision," a voice behind me said.

I turned and faced a grinning middle-aged man dressed in faded
blue jeans and a partly opened red-and-white flannel shirt that revealed
a red T-shirt underneath. For a moment I thought he was a stranger,
then I recognized him.

"You're—" I began.

"That's right. Your friendly bus driver on the number 5—Wes
Philips, by name. I've missed you lately. Been on a trip?"

"Oh, no," I said quickly. "We never travel. I—my husband was in
the hospital so I had the car . . . he usually took it to work, you know."

I knew I was babbling like an idiot, but that had been my reaction
every time I had met someone who didn't know that Grant had died.

"He died two weeks ago," I continued. Then, before Mr. Philips
could look embarrassed and say how sorry he was, I said, "I've got to
go now."

I still felt nervous and shaky as I walked to my car after I'd checked
out the books. I knew I was behaving ridiculously. After all, Grant
had been in the hospital for over two months, most of that time in a
coma after his second stroke, the one that came three days after he
was hospitalized for the first time. That should have given me time to
prepare myself for losing him, time to prepare myself for the shock.

When I got to the restaurant where I was to meet Maria, I wished I hadn't promised to have lunch with her. Actually, I had told her no, but Mother had been with me. She'd insisted I go.

"You can't bury yourself in this house and not see your friends," she'd said.

"That's what I'm trying to tell her," Maria said to Mother like I wasn't even there. "She needs to get out once in a while. It's morbid the way she tries to shut herself up in the house."

"I don't shut myself up," I said. "It's just that I'm tired from the long hours I spent waiting in the hospital and from all the relatives who were here for the funeral and—"

"She'll go with you," Mother interrupted.

"Good," Maria said. "Let's make it twelve at Carney's. It's a nice place and not too expensive."

Maria seemed to be telling me I'd have to watch expenses from now on. And I would if I didn't find a job soon. I'd talked to Mr. Rodriguez, our lawyer, just two days before. He'd told me he thought he'd found a buyer for Grant's photography shop. The price he was getting for the shop would just about pay for Grant's medical expenses, the ones the insurance policy hadn't covered.

"I'm glad," I told him. "I would hate to be in debt."

He took off his glasses, rubbed his eyes, then put the glasses on again. "Oh, no, no—you won't be in debt, Mrs. Kim. Grant was always concerned about you. He took out a five-hundred-thousand-dollar life insurance policy years ago. Of course, five hundred thousand isn't what it used to be, but with careful spending habits, you can survive. And of course when you're older you'll have his Social Security. Let's see, how old are you now?"

"Fifty," I said. "Five hundred thousand dollars! I can manage fine with that and the job I'll get. I didn't expect anything like that. Grant never told me."

"That's very common," Mr. Rodriguez said. "A lot of men never discuss finances with their wives. Sometimes that leads to tragic results. The women don't know how to manage, and they spend all their insurance money in a year or two. Fortunately, Grant fixed things, so that won't happen to you. I'm to manage the money for you. I'll invest it in something safe, and you'll have the interest checks to live on."

I guess I should have felt relieved when I left his office, relieved and grateful that Grant had thought enough of me to provide for me after he was gone. I didn't, though. I felt sad because he hadn't told me what he was doing and because he hadn't trusted me enough to let me manage the money myself.

I got to the parking lot at the restaurant five minutes early. I sat in the car until twelve even though I saw Maria's car in the row behind mine. I dreaded going in and facing her. I wasn't sure why. After all,

Maria and her husband, Martin, had been friends of Grant's and mine for at least twenty years.

Maria looked at her watch when I stepped into the restaurant. "You just made it," she said.

"I stopped at the library," I told her, because it sounded as if she wanted an explanation of where I'd been.

"You'd be better off getting out more and reading less," she said. "There's our hostess. Table for two, please."

When we were seated she asked what I was going to do with all of the time on my hands.

"Look for a job," I replied.

She shook her head. "You've got to face reality, Faye. You're not a young woman anymore. Jobs aren't easy to come by. No one hires a woman over forty with no experience."

"I have experience," I said in a low, small voice. "I've kept books for Grant for the past fifteen years."

"Oh, that!" Maria dismissed my experience with a sweep of her hands. "You didn't really go to work. You did it all at home. And Grant was your husband. I don't think any firm would consider that as real working experience."

We ordered. Maria had a cheeseburger with French fries. I had a tomato stuffed with tuna salad. That seemed less fattening than a burger, and I'd made up my mind I was going to lose fifteen pounds. I had to get a job, no matter what Maria said! If I looked slimmer and younger, maybe it would help.

"You're not eating enough," Maria complained. "It's important to get plenty of nourishment since you've gone through so much. You have to keep up your health. Your face is looking drawn. Why don't you have something else with that?"

"You sound like my mother," I said.

"Someone has to take care of you now that poor Grant isn't around to do it."

After lunch, Maria suggested we go shopping. She'd read in the paper that there was a sale on jackets at her favorite department store. I agreed to go because I figured I'd have to look good for job interviews. My old jacket was worn and shabby. Every time I'd planned to replace it, some crisis had happened in our lives, a crisis that had taken money.

First, our son, Luke, had married before he finished college. Grant and I had helped him and his wife, Jade, by giving them a check every month.

The next crisis was when our teenage daughter, Elle, divorced her husband of a year and came home broke with a six-month-old baby girl. By the time Elle was on her feet, Grant's widowed father was too ill to live alone. He stayed with us for over a year until he died of a heart attack. Just as we were recovering from that, Grant had his first stroke.

When Maria and I got to the store she said, "You really do need a new jacket, Faye. Nothing too expensive, but if you find something on sale that's practical, you can look on it as an investment. After all, the way the economy looks, prices will be even higher by next year.

"Here," she said as she pulled a drab, blue-gray jacket from the size sixteens. "I'm going to try this on. Why don't you see if there's one like it in your size?"

I went to the size twelves. My eyes immediately lit on a lovely red jacket. Something about it was so cheerful and brave, I felt like I had to have it. I took it off the hanger and tried it on. It fit perfectly, and it seemed to bring a happy sparkle to my eyes and make my salt-and-pepper hair look less drab.

"You don't want that!" Maria said. "It's too young for you! Besides, it isn't practical. Now, this gray with just a hint of blue would be something you could wear with everything. Here, try it on."

I slipped out of the red coat and put on the gray one. My eyes didn't sparkle. My hair looked drab and dead.

"Very sensible," Maria said. "If you're going to look for a job, that's what you need. Nobody's going to hire a mature woman who's trying to look young. She'd seem too foolish."

Was she right? I wondered. Was I fooling myself about the red jacket? Was I fooling myself about everything? Was my judgment bad? Mother had always thought so, and Grant must have agreed with her. If he hadn't, he would have told me his plans for my future security. And he would have trusted me to invest the insurance money he'd left me.

"I'm going to take it," Maria was saying. "It's a good buy. Why don't you get it in your size? What difference does it make if we have the same jacket?"

"None at all," I said. "It's just that I'm not sure it's what I want. I think I'll take a few days to think about it."

"I suppose that's understandable," Maria said, although she sounded as if it really wasn't understandable to her. "This article I read said that after a woman has gone through a major crisis like a death in the family, she often reacts by not being able to make decisions. I guess that's better than making a lot of wrong ones. So you'd probably better hold off getting a job or doing anything else important for now."

But when Luke and Jade dropped by to see me that evening they seemed to think getting a job would be a good idea—if I could find one.

"Where's Jarred?" I asked when I noticed my grandson wasn't with them.

"We left him with a sitter," Jade explained. "We're on our way to have dinner with a contractor and his wife. It's sort of a business meeting. He and Luke may work together building a shopping center."

"Yes, we can't stay long, Mother," Luke said. "I stopped by because

I've just had a long talk with Mr. Rodriguez. The money Dad left you really isn't that much. I think you're going to have to consider going to work to supplement it. Either that, or sell this house. If you do decide to sell, I'll put it in the hands of a realtor I know, and I'll help you invest the money you get from it."

"I'm going to look for a job," I said. "Maria and Mother don't seem to think I have much chance of getting one, but I thought with my bookkeeping experience—"

"I suppose that's a possibility," Luke said. "But I was thinking more of a job as a companion to someone who doesn't need a nursing home, but who isn't able to be alone. For that type of work, your age won't be against you. It usually doesn't pay much, but includes free room and board. That way, you could save the interest from your insurance money for the time when you're no longer able to work. I'm sure that you never want to be a financial burden to others—"

"No, I don't want to be a financial burden," I agreed.

I felt guilty for even thinking of how he and Jade had been a financial burden to Grant and me.

No, actually, that was wrong. Grant hadn't given up anything because of them. I was the one who always gave things up. At the time, it had seemed fair.

After all, Grant worked hard and supported us and, like he said, all I had to do was keep up with housework and the small amount of bookkeeping I did for him.

True, I was always busy with my gardening and my sewing, but they were things I enjoyed. So why did I suddenly feel like I'd been cheated?

I pushed those negative thoughts out of my mind and got busy. During the next few days I worked out a budget, cleaned the house thoroughly to get it ready to sell, and concentrated on my diet.

Maria phoned almost every day to see how I was doing, and Mother either called or came by. Elle called once from California where she'd moved with her new husband. She seemed relieved when she found out Grant had left me some insurance. She said almost the same things Luke had said. "I know you wouldn't want to be financially dependent on us."

"No, I wouldn't," I said, "and I'm sure I can make it just fine as long as you or Luke don't come home to be financially dependent on me."

Later, I wondered what had gotten into me. I'd never talked like that in my whole life.

When the phone rang Friday morning, I thought it would be Maria or Mother. Instead, it was a stranger with a lilting, sensuous voice. "I'm Gloria March," she told me, "a business friend of Grant's. I just got back from a trip to Europe so I didn't find out about him until last night. Naturally, I'm terribly sorry. Perhaps this is too soon to bring this up, but if you decide to sell the shop, I'd be interested in buying it."

I explained I had decided to sell and my lawyer already had a buyer. All the time I was talking, I wondered why Grant had never mentioned Gloria to me. But then Grant undoubtedly had a lot of business acquaintances he never talked about.

"I'm sorry I'm too late," she said. "While I was in Europe, I decided I wanted to go into business for myself and his shop is in a beautiful location."

I told her I'd take her name and phone number and have my lawyer get in touch with her if the first deal fell through.

She thanked me and then said, "I'm going to ask one more favor. Grant has some pictures of mine that I'd like to have back. Would it be possible for you to meet me at his shop with a key?"

"I'd be glad to meet you," I said.

I realized I wasn't lying. If I got out of the house, I'd miss Mother's and Maria's morning calls. For some reason those calls were depressing me more every time they came.

Gloria March was a small, dark woman, as charming as her voice. "I've been doing freelance photography," she explained to me. "Grant liked my style and he entered some of my pictures in a contest while I was out of the country."

I unlocked the door to Grant's shop and we went in. Gloria hurried to a back room as if she'd been there many times. She found her photographs in a large folder, thanked me graciously, and said she had to run because she was meeting a friend for lunch.

I knew I should go, too. There was no reason for me to be in the shop. Mr. Rodriguez would take care of everything there. Nevertheless, I felt a strong urge to stay, to be in this place where Grant had spent most of his time, to try to understand the man who had once been so close to me, the man I suddenly knew I had lost long before he died.

How long had it been since Grant and I had been close, really close? How long had it been since we'd talked things over like friends or lovers? How long had I been living in my own little world of housework, knitting, gardening, and seeing friends while he spent his time at the shop or behind a newspaper or in front of a TV screen?

What had his life been like in this place where I practically never came because he didn't seem to want me here? I knew the number of clients he had. After all, I kept his books. And I knew how much money he made, but that was all I knew. Even when we were first married and passionately in love, Grant had believed that a woman's work was in the home, a man's job was to make a living for his family, and the two didn't mix—even in conversation. I'd become his bookkeeper only because his old one had quit one year, and after two desperate attempts to replace her with women who had made costly mistakes, he'd turned to me.

I went to the outer office and looked around the room at the large portraits Grant had on the walls to illustrate his work. I hadn't paid attention to them on the way in, but now I saw that one of them was a portrait of Gloria. I stared at it for a long time, hating myself for the jealousy I felt. It was nonsense, of course. Gloria's wasn't the only portrait. There was one of a baby, one of a mischievous-looking boy of about eight, one of a high school girl, and a wedding picture of a couple cutting a cake.

I remembered the picture Grant had taken of me just a few months before his stroke. He took it because Mother had suggested it. She wanted one of me, one of her grandchildren, and one of her great-grandchildren for her birthday. It had been a good picture of me, so good that I'd had some small prints made to give to friends. Grant could have had it on his wall, but instead he had the portrait of Gloria March.

No wonder! I found myself thinking. *She's sexier and more glamorous.* I'd looked somewhat like her when I was younger. I'd still been slender then, and my hair had been long and dark. Our eyes were very much the same, and she was wearing my favorite color—red.

I sighed and went to the small office in back where I knew Grant's private things were. I looked through the drawers, not sure what I expected to find. Mr. Rodriguez had said his secretary would go through things, so there was no reason for me to upset myself by coming by. Miss Lewis had worked for him for years, so she would know what to keep and what to throw away.

There didn't seem to be anything interesting in the desk drawers, just business papers and a few magazines on photography. Then, beneath one of the magazines, I found a picture of myself. It wasn't one that Grant had taken. It was an old photograph taken before we were married. My hair flowed long and full around my face, and I was smiling with an inner light because I was so happy that Grant and I had found each other.

All the portraits he had taken of me, yet it was that old photograph that he had saved!

I started to close the drawer, but the magazine I'd lifted up stuck. As I loosened it, another picture fell out, one of the small ones I'd had made from my last portrait. I stared at it in amazement. Grant had drawn over it the way a child draws over a picture in a magazine, making bearded ladies with buckteeth.

Oh, he hadn't put a beard on me or changed my teeth. He had used a pencil to make my short hair long, and he'd used his red pen to put more color in my lips and to color my sensible beige blouse red.

I stared at the picture for a long time trying to understand. When he'd married me, I'd been a warm, impulsive person who didn't agree with many of his conservative ideas. Slowly, over the years, I'd become the woman I thought he wanted me to be. Yet all the time he'd wanted

180

me to be the woman he'd courted and married.

When I left the shop I did something I hadn't done for years. I acted on impulse and went to the store where I'd looked at the jacket with Maria. There was still a red one in my size. I bought it without even the smallest twinge of conscience. I also bought some lipstick and some eye makeup.

When I got home, the phone was ringing. It was Maria wanting to go to lunch the next day. "Weekends are supposed to be the worst times for a widow," she explained. "It'll be good for you to get out of the house."

I told her no as politely as I could and explained that Saturdays weren't that bad for me because Grant had always worked six days a week. I was used to spending Saturdays without him.

"Martin still works Saturdays, too," she said. "That's why I thought it would be a good time for us to get together."

I thanked her again and told her I had other plans. Maybe I was being a coward, but I wanted to wear my new jacket and new makeup, and I wasn't sure I had the courage to face Maria the first time I wore them.

I should have known I couldn't get away with anything. The next morning just as I'd finished dressing to go out, Mother and Maria came by.

"You bought the red one!" Maria exclaimed. "Really, Faye, I think it's too bright for someone your age."

"A black or a gray one would be more practical," Mother said. "Red doesn't go with everything. Where are you going, anyway?"

"To the library," I said in a small voice.

"You were just there last week," Maria said.

"I read fast," I said, trying to explain.

"You read too much," Mother said.

"I won't much longer," I replied. "I going job hunting Monday. That's why I bought the red jacket—to give me some courage."

Mother just shook her head, and Maria suggested we meet for lunch after I went to the library. Mother looked at me as if she dared to say no. I'm not sure what it was. Maybe it was the memory of what Grant had done to my picture, or maybe it was the courage my new makeup and jacket gave me. Anyway, I apologized in a firm voice. "I haven't got time. I'm going spend several hours in the library doing research on writing job résumés."

My new firm voice worked. Mother didn't say a word, and Maria said I should phone her sometime.

I didn't feel brave on the way to the library. I felt like a middle-aged woman who was making a fool out of herself. Nevertheless, when I got to the library I held my head high and tried to walk the way Gloria March had done, like I knew I was attractive and I had all the confidence in the world.

I did something else different. I went to the dessert part of the library first. I felt like I needed a book for sheer pleasure to lift my spirits to match my red jacket.

As soon as I got there, I recognized the bus driver, Wes, pulling out a book about Australia.

I smiled and said, "Hi. Do you take real trips or imaginary ones?"

He smiled in a rather reserved way and said, "Both."

I felt put down. Did he think I was being too forward? Good-looking, single middle-aged men were in short supply. Probably a lot of women made fools of themselves over him.

I wanted to hurry away, but I forced myself to pick out a book, any book. I didn't bother to read the title. I put it in my bag and turned.

As I did, Wes smiled and said, "For a few minutes I didn't recognize you. You look great. What did you do to grow ten years younger?"

"It's the red jacket," I said, beaming.

A heavyset lady who reminded me of Maria came up. She glared at both of us and said, "Shh!"

Wes winked at me and formed the word "lunch" with his mouth.

I knew what Mother and Maria would say if they were with me: I didn't know him well enough. Besides, Grant had been dead too short a time for me to go out with a man, even for a casual lunch. But I wasn't listening to Mother or Maria any longer. I was listening to my own inner self.

I smiled and nodded.

We walked out of the library together. There would be time for me to go back later and read up on résumés. One has to grab good things when they're offered. That's something the girl I had once been had known, the girl Grant had loved and married. She was the same girl who could have held his love forever if she hadn't foolishly tried to change. She was still there inside me, struggling to get out. I had a feeling she wouldn't have to struggle much longer.

THE END

AND FLUFF
MAKES THREE . . .

It was already four o'clock in the afternoon when Vito motioned me over to the central desk. I was just checking off shift and in a hurry to get home. Aside from that, I always gave Vito Carmichael a wide berth anyway.

Vito is big and portly, with a shiny bald head. He's also a typical male chauvinist, and he gave me a terrible time when I first started working as a traffic officer seven months before. Lately, he'd eased up on the sexist jokes a bit, but I approached his desk warily. Somehow I didn't like the grin on his face.

"You live at thirty-two Morris, don't you?" he asked, one hand over the desk phone. I nodded, feeling a nudge of apprehension.

"This guy lives at thirty-one Morris. He's complaining about a dog at thirty-two. Is it your dog?"

"Probably," I admitted, trying not to get into a flap in front of Vito. But Vito wasn't fooled. He knew I felt embarrassed. His grin broadened.

"You have one angry neighbor."

"Tell him I'll be right there," I snapped, and hurried away.

In the lobby, I ran into Maggie, the only other woman in the city police department, but I didn't stop to chat. I liked Maggie, but we didn't have a lot in common. She was married to a fellow officer and was in a different division. Besides, she was older, with a dignified bearing that somehow just seemed to command respect from the guys, a respect I had to fight for tooth and nail. Outside, I hurried to my car, cursing Fluff under my breath.

Fluff wasn't even my dog. He belonged to Aunt Ruth, who was vacationing in Florida, along with my parents. My sister, Cathy, had a preschooler, plus a new baby, and understandably couldn't care for a spoiled mutt to boot. So I was stuck with Fluff, and the week that had just passed seemed like an eternity. He barked half the night, chewed up slippers and handbags, tipped over garbage bags, and shredded newspapers. The amount of havoc he created was incredible for a pint-sized poodle, and now this—a complaint to the police from the artist who lived next door.

I'd seen him, but he hadn't seen me. Our kitchen window overlooked the small cottage next door. The old couple who'd lived there for years moved away and rented the cottage now and then to college students. The artist had moved in a week or so before my parents left, but I hadn't paid much attention to him. Nobody stayed in the cottage long enough to really get acquainted with them. Besides, I wasn't keen on strangers knowing my parents were away and I was alone in the house. I'd seen the fellow outside, though. He often painted in the garden early in the morning or late in the afternoon. He was tall and, I had to admit, attractive.

And he evidently doesn't like yapping poodles, I thought as I parked the car in front and started walking around to the backyard where Fluff was kept.

Fluff's shrill, excited yapping immediately assaulted my eardrums.

The artist was leaning against our back fence, looking into the yard at Fluff. When he noticed me, he stared at me for a long moment, his eyes taking in my uniform, my legs, my face, my hair, and goodness only knows what else.

"Hello," I said stiffly.

He straightened and smiled. "Hello. My name's Joe Rawlings. I'm the one who called in the complaint. I'm sorry to trouble you, Officer, but this animal is definitely disturbing my peace."

"It's all right—I'll quiet him down," I said quickly.

"But nobody's home. I've knocked and knocked. Nobody answers the door."

"I know," I answered. "I live there."

His eyes widened. "You do? You mean I'm living next door to a police officer?"

"Yes. I'm in the traffic division," I explained. His eyes were very warm, I decided, and except for the paint-splattered jeans and faded shirt, he was quite good-looking.

"Then this is your dog."

"He belongs to my Aunt Ruth. I'm just caring for him while she vacations with my parents."

"You live here with your parents?"

"Yes."

"No husband?"

"No," I admitted, forgetting all caution.

"I'm not married, either," he volunteered, smiling again. His teeth were white and even.

"You're an artist, aren't you?" I asked, definitely interested now.

"In a way. I teach high-school art in Pine Lake. I'm only here for three months, taking an advanced art composition course."

By this time Fluff, hearing my voice, was flinging himself wildly against the gate. I smiled at Joe, fumbling with the latch gate. The lock came up, but the gate didn't open the way it usually did. Impulsively, I pressed all my weight against the gate. It gave suddenly. I would have fallen if strong hands hadn't steadied me.

"Thank you," I stammered, feeling like a fool. He was close to me, too close. I took a step backward. He released my arms, his eyes amused.

"My pleasure," he murmured.

184

Just then Fluff decided to give me his usual greeting. He flung himself at my legs, almost knocking me down.

"Fluff, stop it!" I shrieked, trying to fend him off. After a couple of sharp taps on his rear, Fluff backed away, sat down on his haunches, and whined reproachfully.

"Does he always do that?" Joe asked, his eyes still amused.

"No. Sometimes he greets me by ripping my skirt or hose. He isn't stupid, he knows better; he's just spoiled. My aunt doesn't have any children, you see—"

I didn't get to finish the sentence. Maybe Fluff thought Joe had been trying to harm me when he steadied my arm, or perhaps Fluff was just suddenly possessed by some wild, canine insanity. Whatever motivated him, he suddenly made a charge for Joe's legs, his needle-sharp teeth bared.

Joe let out a yell, even though it was only his jeans that Fluff clamped down on.

"Stop it!" I ordered, trying to pull the demented little jaws apart. My impulse was to choke the mutt, but I was afraid I might accidentally kill him.

And then I remembered the broom. It was still on the back porch where I'd swept the back steps that morning. I raced for the broom. When I returned, Fluff still had his teeth sunk into Joe's jeans. Joe was desperately trying to get a hold on the writhing, squirming ball of fur, but wasn't having much luck.

"Stand up!" I yelled at Joe. He straightened, surprised, and I aimed a good, hard whack at Fluff's rump with the broom. Only Fluff was quicker. He leaped away just as I let the broom fly. The broomstick struck Joe's shinbone with a dull thud.

"Oh, no!" I gasped, throwing the broom down and rushing to Joe. "Did I hurt you?"

Joe looked at me, his warm, friendly eyes cold. "I've had enough of this nonsense," he said stiffly. "That dog attacked one of my legs and you tried to finish me off on the other. . . ."

I didn't even get a chance to apologize. Fluff charged again, and what happened next happened so fast that I didn't really see it.

It was just an impression. Joe was stomping and kicking, trying to fend off Fluff's attack, and somehow the two of them got tangled up together and then Joe fell right on top of Fluff. Fluff yelped, squirmed from beneath Joe, and then ran to the fence gate, whining. I hurried to Joe, who was still crumpled up on the grass.

"Are you all right?" I asked, leaning over him anxiously.

He sat up and glared at me. "Don't come near me," he said hoarsely. "Please—just stay away."

I backed away, feeling sick inside.

"I think I'm going to sue you," Joe went on. "I'm going to sue you,

185

your aunt, that poor excuse for a dog, and the entire police department."

"The police department doesn't have anything to do with this," I snapped. "I'm sorry. I know Fluff has acted badly."

"Acted badly?" Joe repeated loudly. "If that isn't the understatement of the year!"

He made a move to get up and then sank back on the ground, wincing.

"What is it?" I asked, heart sinking.

"My ankle. It hurts."

"Let me see." I knelt and pushed the left pants leg away from the ankle, the one Fluff had been aiming for.

"It's my other ankle that hurts," Joe growled.

I quickly pushed up the other pants leg.

"Oh, no!" I moaned. The flesh around his right ankle was swollen and ugly. Joe looked for a moment, too, and then pulled the pants leg down over the swollen ankle.

"It's okay," he said. "I must have sprained it when I fell. It's a weak ankle and I've sprained it before. If you'll get that fool dog out of the way, I'll try to get up."

"No, you mustn't move," I said firmly. "Your ankle could be broken. I'd better call an ambulance."

I moved to get up, but Joe was quicker. His strong fingers closed over my wrist.

"My dear young lady . . . What's your name, anyway?"

"Tiffany—Tiffany Mitchell." His face was close to mine and I could see golden flecks in his eyes.

"Listen, Tiffany. You're a very pretty young woman and I like you a lot, in spite of the fact that you've tried to kill me, but you're not deciding right now what I need. Is that clear?"

"Your ankle looks awful. It could very well be broken. I'm trained in first aid, and moving someone with broken bones—"

"You didn't understand what I just said, did you?" he broke in.

"Yes, of course I understand, but you're making a mistake."

"Then let me make it. Just lock that dog up somewhere so I can get to my car. I'll go to a doctor and maybe have an X-ray done, okay?"

"Okay," I agreed reluctantly. His fingers loosened from my wrist, the warmth of his touch lingering.

I went to get Fluff and put him in the house. Fluff obviously wasn't physically hurt by the fracas, but he was still hyper. Just when I would get near enough to pick him up, he would bound out of my reach. Finally, I conceived the idea of luring him into Joe's backyard. It was fenced, too, and would solve the problem for the moment. I opened the gate and when Fluff raced in after me, I locked it. Then I went back to Joe.

"I still think I should call an ambulance," I said as Joe hobbled

186

beside me, one arm around my shoulders. I could tell he was trying not to lean against me, so I circled one arm around his waist.

"Are you trying to take advantage of me in my weakened condition?" he asked, smiling down at me.

I could feel the warm blood rush to my face. "Don't be silly," I snapped. "I'm just trying to keep you from falling."

When we got to his car, I opened the door and he slid behind the wheel with difficulty.

"This is ridiculous. You can't drive with that foot," I said, watching him.

He nodded. "I think you're right. Would you please call a cab?"

"Push over and I'll drive you to the hospital," I said firmly. "There's no point in going to a doctor's office. You would just be sent to the hospital for X-rays, so we'll save time going directly there."

"All right," he agreed and, wincing, moved over.

I backed his little car out of the driveway and headed toward City Hospital. I was trying to concentrate on my driving. I wanted to get Joe to the hospital as soon as possible, so I didn't say much. I could feel Joe's gaze on my face, but I ignored it.

"At least you seem to know how to drive," he said when we were about halfway there.

I felt a rush of anger. "I know how to do a lot of things," I answered evenly, trying not to let him get to me. "Just because Aunt Ruth's dog is crazy doesn't mean I am."

"I wasn't insinuating you were crazy. I was just wondering how you ever got on the police force. I mean, you just don't look like a police officer."

And then the anger did boil over inside me. The frustration of all those months of trying to prove myself at the station, knowing that I was watched more closely than any of the others, listening to all the sexist jokes, trying to ignore the thinly veiled disrespect from men at least half the time I gave tickets, having the judges scrutinize my work to a ridiculous degree—suddenly it was all too much.

"You're a typical male chauvinist, you know that?" I flung at Joe. "You don't know anything about my work, but because I'm a woman, you just naturally assume that I'm an incompetent officer and have no business working for the police department!"

"You just ran a stop sign," Joe interrupted. "And there's a police car behind us. I think he's signaling."

I didn't blindly run the sign. I'd paused, but not as long as I would or should have if I hadn't been in a rush to get Joe to the hospital. A glance in the rearview mirror told me that a police car was indeed signaling us. Feeling like an utter fool, I pulled over to the curb. The police car stopped behind us and an officer got out. It was Bill Friedrichs, one of the old-timers on the force.

187

"Why, hello, Tiffany," he said, surprised to see me behind the wheel. I nodded, trying to smile. Bill looked from me to Joe, and then back to me.

"Tiffany, did you know you ran a stop sign back there?" he asked awkwardly, his expression slightly embarrassed. No officer enjoys catching a fellow officer breaking the law.

"Officer, it's really my fault," Joe broke in quickly. "I was attacked by a mad dog. Tiffany here rescued me and was rushing me to the hospital. I'm in terrible pain. See, Officer, just look. . . ."

Joe was rolling up his pants leg, and by this time his ankle looked a mess, swollen like a balloon.

Bill nodded. "I'd better give you a police escort," he said crisply. "Follow me." He turned on his siren and we went flying behind him.

At the emergency entrance of the hospital, Bill went in to arrange for a wheelchair while I helped Joe get himself out of the car.

"I don't need a wheelchair, for Pete's sake," Joe protested as a couple of attendants started out with the empty chair.

"Of course you do," I answered. "Are you still in terrible pain?"

"No. I just said that for the cop's benefit. Actually, I can't feel anything."

"That means it's probably broken," I said, fighting back tears. That's all I needed, to break down and bawl.

"Don't worry your pretty little head about it," Joe snapped.

The attendants helped him into the chair and wheeled him away. Inside the emergency reception room, I told Bill everything that had happened and he told me to come down to the station and make out a report.

"I'll give you a ride down and back," he said. "It won't take long. It's correct procedure and, in the event your friend sues you, it will help."

I went down to the station with Bill and filed a report. I knew Fluff had had all his rabies shots—just in case he'd managed to nip Joe—but that wouldn't help my status around the station. I would be in for a lot of kidding. But I wasn't really thinking about that; I was worried about Joe's ankle. When I finished the report, Bill patted my shoulder.

"Don't take it so hard, kid. Things like this happen all the time."

His kindness touched me and I managed a smile. By the time Bill dropped me back off at the hospital, Joe was finished with his X-rays and treatment. He came hobbling into the reception room on a crutch, his ankle bandaged.

"Just a bad sprain," he announced, grinning an I-told-you-so grin at me.

Relief washed over me. "That's wonderful," I breathed.

"Yeah." We stood there for a moment, smiling at each other. "The office down the hall wants some information about the dog. I told them you'd attend to it."

That took another five minutes or so. By the time we got back out to the car, it was almost dusk.

"I'm glad it wasn't worse," I said as we drove out of the hospital parking lot. "And I'll pay all your medical expenses, of course."

"That won't be necessary. I'm insured to the hilt. And you can forget about what I said about suing you. I was in a state of shock when I said that."

"But I wouldn't blame you if you did," I protested.

"Not if you were a guy and the girl had the softest hair you'd ever seen and the loveliest green eyes."

"They're gray," I corrected, my heart skipping a beat.

"Will you stop arguing with me, woman?" he demanded, and we both laughed.

"But you should at least let me pay for some of the expenses," I said after a moment, still thinking about it.

"Let's make a deal," he answered smiling. "There's a diner down the road. All this ruckus has made me hungry. You can buy me a hamburger and a root beer, and we'll call it even."

I turned into the diner, and we ordered hamburgers, French fries, and big mugs of root beer.

"Do you have a boyfriend?" Joe asked when the waitress went away with our order.

"No," I answered quickly. "I was engaged last year, briefly. But it didn't work out."

"What happened?" he asked quietly. "Or would you rather not talk about it?"

I looked at him. His eyes were thoughtful, patient, interested. *He's probably a very good teacher,* I thought.

"I don't mind," I said. "I just decided I really didn't want to get married, at least not to Tony. He's a nice guy, but his mother spoiled him. He wasn't as interested in me personally as in having a woman to wait on him and baby him. I guess I'm too independent."

"There's nothing wrong with being independent," Joe said slowly. "I don't care for the clinging-vine type myself. I rather enjoy independent women."

"You do?" I asked, feeling as though I could drown in his warm eyes.

"Sure."

"But you wouldn't marry one, I bet."

"Why not?"

"But you haven't married at all—"

"I just haven't found the right girl."

I looked away, heart pounding. He was a most disturbing man.

Our food order didn't take long to come. I picked up one of the big mugs of root beer and started to hand it to Joe. But he picked that moment to bend down and check the bandage on his ankle. I didn't see

189

him bend down because I was reaching for the hamburgers with my other hand. When he straightened up, he bumped into my hand that was holding the root beer. The icy contents of the mug poured down his front and into his lap.

"Oh, I'm so sorry." I gasped, looking at his wet shirt and pants. "Here, I have some tissue," I babbled, reaching for my purse.

Only I didn't have my purse. In my excitement, I'd left it on the back porch when I'd made the ill-fated decision about the broom. I carried my identification wallet in the jacket of my uniform, but all the other incidentals were in my purse.

Joe reached over and took the empty mug out of my hand, put it on the table, picked up the extra paper napkins on the tray, and started trying to soak up some of the excess root beer from his clothes. I watched him, wishing I were dead. Why was I so stupid and clumsy around him? Usually, I was a very competent person.

Joe paused, looking at me.

"Tiffany, tell me something. Why do you want to kill me?"

"That's silly," I protested.

"It sounds silly. Nevertheless, too many horrible things have happened to me in the very short time that I've known you. Don't you like me?"

I stared at him, and then suddenly the absurdity of the situation struck me—or maybe it was just sheer anxiety. I started laughing. I couldn't help it. I laughed until the tears came and then I laughed some more.

"You're a sadist, too," Joe said when I calmed down.

I wiped my eyes, choking back more hysterical laughter. I could tell he didn't really think I was a sadist. "No, I'm not," I answered. "And to prove it, I'm going to buy you another root beer."

"Never mind. We'll share the one that's left. There are two straws, aren't there?"

And that's what we did. We ate the hamburgers and French fries and took turns sipping the root beer through long straws.

"This is ridiculous," I giggled over the root beer.

"I think it's fun," Joe answered. "It reminds me of my students."

"Do you like teaching?" I asked, curious.

"Very much. The kids are great. I want to have an art show this fall and exhibit some of my students' work along with my own. As a matter of fact, I was just trying to finish a painting today that I want to include in my show. It's one of the best I've ever done."

"May I see it?"

"Sure. When we get home, if you like. It's still out in my backyard. The scene is the back hedge and the birdhouse."

I swallowed hard, remembering I'd locked Fluff in Joe's backyard.

"Is the painting on an easel?" I asked, trying not to sound alarmed.

"Yes. Why?"

190

"Oh, no reason in particular, but I think we'd better go if you're finished."

"I'm finished. And thank you for a delicious snack. I enjoyed it, even if I did have to swim through a river of root beer."

"You're welcome," I answered, ignoring his last remark. I signaled the waitress, and she came over with the bill.

And then I remembered something else. My money was also in my purse on the back porch.

Red-faced, I turned to Joe. "I'm sorry, but I left my purse at home," I mumbled. "You'll have to pay the bill."

Joe's eyes widened and then he started to laugh. I sat, red-faced and annoyed, as Joe, still laughing, paid and tipped the waitress. "Tiffany, you're fantastic," he said. "I've never been out with a woman like you before."

I drove out of the lot and started home. When we got there, I tried to park in front of Joe's house, as it would be easier for him to get inside the cottage with his crutch.

"No, go down the driveway to the backyard," he insisted. "I want to show you my painting."

"It's getting dark," I said nervously. "It can wait until tomorrow."

"There's still plenty of light. I have to take the canvas in, anyway."

I pulled around to the gate and Joe got out with his crutch. "Wait a minute," I cautioned as Joe started to unlock the gate.

He turned, startled. "Why?"

"Because I locked Fluff in your yard," I explained quickly. "Wait while I get his chain."

"Good thinking," Joe said. "I'll definitely wait."

When I got back with Fluff's chain, Joe opened the gate and we went into the yard. I stepped inside first, hoping against hope that Fluff hadn't done anything to Joe's painting. But I should have known. No day so full of catastrophes could possibly have a good ending.

The easel was lying on its side and the canvas was ripped in shreds, scattered from one end of the yard to the other. Fluff was curled up into a ball on one of the larger scraps of canvas. Evidently exhausted from his day's activities, he was sound asleep.

"Oh, no!" Joe moaned, looking around the yard. "Oh, no!" His expression was that of a woebegone child. It was the last straw. I burst into tears.

After a moment, I felt Joe's arm around me. "Don't cry, Tiffany, please."

"I feel so awful!" I sobbed. "It was one of your best paintings!"

"So what? I can do hundreds of others. Now please—just don't cry. It doesn't matter."

"But you said—"

"Never mind what I said. All the paintings in the whole world

191

aren't worth your tears." His hand was underneath my chin, holding my face close to his.

"How can you say that?" I blubbered. "I know you think I'm an incompetent officer. . . ."

"That isn't true. I think you're a warm, lovely person who can obviously do many things. I would be very proud to have you for my friend."

"You would?" I asked breathlessly, feeling I could drown in his eyes, his closeness. When he kissed me, gently, my heart felt as if it would burst. On the second kiss, he didn't let go and I seemed to melt into him. And then Fluff came to life again. He sat up, barking.

Joe and I broke apart, and Joe braced himself as though for an attack. I hurried over to Fluff with the chain, but evidently his nap had put him in a good humor. He licked my hand and didn't even bark at Joe.

"Well—uh—I guess I'd better take Fluff home," I said awkwardly, a little embarrassed now at how eagerly I'd returned Joe's kisses. "Will you be all right?"

"I think so." He was smiling deep into my eyes.

"Would you like me to bring over some coffee and cake later?" I asked.

"I'd love it. If you promise not to spill it on me, that is."

"I promise," I said happily.

And I haven't spilled anything on him for two whole years now, including the eighteen months we've been married. Actually, Joe does most of the cooking now because he likes to cook and I'm expecting our first baby soon.

And guess who else lives with us? Fluff. Aunt Ruth decided to move to Florida and couldn't take Fluff with her. Nobody else in the family wanted him because he's so spoiled, so Joe and I took him. After all, as Joe is fond of telling everyone, he and I probably wouldn't even be together if it weren't for Fluff. And wouldn't that have been awful?

THE END

TRAPPED IN MY CAR ON
A LONELY ROAD

I pushed back my breakfast plate. "Oh, Grandma," I said, more sharply than I meant, "why do you have to be so stubborn?"

Grandma's eyes looked hurt, but she said reasonably, "I've told you already, Lana, I want to be there for Decoration Day to clean your grandpa's grave and put flowers on it."

"There's not even such a thing as Decoration Day anymore," I argued. "It's Memorial Day now, and that's on Monday."

"At my church there is," Grandma said patiently. "We take baskets of food to eat at lunchtime, and we stay all day at the cemetery."

"But you'll be eighty-two in July, Grandma," I pleaded. "You're too old to ride the bus all the way to Rock Hill alone."

"I know very well how old I am," Grandma said crisply. "You don't have to keep reminding me. I've put flowers on your grandpa's grave every Decoration Day for fifteen years." Her eyes misted. "I feel like he's expecting me."

I had a vision of perky little Grandma, if there hadn't been a bus to Rock Hill, taking her striped suitcase and starting out to walk almost two hundred miles to Rock Hill for her church outing.

My husband, Chuck, and I had planned all week to drive Grandma home that Saturday. But about midnight on Friday we'd had a phone call that Chuck's older sister, Janice, had been admitted to intensive care with a massive heart attack in Florida, seven hundred miles away. Chuck had hastily shaved and dressed while I packed his bag. He had kissed me, said, "I'll call tomorrow night," and driven off into the night, both of us in our concern forgetting our plan for taking Grandma home the next day.

Even though I was up late helping Chuck prepare for his trip, I got up early as usual to wake our seventeen-year-old son, Tommy, for his job as stocker at the supermarket downtown. And there Grandma sat in the living room, already dressed to go, with her purse in her lap, her suitcase by her chair, and an expectant look on her face.

My fingers flew to my mouth in dismay. "Grandma! We completely forgot." I told her about the phone call after she'd gone to bed, and Chuck's sudden trip to be at his sister's bedside.

"Well, I'll just ride the bus," Grandma said calmly.

Tommy was putting powder in his shoes and pulling on a second pair of socks, preparing for his grueling day at the supermarket. His job was to pack bags of groceries and carry them to cars in the parking lot. But even though he sometimes had blisters as big as half-dollars on the bottoms of his feet when the store closed at midnight on Saturday, Tommy was proud of his job. It hadn't been easy for him to find work.

"Mom's right, Grandma. You shouldn't ride the bus. There's only the local today. It stops at every stop and takes about five hours to get there." Tommy tied his shoes carefully. He and I saw by Grandma's face that we were far from convincing her.

"Tell you what, Mom," he suggested. "If you'll drop me off at the store, you can drive Grandma home in my old pickup."

There wasn't time to think it over. It was twenty minutes before time for Tommy to clock in, and I was still in my pajamas. Allowing fourteen minutes for the drive downtown, I had six minutes to get ready. After bolting the back door, I shoved the milk and butter into the refrigerator on my way to the bedroom. I snatched a pair of jeans, a knit top, and some underwear out of my bureau. Darn! Tommy was in the bathroom. I dressed in the bedroom, put on sneakers, and picked up my purse. No more time.

Tommy put Grandma's suitcase in the bed of the truck, and I helped her up into the seat. I asked Tommy to drive until we got to the store so I could see how he shifted the gears. I had, years earlier, driven a car with a standard shift, but I was afraid I'd forgotten how to operate the clutch pedal. In fact, I had hardly driven at all for years. We had only one car, which Chuck drove to work. When he wasn't working and we went somewhere together, Chuck drove.

"See, it's simple," Tommy said. I watched his left and right feet alternate smoothly as he shifted the gears.

Grandma wrinkled her nose at the condition of Tommy's truck.

"We went out to a fast-food place last night," Tommy said, grinning apologetically. The litterbag was overflowing, food wrappers and soda cans were under our feet on the floorboard, and a half-empty soda bottle was still in a holder on the dashboard.

"Looks like you've set up housekeeping in here," I commented, looking at Tommy's row of gadgets. He proudly pointed out his CB radio, his stereo system, and demonstrated his extra horn that sounded just like a cow.

The truck rode roughly. Tommy said that was because of the extra-wide tires he'd put on it. When he got out at the store and I slid over under the steering wheel, I found that they made the truck hard to steer, too.

Tommy quickly kissed Grandma and dashed for the entrance of the supermarket, saying, "Bye, Mom. I'll get somebody to take me home tonight."

For the first few blocks, my mind was occupied with getting the feel of the truck. My starts at green lights were pretty jerky at first, but once I got over being nervous, I kind of liked being up high where I could see better. One thing I found out in a hurry: If I let the clutch

194

out too fast with those big tires, the truck didn't go anywhere. It just sat there and spun.

I was more than a little worried about what Chuck would say about my driving Grandma home to Rock Hill alone. He had never wanted me to make that trip without him. Not only were the roads steep, winding, and lonely, but there were, Chuck said, some tough characters living up in those hills.

I'm going to miss Grandma, I thought, choking up a little. I'd hoped that this time she might agree to stay on and live with us. We all loved her dearly. My mother, Grandma's only child, had died when I was seventeen, so Grandma seemed more like my mother than my grandmother.

We'd brought Grandma down six weeks earlier for a cataract operation on her left eye. But for several days now she'd been hinting wistfully about going back home to see about her flowers and her cats. A neighbor had promised to look after everything while Grandma was with us. We had no excuse to insist on her living with us. Grandma was active and alert. She kept herself and her home spotless, and her flower garden was her pride and joy.

I knew how much Grandma's church meant to her, too. I still enjoyed, when we visited her, attending services at Mt. Cross. They sang from hymnbooks they called "The Sacred Harp." There were only four notes in their scale, and each of the notes was pictured in an odd little shape. Grandma said that was because long ago a lot of people couldn't read. They said the notes instead of words when they sang, like: *Fa So La Do.* I thought the singing was beautiful. There were many older people in Grandma's church. The men sat on one side and the women on the other.

The scenery was fantastic driving up through the hills to Rock Hill. Much of the time we had the road all to ourselves. Grandma and I rolled down our windows so we could enjoy all the good smells—the pines, the sweet shrubs, the wild honeysuckle.

We reached Grandma's house about noon. I figured I'd have time to drive Grandma to the country store to stock up on food and still get home before dark, in time for Chuck's phone call.

At the store, I helped Grandma select all the food she thought she'd need for a while, plus special items for her to prepare for the basket she'd take to the cemetery the next day. All the time I was dreading leaving her, hoping I could keep from crying. I didn't want Grandma to feel bad about insisting on coming home.

In concentrating on what Grandma might need for her kitchen, and in my efforts to control my emotions, I forgot the one thing that comes automatically to anyone who drives a car regularly. I didn't check the gas gauge in Tommy's truck.

In spite of my good intentions, I wasn't able to leave Grandma without tears. But she assured me that she'd be fine. "I appreciate your driving me home, Lana dear. Drive safely." Grandma stood among her flowers and waved as long as I could see her in my rearview mirror.

It was lonely driving back down through the hills. I wished I'd asked Tommy to show me how to work his CB radio. Although it was only mid-afternoon, the tall pines on the steep hillsides shaded the road from the sunlight, making it seem gloomy and foreboding.

I'd been driving about an hour when the motor sputtered out. I let the truck roll to the shoulder of the road and set the emergency brake. It was only then that I remembered to look at the gas gauge. It stood at E. *Oh, how stupid!* I thought. At first I was too angry at myself to be frightened. Then I thought about my expected phone call from Chuck. *He doesn't even know where I am,* I thought in consternation.

And Tommy. He usually went out for pizza with his friends after the store closed at midnight. It would be at least one o'clock before he knew I was missing.

Someone will come by soon, I consoled myself. I sat and waited for a passerby to stop and help me.

But there weren't any passersby, not for nearly an hour. Then, at intervals, there were several cars going in the opposite direction. I looked as helpless and wistful as I knew how, but although the drivers stared, none of them stopped.

Then four young men, walking, emerged from a side road that wasn't much more than a path. They sauntered curiously toward the truck. I'd been so worried, it was a big relief to know that I wasn't utterly alone with night coming on.

As soon as the men got within speaking distance, I rolled down the window. "I'm out of gas," I called. "Do you know where I can get some?"

"Got any money?" the man in front asked.

"Well, yes, a little," I answered. Something about their faces, now that they were closer, made me quickly roll my window back up.

The men surrounded the truck. The one I'd spoken to, a burly young man of about twenty, slapped the window with his open hand. "Open up!" he demanded.

I shook my head.

Grinning, the men began rocking the truck from side to side. *They're going to turn it over,* I thought in panic. On my right was a steep ravine, the edge less than two feet from the truck's right wheels. I couldn't believe what was happening. The men were going to roll me down into that ravine, just for fun! I hung onto the steering wheel as hard as I could.

Just as I thought the truck would surely go over, the men stopped their rocking. "Open up!" the burly one yelled again, looking mean and ugly. He kicked the door of the truck. One of the others went to the

196

side of the road and picked up a rock the size of a football. He brought it over to the truck and raised it over his head to hit the window.

I was terrified. I flipped open my seatbelt and scooted across the seat to the right side, thinking I might jump out the door and roll down the ravine to try to escape them. But the other three men quickly circled the truck to block the right-hand door.

The window shattered. The man laughed as he reached in through the broken window to pull up the lock. Some deep instinct had made me grab the glass bottle from its holder in the dashboard. Holding it by the neck I hit him with all my strength right in his ugly, laughing face. He staggered backward.

In that instant's reprieve, knowing now how deadly serious my situation was, I shoved in the clutch and grabbed the emergency release, letting the truck start rolling downhill, back onto the road.

The truck started rolling so dreadfully slowly that I thought all was lost when the other three men rushed around toward the broken window. But somehow, as they raced around the truck, they got in each other's way.

The truck slowly gained momentum. One of the men actually got his hand in the hole in the window, but he was having to trot alongside the rolling truck, and he couldn't twist his arm around to get his hand on the lock. Too late then, he tried to hang onto the truck and scramble up into the bed. It was gaining speed every second, and a sharp curve flung him off.

I hung onto the steering life for dear life, the coasting truck nearly getting out of control on the curves. Down through the hills I sped, putting mile after mile between me and my tormentors, laughing and crying at the same time in hysterical release.

The hills were leveling out and the truck was barely creeping along when I saw a country gas station a few hundred yards ahead. I just made it to the gasoline station. "Fill it up," I said shakily to the attendant. I rolled the broken window down to where I couldn't see it to be reminded of my terrifying experience.

Delayed reaction set in then. It was only with great mental and physical effort that I made my jerking limbs drive the remaining hundred or more miles home. But I was home by the time Chuck called. He said that Janice was in poor condition—that he'd call again the next night. I didn't tell him then about my horrifying experience because I thought he had enough worries.

I told Tommy, though, when his friends dropped him off about one a.m. I walked out with him to show him the broken window in his truck. Tommy turned pale, then he whistled. "You were really cool to get out of that, Mom."

"I wasn't cool," I admitted. "I panicked. I cried all the way home, and I'm still shaking. I dread telling your daddy. He's going to be really angry with me for driving to Rock Hill while he was gone."

"It's my fault," a subdued Tommy said. "I suggested it. But I couldn't stand for Grandma to ride that jolting bus so soon after her operation."

"I know. I couldn't, either," I comforted him. "Anyway, I'm home safely but you've got a broken window."

"Oh, well, summer's coming," Tommy said with a smile.

Soon after daybreak, Chuck called. His sister had died in the night. "Chuck, I'm so sorry," I said.

He asked me if I'd take the bus down to Daytona for her funeral.

"Of course I will," I agreed. "I'll take the six o'clock bus tonight."

I didn't insist on Tommy going with me, because he was so new on his job at the supermarket. All that Sunday I packed and got myself ready, and cooked things to leave in the refrigerator for Tommy to eat while I was gone.

Tommy drove me to the bus station that afternoon. I almost cried, leaving him home alone. "Don't forget to set your alarm to wake up tomorrow," I said as I climbed on the bus. He grinned and waved.

I rode all night and until noon the next day. Chuck met me at the bus station in Daytona. He looked so grieved and so weary that I couldn't bring myself to tell him what had happened to me.

Janice's funeral was so sad. I could hardly bear to see the grief of her son and daughter and her grandchildren. I'd been very fond of Janice, too. It was a mournful day.

We left for home soon after the funeral. We drove all night and reached home just as Tommy was leaving for work on Tuesday morning. Both Chuck and I collapsed on the bed and slept most of the day.

The next day Chuck went back to work. I finally got up enough nerve to tell him my story that night when he got home. Somehow, after what we'd just been through, my experience didn't seem quite as terrifying anymore.

But Chuck was rightfully upset. "Don't ever take a chance like that again!" he ordered.

"I won't," I promised.

He called the Dutch County sheriff, but by that time there wasn't much he could do. Tommy's automobile insurance policy had a five-hundred-dollar deductible clause, so we had his window repaired ourselves.

The whole thing is beginning to seem like a bad dream. But finally I got Tommy to teach me how to operate his CB radio—just in case. One never knows what can happen.

THE END

Made in the USA
Columbia, SC
25 May 2020